BAKED GOODS & BLACK MAGIC

Stories From Saforia

By: A. R. Lines

If you find any spelling or grammatical errors in this book, please let the author know via email (authorarlines@gmail.com)

Cover Design: **Meraki Cover Design**
E-book ISBN: 978-1-7383405-0-7
Paperback ISBN: 978-1-7383405-1-4

CONTENTS

DEDICATION

This book is dedicated to all the romance authors that have given me countless hours of escape into wondrous worlds full of spice and adventure.

Also, to my husband who does not understand my obsession with spicy books but encourages me anyways and has been a cheerleader, telling everyone he can that his wife writes smut with multiple men.

(If you're my family please don't read this book. Or if you do, don't tell me you did. Family gatherings will be very awkward otherwise.)

AUTHORS NOTE & CONTENT WARNING

This is an omegaverse book. This means that a large part of the story is based around scents, heats, adaptive body parts and knotting. Omegaverse is an alternative universe where the creatures and humans involved fit into three categories: Alphas, Betas, and Omegas. They have animalistic characteristics regardless of what kind of creature/shifter/magical being that they are. Relationships are mainly driven by the sexual beast-like connections formed between Omegas and those they consider pack.

This is a world where it is common for one female (Omega or Beta) to end up with multiple mates. This is considered their pack, their family. In this world magic abounds and there are many different types of creatures, or beings, but they all fit into one of the three categories or designations. They will still exhibit characteristics of what they are on top of their designation.

There will be references involving sexually explicit scenes (consensual), these characters enjoy intimacy and a large part of omegaverse surrounds this aspect. Anxiety, as with anyone or anything exists and the characters will exhibit signs of worry and tension in the form of anxiety. There is a scene with kidnapping, this is not all sweet and fluffy and throughout the book you will encounter scenes of violence and injuries to more than one of our MC's.

Due to the genre there will be scenes with spankings/domestic discipline, light degradation, biting/marking and a breeding kink. Our MMC's really like the thought of offspring (or they just enjoy trying).

There is a disability rep, as one of the characters cannot speak. He uses sign language and body language to communicate.

This book is steamy and the focus is on their female, there is no MM. Our FMC will be adding mates to her pack throughout this book and the ones following. This ends on a cliffhanger.

Also, this is high-fantasy, a whole new world and while some creatures and animals will be familiar there are also others that exist unique to this place.

PROLOGUE

Running a bakery is exhausting. I don't know why I thought this was a good idea. I'm up at a ridiculous hour everyday, I'm tired all the time and I have absolutely no life outside of this building. Everyone that I used to talk to, except Dani, has moved on with their lives and I feel like I've been left behind in this rut. It is a rut that I chose so I don't know how much I can really complain. No, scratch that, I can complain all I want. This is my life and even if I made all the choices to get me here, I will complain to my heart's content. Because that makes me feel a little better and no, I do not care if people say that's unhealthy. I'm going to do whatever I can to make myself feel better. It's the same reason I started baking in the first place. Yummy, homemade, baked goods make me feel happy. I mean, who doesn't enjoy a fresh cinnamon roll? Or a fruit tart? Or even a simple chocolate chip cookie?

I remind myself of why I started my bakery. I do it because the goodies make me happy. Because it brings me joy to see other people enjoying the things I've made. It also helps that it pays for me to survive. Honestly, I'm lucky that I had help building a room for me to live in above the bakery, otherwise I'm not sure what I would have done.

Life would have been much easier if I hadn't lost my parents. I would have remained with them and gotten sick too, if they hadn't insisted I stay with my friend Dani. She's been my closest friend for my whole life and I love her to pieces. Her, and her family, have always been there for me.

My parents were so supportive when they were around but when sickness swept through our village it hit many families and the healers didn't get here in time to save most of them. We're too small and not very enticing for a healer to live here.

Sometimes I wish we were bigger, or at least, closer to a bigger village that housed a Healers' Guild. But, I think I would absolutely detest the crowds.

I have my life down to a routine. Everyday I wake up before the crack of dawn. I make myself some tea, then have some toast and porridge. After that, I get to work in my bakery that I named in honor of my family, 'Bakken Bakery'.

I start with the cinnamon roll dough because those sell out the fastest in the mornings. Almost the entire village likes to stop in most mornings. Usually, they'll buy their breakfast and something for lunch as well. I do alright, considering I'm one of the few places someone can purchase food. It's either my place or the Inn, and they do make decent food but it's all stews and soups. Nothing sweet. Honestly, sweetness makes this life bearable. I don't know why they don't just purchase some goodies from me to sell to the evening crowds. I refuse to stay open past dinnertime. I have a life too... well, kind of. I would like to not work every second of every day.

Every few months our village hosts a market. Travelling merchants come from all over to sell their wares and many of our talented locals also set up stalls to sell whatever it is they make. I used to set up a stall for the whole week of the market but since I lost my parents I don't have anyone to watch it while I shop for ingredients. I could hire someone but I really need the money to keep the store going. So, what I've started doing is getting all my ingredient shopping done on day one and then the rest of the week I set up my stall to sell treats.

I haven't travelled far outside of my village so I don't know much about the wider world, but with how often we have travelling merchants, I've seen many of the beings that call this land home. Our village is named Pekayan but the Kingdom is called Saforia. It's a truly magical land, with beings that can actually *do* magic. Some beings are magic, like the Shifters or certain types of Fae. The ones that can do magic are called Users, as in they can *use* the magic from the world around them. Users come in all forms, be they Human, Fae, Shifter, or other. There are so many different types of beings, it's really hard to name them all. I'd be standing here for an hour and still I'd probably forget some. I really do appreciate that many of them are travelling merchants, otherwise, I'd never get any new ingredients.

Many of the merchants that come through here regularly are Goblins and Shifters, sometimes I'll see a Fae, but they mostly stick to the capital.

Along with all these different beings that live here, there are the designations that we all fall under. Alphas are the top of the food chain. They are the strongest of all of us, usually bigger too. All of them tower over me at my five foot two height and they tend to range between six and eight feet. They are *big*. Most of them have a pretty dominant temperament, by that, I mean they are blunt and make decisions quickly and with confidence. But they also tend to care about the well-being of those around them. And the one thing we all whisper and giggle about is that only Alphas have a knot at the base of their cock. It is unique to them and it's meant for an Omega, but if you work hard enough and prepare, a Beta can take it too.

Then, we have the Betas. They are like me, middle of the road, easy going, calm and hardworking. We're the average citizen, average height, average looks and average temperaments. We're also the most prolific designation.

Lastly, we have Omegas. They are the most delicate of the designations. By that, I mean they tend to be the most emotional. They feel for everyone around them and they are caretakers. They want to make sure everyone is happy. They tend to be very empathetic. Omegas can feel the emotions of those around them and oftentimes it's hard for them to ignore that. They, like Alphas, are a little more animalistic in their temperaments. They like cozy places, filled with comfortable things. They tend to build nest-like sleeping spaces where they feel safe. Omegas have heats, once every three months. This is when their more bestial characteristics appear. They nest in quiet, dark places and something in them demands they take an Alpha's knot. This can last for days. It sounds rather uncomfortable to me, but I don't actually know anything about heats aside from this.

All of the designations react to scent, it's how we can tell who is meant to be around us, as friends or potential mates. If someone smells amazing, it's likely they are a good match romantically. If they smell good, they're probably meant to be friends or confidants. If they smell bad, it's a warning to stay away. I'm pretty sure it's our evolutionary way to keep ourselves safe.

I miss my family but at least I have my health and I bring joy with my bakery. I grew up happy with a loving family but I had to work hard to help all of us survive. I know the value of hard work and I keep that up with my life now. I don't feel the need to leave my village to explore the land, there's too much danger out there to go alone and I don't really have many friends. Not many want to leave anyways. But I always enjoy seeing other beings and hearing all their stories of adventure and excitement. I try to grab a new book whenever I see a merchant selling one. I'm much happier reading about someone else's journey.

I'm also alone. No romantic partners. I would honestly love to have someone I could rely on, but I don't have a lot of trust for my fellow villagers. None of them smell right to me. They all smell OK, except for a few folks, but no one stands out as that one scent that will drive me crazy. I'm happy enough alone since I haven't found a scent compatible match. I get by just fine... although, it would be nice to have someone to cuddle at night and to maybe hunt so I could supplement my meals with meat once in a while. I go to the Inn if I have a craving but it would be so much more affordable if I could prepare it myself. I'm pretty good at foraging in the woods behind my home. I try to find enough for my own meals and for the bakery. I also try to get enough other ingredients to make healing salves, since we don't have any healers, we need to try to keep ourselves fit and healthy any way we can. I doubt I could afford a healer if I ever needed one.

My village is on the small side, there's around sixty people living here. There's a single Inn, a blacksmith, a tannery, a few small herbal shops and a seamstress. Many people that live here are farmers and sell things out of their homes or to merchants. Being as small as we are, everyone knows everybody's business and all my neighbors are extremely nosey. The only excitement we see around here is the market, and that only happens every so often. I don't actually mind it that much, many of my closest neighbors helped me through my grief when my family passed. It was nice knowing I had people I could rely on when I was at my lowest. It's been years since I felt like I needed to call on them for help. I have grown fairly independent since. I enjoy my solitude and find baking in my kitchen alone to be the most relaxing thing I can do. Which is why I turned it into my business. But, sometimes, I get the feeling that I'm missing something.

CH.1

The sun hasn't risen yet when I get out of bed. I'm slow to drag myself into my little bathroom. I need to get downstairs and make tea before I'll be awake enough to function. I'm feeling a little extra run down today.

The bakery kitchen is the only one I have, so I use that for my own meals as well.

Getting the water boiling for tea, I start pulling out the ingredients I'll need for this morning's breads. I'm nibbling on the goods that didn't sell yesterday for my breakfast. Once I've got my tea in hand I take a moment to sit out front and sip it, enjoying the fresh air even though there's always a little chill this early. Getting to watch the sun rise makes it worth it though.

Closing my eyes, I lean back in my seat and inhale deeply, all my tense muscles slowly relax as the early morning light bathes me in its warmth. While I'm sitting out here enjoying my hot tea watching the sun slowly rise over the houses, the sounds of the market being set up filter over to me. I almost forgot that was happening this week. I don't know what's been going on with me lately but I've just been so tired and my mood has been lower than usual. I'm hoping it will pass, there isn't much I can do anyways so I may as well just keep trying to push on.

Finding some of my excitement returning, now that I've remembered the market, I smile to myself. I'm really looking forward to seeing all the newcomers to our village, getting some new trinkets as well as making some sales. I'll have to put in some extra time today to prep everything I'll need to sell in the next few days.

As I'm contemplating what needs to be done today I almost miss the sound of footsteps coming down the main pathway through the village. I'm right on the main road closer to the far side of town so I don't get to see all the new beings coming and going.

Opening my eyes, I glance over at the sound and see Jerrik. He is the local Lord's son and spends far too much of his time wandering our village. Doesn't he have Lordly stuff to learn? A frown flickers across my face when I catch him heading my way. I really don't feel like dealing with him today. He has been pursuing me for years and I have never once given him the impression that I was interested. I don't understand why he persists. From what I've learned, we all judge compatible partners by scent. His isn't totally offensive but it's not my favorite, like a candle after it's blown out. Kind of waxy and bitter, it makes my nose wrinkle in an effort to avoid it.

"Hail, Luella." He waves, wafting his bitter scent at me.

"Jerrik," I bite out, keeping my response short so he leaves faster. I dislike his high and mighty attitude. Just because he's the local Lord's son he thinks he can do whatever he wants. I mean, he kind of can but that's only because we don't have any knights or mercenaries that patrol our village. Mostly, we look out for each other but he must know that everyone else is helping set up the market. He's acting suspicious and I don't like it.

"Are you planning on attending the Harvest Festival in a few weeks?" I think he's trying to sound sincere but it comes off as smarmy. He knows I attend every year to sell my goods.

"Of course I'll be there. I've got to make a living," I state with a firm tone. "Sorry," *not*, "I've got to go." I chug back my tea and get up to go inside. He grabs my arm hard, jerking me to a stop.

"Listen, Luella, you and me are going to happen. You can fight me all you want, but I'll enjoy breaking you," he sneers at me with cold eyes, a vein throbbing on his forehead. His anger adding bitter notes to his scent. I can't help wrinkling my nose in distaste.

My heart races as my fear builds. Swallowing hard, I glance away from him, trying to keep my body from trembling. I don't want him to know I'm afraid, he seems to enjoy that. Why can't he understand that I am not for him? I can't smell any better to him than he does to me. But, he is one of those people that thinks he deserves everything he wants.

Stomping on his foot, I'm pleased with his curse of pain. Wrenching my arm out of his grasp I scurry inside as fast as I can, slamming the door and locking it. He bangs on the door, making it rattle in its hinges.

He screams, "YOU CAN'T HIDE FOREVER, LUELLA!" Another thump and he says quietly, "I'll be watching."

The only reason I heard that is because my back is pressed tight against the door, panic freezing me in place. My heart is pounding, eyes wide as fear strokes cold fingers down my spine. He's gotten bolder in his advances and I'm worried he's going to do something to me. Force me to be with him, or... I don't know. Something awful. I'm starting to wonder if I should leave the village, start over somewhere else. Far, far, away from him.

I'm not going to answer him because I just want him to go away. I've learned in my twenty eight years on this land that I am bad with conflict. I know this about myself and have accepted it. I have found ways to work around this issue. Mostly by getting out of the uncomfortable situation. I'm good at slinking away unnoticed, or at least I think I am.

Barely breathing, listening for any sounds on the other side of the door, I jump when he slams a hand against the door once more before his footsteps trail away. I wait another few minutes before I can convince my limbs to move.

Shaking, I make my way to the kitchen. *Making dough will help calm me down.* The process of baking cinnamon rolls is very soothing and I find myself finally breathing again. Working very hard not to think about Jerrik and what he meant by, 'I'll be watching'.

As I'm kneading the dough I think through all the things I need to do today.

1. Make rolls

2. Make lemon squares

3. Make cookies

4. Make fruit pastries

My excitement for the market returns. I can't wait to go through and do my shopping tomorrow. I wonder what new treasures I'll find, and what new beings I will meet. I try to work around my shyness and ask the merchants about what they've seen and done. Collecting stories is one of my favorite pastimes.

Many of the regulars that come to our market know me well at this point, since I've been attending as long as I can remember. There's only a few regular travelling merchants that have been coming here as long as I've been alive.

I am always curious if I'll get to see any of the beings I haven't yet had contact with. Like Elves, they never come out this far. They tend to stay in the forests and seclude themselves from the rest of the world, as far as I know. We have a nice sized one surrounding us but I think the one they live in is quite ancient and their homes have been passed down through generations. I know they live harmoniously with nature so I think all the cities and villages offend them to some degree.

My mind wanders as I bake and before I know it the hours have flown by and it is time to open up for my morning rush. I pull out the trays of rolls and muffins and carry them out to the front display. I like to make some pastries and muffins, along with the cinnamon rolls. It's important to have variety. Once I have organized my display the way I like, I ready my cash box and go unlock the door.

CH.2

Spending my morning making small talk while selling goodies to my neighbors and friends is fairly routine. Wayin tells me about her goats, when I'll be able to pick up the next batch of cheese and how her mate, Powel is doing with his garden.

Cheya is all smiles as she picks up enough food for her and her mate. Boon is an Alpha and the blacksmith. The two of them have done so much for me. Whenever I have an idea for a new type of baking tray or cake pan, Boon has been wonderfully patient with me while I describe what I want. He usually has it finished within a few days. He's magic with metals.

Miss Jena is a widow who lives alone at the edge of town. She stops by often to chat, I think she's lonely without her mate. She lost him to the sickness that took my parents.

She's one of the only Shifters that live here, a beautiful russet fox. I never mind when she comes in to visit. As long as she's happy to follow me as I putter around cleaning up after the morning sales I'm delighted to have her stick around.

By the time I'm done cleaning, she's talked herself out and gone for a run in the forest, I'm ready to relax into the afternoon baking. This is when I bake loaves of bread and other more savory items that people can purchase for their dinners.

Just as I'm heading into the kitchen I hear a jingle. I look up into the crystal blue gaze of the most intriguing stranger I have ever seen. He has to be an Alpha as he stands at well over seven feet, which means he towers over me and probably everyone else. He has gorgeous red hair tied back in a bun. High cheekbones and a roman nose give his face an alluring definition. Full lips that look like they were meant to be bitten, paired with a sharp jawline impress upon me this male's stunning beauty.

What intrigues me the most are the beautiful grey leathery wings tucked tightly behind him, they compliment his pale greyish skin tone.

I have the strangest urge to pet them,

wondering if they are soft or rough. Never have I seen another male as muscular as him, I think he could lift my oven over his head with one hand and it is extremely heavy. He has got to be a mercenary, there's a large sword sticking up between his wings and I'm guessing he probably has more weapons hidden on his body. He's the biggest being I've ever encountered, I wonder what he is... Those wings indicate he might be some sort of Shifter but it's hard to tell.

Standing there staring at him like an absolute loaf of bread, I catch him smiling gently at me.

This snaps me out of my open mouthed stupor enough to say, "Welcome to Bakken Bakery, how can I help you?" I paste on my customer service smile to cover up my gawking.

He chuckles at my attempt to gloss over staring at him like an idiot and asks, "Do you happen to have any rolls left over from breakfast? I was told this was the place to go if I didn't want to eat another cold meal of travel rations." He has the most charming smile, shy but genuine.

Now that he's close enough, I catch a hint of his scent and *oh my*. My knees feel weak and my core warms. It is absolutely mouthwatering. He smells like melted chocolate and I have to wonder if he tastes as good.

Nope! No. What am I thinking? This is a stranger and he is obviously here for the market so he won't be here longer than a week. This is not something I should be thinking about right now. *I don't have time for a mate, remember?* I chide myself. I shake my head internally and focus on selling this delicious chocolate-scented male some food so I can go back to my boring life of baking and loneliness. Even my thoughts sound bitter.

"It, um, it looks like I have two rolls left. One is four marks." There are marks, orim, silvum and copen's. No one in this village has ever seen a silvum or a copen, that's the kind of money only royalty has.

Pointing at my display redundantly, I show him what I've got left. He follows my finger and gets a little crease between his eyes. I would assume he's thinking about whether he wants a roll or one of the cherry pastries leftover.

"How much for both rolls and the three pastries?" He's eyeing the display hungrily.

I wonder how long he's been travelling for to look at food like that. Jerking, I realize I said that out loud, and my cheeks flame.

His eyes brighten and he snorts out, "We

have been on the road for a week and I haven't had anything more than cold cheeses, hard bread and dried meat. I could smell this place from down the road." He inhales deeply and sighs. "Ahhh, heavenly."

I try to get back into my customer service facade. Which is really the blankest face I can manage. I am a pretty expressive person, so it's really hard.

"Wow, you must be extremely hungry! All of that together will be fourteen marks," I remark, losing my customer service persona and adapting a warm smile. This male has me tingling in places I don't want to acknowledge. I don't really know if that's good or bad yet. But I feel like I should find out. Did he say we? Oh! He probably came with a group of mercenaries guarding a merchant.

"Are you with the merchants? You definitely look like someone strong enough to be a guard," I query lightly.

He lets out a boisterous laugh, "Oh thank you! You are precious, aren't you? I am one of the merchants setting up for the market. This is my first time to this village, I haven't ever travelled this far from Tayrin and Varough before."

Feeling a blush warm my cheeks for my assumption I look down as I inquire meekly,

"What made you travel this far from the capitol? Coming through the mountains must have been difficult and frightening."

"Adventure, of course! I was feeling a little stagnant back home. I just felt this need to change something. To make things better for myself..." Trailing off, he sounds a little morose. All I want to do is make him feel better and I have no idea why. I don't usually concern myself this deeply with my customers. But I have this insane, driving urge to put a smile back on his face.

Walking around the counter that blocks me from the rest of the room, I stop in front of him. Placing a hand on his arm, not fighting my urges, I remark, "It is good to do things that will make you happy, or happier..." Pausing, I think about my own life and the sadness I've been wallowing in. "We all have to try a little harder to find things that make this life worth living. I have a feeling this breakfast will help cheer you up!"

Looking at me curiously, he cocks a brow, before smiling again. "You are absolutely right... umm?"

"Uhh... Oh! Luella. My name is Luella." My blushing cheeks are burning. I bite my lip to hold back more questions about his travels. I'm usually much more reticent around strangers.

"Well, Luella, I'm certain you are correct. The smell alone is tantalizing." His eyes darken a smidge as he stares at me.

Inhaling deeply, his nostrils flare. I assume he's taking in the smells of my kitchen but he's still looking down at me and not the baked goods.

"You are certainly a treasure, aren't you?" I don't know what to say to that so I just stand there feeling flushed, avoiding eye contact.

He smiles. "If you were wondering, my name is Feandal. But my friends just call me Fen."

"Well, Fen," I chirp, testing out his name. "It is very nice to meet you." I go to hold my hand out for him to shake but I realize it's still on his arm. Quickly lifting it off I awkwardly hover it in between us.

Luckily, he puts me out of my misery and grabs my hand. Lifting it to his lips, he flips my hand over and places a gentle kiss on my wrist. I can tell that as long as he is here the redness on my face will not go away. My awkwardness and his gallant gestures will see to that.

None of the males of my village act like this. Mostly, I ignore them since none of them interest me all that much. I tend to avoid them because of Jerrik. He makes me so uncomfortable and anytime in the past if I have spoken to a male, when Jerrik finds out he comes to hassle me about not being faithful to him. I don't know how many times I can tell him I have less than zero interest in him. It is becoming exhausting.

My flush deepens as my chin dips down and I fiddle with the pockets on my dress. "Th-thank you."

"Oh, Precious. I am going to work hard to make you blush every time I see you," he declares. He has an absolutely gorgeous smile on his face and I know I am going to be in trouble if he's around for too long.

Looking up into his eyes. "You never did answer, what kinds of goods are you selling?" I wonder if he has anything I'll want. It will give me a reason to explore his cart.

"Ahhh, yes. I have an assortment of trinkets, weapons, and Fae-touched items," he replies. He had me hooked the moment he mentioned trinkets but, if he truly does have any Fae-touched items I will be in awe. It is rare for any to make it out this way and they usually carry a lot of power, making them very expensive.

"I will be sure to stop by your cart in that case," I tell him, I think he can see the excitement on my face because he's grinning at me.

"Let me gather your breakfast goods in a box and I will let you be on your way," I murmur, turning to get it packaged up. I realize he's still holding my hand and I giggle, gently pulling my hand from his. He tightens his hold for a moment, giving me a thoughtful look, before letting me go.

When I head behind the counter I can feel his gaze on me. It's warm and comforting, unlike some of the other men I've had flirt with me. He is so unusual, but I think I like him.

Fen's eyes follow me while I putter around grabbing a liner for the box, then placing the goodies in and closing it. I sense that he's moved closer before I turn to hand him the box. This gives me another chance to observe him. I catch him sniffing the air a little and I wonder if he's smelling me or the rolls.

Placing the box in front of him, I smile shyly. "I do hope to run into you when I do my shopping at the market."

"You surely will, Precious." He gives me a little salute with the box of goodies, leaving the payment on the counter.

After Fen's gone I give myself a moment to enjoy his lingering scent before I return to the kitchen.

I have never reacted so viscerally to a male before, or to anyone for that matter. From what I can remember my parents telling me, to react that strongly to someone's scent means they would make a good match. I'm not sure what to do with this though, because he's only here for a week, and I have no idea where he lives when he's not travelling to sell things. Or, even searching for things to sell. I am not a very active person; would I consider travelling? Maybe. Would I consider moving? Yeah, probably. What would this mean for my way of life? I have too many questions and no answers. I also think I'm being much too presumptuous.

I should wander over to Dani's, and see what she thinks of this. I can already guess what she will do. She will squeal and shout and be generally excited about the opportunity for me to find a mate.

She has known me long enough, our entire lives, and she's realized that I avoid getting involved with anyone. Has she guessed that I have never touched a male in *that* way? She probably knows. It isn't like she has ever seen me go off with any males before.

I do not know what to do with these emotions. So, I will bake. I will make my breads and sell them for the dinner rush and I will bake all the treats to sell in my stall. I will not stew on this and I will find Fen's cart tomorrow. What will be, will be, and I will accept the path the Goddess has chosen for me.

The Goddess created our world and all the different inhabitants of this land. She's all-knowing and all-powerful. I've always thought of her as a watchful parent, pleased when she sees her children doing well. I've heard stories about her, gently nudging heroes and adventurers in the right direction to save the world. There is even one story from centuries ago of her interceding in one of our past King's lives to guide him to his Queen. She is known for benevolence, love, fertility and wisdom.

Although, there are a few stories about her exacting vengeance against a black magic User, how she came down from the stars to aid our long ago King in defeating a great evil intent on destroying and conquering this kingdom. But, we all know these are just stories. No one has seen or heard from her in the last century, at least. I may pray to the Goddess and follow the path I think she designed for me but I don't believe she will ever physically come down from the heavens to meddle in our lives.

CH.3

Working late into the night, I bake cookies and other easy to transport treats. I probably stayed up much later than I should have considering how reluctant I am to get out of my warm bed right now. But, I've already slept later than usual, I can see the greyness of early morning. I need to get up, drink my tea and make my morning rolls.

Throwing the covers off in an effort to encourage myself to get up, I lay there for a moment. The cold air really does the trick. Goosebumps creep along my arms and legs and I shiver violently. The floor is cold on my feet as I try to find my slippers.

Rushing through dressing, I make my way downstairs. Taking a deep breath of the crisp air, I exhale all my stress out as I sit in my chair with my hot tea. This little ritual helps prepare me for the day to come. Luckily, no one interrupts me today.

As I work, I feel my excitement for the market grow. And, if I'm honest with myself, seeing Fen again. I can't wait to explore all the different stalls.

I wonder what new ingredients I'll find and what I'll be able to create with them.

The morning breezes by as I'm lost in thought. Before I know it, there's a line outside my door so I hustle my way out front with the trays of warm goods. Once I have everything where I want, I unlock the door.

It isn't long before I'm sold out. That makes this morning even better. I can get my evening breads proofing before heading over to the market. More time for shopping! I have a whole shelf in my bedroom dedicated to little statues and art that intrigues me.

Grabbing my bag and a light sweater I head out. As I'm locking the door I hear footsteps coming up the main street. My body tenses, fight or flight instincts readying me for another confrontation with Jerrik. But when I peer over my shoulder, it's only Dani. Slumping against my door, all the tension leaks out of me abruptly as I let out a shaky exhale.

"Luella!" she shrieks, waving her arm madly. I'm always amazed at how much energy this Pixie contains in her tiny body.

Dani is minuscule, only coming up to my chest. I swear she's four feet but she claims she's five. If I stand at five foot two then she absolutely cannot be five feet. It's an ongoing argument between us, but it's all in jest.

She may be itty bitty but she is unquestionably gorgeous. With very light pink hair, bright green eyes that look far too big for her face and her mesmerizing wings, she embodies beauty and joy. Her wings color shift depending on how the light hits them, and whenever I'm near her I can't help staring. They're just so pretty. Honestly, I feel so plain when I stand next to her with my wavy brown hair, hazel eyes and short, plump stature. Well, short compared to everyone except her. We were always close as children and basically grew up together. She's like a sister to me.

Laughing at her enthusiasm I try to match her energy, seeing her has me easily forgetting the tension that plagued me when I thought Jerrik was here.

"Dani! Are you heading to the market? Or just wandering around as usual?" She does tend to float around the village, talking to anyone she can convince to stay still for a minute and she often wanders through the woods. I think it has something to do with being a Pixie.

"Yes! I came to see if you wanted to go with me? Please come with me?" she practically begs me.

My head tips to the side as my lips tilt upwards. I feel lighter just being in her presence.

Replying with a growing smile, I swing my bag over my shoulder, "Of course I'll go with you, silly. But do not feel bad when you inevitably wander off. I have certain things I need to bargain for and I know you can't stand still for that long." I can't help chuckling at the mulish look on her face. A typical trip with her is like this, we start together and before I know it she's gone. She will talk my ears off for the first ten minutes and then as soon as I stop at my first stall she loses focus and wanders until she's lost in the crowd. Then she will find me later and beg forgiveness for being a bad friend. Which is just silly, she knows I wouldn't ever stop being her friend just because she's easily distracted.

With hands on hips and a moue of displeasure she exclaims, "I'll have you know I would never just leave you on your own! I will stick by you during the boring bartering and help you carry things and I won't get distracted."

"Dani, I love you. Whatever happens while we're out today is what's going to happen, so don't stress yourself out over anything okay?" Giving her a side hug as we walk towards the bustling market, I rest my head against her.

She hugs me back, squeezing way harder than someone as small as her should be able to, and says with a sigh, "Okay, Lulu, I'm glad you know me so well. I really will try but..." She trails off with a shrug.

We both giggle and break our hug as we come upon the entrance to the market. I contemplate telling her about my encounter with Fen, but I think I'll wait and see if she's still hanging around by the time I make it to his cart. I will tell her about Jerrik though, she knows well that he's been harassing me for years.

With her cheeks red from anger and her fists clenched she growls, "That asshole! I'm going to punch him right in the nuts next time I see him."

Snorting a laugh, I cover my mouth. "I called him a weasel in my head yesterday, but asshole is more fitting. I don't think you should bother with him, Dani. He isn't worth it." *I'll just have to work harder to avoid him.*

"Ugh, fine. I know you worry he'll get us

in trouble but I think he'd be too embarrassed that he got beat up by a girl, and one as small as either of us!" She rolls her eyes as if thinking about Jerrik and his stupidity is too painful.

CH. 4

The scents and sounds of the market have me sighing with happiness. I adore it, it's so full of life with the energetic crowds, the scent of food stalls and beings wandering through. And of course all the treasures I can find!

Thinking about it, maybe I would enjoy living in a bigger town...

I'm already dragging Dani through the crowd to my first stop. I'm excited to see what Kip has brought this time. He's been coming to our market since I was a little girl. He's a Goblin and he has the same knobbly green skin that all Goblins do. With a very short stature, he's probably the same height as Dani. Somewhere around four feet but his personality makes him seem taller. With no hair, just a shiny bald scalp, it reflects the sunlight very well. It is almost surprising how loud and grumpy such a small being can be but he is actually very kind to me. Kip's just got a very blunt personality. Once you get past that he is wonderful. It's why I always go to him for ingredients. For a Goblin, he is very honest and does not try to scam me. I appreciate his scent, it is neutral to me; like a deep cave. A little musty but mostly just earthy, I'm pretty sure he's a Beta.

Weaving through the mass of beings, I keep an eye out for Fen. Feeling a little guilty my steps drag. I should have told Dani about him, but I kind of want to keep him to myself. *That's a bit selfish isn't it*? Turning to Dani to tell her about him, she jerks me to the right squealing with excitement, seeing a cart full of fabrics. She's a seamstress, just like her mother, and her designs are incredible.

"Oh Goddess, Luella! Look at this fabric! The color is so bright and the texture so soft." Sighing, she closes her eyes with pleasure as she strokes a hand over the pretty fabric. Still hanging on to my arm, she tugs me closer to share the fabric with me. She is much more into clothing and fashion than I am. I usually have her do any mending for me and I wear any new clothing she experiments with. She likes to play with new styles to sell. I'm happy to support my friend any way that I can, if that's wearing strange new clothes then so be it.

Reaching over I stroke the fabric with

her, and *oh my!* It is incredibly soft, I just want to rub my face against it and surround myself with it. I must make a noise to that effect because she gives me a sly smile, eyes crinkling with delight and declares, "That's it! I'm buying it. I'll make you a new outfit."

Still petting the fabric distractedly, I reply, "Hmmm, well, if you are going to make something for me, can I request a blanket? Or maybe a nightgown? This fabric feels so cozy that all it makes me want to do is curl up in bed and bury myself underneath it."

Laughing loudly, her face sparkles with amusement. "Of course! You're just like a kitten, seeking warm, comfortable spots to nap."

My cheeks redden in embarrassment as I look down and kick at the dirt. I mumble, "I'm not a kitten."

"Oh, don't be so sensitive, Lulu! You know I mean that with love." She hugs me tight before turning to bargain with the merchant.

My attention wanders while she barters and I look at the stalls on either side, just to see if they have anything interesting. I don't see much for me, so I spin around and look across the pathway at the carts there. Something shiny, glinting in the sunlight, catches my eye. I glance over at Dani, she's deep into a discussion on fabrics and thread so I figure she won't miss me for a few minutes.

Dodging beings walking by, I make my way over to the cart of shiny things. I don't take any notice of the merchant running the cart when I reach it. The glittery thing that drew me over is a treasure box. Delighted, my eyes widen and I shimmy in excitement. It's square, about six inches across and it has an inlay of beautifully colored jewels on the lid. The latch drops down from the lid and it comes with a lock. I absolutely *have* to have it. I reach out to touch the lid, but before I do I stop and look up. I figure I should probably check with the merchant before I touch something that looks as valuable as this.

Making eye contact with him, my mouth pops open in surprise, it's Fen!

"Oh! Hello, Fen, I'm so glad I ran into you today!" I exclaim, smiling like a loon. I am very happy I have the chance to see him again. I can't scent him in this crowd, but I already know he smells amazing.

Laughing, he replies, "I was wondering when you would notice me. You seem awfully engrossed in the jewelry box I have for sale. It is only 10 marks, or... I will trade it to you for some of those breakfast rolls. They were delectable." His voice deepens, causing a shiver to trickle through my core.

Feeling sheepish, I avoid making eye contact. "I really like shiny things..." I mutter quietly.

He reaches out, gently lifting my chin so I have to look at him. His smile is warm, putting me at ease.

"Oh, Precious. You are the most adorable thing I have ever seen. Would you be alright with a trade?" He's being so kind and his hand is so warm. It also brings his scent to my nose and relaxes me even further. I'm no longer burning red, only a little pink now and I think it's more from wanting him than embarrassment.

Feeling braver with his hand on me, I respond, "Yes, a trade. Cinnamon rolls for the jewelry box sounds very good." I don't know if I will ever stop blushing. I really want to ask Fen to spend some time with me. I know he'll be incredibly busy with the market all week and then he'll probably move on to the next village. I'll have missed my chance to get to know him beyond his gorgeous looks. I really want to overcome my shyness, but... what if he doesn't want to spend time around me? What if he has a partner already? What if....?

"I can see you spiraling and I would love to know what's going on in that mind of yours,

Precious," he purrs, his earnest voice startling me out of my anxiety. Refocusing on him, I note that he's moved closer. His hand is still holding my face and he smells like happiness and comfort. Having no desire to pull away from him, I let him relax my anxiety. In fact, I'd really love to burrow in and encourage him to give me a big, squeezing, hug.

"Uhhhh... I-I'm just... a-a little embarrassed... th-that you witnessed m-my total focus on shiny things," stammering, I let my eyes drift away from him as I fidget with my dress. I hope he didn't see my little shimmy of happiness. *That's embarrassing.*

He's still holding on to me and when I look at him I watch as his smile grows. "Luella, would you be interested in spending a little time with me this evening?"

Nodding my head before he's even finished speaking. "Uh huh, yep. That sounds nice. But... I do have some baking, so maybe you could come hang out and talk while I work?" I want to get closer to him. I want to shove my face into his chest and inhale his scent directly from the source. *What is up with me?*

He moves his hand off my face only to grab onto my shoulders and gently tug me forward into a hug.

OH.

Yes.

This is exactly what I wanted. Did he read my mind? As I'm pondering this I start vibrating. No. Wait. He's laughing at me!

"Excuse me? Are you laughing at me? And wait, are you able to read minds? Is that a trait of... whatever you are?" Stopping myself from peppering him with more questions, I realize I was being incredibly rude. "Oh Goddess, please ignore me! I'm so sorry. My mouth got away from me for a moment and I'm not even sure what I just said." My face is furiously red again and I grimace, clearing my throat. I absolutely refuse to look at him. I don't know why I can't behave like a normal being around him.

He laughs harder and I glare at him until he finally stops, but he's smiling at me like I'm the best thing he has ever seen. It softens my ire a little.

"You are so precious. I'm happy to watch you work. I want to spend every free moment I have with you. I'm sorry for laughing but you're just so cute. I'm usually the awkward one. I feel better about it now that I know I'm not alone." His eyes crinkle with happiness as he smiles at my rosy cheeks. "And to answer your rambling questions; I cannot read minds but you have an incredibly expressive face, and I am a Gargoyle. Hence the grey skin and wings." He flexes them out a little to show me.

My mouth goes slack and my eyes widen, because he's hugging me and not only does he smell like chocolate but also because I am hugging a Gargoyle! *Whoa*. I'm at a loss for words until I realize he said he wanted to spend all his time with me, then I feel a flush of heat roll through me.

"You're really a Gargoyle? That's *so* cool!" I know I have hearts in my eyes, but this is honestly the most incredible being I have ever met. "I don't believe you. You have not once been awkward around me. You're sweet, smell amazing and I feel very fortunate that you want to be around me."

"Precious," he whispers, leaning down so he's resting his face in my hair. "You honor me. What time should I come to your home this evening?" He sounds so reverential, I don't know what I did to honor him... was it because I said he smells amazing? It doesn't matter, I'm very excited to spend time with him.

"Come to the bakery when you're done here? I'll likely be in the kitchen cleaning up after the dinner sales. And I live above the bakery so I'll be around anyways," I tell him, tucking my nose into his chest and inhaling deeply. Fen's addictive scent eases something inside me.

He squeezes a little tighter before releasing me and stepping back. "Let me wrap up the jewelry box for you." His smile is warm as he grabs some fabric to protect it before putting it in a small bag. "I really want to hug you again but then I might not let you go. It's my turn to run the cart today so I should probably pay attention to other customers," he admits wryly, smiling wistfully at me.

"Thank you, Fen." Smiling up at him brightly. I clutch the box to my chest.. "I can't wait to see you later tonight! I should go see if my friend is done bartering for fabric. Bye!" Turning, I scamper away grinning to myself.

CH. 5

Strolling back to the fabric merchant to find Dani, I can't see her anywhere. Feeling badly that I was the one to wander off this time, I let out a heavy sigh. I'm sure I'll find her later. I will try to keep my eyes peeled while I finish up my shopping.

Setting out to find Kip, I let my excitement build. I'm curious to see what he will have for me this time. I like to think I'm his favorite customer. I always visit him when he comes, even when I don't need to purchase anything. He's such a lovable grump, I take great joy in teasing him about it.

Weaving my way through the crowded market I head straight for Kips cart while keeping an eye out for anything interesting. I'm also checking to see if there are any other being's I haven't seen before. Considering I've already met a Gargoyle, I feel pretty good about my chances of coming across others.

Nothing catches my eye as I make my way over. He's helping someone, so I take my time looking over his goods. There are some interesting green things that I don't think I've tried before and he has *chocolate*! Oh, Goddess! I can't believe he has chocolate and that he hasn't hidden the entire stash for me. I pout a little. I'm too caught up in drooling over the chocolate to notice Kip standing next to me. He clears his throat.

"Luella. I see you eyeing the chocolate display and I know that look on your face. Do you not trust me, my dear?" He props his hands on his hips and harrumphs at me. "Of course I put aside an entire crate for you! You're my favorite customer and I know anything you purchase from me will go to good use."

"KIP!" Squealing his name, I shake with excitement. "You absolute saint. I should have known you would, especially when it comes to chocolate." My voice rises another octave, I lunge at him and throw my arms around him. He cringed the moment I started squealing but he puts up with the hug I force upon him. "Thank you, thank you, thank you!" Gently disengaging, he sets me on my feet.

"Yes, yes, I know I am the best. Give me a moment to go get your crate. It's pretty heavy, Luella, do you have a small hand cart or someone strong enough to carry it for you?" His eyebrows draw together and his lips press tightly into a flat line, like maybe he's re-thinking giving me a whole crate.

Jumping a little, I squeak out, "No. but I'm sure it's fine, Kip! I'm pretty strong, you know." Giving him a wink for good measure. I don't know why I feel the need to prove myself as some strong independent woman, maybe because I have been alone for so long...

Following him around to the back of his cart I watch him uncover a crate with a little brown bean on the side. I'm so glad Kip loves me, otherwise I wouldn't have opportunities like this.

"Here you are, Lass. A full crate of chocolate." He waves his hand lazily at the crate, as if to say let's see you heft this thing.

Bending my knees, I squat down to get my hands under the sides and then... I get stuck. It is obvious that I cannot lift this heavy crate of deliciousness on my own. But who can help me? Should I try to find Dani? Or maybe I can go home and grab my small hand cart? Oh! I'll go see if Fen would be able to pick it up before he comes to see me tonight!

"Okay, Kip. You were right. I most definitely cannot carry this. I have a friend here selling things in his own cart. He's planning to stop by my bakery after the market closes tonight, could you hold on to the crate for me until he can come get it?" Making my eyes really big, I push my bottom lip out into a pout, and press my hands together, pleading.

With a harrumph, he quirks an eyebrow. "Of course, Luella. But shouldn't you check to make sure your... friend... is willing to come get it for you? I'm happy to hold the crate until tomorrow when you bring your cart to set up your stall. How will I know who your friend is? I can't just give your crate of chocolate to anyone."

My ears redden at my assumption and I glance away. "Oh, right, uhhh. Let me pop back over to ask him. If not, then I'll get it tomorrow." Clearing my throat I add, "And I really do want to see what else you have for me."

Nodding, he leads me back around to the front. With another 'help yourself' wave, I get to it.

Spending about half an hour looking, smelling and touching ingredients, I settle on a few other items. Kip kindly offers to keep everything with my crate of chocolate while I continue shopping. Making sure to give him another hug, I head out to find Fen, and more treasures.

Meandering back and forth across the pathway, from cart to cart I'm hoping some new treasure will catch my eye.

I happen to glance over to my right and see an intricately carved wooden statue. It looks like it's a depiction of the Goddess. Heading straight for it, I try to decide if I need another statue. I already have a carving of her, but this one has such beautiful detail. I need to add it to my collection. *It belongs on my shelf*, I nod, agreeing with myself.

Feeling eyes on me I look up to find the merchant staring at me. *Whoa*, he is as handsome as Fen. Short glossy black hair shines back at me. *It looks so soft, I wonder if he would let me pet him?* I have to mentally shake myself out of the daze.

Brilliant orange eyes that make the sun look faded, observe me as intently as I do him. His skin is a smooth, pretty, ochre and his cheekbones defined. That face looks like it could belong to royalty, but I doubt royalty would be manning a cart at the market in Pekayan.

I can't help but snort at my thoughts. He's tall but not as big as Fen. Possibly around six feet. Still, I feel tiny standing in front of him. And that scent! I thought Fen smelled amazing but this guy smells like my favorite sweets. Like salted caramel and freshly baked sugar cookies.

Knowing I've probably got a very unattractive look on my face, I still can't help gawking at this beautiful male. I don't think I've ever seen anyone as striking as this. Making an effort to school my face into something less stupid, I snap my mouth closed.

"Hello, Little Kitten. If it isn't too forward, I must say you smell absolutely mouth-watering. You should not be out alone, where is your keeper?" he asks, with no condescension, even though it sounds like it should come off that way. Continuing before I have a chance to reply, "I do not smell a mate, or any other scents for that matter. Are you alone, Little Kitten? That is completely unacceptable. I would like to court you." With his dark and raspy voice, it gives me chills listening to him.

His gaze isn't lecherous, it's hot. Like, scorching, sizzling, sexy hot. Fanning myself, I know I look very silly but I don't care. If I had any sense whatsoever I'd jump on this hunk of man. But being who I am, an awkward, rambling, mess of a woman, all I do is stammer out a reply.

"Uh. Um. Uh... Hi?" Mentally, I facepalm. "Umm, thank you? You smell... very good to me, as well. Um, I don't have a keeper? I live alone and have no family, so I guess... I am my keeper? And you... wanna court... me?" Pointing at myself stupidly, eyes wide with surprise. Like, what could he possibly see in me? I'm just a regular human Beta with no skills besides baking and being awkward.

He smiles at me gently, but with plenty of heat and says, "Yes, Little Kitten. I want to court you. I can smell the scent of a perfect match and I'm positive it is coming from you. You smell of strawberries and cake and it makes me ravenous." Staring helplessly, with wide eyes, as he slowly licks his lips before continuing, "How in the world has no one snatched you up? You are alone and vulnerable and I find this unacceptable. My pack will take you in when I inform them you are to be my mate. It's possible my whole pack will find you a scent match. Hmmm... more protectors, yes I like this. My whole pack will mate you and you will be our Center..." He nods, like this is already a forgone conclusion.

I wonder if I get a say in this? He's sort of trails off contemplating my future. I mean, he is incredibly attractive and his scent does tell me that we would likely be compatible but I don't actually *know* him. I feel like I should be offended that he thinks I need a keeper, but for some reason I'm flattered. I should do something to slow him down a little.

"Ummm, what's your name? I can't keep calling you Cookie in my head. Well, I can but I think I'd rather have a name for you since you're planning my entire life and all." Chewing the inside of my cheek, I smooth a hand down my dress. And even though I'm a little unsure, I'm still trying to make a joke. I don't think he gets it though.

Smiling widely, it shows off his dimples. "Yes! I am Rafeel, your soon to be mate. I will likely continue to call you my Little Kitten, even if I know your name, but as you said I am planning *our* life so I should know the name of my mate."

His self-confidence is astounding and actually pretty complimentary. I've never had a male react to me this way. Fen was interested in me right away but seems to lack the confidence this one has. I figure it can't hurt to give him my name, he seems harmless to me, if not a little obsessive.

"My name is Luella," pausing for a second before I add, "and I don't actually mind your nickname for me." Flushed, I look down as I fiddle with my fingers in the face of his confidence. I feel like I need to decide if I want to encourage this male's behavior or if I should try to brush him off before finishing my shopping. If I had to admit it, I think I like him. I like his directness and his attention. There's something inside me, at the back of my mind whispering approval of his actions. But I should mention Fen.

"Ok, so, if you're very sure you're interested in me..." I start hesitantly.

"Very," he interrupts me, playfully, before nodding at me to continue.

"Uhh... If you're sure of your interest in me then I feel I should tell you I am sort of being courted, maybe, by someone."

Frowning, he takes a deep breath and sighs sadly, "Who is he, Kitten?"

Well, he didn't drop my nickname so hopefully that means he isn't really that upset. I wonder if he knows Fen, since they both likely travelled a similar path, as all who come for the market.

"His name is Feandal. I met him when he came to my bakery for breakfast yesterday." Chewing my lip, as my eyes shift around looking at anything other than him.

But this news doesn't make him frown any deeper. He's sporting a big grin, showing off those dimples again.

"Excellent! I knew my pack-mates would love you. I will have to ask Fen why he hid you from us," muttering this last part, he chuckles to himself.

Obviously they know each other, but I didn't think they were going to be pack-mates. This is a little troubling. Am I ready to deal with more than one suitor? Probably not, considering I've been alone and had absolutely zero interest in a mate before these males came along. But, am I going to give them a shot anyways? Yep, definitely, it's time for me to be brave and maybe I will find that one, or one's, who will cuddle me at night and hunt for me.

I wonder if Rafe would be willing to haul my crate of chocolate over? Only one way to find out.

"So, I take it you are well acquainted with Fen? That's quite interesting. Did he share any of the breakfast treats he bought from me yesterday? I'm pretty proud of my baking. Also, when are you done manning this cart? I could use someone with muscles to help me bring some purchases back to my bakery. I was going to ask Fen but you're here and you seem to want to be around me so..." Trailing off, I run out of steam from my nervous rambling. Sometimes my mouth really gets away from me.

Fidgeting with the bottom of my shirt I shift from foot to foot, because I don't really know what to do with myself. A light touch on my chin sends a jolt of warmth through my body. He tips my head up so I'm looking at him once again.

"My Little Kitten. Do I make you nervous? I suppose that would be normal for someone to feel after I have made my intentions so obvious. Do not worry, my Little One, I will answer all your questions and I am happy to answer any future ones you may ramble at me as well." Smiling gently, he cradles my cheek before continuing, "Let's start in order, hmm? I am pack-mates with Fen and I have known him almost my entire life. We are as close as could be. Although, he did not share any of the breakfast treats, which makes me think he's not as close to me as I thought. I *am* very interested in tasting your goodies," -he winks, as if insinuating something else- "I will be done here whenever Tawson shows up and I would be delighted to help you carry heavy items. This will allow me to spend more time with you and I will get to see your bakery. That is an excellent plan."

The warmth still flows through me from his touch, making it very difficult to pay attention to his words. But, I think I got the gist of it. He is going to help me carry my crate and he's going to come to my bakery. I'm not sure I'll be able to get him to leave after, or if I'll even want him to leave. I'm feeling very clingy with his attention right now and I'm not sure why.

"When do you think this Tawson will come to take over?" I ask, lips parting as I take a deep breath. He's muddled my mind with his scent and sunshine-y warmth.

Finally, he lets go and steps back. "If you give me a moment I will call him. I find myself very uninterested in working right now."

Missing his warmth as soon as it's gone, I shake my head. What is *wrong* with me? Have I been meddled with? Has someone cast a spell on me? Why would anyone even bother? No, none of that makes sense. What does make sense is that I have finally found scent compatible males that I actually think I could like. That must explain my odd behavior. Today has been confusing, but interesting, so far.

CH.6

As I wait for him to call on Tawson I look around at the items he's selling and remember the wooden figure that first caught my attention. I should really make sure I purchase that before leaving. I catch a glimpse of him out of the corner of my eye and he's got a strange look on his face. It's almost like he's blank and his eyes have a slightly glazed look. It's only a moment before he turns back to me.

"Alright, Tawson will be here momentarily and you can take me to your heavy lifting!" His cheerfulness is contagious. He makes me smile so easily.

"Oh! Before we head off I would very much like to purchase this figure, how much is it?" Pointing at the one I'm itching to have, as his smile grows. I don't understand why such a simple question could elicit such a grin from him.

Replying, he snags the figure, "Kitten! Think of it as my first courting gift, although really it should be from Gin since he carves them. He will absolutely love you. I can't wait until you meet." He's looking at me but I think he's grinning to himself at the thought of me meeting his pack-mates. He turns to wrap the figure in cloth before tucking it into a cross-body bag. He looks up suddenly. "Ahh, there he is!"

Turning to follow his gaze, I spot another incredibly handsome male. Where in the world did these guys find each other? Did they all find some special magic that made them extremely attractive? Shaking my head I scrutinize another male that belongs to Fen and Rafe's pack. Assuming that this is Tawson.

He's about the same height as Rafe, around six feet but that is the only thing that they have in common. Beautiful long teal hair, done in many small braids. No facial hair so I can clearly see his striking face. Deep, forest green eyes regard me. Even his skin has a light tint of green, it's the color of new leaves and it suits him so well.

Noticing his pointed ears peeking through his hair, a quiet squeal escapes me. This must mean he is Fae or Elven. Once he gets close enough I catch his scent. Oh no, another one that smells like all my best wishes have come true? Rafe might be right, his whole pack could be compatible.

Tawson smells like a field of wildflowers next to a river, lightly flowery but with the other scents of forest and freshwater. He smells like I want to roll around on him and coat myself in this scent. I think I might be drooling, *again*. I don't know if I'll be able to string together a full sentence, hopefully Rafe will do all the talking.

Having zoned out smelling him, I come back to myself. They're both looking at me, Rafe with a knowing smile and Tawson with a very slight tilt to his lips. I get the feeling that he is more serious than the other two. Fearing I missed out on some of their conversation, I try to focus. I bet it was about me.

Tawson looks me straight in the eyes and asks, "Who might you be, Sweetheart?"

I swear I can scent the desire coming from him and I know this is going to elicit stranger behavior than before. I don't know how to behave around males as attractive as this! Where is Dani when I need her? She would know how to talk to these guys. I also think she would probably be throwing me at them if she'd heard how Rafe was talking. I'm a little afraid of what she's going to do when I tell her about all of this.

As I'm contemplating this, staring at him open mouthed, I try to discreetly wipe my chin. Managing to stutter out a response, my face heats, "Uh... Um... I-I-I'm Luella."

He steps closer to me, close enough that I can feel the heat of his body. His gaze is intense. "Rafe has informed me that you are going to be the mate to our pack of misfits. When he first mentioned he had met our perfect match, I thought he was joking, but as soon as I scented you, I knew. You *are* perfect and I have a feeling every single one of us will agree on this. Gin may be a little grumpy about it, but he's pretty much always like that." Rafe laughs at this and I feel like I'm definitely left out of the joke because Tawson is chuckling lightly, too. He continues, "I hear that Fen has also already made your acquaintance and tried to keep you to himself. Such a naughty thing for him to do. I'll be having words with him later."

To say that I am confused and a little out of my depth would be a massive understatement. I understand about half of what Tawson has said to me. I'm also confused because Tawson said Rafe told him about me but I only met him half an hour ago and I have been standing in front of him the entire time.

At no point did I hear Rafe tell him about me and Fen either. Something is strange, and it's not me this time!

Before I get a chance to comment on anything, Rafe declares, "Well, Tawson, I'm leaving the cart in your capable hands while I help our pretty little mate carry heavy things. I also get to visit her bakery and hopefully I'll have a chance to taste something..." his voice drops lower, and gives me shivers, "delicious." Does he actually mean my food or is he hinting at something else? I'm so in over my head with these guys.

Tawson groans. "That's why I had to come take over? Why don't I go help her and you can stay here?" I'm pretty sure Rafe is going to say no, I'm also very sure I'm not ready to deal with Tawson by myself yet. He's far more serious and intimidating. I fear I'd make a fool of myself alone with him.

"No," that's all Rafe says. Just, no. Clearly he's not ready to let me out of his sight just yet. Tawson sighs and makes his way to the spot Rafe was in when I first walked up to his cart.

Rafe, with a hand on my back, steers me away from Tawson.

Looking over my shoulder at Tawson I chirp a quick, nervous, "Bye!" as we walk away.

I don't think Rafe knows where he's

going though since I haven't told him where I need to pick up my crate. I wonder if he's going to ask or if he's just going to guess on the direction. So far, we're going the right way and I know it was a 50/50 choice but I am impressed.

Deciding to break the silence, "So... Can you guys communicate telepathically or am I losing my mind?" Okay, so I went right for it. I think that's the thing that has me most curious. I need some answers.

Smiling widely at me, his eyes bright with amusement. "Yes! Kitten, you are very smart aren't you? You're going to keep us all on our toes. I can see it now, it will be great entertainment for me and Fen but I have a feeling you will give Tawson and Gin anxiety. I'm very excited."

"I don't want to give anyone anxiety. I don't want to upset anyone either. I'm just curious and Tawson said a few things that didn't make sense to me and the only way he would have known any of it is if you'd told him but I don't remember hearing you say anything so it had to be mentally. It's not really being smart, it's just the logic of deduction." Shrugging, as if his compliment didn't make my ears burn with pleasure.

Smiling down at me gently, he tosses an

arm over my shoulders and tugs me close to his side. "My Little Kitten, you're much too sweet. But don't worry, any anxiety those two get will only be because they are worriers. Anything that doesn't follow the plan concerns them. Fen and I have learned to just allow them to do their thing."

Before I can ask about the other guys in their 'misfit' pack, I see Kip. "Oh! There's Kip. He's holding onto my purchases. He has the *best* ingredients and he always makes sure to bring extra of certain items for me if he thinks I'll enjoy it. This time he brought me an entire crate of chocolate!" I exclaim excitedly, adding a little hop to my step. I know I'm rambling but that doesn't seem to bother Rafe. He just smiles down at me. The more comfortable I get with these males the less shy I feel. It happened much faster than I expected though.

Kip catches sight of us and scowls at Rafe. I know he is a little protective of me, he knows my history and he's been almost like a beloved uncle to me. Currently, he is assessing Rafe and I can't tell what he thinks because he hasn't stopped scowling since we walked up.

Kip finally looks at me with a grumble, "Where'd you find this one? And why is he touching you? Shouldn't he be here just for the muscle? Muscle doesn't need to touch you." He's frowning at me but it's gentler than his usual scowl for anyone else. That's how I know he likes me. His frown is usually a little softer for me.

Smiling, my cheeks warm. "I met him just a little while ago, he and his pack are courting me. He's going to prove that he can help me around the house by carrying heavy things for me!" I'm a little surprised with myself for not thinking that Kip might have a problem with any males I may bring by. I guess he really only has a problem because Rafe has an arm around me. I didn't think Kip would be so defensive of me. I am an adult and have been caring for myself for many years now. But it is nice to know he cares this much about me. It gives me warm and fuzzy feelings.

Kip's reply is gruff and grumpy, "Well, what's his name then?"

Rafe steps forward and gives a bow before answering, "My name is Rafeel Dinsha and it is my pleasure to meet someone who cares a great deal about my Little Kitten." The bow he gave Kip was deep enough to be considered a sign of respect. I'm pleasantly surprised he was willing to give that to a Goblin. Most races find Goblins to be distasteful and generally treat them badly or snub them altogether. I can tell Kip is also surprised by this as his brow raises and his scowl lessens a tad.

Kip clears his throat. "Hmph, well then... I see you at least have manners." Turning to me. "Did you say a whole pack was courting you? How many are we talking about? This is ridiculous, you do not need a whole pack. Maybe one good Alpha or an extremely impressive Beta, but a pack?" Near the end I can tell he's a little lost in his own head grumbling about packs and unnecessary Alpha's.

Chuckling, I bring my hands up to cover my mouth so neither of them notice but that fails when I spy Rafe holding back a laugh and Kip's scowl is almost a smile.

"Luella, how in the Goddess did you end up with a pack of Alpha's chasing you? I'm not sure this is a good thing." Kip's back to glowering at Rafe, hands fisted on his hips.

Rafe replies, "I can assure you, this is a good thing. My Little Kitten has been alone for far too long and I'm positive we are highly compatible. Not just myself but my pack brothers as well. She hasn't met my last brother yet, but since she is a match to the others, I'm confident she will match him as well. Even if she doesn't, we will spoil her and treat her like the Queen she will be to us."

His response is stated with such confidence it makes me blush. How can anyone think I need such spoiling? I'm not sure what

I'll do with being spoiled since I haven't had someone looking after me like that for years. I don't know if I'll be able to let them spoil me, I am pretty independent and don't truly know how to ask for help when it matters. I mean, if I could have lifted the crate off the ground I would have tried to carry it home on my own.

Kip eyes him up and down before responding, "Ok. I cannot argue with scent matches, you have manners, and you seem to have Luella's well being in mind, so I will not stand in your way. But, I warn you, if I come back here and find out you have injured her in any way, and this includes her feelings, I will make you and your pack disappear. I may be a Beta, but I am also a Goblin, and we are the masters of making things disappear into the dirt."

Kip nods like this is the end of the conversation before turning to lead us behind his cart where I had left my crate and the other goods I purchased. Rafe looks at me with an eyebrow quirked and I shrug trailing after Kip.

CH.7

Rafe made carrying all of my goods seem easy. It was a little unfair because I hadn't been able to even lift the crate off the ground. But I guess that was a good thing because I didn't have to find Dani and try to haul all of this between the two of us or wait until tomorrow when I could bring my own small cart to drag it back to the bakery, which would definitely get in the way of my sales.

The walk back went well, it wasn't too far and Rafe kept up a stream of increasingly ridiculous questions about my likes and dislikes. Turning each question on him after, because I want to get to know him too. Since he seemed so determined to become my mate I figured it would be a good idea to learn as much as I can. Deciding to mate a bunch of Alphas on scents alone is foolish. I'll have to remember to ask the others these silly questions too.

Leading him up to the front of my bakery I unlock the door. Directing him to drop everything off in the kitchen through the opening behind the counter while I re-lock the door behind us. I don't want customers just walking in while I have nothing to sell. I have to check the breads and prepare the fires for baking. I may even have some time to whip up a few savory pastries with some of the new ingredients. *Oh! The Chocolate! What should I make with it first?*

Staring out the window by the door, I jump, flailing when I lose my balance and almost rip my curtains down when he comes up and lightly touches my back. Luckily, Rafe catches me before I fall and destroy my drapes. His warm scent wraps around me like his arms do and I can't help laughing when I remember I'm not alone here. Getting so lost in my head thinking about what I need to do next that I almost forgot about Rafe.

Turning to him, blushing, again I blurt, "I think I forgot you were here for a second and I got distracted in my dinner prep planning."

Laughing, he tugs me against him. As he wraps his arms around me in a warm hug he replies with mock hurt, "Kitten, how could you forget my magnificence was here with you? Have I been dimming my brilliance too much? Shall I rectify this?"

While he's being dramatic he's tugged me even closer and is now snuffling against my neck, it tickles and I giggle, warmth suffusing me at his playfulness. It also has heat flushing through me to my core but I'm choosing to ignore that for now. I like this impish side of Rafe. I hope I will enjoy being around the rest of the pack, too.

After taking a deep inhale of my scent, he asks, "So, what do you need to do before your dinner sales? And how can I help you?"

"That's very sweet of you to offer, but don't you need to get back to your cart?" My brows squish together as I get a fluttery feeling in my stomach. I wasn't expecting him to stick around and watch me bake for the afternoon but I can't deny I enjoy his presence.

"There is nowhere else I'd rather be. Tawson said he'd handle the cart for the rest of the day and depending on what's going on tomorrow he may work it again for me. I would much rather be near you, at all times. You're precious and my inner Alpha has this driving urge to protect you and provide for you."

He's very blunt about his feelings. I already knew this but whenever he spouts this 'I am Alpha' stuff, it still surprises me. I'm not used to anyone wanting to take care of me, it's strange.

Humming a little in response I lean in to give him a sniff before untangling myself from him. I didn't even think before I did it, but it's happened, and I'm going to act like I totally planned to do that. I take his hand and lead him into my kitchen. Pushing him into a chair at my little table I mutter, "Okay. Let me get things going here for my dinner rolls and I'll see if there's anywhere I can put you to work."

He watches intently as I go through my routine. I'm very aware of his focused gaze as I putter around. When I'm done placing the bread on cooling trays, I clear a space for the savory pastries. Deciding I can use him, I have him help mix things. It cuts my prep time in half, having an extra pair of hands and I'm finished much earlier than expected.

He helps stock my display while I get my cash box out to the front counter and prepare for my evening sales. We aren't talking much but it is surprisingly comfortable to have him in my space. When he passes near me he runs a hand along my back or shoulder and it's... nice. I like when he touches me, it's strangely soothing in a way I hadn't expected. I didn't think I would enjoy having someone, a male especially, in my space constantly but Rafe has a very soothing aura surrounding him. Which I didn't suspect because from the moment I met him he seemed excitable.

Once everything is in its place for sales, I unlock the front door. Rafe stands behind me, leaning against the wall like a personal bodyguard. I hope his presence doesn't put off my customers.

I shouldn't have worried though because I completely sell out of everything in a few hours. Rafe seems a little surprised and sad.

"Why are you sad I sold all my goods? This is a good thing, Rafe." Frowning at him in confusion as I tidy.

Looking a little sheepish, a slight blush tints his cheeks as he bites his lip. "I was hoping there would be something left for me to eat. Everything smelled so good while you were baking it."

Giggling brightly, I grab his hand and drag him back into the kitchen. "I put aside food and some pastries for us for dinner."

Grabbing me in a big hug, he swings me around as he laughs. "Oh, I should have known better! My Little Kitten will take care of me." I don't know if I've ever smiled this much in my life, my cheeks are starting to hurt.

Once he puts me down I uncover the plates of food I set aside. He looks at me, head tilted to the side and eyebrows raised. "Why are there three plates? There's only two of us here, are we expecting company?"

"I told Fen I would spend time with him when he was done at the market tonight." My ears turn red as I shuffle my feet, fidgeting with my pockets. Truthfully, Rafe had almost distracted me enough that I forgot about Fen coming by. But when I was putting aside food for Rafe and myself I remembered.

As I'm explaining this to Rafe I hear the door open. Oops, I guess we forgot to lock it after I had sold out.

Rafe gets a serious look on his face, all humor and playfulness gone, and gently puts me behind him. "Let me check who's here before you go out there."

Knowing he takes my safety seriously is reassuring and sweet, but this is a little funny to me, since I run a bakery that has people coming in and out all the time. I'm sure it's either Fen or someone looking for more dinner rolls.

Trailing after Rafe I bump into his back when he stops abruptly. Peeking around his broad shoulders to see what made him stop, I catch a glimpse of Jerrik's sneering face.

He stops when he sees me and mutters a curse before attempting to growl out, "Luella. Get over here, right now. Who is this beast coming out of your kitchen? I thought I told you that you were MINE?" He almost screams the last part at me. Which was a very stupid thing for him to do in the presence of an overprotective Alpha. I guess I can't really blame him, he doesn't know Rafe and he's also a very dimwitted human. I wonder what Rafe is... I never did ask him. I bet it's impressive, there's something in his eyes that burns with a manic sort of power.

Rafe starts growling at those words, it's a rattling, angry sound that makes my windows shudder and shake. I wonder if I'm going to see him murder Jerrik today? I don't actually think I would be upset. But I also don't want Rafe to get into any trouble with the Lord so I place my hand on his arm and murmur, "Rafe, Honey? Regardless of how much I dislike this male, I can't let you kill him because he's the local Lord's son and I don't want to see you imprisoned or executed for harming him."

This quiets the growling a little, but doesn't stop it. Rafe tries to push me behind him again, like I need protection from this fool who doesn't know any better. But before Jerrik has a chance to say anything else absurd the door behind him opens and Fen steps in.

Looking between Rafe, Jerrik, and then me being guarded by an angry Rafe, he grabs Jerrik by the back of the neck before literally throwing him out the door. Locking it, he says,

"Well, that was interesting. I haven't heard Rafe growl like that in about six years. Although, I know he's very protective of you and that will only get worse. Big ol' papa wolf this one." Fen smirks, crossing his arms as he holds back a laugh. He continues, dropping the amusement. "I hoped you hadn't forgotten about me coming to spend time with you this evening. When I heard that you had met most of my pack, I worried that you would overlook me," he voices quietly. This makes me sad because he is gorgeous and not easily forgotten.

Walking over to him I am bold as I throw my arms around him and squeeze. I hope this will show him that I will not be overlooking his sweet face and delectable scent. I don't know how anyone could miss his presence. I mean, yeah Rafe and Tawson both smell amazing but there's something about Fen that makes me feel warm and cozy. I just want to wrap his scent around me like a blanket. I bet I would get an amazing night's sleep if I had his scent in my bed... I wonder if I can steal a piece of his clothing without him noticing? I wonder if I could steal a piece of clothing from all of them for that matter... I shake off my thoughts of thieving their clothing with a frown.

What a strange thing to desire...

He hugs me back and, just like I thought, I immediately feel warm, comfortable and happy. Before I realize what's happening I'm flying. Ending up with my face tucked into his neck, I can't help but take a deep inhale of his concentrated scent. I almost shudder with pleasure at his melted chocolate smell. I'm nuzzling him before I know what I'm doing and then my cheeks are blazing with my embarrassment for doing something like this without asking. I get the feeling he's okay with it but, still, one should ask before rubbing their face on someone. I don't know if I'll ever learn not to be so awkward.

Now hiding my burning face in Fen's neck so they can't see my mortification even though I just chastised myself for sticking my face here in the first place. *I can't win.* Like I told myself before, I've just gotta roll with it, so I'm going to stay right here until they make me come out.

Fen remarks softly, "Precious, you have no need to feel embarrassed about enjoying my scent. I rather like the fact that you can't get enough of me. And the feel of your little nose rubbing against me is making me all kinds of warm that I'm not sure you're ready for so I'm going to set you down now. I just needed to hold you close for a moment after ridding your place of such foulness. I needed to know you were unhurt." Realizing that hiding my face doesn't really do much to hide my embarrassment, I nod.

I forgot that they can scent my emotions. Damn Alpha senses.

Gently, he sets me on my feet and my rosy cheeks finally cool after hearing his words. "I can't help how I feel and I'll probably make a fool out of myself a bunch more because I doubt I'll ever change. But I am pleased you got rid of Jerrik, he's such a nuisance and I do not have the strength to throw him out myself. So, thank you, Fen. You probably also saved Rafe from being thrown in jail or executed for murdering the Lord's son. I kind of like him, too, so I'm glad he's going to be sticking around." Rushing the words out quickly, almost jumbling them in my haste. Hopefully, one of them will realize I could keep going forever, talking about nonsense.

Luckily, Rafe stops me with a gentle touch to my lips and a serious look on his face. "Kitten, does that vermin bother you often?"

Clearing my throat. "Well... not *often*, but enough to be a true bother and he did say something to me a few days ago that has me a little concerned he's going to escalate his attempts to get me to mate him. Even though I've told him countless times, I have less interest in him than a pile of trash, he doesn't seem to truly understand that I don't want him. I don't think he's ever been told no before."

The dark look on Rafe's face is eerie in contrast to his usual upbeat demeanor and Fen doesn't look much better. They're silent but I have a feeling they're having a conversation that I can't hear. They're making heavy eye contact and I can see their glazed eyes telling me they are doing their mind talking thing.

Rafe turns to look at me with one brow raised. "Okay, my precious Little Kitten, is it too forward of me to ask if one or both of us could spend the night here? We don't have to stay in the same room if that makes you uncomfortable." I swear I hear him mumble *'even if that's exactly where I desperately need to be'* before he continues, "Neither of us feels very comfortable leaving you alone with that snake lingering nearby."

Shooting a smile at them both. I've already deviated so far from my normal so why not allow them to stay? I have a feeling none of the Alphas in this pack are willing to let me go it alone now that they know me and I'm strangely alright with that.

"Okay." Shrugging, I turn to head into the kitchen tossing over my shoulder, "Now that all the excitement is over let's have some dinner."

◆ ◆ ◆

After a nice dinner with them both, in which Rafe pulled me to sit on his lap, since I only have two chairs I didn't fight this. I argued when he started feeding me though, because I'm not a child and I can feed myself, thank you very much. He honestly wouldn't hear any of it and threatened to spank me if I wanted to continue to behave like a child. I pouted for a while but relented when my grumbling stomach protested the lack of food. After that it was a lovely evening. Fen asked me about meeting Rafe and Tawson and whether I'd met Gin yet.

Making sure to double check the locks and that all the kitchen fires are out, except my big fireplace, I lead them up to my living space.

Anxious about them seeing my space and whether or not they'll like it, I fidget all the way up the stairs, chewing my lip. It is such a silly thought that I have to stop myself from laughing out loud. They asked to stay here so they will just deal with it. I think my bed will be big enough to fit all of us. It isn't until we get to my bedroom that I realize they're much bigger than I thought and I'm not sure even one of them will fit with my massive pile of furs, blankets and pillows.

Humming a little before I chirp, "Okay, wait here please. And take off your boots." I didn't realize I had it in me to be demanding with anyone, let alone these large Alphas.

Ignoring their light chuckles, I go about preparing my sleeping space for all of us. I have to completely rearrange everything to make it so we will all fit. I wonder if they'd complain if I asked to sleep on top of one of them? Although, I don't know how comfortable they'd be, they're all muscled hard bodies.

Once I'm finished, I stand back to admire the space I've created for the three of us and smile, but it does feel like it's missing something. I turn towards the Alphas patiently waiting and stalk over to them.

Reaching out, I tug at Fen's shirt. "Off. Please?"

I don't have to say anything else before Rafe is also pulling off his shirt. Once I have them in hand I head over to my creation and gently kneel down patting each shirt into its own spot. When I stand again, this time it feels right. There's a brief thought of how strange this is but I shrug it off as exhaustion.

Turning to the males, I swear I drool a little. They looked good with clothes on but shirtless, oh Goddess, they are fine examples of the male species. Shaking my head trying to focus I announce, "Okay! I'm ready now. Which one of you wants the bottom?"

They look at each other before giving me

a strange look. Rafe asks, "What? The bottom of the bed? Or...?"

Cackling with laughter I have to hold my sides as I gasp for air. Once I've caught my breath I reply, "No, underneath me silly. I wouldn't be cruel enough to make one of you sleep at the bottom of the bed when I've made space for all of us."

They glare at each other and play some strange game, I'm assuming to figure out which one gets to sleep under me.

Fen wins and I can see he's trying not to gloat too hard, but he's having trouble hiding the gigantic smile on his face as he turns to me.

"Pants on or off? I promise we both have underpants so we will not push any of your boundaries too quickly."

Rafe snorts out a laugh, as if he knows they've both pushed well past any normal boundaries. Shaking my head, I frown at them. "Who sleeps in pants? Isn't that really uncomfortable? No, I am not afraid of your male parts, I think. I've just never gone... *there*... before, so I don't think I'm ready. Especially because I've only known you both for a day or so. I feel like just having two males in my bed is an incredibly large step for me." When neither of them move I make a 'come on already' motion with my hands.

I have never seen a male strip before but I feel like they remove their pants in record time, they move so quickly.

Stepping up beside me, they wait. For what, I don't know. Rafe clears his throat and implores, "May we enter your ne..." he stops when Fen jabs him with his elbow, taking a breath before he continues, "your space?"

My nose scrunches in confusion, but I want them surrounding me so I shake it off and nod, gesturing at Rafe to get in first because I need to situate him and Fen before I can crawl in on top.

Once I'm snuggled on top of Fen with Rafe tucked beside us he pulls the top blanket over us and rests his hand on my lower back.

Taking a deep breath, I sigh at the perfect feeling I have with these two in my bedding. I drift off pretty quickly because this is the most comfortable I have ever been, their scents make me feel like I have no worries at all.

CH.8

Waking with my face smushed into Rafe's shoulder and a large rod poking into my backside is odd, to say the least. I wiggle a little, trying to pull myself out of their embrace knowing I have a lot to do this morning. But getting myself up feels incredibly difficult right now because they have me trapped in between their bodies and someone has an arm wrapped tightly around my waist.

My wiggling must wake Fen because I feel his hands clamp down on my hips to stop me. Am I hurting him? I pop my head up and look at him. He's smiling so I think he's okay.

"Precious, you have to stop wiggling against me like that or I'll be embarrassing myself very quickly." His voice is deep and husky with sleep and I shiver with want.

I don't know what it is I want but, I

want something. Before I get the chance to say anything Rafe groans. "Pfft, you'll embarrass yourself? I'm right there with you, brother." He sounds a little pained and it has Fen laughing.

His mirth shakes me, and my laughter joins his. Rafe's deep chuckles mix with ours, after a moment. This is the best morning I've ever experienced. But I do have to get moving, the sun looks higher than it usually does when I need to get things started in the kitchen, so I begin the struggle of getting out from between these two. But, they aren't letting me go anywhere. Two sets of hands, one at my hips and one at my waist tighten keeping me pinned in the space between them.

"I have to get my breakfast breads started! I'm already later than usual to get moving so I'm going to be rushing," I whine at them. The moment that sound hits them, Fen is dragging me into him and rolling so I'm near the edge of the space. He doesn't let go for a moment, leaning in and rubbing his face in my hair. Then he releases me and I hop out of bed. Looking back at them, all mussed and smelling heavenly, I scamper off to my bathroom to freshen up before I decide to spend my entire day in bed. It's barely a thought in my mind to wonder why they reacted so quickly to my whine.

When I get back to my room they're

both up and dressed but I note they left their shirts in my bedding and I couldn't be happier about this.

Why am I so happy to keep their shirts?

The thought briefly crosses my mind but I shake my head, I'll figure it out later. I hope I don't get too distracted by their shirtless forms while I'm baking.

Fen probes, "Alright, Precious, what can we do to help this morning since we made you late?"

Smiling softly at him feeling the tension in my face relax I motion them both to follow me downstairs. I'm giving orders as soon as we hit the kitchen.

"Fen, please light the fires and fill the kettle with water. Rafe, will you please wipe down the counter here so I have a clean space to work?"

Grinning, they nod and get to work while I start setting out all my ingredients. It's a surprisingly peaceful morning, we chat and ask questions getting to know each other better while I putter around and order them about.

While the dough is rising I invite them to join me for a cup of tea out front. I have them bring a chair from inside. Rafe pulls me onto his lap, like last night, and cradles me with one hand while sipping tea with the other.

This is nice. I never thought I'd enjoy sharing my peaceful mornings with anyone but these two make everything feel so natural. We're silent, enjoying the morning and it doesn't feel awkward. It's relaxing and I think I could get used to this. But, I remind myself, they aren't going to be here forever. They will leave at the end of the week and I'm not sure what to feel when I think about them leaving. Although Rafe did mention being their mate so, who knows what will happen.

That is a problem for future me. I'm going to enjoy this while I can and not worry about something I can't do anything about.

Following me back into the kitchen, I put them to work helping me pack for the market while I finish the breakfast rolls. They get the front set up for the morning sales and it makes my life so much easier. Who would have thought having more hands would make the work a breeze? I snort at my sarcasm.

They help me clean up after I'm sold out and then we're off to the market. I wonder if they're going to find reasons to hang around my cart today or if they'll go and help their pack at their carts?

Either way I don't think I'd mind them

sticking around but I know I'll be really busy and won't have much time to do anything except focus on my customers. My stall is always bustling and I'll likely sell out by early afternoon so I might have time to spend with them later.

Leading them through the slowly filling market I direct them where to put my baskets of goods. "Okay, I have to set up my display and get ready for the rush of customers. Are you guys working your carts today too?" I query as I hustle around, my focus half on them and half on my display.

Fen's eyes are laughing as he holds back his chuckles, crossing his arms. Rafe's head tilts to the side sporting a frown.

Fen replies, "I will be going to work at my cart today but I think Rafe will never be leaving your side. Literally, ever." Laughing outright now, he elbows Rafe, whose ears are burning while he shrugs with a self-deprecating smile.

Rafe murmurs something to Fen before looking at me. "Someone should stay with you. You need protection..." He trails off when I can't hold back my giggles.

"Rafe, I've lived alone for years now and no one in this village has ever given me problems. Well, except for Jerrik but he's never gotten too bad..." Pausing to think about how much worse he's been lately before I shake it off. "But, honestly? I really don't mind your company. Just know that you will likely be bored because my stall gets very lively." My face softens as I step closer to him, patting his arm. "I don't think I mind your protectiveness but understand that I will probably argue with you because I'm not used to it."

His eyes light up and a grin spreads across his face as he takes my hand. "I will argue right back when I feel you need to be protected and that means that I'm probably going to follow you around for the rest of your life. If you don't like that, I'll follow, unseen, from the shadows."

That statement has me snickering. When I get myself under control I ask, "You mean you'll stalk me if I'm not okay with you hanging around?"

Looking sheepish, he shrugs. "Uhhh... yes?" Rubbing the back of his neck. He looks so adorable I feel the need to help him out a little.

"Rafe, it's okay. I know that sounds really strange but I can honestly say that I am fine with having a very attractive, large, and polite male following me around." Leaning back so I can make eye contact with him, I smile gently. Although, I don't understand *why* it doesn't bother me. If it was anyone else I'd be so uncomfortable at the thought.

He hugs me close to himself and huffs out a laugh. "Good. I'm not sure if you know this but you will not be getting rid of me."

Taking a second to think about the end of the market, I impulsively utter, "Even after the market is over? You don't have a family or a life to get back to?" The vulnerability in my voice is apparent and I'm not really trying to hide it. I want them to know they've already become important to me and just thinking about them not being near me actually hurts.

Fen joins our hug, wrapping his long arms around both of us. "Luella, Precious, you are a part of our pack that we didn't know we needed. You make us feel whole. You give us something we hadn't really expected. We will discuss what we're going to do after the market but know this, you are coming with us wherever we go."

At Fen's statement, I feel warm and fuzzy. A big smile stretches across my face. I don't acknowledge that he said I'd be leaving with them, it's a bit strange, but I think I would be okay leaving my home and bakery to travel, as long as I was with them. Plus, it's as good an excuse as any to get away from Jerrik.

Neither of them can see it because I've

buried my face in Rafe's chest but I know they feel my happiness. I wonder if this other sense I'm developing for these males is a pack thing?

Mumbling into Rafe's chest, "Thank you. Every time I thought about you guys leaving, it actually hurt. So I'm really glad to hear that this isn't one sided." They squeeze me a little tighter and I gasp for air and laugh before stepping back.

"This is definitely not one sided. You are *ours*." Leaning in, Fen gives me a quick peck on the corner of my mouth. My blush grows brighter before he continues, "Okay, I've got to go relieve Gin and touch base with Tawson. I'll see you both later."

After he leaves both Rafe and I are quiet as we finish setting up my display and start selling to the customers walking through.

The day grows busier and we have little time for conversation. As I'm selling, Rafe is being helpful by wrapping up goods and refilling the displays.

Until we start running out of treats, we have a constant stream of customers. When we're finally sold out Rafe looks at me, eyebrows raised and mouth gaping. "How in the world did you sell out of all of those this early?"

Laughing, my delight apparent in my

smile. "Rafe, this is very normal for me on market days. Selling out this early gives me time to go back to the bakery and make more for tomorrow. Oh, and prepare for my evening sales."

"Kitten, you are amazing! I don't understand how you do everything you do. It's incredible and your determination to keep people fed is commendable but do you ever take time for yourself?" Touching my shoulder gently he turns me towards him, away from my tidying.

"Hmm... I took a day off last month to spend in the forest with my friend Dani, that counts right?" Tapping my chin, I think about any time off I've taken. Realizing it doesn't happen very often. But I don't really mind, even if I complain a lot to Dani.

"Well, I think, after the market is over you should plan some time off to get to know us and to take a well deserved break. Things will be changing for the better in your life," Rafe gently explains, it's almost like he knows I'm about to argue with him when Dani pops up in front of us making me jump and clutch my chest.

"Lulu! I'm sorry I disappeared yesterday, but I just got so distracted talking to the cloth merchant and then they wanted to show me some of their new stock they hadn't put out yet and I spent the rest of my day bartering for some awesome new fabrics that I can't wait to show you!" She rushes all her words out so quickly that I almost can't understand her. She's jumping side to side, talking with her hands. Everything she does is so animated.

A laugh sneaks out of me and before I have a chance to reply to her she continues with, "I see you didn't waste your day though. Please introduce me to this absolute hunk of a male you have hovering over you." Giving me a sly smile she winks and nudges me with her elbow.

"I wasn't worried when I couldn't find you. Plus, I was the one who wandered off this time and yes, I had a very fruitful shopping day yesterday. Kip saved me a whole crate of chocolate! I can't wait to experiment with some new recipes..." She cuts me off before I get lost in my ruminations over recipes.

"LULU! I love you and I love your food but for the love of the Goddess please introduce me to this male!" Shrieking, she jumps up and down, her wings fluttering with her exuberance. She's smiling so hard her cheeks must hurt.

Blushing lightly, I peek over my shoulder at Rafe, who is currently trying to hold back his laughter.

Clearing my throat. "Uhhh... Yeah, so... I may have forgotten to tell you yesterday that I met a male who came into my shop the day before and I couldn't get over his scent... and then at the market yesterday I ran into him again at his cart and we planned a very small date before I continued my shopping. Then, I met another very attractive male who immediately told me I was going to be his pack's mate because my scent was perfect... and then he hasn't left my side since." Getting it all out, speaking almost as fast as Dani, I know she's going to have a million and one questions for me.

Before she can respond to all of that, Rafe pipes in, "Hello, I am Rafe, Luella's soon to be mate." Holding his hand out to shake, she just stares at him before looking at me with her mouth opening and closing like a fish.

After a long awkward silence, while Rafe holds his hand out waiting for her to shake it, she screeches, "LUELLA BAKKEN! How could you not tell me you found compatible males! And a pack! This is amazing!"

Flinching at her high pitched shrieking I look down, fiddling with my dress, feeling chagrined for hiding this from her. Before I can give a response to this she engulfs me in a big bear hug, squeezing me so hard it feels like my insides are being smushed.

"I'm sorry, I didn't mean to yell at you, but Lulu, this is huge! I'm so happy for you, as long as they are good males." She glares at Rafe. "I'm going to have to meet them all because I have to make sure my best friend will be well taken care of."

Rafe steps forward and bows gallantly to Dani. "Let me properly introduce myself. I am Rafeel Dinsha from Pack Foreastra. We got together in Tayrin almost eighty years ago. I know that makes us sound old but we met when we were quite young and knew we were meant to be together, it's the same feeling I got the moment I met my Little Kitten." Looking over at me, his smile softening as he holds one hand over his heart.

Dani is trying to telepathically tell me something, but since we don't have that power she just looks a little constipated and I sputter out a laugh.

Grinning at Rafe while I get my laughter under control, I reply to Dani, "Honey, sweetheart, my bestest friend. You know I can't read your mind but I am very happy that I've met them, even though Rafe here can come on a little strong. But, both him and Fen, one of the others, stayed with me last night and even threw Jerrik out when he tried to harass me again. They make me feel safe and happy."

She starts tearing up at that, sniffling and clutching both hands to her chest, vibrating with emotions. "Lulu, just for the fact that they threw Jerrik out makes me love them for you. Okay, I need some time to fully process this and I know you're busy here but at the end of the market you *will* bring that pack over to meet me and my parents before you swan off into the sunset with them." She's stern, wagging a finger at me, one hand on her hip. Her dainty Pixie face looks adorable instead of the serious she was going for.

"I promise, I will." Giving her a hug goodbye before turning to Rafe. "Well, that was my best friend Dani and I'm sure you have some questions but let's finish tidying up here before heading back to my shop." Nodding his head, he leans down and kisses my forehead before going back to what we were doing. I wanted to ask him about how my life was going to change, but I'm pretty sure I can guess.

CH.9

We don't head straight for my shop, Rafe takes me on a detour to see Fen first then after that we are going to stop at Tawson's cart.

Fen's eyes light up when he sees us approaching, and I melt a little. He comes around to give me a hug and kiss on the head before asking, "How were your sales today?"

"Oh, we sold out about an hour ago so we cleaned up and are going to head back to bake more for tomorrow." Smiling up at him, I lean into his side.

"I'm not surprised you sold out, your food is amazing! I'm glad you stopped by, Gin is about to take over for me and I'm excited for you to meet him." Wrapping an arm around me he tugs me tight to his body as he praises me.

Nervous to meet the last male in their pack, I look down and nibble my lip, what if he doesn't like me? What if all of this has been a mistake and they no longer want me in their pack? I mean, what does a pack of Alphas want with a short, awkward, Beta? The most I have to offer is my baking... I know I'm spiraling and it's silly but I can't help these self-deprecating thoughts.

Interrupted in my spiral of doubt by Fen picking me up and tucking my face into his neck while he squeezes me tight. I settle immediately, all my panicked thoughts calming. His scent is so good and the tightness of his arms is comforting, it relaxes me so much. I feel like I've found a new happy place.

A deep, gravelly, voice interrupts my relaxing thoughts of making chocolates in my kitchen. "This her?"

Peeking up, and up, and up, at the last male in my potential pack, I can't stop my mouth from dropping open. This is the most incredible male I have ever set my eyes on. And I've said this about every single one of these males. He's got to be at least eight feet tall. Even in Fen's arms I feel tiny in comparison. With such a deep black his hair looks like it almost absorbs the light.

Deep dark blue eyes inspect me, they are so dark they must have hints of black. With a body so muscular it looks like he could crush melons with his biceps, I kind of want to ask him to do it so I can swoon over it. This giant male's skin is the color of milk chocolate and I want to lick him to see if he tastes as good. I can't scent him because my face is still pretty tucked into Fen's neck so I wiggle a little to be let down.

Stepping towards him I hold my hand out to shake when I catch his scent and I don't really know what happens but I find myself climbing him like a tree and taking deep lungfuls at his neck. His hands cradle me so gently while I practically molest this male that I've only known for about three seconds. But, his scent called to me so strongly I think this reaction was unavoidable. He smells like home, like my morning tea and cinnamon rolls and I can't get enough. I don't think I'll be able to let him go.

A rumble runs through me. Realizing it's him, I suck in a shocked breath, he's purring. I've heard that Alphas do this to relax their Omegas and I'm not sure why it affects me, a Beta, but it makes me melt. Mumbling into his neck, "Sorry, not sorry, I don't know what happened. But you smell so good I can't get down, okay?"

Chuckles sound all around me and I can hear Rafe saying, "I know she liked my scent but I didn't get this reaction. I think I'm a little jealous of Gin."

Fen replies, sounding confused but happy, "I'm jealous too but also really surprised, Gin doesn't like anyone and I was a little worried about them meeting. I guess I worried for nothing."

In his deep, guttural voice Gin exclaims, "Mine!" Shivering, I can tell he feels it by the way he clutches me a little tighter.

"Alright, Big Guy, but don't forget you have to share! She's *ours*," Rafe tries to tell Gin who just turns his back to him. He laughs and continues, "Well, Fen, I don't think Gin will be taking over for you, it looks like you'll be here for the rest of the day. I think we should all move our stuff to her bakery so we can stay with her, I'll let Tawson know and you two can haul everything over."

"That's an excellent idea! I'll meet him at the end of the day to help gather everything. We'll both see you tonight," Fen replies with a smile, delight shining in his eyes. He doesn't seem upset that he has to stay, he just looks happy that I get along with his last brother. Fen smirks and gives me a wink. My face reddens as I peek at them both over Gin's shoulder.

They do a manly back slap and Rafe joins me and Gin. "Okay, Big Guy, let's head over to Tawson's cart before I take you to see her bakery, she still has a bunch of stuff to do today so you will have to put her down eventually."

The thought of Gin putting me down has anxiety thrumming through me. A small barely audible whine slips out and a growl rolls through Gin directed towards Rafe. He puts his hands up and utters, "Never mind, just ignore me. Let's go see Tawson and we'll figure out the rest later."

He sounds a little grumpy so I reach over to grab his hand but I'm so high up that I end up patting his head instead, making him laugh. He smiles up at me. "Alright, Kitten, I'm fine. Everything is actually pretty great."

Once we reach Tawson I wiggle to be let down but Gin isn't having it. He grumbles at me and I respond with, "I need to give Tawson a hug, I haven't seen him since yesterday!" I don't know why I *need* to give him a hug, but I do. A lot of things have been very confusing lately. But, that's a problem for future me.

"He doesn't need a hug, he's fine," Gin grunts. I get the feeling that he doesn't talk much and usually gets his way. But I'm very stubborn and I *will* be giving Tawson a hug.

Tawson and Rafe are laughing at my predicament. "Hey, Big Guy, I would really like to hug my Little Sweetheart. I barely got time to see her yesterday." Tawson sounds like he's trying to guilt Gin but I don't think that will work on him.

Giggling into Gin's neck I pat his chest and plead, "Please, Big Guy? I promise to come right back to your arms when I've gotten my hug from him." Giving him my best pout, along with big pleading eyes, I ruin it by smiling.

But it works because he rumbles out, "Fine." Instead of putting me down he hands me directly into Tawsons arms.

Tucking my face into his neck now, I take a deep inhale of his scent while squeezing him tight. He's like a breath of fresh air. Like laying in a sunny meadow, no problems or worries. Sighing with satisfaction, I squeeze him.

Talking into his skin, my voice is slightly muffled, "Hi, Tawson, it's nice to see you again."

His suppressed mirth shakes me a little. "Hello, Sweetheart. It's wonderful to get another chance to see you. Although I almost wish you hadn't met Gin yet because I think he's going to hoard you to himself, the greedy Dragon. Although I am surprised that he's taken to you so fast, he usually hates everyone." He hums as he contemplates this.

I wonder if Gin really is a Dragon, because that would be the coolest thing and maybe I can get him to shift for me. "Why do all of you call me little? I'm not *that* small." Leaning back I cross my arms, and furrow my brow, trying to look serious.

"You are just so much shorter than all of us, we can't help it. You're tiny and beautiful and sweet. We can stop if you want," Tawson tells me, tugging me forward to nuzzle his face into my hair.

Before I get a chance to say anything else to him, I'm in Gin's arms again. It happened so fast I barely felt anything. Neat trick, I wonder how he did that. I feel like I'm always going to have about a million questions around these males.

Looking up into Gin's eyes I get lost for a second before I remember what I was going to say, "Gin, honey, you will have to share me with your pack mates eventually." Patting his chest, I get lost in the feel of his muscles and run my hands over him.

All three of them start laughing because I'm definitely the most awkward female they've probably ever met. Oh well.

Gin rumbles quietly, "Okay, Little One, I will try to share but not yet."

I can agree to that, at least he knows he has to share eventually. "Are you really a Dragon? Tawson said something about hoarding and Dragons and... that would be really cool, I've never met a Dragon before. Then again, I've never really left this village and it's pretty small. The only time I get to meet new beings is during the market and we don't usually get unique beings here since we're so out of the way," I blurt out rapidly.

"Yes. I can't wait to show you my hoard." Whenever Gin speaks, I feel all melty inside and I love it. His voice is so deep and the guttural tones make me clench my thighs together. Feeling a little wetness seep out from my core, my eyes widen slightly. That's new, and strange, it must be because these males arouse me just by existing.

They all inhale deeply and purrs echo from each of them, my body immediately goes limp in Gin's arms. My eyes feel heavy and all I can do is drape myself over him. I guess they can smell my arousal.

A shocked gasp interrupts his purr and draws our attention over to Rafe, whose mouth is gaping open, eyes wide and arms limply hanging at his sides. "You're going to show her your hoard? You haven't even shown your pack yet! And we've been with you for eighty years! I almost feel insulted... But, because it's our mate I can understand a little." The pouty, offended tone in his voice is highly amusing.

It's my turn to make a shocked little gasp. "How old are you guys? You've been a pack for eighty years and yet you look like you're not much older than me... I feel like a child compared to you, I'm only twenty seven."

"Doesn't matter. You're ours." Gin is very direct and to the point. I get the feeling that he doesn't need to say much to get his point across. I am still curious to know how old they are.

"But..." I'm cut off by Tawson.

"I promise all of your many, many, questions will get answered because you are going to be with us for a very long time. We will all learn many things as we grow closer together." Cupping my cheek while he talks distracts me when I get a hint of his scent and, mixed with Gin's, I feel euphoric.

"But, I'm only human so I'm not going to be around as long as you guys..." Trailing off with a sigh. The realization that they are all, likely, incredibly long lived beings hits me and it makes me want to cry. How can this work? I'm only going to live for a minuscule portion of their lives.

"Tawson?" Looking at him and then Rafe. "Can I ask what kind of beings you are?" Knowing I sound sad but I can't help it. Gin purrs harder to try and comfort me.

Rafe responds, "I am a Hellhound, I have the shape of a dog but much larger and I drip magma and fire. I can also use both as a defence. It makes me particularly dangerous." His brows draw together as he wipes his palms against his pants. He looks worried and I wonder if it's because he's afraid that I will be scared of him. I'm not, he sounds amazing and I want to ask if he'll shift for me. It also makes me feel safe because no one would survive attacking any of them.

"I am a Fae. Summer Fae to be exact." I don't let Tawson finish because I'm so excited.

"Whoa! Really? I've always wanted to meet one of the Fae! I know each court has specific powers but Summer has always been my favorite season because I love the warmth and sunshine. Your court has specific powers in manipulating storms and water, right?"

Laughing, he smiles brightly as his shoulders relax. "Yes, Love. I can manipulate storms, lightning in particular. I can also influence water of all types and additionally I can control certain facets of plantlife."

Before either Tawson or Rafe can continue, Gin cuts them off with a gruff, "Why are you sad?"

Sniffling to try and hold back my tears, I hide my face in Gin's neck before I answer,

"Because all of you are basically immortal beings and I'm just a silly little human with a tiny lifespan compared to you and this is never going to work because you'll blink and I'll be old and weak and gone before you realize." Some tears escape and I choke back a sob and wonder why I'm feeling so emotional. I should have known that this wouldn't work, that's not how things go for me. I'm alone and will always be alone. Even Dani will live decades longer than me. Humans are the weakest species out of all of them.

"Little One..." Gin pauses and inhales deeply, "I do not think you are human. You do not smell human and I have an excellent nose. Also, once any of us bite you to create the mating bond you will gain our lifespan. *YOU. ARE. OURS*," Gin says all of this in a raspy whisper in my ear while I use his shoulder as a cloth to catch my tears.

It takes me a moment to process what he said and when it sinks in I jerk my head up and stare at all of them with wide eyes. "WAIT! *What?* I'm... I'm not a human? Then... what am I?"

This time it's Tawson who responds, "We aren't sure, I've never smelled anything like you before but I know it isn't human. Humans have a particular note to their scent regardless of how nice it is, that gives them away. I think it's the scent of mortality." He shrugs, unconcerned.

"Oh," that's my bright reply. I think I'm in shock. Hearing that I'm not what I thought I was is a major surprise but it's not like I would have ever known, at least until I stopped aging like a human and lived longer than their lifespan. I have no parents to ask... But they were human, weren't they?

"I'm very confused. Can we go home? I need to bake and process. I can't deal with any more information right now."

Gin brushes the hair off my face and grunts. "Of course." Turning to Tawson, "Fen will help bring all our stuff to her place, we are staying there."

He doesn't wait for a response before walking off. Rafe has to jog to catch up. Chortling as he remarks, "Gin, her place is this way."

CH.10

I don't realize that I've fallen asleep on Gin until I wake up in my bed at home. Confused and groggy, I don't remember how I got here or why I'm on top of Gin. Where's Rafe? Looking around I don't really see anything because I'm still half asleep.

Gin rumbles beneath me and I suck in a breath because, whoa, that felt really good. My legs are spread over his stomach. He's too tall for me to fit perfectly against him, he must have kept my face on his shoulder so I could sleep comfortably. I think I would have been okay if I'd been a little lower. I'm curious to know what he's got going on down there. He's so big and I'm a tiny bit scared of what I'm going to find. Would he even fit? I'm so much smaller than him and I've never been intimate with a male before. I've never been interested. I mean, sure, I've touched myself once in a while to burn off some energy and feel good for a bit, but males have never really interested me until I met this pack.

Peeking up at Gin, I find him already watching me. I wonder if he can read minds? I'm slightly afraid to ask if any of them can because my mind is a mess most of the time. "Hello. Um... You make a very comfortable bed. Thank you for letting me sleep on you?" I pose it as a question even though it's not.

He rumbles again and I hold back a moan, because *oh my*, that feels good against my core. "You are welcome to sleep on me everyday. I think I will enjoy waking up to your beauty." Smirking now, he's got a sly look in his eye and I'm sure with his enhanced senses he can smell my arousal.

Blushing hard, I glance away. "Thank you. Umm, I think I need to get up." Shooting upright. "Oh! How long have I been asleep? I have so much to do! Have I missed the evening? Oh, I'm going to be up so late baking for the market tomorrow." Panic and shock flow through me at the thought of missing an evening of sales. Although, now that I think about it, I don't need the money as much because even if I don't go to put up my stall I still get plenty of customers coming to my bakery during the market. Okay, yeah, I'll be alright. I can still afford to feed myself and pay the tithe to the Lord of this land.

"Relax, Little One, you've only been asleep a short while. You have plenty of time to bake for your evening sales." Tugging me down, he places a gentle kiss on my lips. His voice vibrates his chest under me, forcing me to bite back a moan.

It stuns me, I don't know why. But it surprises me so much that the moan I'd been holding back slips out when I taste him on my lips. Eyes darken at the sound and I let out a squeak of wonder when he deepens the kiss. I feel his tongue tasting my lips and open them a bit to see if his taste is as good as his scent.

It's so much better. He licks into my mouth, groaning. I find myself grinding my leaking pussy on his abs and he encourages me to move more when his hands grasp my hips. There's a tingle deep in my core growing and building with each rock of my hips. I gasp when his thumb rubs against my clit.

Rocking faster, he growls and it rolls through my body making my head fuzzy before it finds its way to my core. He grunts out, "Let go, Little One, I will catch you."

At his words I spasm. This orgasm is so much bigger than any I've ever given myself. I'll never be satisfied by my own fingers again and I must mumble something to that effect because he barks out a laugh. "Little One, you will never have to use your hands to pleasure yourself again."

I'm so relaxed I have melted into him, not even acknowledging the wetness that has seeped through my underpants, leaving a puddle under me on his stomach. I murmur, "Thank you," before a shadow falls over us.

"Awww, did I miss out on some fun with my Little Kitten?" The pout in Rafe's voice has an amused smile creeping across my face.

Peeking up at him with lust fogged eyes I bravely state, "Yes. My Dragon made me feel amazing. I dunno if anyone can top that... Or is this just what it feels like when another person helps touch someone intimately?"

Rafe growls loudly and probes in a rough voice, "Kitten, are you telling me that no one else has ever touched your little cunt before?"

That growly voice generates shivers throughout my body and my pussy leaks more wetness. "I didn't want anyone before you guys. Is... Is that bad?" My voice grows a little smaller at the end. Now I'm wondering if my inexperience is a bad thing and my anxiety builds, while my lust wanes.

"Goddess, no. It's incredibly attractive. It makes my beast feel smug to know that our pack are the only males that will touch you. Ever." Rafe's tone is velvety and smooth and I giggle, sighing with relief.

"Okay. Good. Um... I need to go clean up and then get to baking. Thank you." Leaning down I give Gin a quick peck. After Rafe helps me out of bed I tug him down for a kiss on the lips too. Then, I scurry to the bathroom, the cooling release between my thighs feeling awfully uncomfortable now.

When I get back to my room to change they're both gone, probably downstairs. I quickly dress and head down. I have so much to do, but I think it was good that I took a moment with Gin and experienced something so wonderful. I bet that's why Dani fools around with so many males. It feels amazing! I'll have to stop bugging her about it and tell her I finally had a male make me cum.

As I'm lost in thought I wander downstairs and bump into a wall. It's jarring and I stumble back. Strong arms catch me before I can fall and all of a sudden I'm up in Gin's embrace again.

"Oh! I'm so sorry! I wasn't paying attention to where I was going..." I trail off because Gin has a look in his eye that I'm not sure I like.

"Little One, be careful. I am fairly large and it's pretty hard to miss me. I don't think you'd appreciate it if my Dragon took over.

He keeps telling me to carry you off to our hoard where nothing can touch you and we could protect you better," he grumbles out, a little smoke escaping as he speaks. His Dragon is making himself known. It's honestly the coolest thing ever, and I can't wait to see what his Dragon looks like.

That's the most I've ever heard him speak at once and I'm a little dazed from the raspy, rumbly sensation of his voice. But, I have too much to do to be swaddled away in some far off place for my 'protection' so I shake myself out of it.

Patting his cheek lightly. "Okay, grumpy Dragon. I will be more careful, I promise. Now, I need you to put me down because I have baking to do!" I kiss his cheek for good measure.

His chest rumbles pleasantly before he relents and puts me on my feet. But he insists on following me as I gather ingredients and get to work. It makes things a little difficult and I tell him so but it doesn't seem to make any difference.

Rafe isn't any help either. He just sits at my small table in the corner laughing at us both. Eventually I get fed up and sternly tell Gin, "Go sit with Rafe! You can see the entire kitchen from there and reach me in seconds if something happens." Propping my hands on my hips for good measure, I frown at him. "GO."

I've never seen a giant, grumpy, male pout; it really is something. I have to hold back a laugh at the put out look on his face but I manage. Barely.

It doesn't take me long to get the savory pastries ready. Today I decided to make some spiced meat pastries, since I was able to grab some fresh deer before we left the market. It makes the kitchen smell incredible. While those are baking in the oven I start on more cookies, bars and hand pies for the market tomorrow.

After my evening customers are gone it's time for us to eat. Hopefully, Fen and Tawson will be here soon. I tried to make enough for them as well. They are large males though, so I'm not sure how much they will eat.

Thinking about them must have summoned them, because they both walk in shortly after the last customer leaves. I'm so excited to see them I run and jump on Fen first, who catches me easily. Giving him a kiss on the cheek before I lean over towards Tawson, who casually plucks me from Fen's arms.

There's no stopping myself from

sticking my nose in his neck and huffing his scent. I feel like I should be embarrassed but I'm really not. Not when they all smell so freaking good.

When I'm done scenting him I kiss his cheek too. I can't leave any of them out. I want to make sure I'm being fair with my affections.

Leaning back so I can see all of them. "Now that everyone is here, we can have dinner! I tried to make enough for everyone... but you guys are really big so we might have to make some snacks later." I finish with a shrug.

Instead of putting me down, Tawson heads for the kitchen while holding me and orders Fen to lock the door.

Since I only have two chairs Tawson keeps me on his lap while Gin and Rafe stand. Fen takes the other seat. Rafe grabs the pastries I set aside and everyone digs in.

Tawson feeds me bites of food before eating any himself. These guys really like to do stuff for me, and they don't seem to hear me when I insist I can do it myself. It's honestly kind of funny and I have to contain my laughter.

They help me wrap up the goodies for the market and place them in baskets so everything is ready for tomorrow. They surprise me by getting all the cleaning done and I'm left watching them with nothing to do but drool over their muscles.

Once I've finished ogling them I tell them I'm going upstairs to get ready for bed. I have some rearranging to do if everyone is going to fit in my room... Actually, I'm not sure they will all fit. It isn't that big of a space.

I don't know how long it's been since I came up here to rearrange things but I look up and they're all crowded around my doorway watching me move pillows and blankets around. I hear a faint humming and realize they're all purring. It has a smile steal across my face.

"I don't think everyone will fit in the bed... I'm pretty sure three is the limit. Since Fen and Rafe slept with me last night it's only fair if Tawson and Gin join me tonight. Do you guys have sleeping rolls? There is space on the floor here so we could have everyone stay in the same room." I'm almost pleading with them to say yes because the thought of them all not being near me has me feeling a little panicky, and I don't know why. My emotions have been a bit wild since I met them.

They must sense something because Fen is quick to come over and hug me. "Of course, Precious. Of course we'll all be sleeping in here. We should look at getting you a bigger sleeping platform..." he mumbles the last bit.

"We're just going to pop out to grab our bed rolls. We'll be right back," Rafe placates, as they turn and head down.

Gin and Tawson are slowly pulling their shirts and pants off. Once I catch sight of all that delicious muscle being unveiled I forget what I was doing and stare. And possibly drool. But, who could blame me! Look at all that gorgeous male flesh.

I don't even notice Gin getting closer because I'm busy staring at Tawson's abs until he is pulling my top off. And only then because it interrupts my view.

"Hey! You're interrupting the show, Gin!" I gripe, swatting at him. He releases a deep rolling laugh and my stomach clenches in response.

Still chuckling, Gin says, "Sorry, Little One. But you need to get ready for bed. Unless, you sleep in your clothes?"

With flaming cheeks I glance away from both of them as I reply, "No... I have nightgowns. But, I think with both of you I might be too warm in my regular sleep clothes." Still careful not to look at either of them I mumble shyly, "I think I'd rather sleep in just my panties." I can't believe that just came out of my mouth.

Twin growls answer me, and my core tightens along with a whole body flush. Gin strips off my skirt and stockings quickly after that. He picks me up and tosses me into the bedding. I'm very quickly squished between two large, hard bodies and I don't think I could be any happier about it. Except, I want my other two males here.

I don't know what is going on with me, all these impulses are strange and new. I have never invited a male into my bed, let alone multiple, and I do not know why these males make me feel so safe and comfortable. I don't know why having their scents in my bedding has me feeling so pleased, and I do not know why I'm upset at the fact that I can't fit all four of them in here. I'm pretty sure I'm going crazy, it's the only explanation.

I'm upset enough about it that I have to hold back the tears burning in my eyes. My emotions flipping wildly. Gin notices first and I am swallowed up in a strong embrace.

"Little One? What is making you so sad? The scent of your sadness makes me feel murderous," Gin, sounding panicked as he runs his hands over my body, checking for injuries, and I want to laugh but I just can't right now.

Tawson crowds me on the other side, purring manically, trying to sooth and relax me. "Are you upset that Fen and Rafe aren't here?" he questions before looking at Gin. "This is happening faster than I expected."

Confused and upset now, I squint at him. What is he talking about? What is happening? Before I get a chance to ask him he hollers, "Fen, Rafe, here, now!"

Their steps are loud on the stairs as they run up to see what is going on. "Is she okay? What's wrong?" Rafe enters the room tense and searching for danger.

Reaching for him, Gin surprisingly, lets him take me. As soon as I have them all surrounding me I feel the panic ease. I'm a little dazed as I hear Tawson explain what happened. Nothing he is saying makes sense to me.

"We were getting ready and she started to panic, the scent of her sadness permeated the space. It is happening very quickly and we may need to move on faster than expected. For tonight, set up your bedrolls on the floor here and give her the clothing that you wore today. It will ease the symptoms until she is ready to embrace this," Tawson explains, somberly.

All I can do is wonder about what he means but I'm too tired and stressed to deal with the strangeness of that right now. Stripped of my dress and underthings, practically naked, I am less shy about it than I thought I would be in front of these males. I am handed a shirt from each male and I bring the mound of cloth up to my face, inhaling the medley of scents. It's a drugging high and I feel loose and relaxed very suddenly.

Once I have gotten enough of the scent into my nose, I let my instincts take over and start rearranging my bedding, placing the shirts where I feel they will fit best. Then I look at Tawson and Gin and give a little growl while pointing at the bed. I want them there, now. Questioning my strange behavior will have to wait until tomorrow, I'm overwhelmed and I don't want to think about it right now.

As they climb in, I look around and note Rafe and Fen have settled into their bedrolls on the ground. They take up the rest of the space in my small room, and I feel a rush of pleasure that all my males are in one space.

Climbing on top of Gin I wiggle around until comfortable. He grunts a few times, sounding pained but I don't think I'm hurting him. I'm careful not to put my weight onto any soft spots, not that he really has any.

"Little One? How do you feel now?" he rumbles lowly, cautiously, one brow lifted in question.

Sighing deeply I nuzzle my nose into his neck. "Much better. Sleep now. Thank you," I mutter into his skin.

His chuckle vibrates through me pleasantly. A chorus of 'Goodnights' sound from all of them as I fade away.

CH.11

Waking to wetness leaking from between my thighs is disturbing. There is so much of it I fear I have covered Gin in it and I am mortified. What is happening to me? This is so embarrassing. How do I get up and face him now? The scent of my arousal is strong and my face burns with humiliation.

Someone in the room groans, sounding pained. "How are you not ravishing her right now, Gin? She smells divine and I want a taste so badly." I think that is Rafe.

"I have self control, pup," Gin rumbles beneath me and oh! It feels so good on my core. Wanting him to do it again, I wiggle a little, letting out a moan.

Gin's big hands cup my butt. "Are you awake, Little One? What do you need?"

"I don't know..." I mutter before

remembering myself and jerking upright. "Oh! Oh, no. Gin I'm so sorry! I don't know what happened, I was asleep and I am horrified that I got you all wet..." Trailing off, I realize that all four of them are still here and my embarrassment intensifies.

Ducking back down I hide my face in Gin's chest with a squeak.

"No!" Tawson barks out, stunning me. "No. You will not be ashamed of this. It is natural and perfect and all any of us want to do is taste you."

His bark forces a jolt through me with the need to obey. Then, I register what he said and a flush rushes through me from head to toe. More wetness leaks out of me and I squeeze my thighs together in an effort to stop it.

Gin spanks me and grunts. "Don't. I would like a taste. Please?"

In shock, I open and close my mouth trying to figure out what to say to him. "Uhhhh... Why?" Is all I can get out.

"Because it is the best treat any of us could hope for." Fen, this time, who answers me.

"But... isn't that... gross? I've never had this happen before. I don't understand what is happening. I've been getting all these strange urges and wild mood swings ever since I met all of you and I just... Don't understand..." My voice slowly grows smaller with my hesitancy. Sitting up I clutch my hands around my bare chest, hugging myself.

Tawson tilts my head up to look at him and explains gently, "Sweetheart. Do you not... I don't know how to tell you this but, you're an Omega."

My mouth drops open and I just gawk at him. I don't know if I can process this. "What? No. I-I'm just a Beta... I can't be an Omega. My parents were Beta's so I have to be one... Don't I?"

"Do you remember whether your mom had a special room that no one was allowed into except for your father? You only had one father right? While that is unusual it isn't unheard of. It's possibly the reason you lived way out here in such a small town with mostly Betas. They may have figured you would present one day and wanted to give you time to grow into yourself before Alphas started hounding you." His look is so gentle, like he's trying to soften the blow of information. "As you know, the King decreed that all Omegas were to be placed in packs approved by the Crown. It's... prohibited for Omegas to live on their own. It's dangerous for them and for any Alphas. The scent of an Omega in heat can drive them to act aggressively and become a danger to those around them. I think your parents wanted to give you the chance to choose on your own."

When I think back to my life before my parents passed, I remember my mom turning one of the smaller rooms into a den of sorts and I wasn't allowed in there. My father wasn't allowed in most of the time either. Now that I think about it, they always sent me to stay with Dani for a week every so often... Was my mom an Omega? Oh Goddess, that would mean it's true, I am an Omega! "What? H-how? W-where?" Stuttering, I look at Tawson helplessly.

"What do I do? I don't know how to be an Omega! I won't be able to keep running my bakery will I?" Wailing, I collapse into Gin's chest.

He strokes my back in an effort to comfort me. "Little One, we are going to help you make your life better. First, we are going to get you through your heat. You may have never had one before because you weren't exposed to any unmated Alphas. I am sorry that your life will change, but I promise, *we* promise, to make your life better."

His rumbly voice and gentle petting is calming. It could also be all of their scents soothing me. "I can't believe I never realized I was an Omega. It's obvious now that I look at it. I basically slept in a nest, I collected the most comfortable blankets and pillows I could find and I never let anyone in here until you guys." I'm back to talking into Gin's neck, hiding from the world. From my problems.

Another hand joins Gins, petting me and I feel a vibration in my chest. I sit up quickly and stare at Rafe. "Did I just purr?"

He's smiling so wide. "It was beautiful, Kitten. I've never heard an Omega's purr before, but I have read that it's supposed to relax and settle us Alphas. Some Omega's purr to comfort themselves too."

Looking around the room, all of them are smiling, crowding closer to me. I take a deep breath, filled with all their scents and allow the purr to roll through me again. It's not just relaxing for them, it makes me feel happy that I'm pleasing them. That's another behavior I haven't ever noticed in myself, but I really enjoy pleasing people. I think it's why my bakery is so successful.

Gin lets his purr join mine and it coerces me to melt into him. Then I hear the rest of them pick up the purr and my eyes get heavier until they close. It's like magic when they all start and I can't help falling asleep.

Waking slowly, I'm not ready to open my eyes. I'm not sure the guys know I'm awake yet because I overhear their discussion.

"Tawson, we need to move soon. Now that we have her we have to inform the Crown that our investigation needs to be picked up by someone else." I think that's Fen talking and he sounds worried.

"Yeah, we can't leave her alone. What if another Alpha scents her before we have her marked and claimed? What if the beast we're hunting makes it into town? She's vulnerable and I can't leave her to finish our job." Definitely Rafe, he's always concerned about my safety. I smile into the pillow.

My pillow starts vibrating and I realize I'm still on top of Gin. "She may be an Omega but she is not weak and she is not stupid."

"No, I know that. But, it is the law that we alert the Crown when we are mated. We can't continue our hunt with a vulnerable Omega in tow and we can't leave her on her own. We will need to send word to our Keep about the change in status and to ready rooms for her. Alec is going to be very surprised." Tawson laughs. It's a warm, pleasant sound, he really should laugh more often.

The others join in, laughing at this Alec.

"This is going to be a mess," Fen mutters

after he stops laughing.

I let them know I'm awake by asking, "Who's Alec? Do I have to leave my home? What beast? And I'll have you know that I have done just fine by myself for the last twelve years. I could survive a day without one of you." Sitting up I cross my arms with a frown, my lips pinched together.

Rafe picks me up and cuddles me into his chest. "I know, Kitten, but my Alpha instincts are telling me that if myself or my brothers aren't near you someone will steal you away from me and then I won't be able to stop the rampage I will go on to find you. What if someone else tried to claim you before we could?" He's squeezing me to him and I can feel him shaking a little. He's so afraid to lose me already, it's kind of sweet and very intimidating.

Before I can respond, Tawson takes over, "Sweetheart. Let me answer your questions before we all get distracted by our fears. Alec is my brother and he is also part of our pack. He doesn't usually join us on investigations because he's needed to run our Keep, our home. Yes, I'm sorry, you will have to leave your home, but I promise we will open a new bakery for you. We will even help you run it, Rafe can be your full-time employee and you will get to boss him around all you want."

Tawson takes me from Rafe and sits on the edge of the bed. "We work for the Crown, investigating issues all over the land. But, now that we've found our Omega we will no longer be sent out to far villages. We'll likely be assigned guard duties nearby."

I don't say anything. Taking time to process this new information. The thought of leaving my bakery, my friends, my whole life, is terrifying. I can't help the tears that escape.

Sniffling, I look at Tawson. "I don't want things to change. I don't know how to be an Omega, I'm awkward and embarrassing. What if your brother doesn't like me? I'm not going to fit in, in some fancy Keep, look at me! I'm always covered in flour and I say inappropriate things sometimes."

Tawson cups my cheek and gently swipes a tear off my face with his thumb. "Sweetheart. None of that matters, you are not awkward. You are refreshing and beautiful. You make us laugh and feed us amazing food. Alec would be a fool not to appreciate your presence, same with everyone else at our home. I'm sorry that we're making such drastic changes in your life, we really weren't expecting to find such a treasure." Kissing me gently, he tugs me closer.

Distracted, I kiss him back harder, chasing his lips.

My cheeks heat when someone clears their throat. Stuffing down my embarrassment, my attention is drawn to Fen.

"As for you not being a good Omega, it's not about knowing how to be one. It's all instinct and you are already following those. You've been making a nest for years, before you even met us. You're reacting to our scents and," inhaling deeply, Fen closes his eyes and shudders before continuing, "if I'm smelling correctly your heat will be upon us in a day or so. We have no plans to leave you to figure this out alone. We will be here to help you with everything, you have no need to fear the unknown."

Deflating with a sigh, my eyes drop down to my lap. "I know I can't live here alone anymore, not with me being an Omega. And I wouldn't even want to watch you leave the village without me. Just the thought of you leaving has me feeling so unhappy it makes my stomach hurt. It wouldn't make sense for us all to live here, there isn't enough room for everyone. It just makes me sad to leave, I worked so hard to get where I am now and I'll miss Dani and her family." Cuddling deeper into Tawson, I tuck my face into his neck, needing his warmth in the face of these big decisions.

"Okay. Enough information has been

dropped into my head this morning. I need to start baking, as it is, the morning breads will be late. Do I still get to work at the market today? Can I still do that? Or is it going to be too difficult with my scent?" Looking up at Tawson, and then around at the rest of the guys, I chew my lip and fiddle with Tawson's braids.

The chest I'm leaning against rumbles as Tawson answers me, "Yes. One of us will be with you all day today. I have to send a few letters and the rest will do a sweep of the forest around the village."

Perplexed, I frown at him before I remember they said they were investigating a beast. "What... What kind of beast? I haven't heard of any attacks or any issues... And wait, so you guys aren't merchants?" Tilting my head, I squint at them.

"The King has been getting reports from Doebra and Gishum of villagers getting attacked by some beast. None of the reports were consistent in describing what it is. But we've been following the trail of injuries and it looks like this village is where it's heading next. We're trying to get ahead of it, but we didn't want to tip anyone off to our presence, hence why we have two carts at the market. So far, we haven't been able to find anything." Perturbed, Tawson strokes my back as he explains.

Confusion creases my forehead. "What do you mean, you didn't want to tip anyone off? Isn't it a beast that you're looking for?"

"Yes," Rafe laughs, "we are looking for a beast but it may not be just a beast. It's likely it is a Shifter of some sort. At least, if you look at all the reports and the strange descriptions, it seems like it could be a feral being."

Immediately, I'm on edge, my muscles tensing, ready for fight or flight. "So... If it is here in my village it could be anyone visiting the market? And I wouldn't know it because no one can give a solid description so all you have to go on are hunches..." Muttering more to myself, I go back to chewing my lip.

Fen clears his throat and answers anyways, "Yeah. It really isn't much and since we've found you we haven't done as much investigating as we should. We do have a scent to look for but none of us have caught wind of it here yet."

As we've been discussing this they have been tidying the room and getting ready for the day. It's time I do the same so I wiggle out of Tawson's lap and declare, "I'm going to get ready. Can someone please start boiling water for me?" And head to the bathroom.

With so much to process, I don't know where to start. I'm an Omega... *wow*. I'm not sure if I should be happy or scared about this. I think I'm somewhere in the middle. I'm happy that I have this pack now, and they seem to be good males, but I'm also terrified of all the changes that are happening to me. I've been so independent my entire life that I'm not sure I know how to rely on others and I'm pretty sure these males will not be letting me do anything strenuous ever again.

Snorting a laugh at my thoughts, wasn't I just complaining about being in a rut? I guess the Goddess was listening and decided to help. Not sure that this was the way I would have liked change to happen but there isn't much point in complaining. I mean... *'Oh no! I have a bunch of very attractive males wanting to protect me and sex me up'*. Laughing again, I can feel the sarcasm in my thoughts and I don't know why I'm even really upset. No, that's not true, I'm upset because this brought a bunch of major changes to my life and I was not at all prepared. Also, I think I'm very overwhelmed and the changes I'm experiencing as I become an Omega are probably pushing my hormones into overdrive.

I figure I will probably be a little wild with mood swings until I get through my first heat. Thoughts of that have my face reddening. Since I have, basically, zero experience with males I can only imagine how it's going to feel.

I'm excited for that and scared, because isn't it supposed to hurt the first time? I wonder if I should get one of them to fix that before my heat comes? Would that be more comfortable? I don't know... I need to talk to Dani so badly.

CH.12

Extremely late getting all my morning baking done, I had a lineup of customers by the time I opened. Luckily, the guys helped me.

It's late afternoon by the time we arrive at the market. I'm not worried about sales though, but there's a very real fear that strangers will catch my scent. I mean, one of the guys mentioned it is getting stronger and sweeter the closer I get to my heat. Are beings going to bother me more? I'm really glad that Gin decided to stay with me today. He is very large and very intimidating. So much so, that I had to tell him to stand behind the stall so he wasn't as visible. He kept scaring off all my customers with his glower.

Sporadically scrutinizing the crowd for Dani, I'm dejected when I find no trace of her. I really want to tell her about everything that is happening, her opinion would be beneficial. Just thinking about sex and what it will be like with them makes me blush. *Stopping by her home after this is a necessity,* I nod to myself.

Peeking over my shoulder at Gin, I can't keep my eyes from wandering down to his package. It is very large, and I don't think he's even excited right now. Quickly, I turn back to the crowds so he doesn't catch me staring.

"What are you thinking about, Little One?" His warm breath on my neck triggers goosebumps over my skin. I bite my lip, holding back a whimper, as he continues, "You are perfuming the air with what is mine, so I think you need to find something boring to think about until I can take you home."

Stammering out a reply, trying to get my burning cheeks under control, "U-uh... Umm, I-I was... uhh, nothing. I wasn't thinking about anything!"

His laughter tickles the back of my neck and it leads to a flash of warmth rolling through me, to my core. I huff out a laugh, too. Because it is obvious I was thinking dirty thoughts.

Distracted by a customer, I go back to focusing on my job. But, I continue to feel his heat near me and I don't tell him to go back behind the cart because his presence makes me feel safe and happy... and a little lusty. Who knew I had it in me all this time? I guess I just needed the right males to come along.

"Before we go home, we are making a detour to my friend's place. I haven't seen her in a while and I really need to tell her that I will be leaving and..." I swallow hard, my melancholy about leaving trying to choke my words.

"Of course, Little One. Anything for you." Gin places a soft kiss on my lips.

His words encourage me to relax into him. Squeezing my arms around his middle I thank him before I take his hand to lead him out of the market.

"Oh! Can you do that mind thingy and tell the others we will be late?" I peek up at him with raised brows and a pleading look before focusing on where I'm going. I can't wait for Dani to meet him, I think she will enjoy his possessiveness of me. She's wanted me to find a partner for so long.

Distracted as I am by my thoughts of how to tell Dani everything that has happened, I only just barely register his laughter at my silly question. When I do, I laugh too. "Well, what is it actually called then? Don't just laugh at me!" But I'm smiling as I look up at him.

"You could call it telepathy. Or just the pack bond. Once we claim you, you will likely be able to use it to communicate with us as well," Gin explains, keeping a vigilant eye on our surroundings as we walk.

I don't respond right away because I'm stuck on the fact that I will be able to talk to them in my mind too! I have always been fascinated by magic Users and jealous that I don't have any natural talent like that. It is absolutely amazing that I'll be able to use a form of magic!

I wonder if, with the changes to become an Omega I might gain a gift? No, that isn't how it works... You have to be born with it, I think?

So lost in thought about magic and Omega things I don't even realize I have stopped at Dani's door until Gin stiffens beside me.

"What is it? What's wrong?" My eyes widen as I look around, trying to see what's bothering him. I clutch at his hand, making sure he stays close.

He sniffs the air and his eyes change. They look more reptilian, the pupil is elongated and his eyes have a glow to them.

"I thought I caught a whiff of the beast

we are hunting. But it's gone now." Looking down at me, his brows furrow. "Is this your friend's place? We should knock and go in, or we should get back to your home. I will inform the others that I think it is in or near the village somewhere."

Goosebumps trail down my spine and I shiver at the thought. Knocking quickly on the door, I strain to hear any movement inside. Sighing, I guess she isn't home... but her parents should have been here. It is almost dinner and I'm left wondering where they all went? I hope they are safe, if there truly is a beast killing people.

"No one seems to be here, we should go. I am afraid of running into this beast." My eyes flick up to Gin, as anxiety races through my veins.

Immediately he picks me up and starts moving towards my bakery at a fast pace, much quicker than I could move on my own.

When we get to my home he stops abruptly, scents the air again and growls deeply.

Gin's growl is aggressive and instantly makes me leak moisture from my core. That is a new and uncomfortable sensation. Am I going to do that every time someone growls? That is *not* okay.

"Gin? What..." I start to ask but am cut off by a voice I did not want to hear again.

"Luella. Who is this beast touching my bride? Put her down this instant!" Jerrik snaps with an ugly sneer.

How dare he call Gin a beast! Jerrik is the only beast here. He is awful and pushy and smells bad. My chest rumbles into a growl and I'm so surprised by this that it cuts off as quickly as it started.

"She is not your bride. You need to leave before I put her down. Because once she is safely out of the way, I may rip your limbs off and stuff them up your ass." Gin is quite creative in his threats. His fierceness triggers a warmth in my body that encourages more slick to leak from me.

A familiar, welcome, voice from behind us remarks, "I thought I told you to leave Luella alone? She is not your bride. She is not anything to you. You had best leave before I let Gin do as he has threatened."

Peeking over Gin's shoulder I see the rest of the pack. Fen steps up beside Gin with a quick smile in my direction before he goes back to scowling at Jerrik.

Jerrik shows his lack of intelligence when, instead of leaving he barks, "Excuse me!? Do you know who I am? How dare you threaten me! Luella you *will* be my bride. Do not allow these creatures to sully you. I will return with my father's soldiers, and if they have ruined what is mine, you *will* be punished," he sneers darkly. We all watch him stalk off.

I'm not too concerned with his attempts at intimidation because he has warned others in this manner and nothing has ever come of it. Although he hasn't threatened *me* with his fathers soldiers before, that's new. I doubt his father will bother. I'm sure he already has a bride lined up for Jerrik from one of the other Lords. They don't generally trouble themselves with peasants, we are beneath them.

Tawson turns to us, all business. "Gin, you said you scented the beast? Where?"

Gin, still glaring after Jerrik, answers, "Her friend's place. Caught the beasts trail nearby. It was gone as quickly as I scented it. That cretin's atrocious smell permeated the air covering any others, but it was here."

Rafe takes a deep inhale. "There's a trace of something but I am unable to pinpoint where it is coming from. It is also heavily mixed with all the scents from the market that it feels impossible to actually tell if it is the beast."

They continue to discuss their hunt while I unlock the door and lead everyone into the kitchen. And by lead, I mean Gin continues to carry me and the others follow. A sliver of remorse drops my eyes to the floor when I realize I don't have enough chairs. But, they invaded my life so they can figure it out. I snort a laugh to myself.

Rafe and Fen sit on the floor while the other two take the chairs. They continue their discussion while I start making some food. I wonder when I'm going to have to close the bakery. I won't be able to keep it open when the scent of my heat gets strong enough that it affects the Betas too. And of course when I go into heat I won't be coherent enough to do anything besides beg for knots and cum. Even thinking that makes me flush and my body responds with a trickle of slick .

Humming to myself, I think about what a heat is going to be like. I mean, I've never had sex but from everything Dani has told me, I figure it's going to feel pretty great. After the first time at least. This also means that pregnancy is a possibility...

The idea of being a parent makes me uneasy since I don't have much experience and can barely remember mine. I have vague memories of warmth and happiness.

I'll have the four, no, five of them, if I'm counting this Alec male, to help out with a child. I won't be doing this alone, but I'm probably getting ahead of myself... I need to actually have sex first. *Yes, let's focus on that for now.*

Large, warm hands cup my shoulders, distracting me from my run-away thoughts. When did everyone stop talking? A warm breath brushes against my ear.

"What dirty thoughts run through your head, Little One?" Gin's voice makes me shiver, and causes slick to leak from me.

"I... I was..." Stopping for a second to take a deep breath. I should just tell them what I was thinking. There's no need to lie about it, even though it's very strange to tell them of my intimate musings. "I was thinking about what a heat with you guys might be like."

A chorus of growls thunder through the room as Gin presses tightly to my back, pushing me into the counter.

"Oh, Little One, anything you think that your heat will be like, I can guarantee that the reality will be better," he rasps in my ear.

Oh.

Oh, no. I need to change my underclothes because that sentence, in his deep voice, with him pressed against me so tightly that I can feel his hardness, made me leak so much slick that I'm concerned I could drown someone in it.

Staring down at the dough I was kneading, trying to find some composure when Fen speaks from my right, "I can promise you that we will ensure your first heat will be something you'll never forget. We will care for you as something precious, because you are. But also, we will wreck your beautiful body in a way you will thoroughly enjoy." Fen places a kiss on my temple. His dirty words fill me with a potent rush of desire.

Rafe, on my left, pushes hair behind my ear before adding, "We are going to claim every inch of your body. Personally, I want to taste you from your head to your toes. I'm going to nibble and lick places you wouldn't think you'd enjoy but you will cream for me regardless."

Fanning myself, I stupidly say, "Is it hot in here? I'm very warm. I should take a layer off, right? Overheating isn't good. I need to change."

But I don't move because their bodies pin me on all sides and I can't say I'm not enjoying myself. Because, whew! These males are a lot for someone who has approximately zero experience. I bet they'd be a lot even for someone who does know what to do with a cock.

"Give her a little space," Tawson orders from behind us. "She needs to finish what she's baking and then I will take her up to... *change*." The way he says change, so much heat and darkness, has my core clenching with need and a faint whimper slipping out.

They all step back, Gin runs his hands slowly along my sides as he moves away from me. I have the strongest urge to grab his hands and put them back. The loss of his touch brews panic within me. But, I resist and concentrate on my dough in order to stop myself.

Their discussion on how to handle the beast becomes background noise. I don't listen all that closely. My mind has returned to my heat and what Tawson is going to do when we go up to 'change'. I'm pretty sure I'm not going to be putting any clothes back on once I take these off. The warmth that I am feeling must be a sign of my impending heat.

Once I've got everything rising I look at the males in my kitchen. Seeing them in my space is comforting on a level I can't quite explain.

"Please put those in the oven when they look doubled in size, usually about an hour. They bake for twenty minutes." I doubt I'm coming back down after I make it to my bed... no, my *nest*. I have a feeling that I am going to get some time up close and personal with Tawson's abs and... cock. Even saying it in my head makes me want to giggle madly.

CH.13

Tawson heads into my bedroom while I rush to the bathroom to clean myself up. Slick has leaked completely through my underthings and down my thighs. Being an Omega is messy and uncomfortable, how do they deal with this all the time? I feel like I'm going to have to wear a menses cloth, although now that I think about it, it is very strange that I hadn't ever gotten mine. That alone should have been a clue that I wasn't a Beta. Omegas only get their menses after a heat and I've never gotten mine at all. Huh... I feel a little stupid for not realizing this.

Tawson is leaning against the wall as I head into my room. I'm surprised he isn't in the nest and I inquire about that. But even as I ask, something inside me is happy he hasn't invaded my space without permission.

He smiles, just a slight upward tilt at

the corners of his lips. "Because, as an Omega, no one should touch your nest until you have officially invited them in. A nest is a sacred space to an Omega and their comfort and well-being is important. No self respecting Alpha would ever touch it unless explicitly told."

Now I understand why he hasn't moved to touch me since I walked in here and my insides melt into a gooey puddle at his deference. I briefly acknowledge Tawson with a nod, but my attention is drawn to my nest, as if it calls to me. The fabric of my dress has steadily grown more irritating and I need it off, right now. Once I'm free, the strongest urge to rearrange my nest overwhelms me.

"Tawson," I demand as I look back at him, "I want your shirt and something that smells like each of the pack." The commanding note in my voice takes me by surprise.

As he steps away from the wall, Tawson brings his hands around from behind his back holding out a pile of clothing. It smells like a medley of all of them and, like a complete weirdo, I stick my face in it and suck down the heavenly aroma. All of their scents are there except Tawsons. When I demand his shirt, he's already handing me the one off his back. Momentarily, I pause to greedily drink in his form.

He's not the tallest of my males, but he still towers over me. His skin is a beautiful green, so similar to mint that I have to fight the urge to lick him. It must be an Omega thing, to want to lick my males since this isn't the first time the thought has crossed my mind. Tawson is slim, but without his shirt hiding him, I can see how muscular and fit he actually is. Not that he didn't look strong with his clothes on, but now the definition in his muscles are visible. His abs are beautiful and I want to trace the grooves and valleys of his stomach with my fingers and tongue. I'm in a daze.

I don't realize how long I've been staring at him until he clears his throat and jiggles the shirt he's holding out to me. Blushing, I snatch it from him, turning to the nest, lest I get distracted by his muscles again.

Arranging the fabric where it feels right, my nest consumes my attention. Something inside me insists that it isn't right.

Tearing off the rest of my clothes as I go, because I feel like I'm overheating. Making a nest is hard work, at least that's what I'm going to use as an excuse for taking all my clothes off. While I am nervous at being nude in front of someone for the first time, I'm also excited. I am not going to think about going into heat and being an Omega at this moment, that's just too much for me right now.

So intent on making my nest, I ignore Tawson's imposing presence, until a choking sound draws my focus. Peering over my shoulder, I climb into the center of the nest, enjoying his keen attention on my ass and, likely, the wetness leaking from my core. A flush of heat covers me from head to toe but I continue what I'm doing because it has to be just right before my males can join me.

Once all the fabrics are placed perfectly, I look around the space trying to figure out what's missing.

"Their scents are here but it doesn't feel right. Can you please call them. I need all of you." Kneeling in the center, my knees spread wide, I sit up and pout at Tawson.

Humming as he does his mind speak thing, I hear their footsteps coming up the stairs shortly after. I have no idea how long I have been working on my nest and I completely disregard my breads. It is no longer important.

When they all crowd into the small room I start making demands, "Fen, here. Now." Pointing at a spot in the nest on the right side. "Rafe, there. Tawson, here. And Gin, right there." Directing them all to the spaces that feel right, even knowing there isn't enough room and it's going to be a tight squeeze. Tawson is in the center with me while the others surround us. I'm not sure why but having Tawson first is what my instincts are telling me, and I'm inclined to listen to them.

If I took a second to think about it, I would be surprised that these large males are listening to everything I say but, I don't have the presence of mind for that right now.

I don't realize Tawson is nude until he comes down on top of me, flattening me back into the nest, pressing his large, hot, cock against my core. The feeling of his hardness against my delicate lips has a moan slipping from me. Tilting my hips to rock into him, I moan again because, *oh*, it feels so good to rub my nub against his hard heat. So much better than my own hands.

He lets me run my hands over his chest and abs, giving me time to explore his body. My fingers trace over the muscles in his back and down to his butt. I didn't realize how much I would enjoy touching male flesh. Tawson is so firm and smooth, aside from the rough hairs on his chest. The contrast of his roughness against my softness is titillating.

Once he feels I've had enough time to explore him he barks out, "Gin, Fen, grab an arm." I'm not sure what's going on so I fight them, but it's useless. After they've pinned my arms down I realize the feeling of being held immobile is stoking my desire even hotter. How did he know I would like this?

Motionless, I'm transfixed as Tawson takes a turn exploring my body. Starting with kisses, he runs his tongue along my lips until I open for him. Moaning at his taste, I revel in his control of me. When I can no longer breathe, he trails kisses from my lips to my ear and nibbles on the lobe. Pleasure thrills through me straight to my core, and more wetness trickles out.

The kisses linger down my neck. Stopping on a spot that elicits a questioning moan. Why in the world does that spot feel so much better than any other? Why do I have the desire to ask him to bite me?

"Oh, Goddess, Tawson! Why?" I don't get any other words out before I'm moaning again as he bites down, without breaking the skin.

"This is my spot, Sweetheart. This is where I am going to mark you as mine." His voice, a rough growl, causes everything in me to tighten. Trying once again to reach for him, I'm reminded of my other Alpha's. A quick glance shows molten heat burning in Gin's eyes, the same reflected in Fen's.

A light touch on my foot tickles me, while reminding me of my last Alpha. Not wanting to be left out, Rafe scrapes his teeth over my ankle, sending shivers up my leg.

Tawson moves down my chest, giving my breast a playful lick, before nibbling towards my nipple. I did not realize that my nipples were this sensitive. Each nibble and lick is like a shock straight through me and I rock against him. The sounds I'm making are not in my control. None of this is in my control and I really like it. Being held down and helpless against his erotic assault is everything I never thought I'd get to experience.

Tawson moves on to my other breast, making sure that one doesn't feel left out. I continue rocking my clit against him, feeling everything tighten inside and I know I'm going to cum. I want it so badly. But, I also want to feel that hardness inside me.

He nibbles down my stomach, causing shivers and twitches. Sucking my tummy in a little, I didn't feel self conscious until he touched my squishy belly. After seeing their muscles on display I realized I have done very little to keep myself in shape. I hate exercise and love sweets, what did I expect?

Tawson leans back, lifts my leg and spanks me, hard. It shocks me out of my head. "No! Do not try to change or hide your body. I desire you as you are. Why would I want hardness against hardness? Your softness compliments me, *us*, perfectly." Growling in a hard voice, brows creased as he frowns at me.

Meekly, I squeak out, "Sorry!" before he leans down and kisses me breathless. Then, he goes back to kissing down my belly. Trying not to feel worried about what they see, to put it out of my mind, and it's easy to let him distract me from anything except his tongue as he makes his way to my wetness.

One lick across my clit and I'm squirming, the puddle of slick under me grows. I didn't realize they would lick me there! I know Dani has complained about males not being able to attend to her properly but I didn't realize this is what she meant.

Moving lower, he licks my lips, pulling me open with his fingers. I can hear him slurping up my silky wetness and my face reddens as I squirm. Groaning as he tastes me, "You are the best tasting thing I have ever had, and I don't think I will ever need any dessert but you for the rest of my life." Tawson resumes cleaning up all the slick I've smeared down my thighs, coming back to my core. He licks into me forcing louder moans to escape my throat.

Tawson's mouth focuses on my clit while he slowly pushes one of his fingers inside me, I cum with very little warning. I can't help it, his finger is so much bigger than mine and along with his attention to my clit it threw me over that cliff so quickly. I can feel myself contracting rhythmically over his finger as I shout his name.

He reaches down and I can only assume he's touching his cock. That thought has me moaning even louder. I squeak in surprise when Tawson slides a second finger in, the fit is tight but not painful. Until he starts to stretch me, then it hurts a little, but in a way that adds to the pleasure.

"Don't cum," he mumbles to himself, "just hold it. Gotta make sure I can fit. Need to save it for her. Need to come inside her." I don't know if he realizes that I can hear him but the thought of him cumming in me has me strangling his fingers.

"Please. Please, I need you. I want..." Begging him, I rock my hips, fucking his hand. I need to feel his cock. "I want your cock. Please?" Tawson groans and the others make pleased sounds. I've been so focused on Tawson that I'm barely cognizant of the others watching.

"Sweetheart. You can have whatever you want. You won't be leaving here until you are thoroughly claimed," he grits out, sweat starting to bead on his brow.

He's still moving his fingers in and out of me and I have decided that it's not enough.

I want his cock, now! I try to reach for him, forgetting that my arms are being held down. I struggle against them, knowing I won't be able to get free. It drives me to clench around his fingers and leak more.

He groans and explains, "I need to make sure I won't hurt you."

"It's fine, you won't hurt me. I know it. Please! I need your cock, your cum. I need something in me!" A whine threads through my voice as I wiggle a little more, trying to encourage him to give me what I want.

Tawson pulls his fingers from me and sucks the wetness off them before moving up. He kisses me, and I taste myself on him. I didn't think I would enjoy that but it actually tastes good, mixed with him.

His hardness bumps against my opening, and I tense. I'm afraid, but I want it so badly.

A spank on the side of my ass surprises me. "Relax, little Omega. It will be a tight fit but it should only hurt for a moment before he will make you feel very, very good," Gin rumbles in my ear. Giving me a quick lick on my neck.

Tawson pulls back from kissing me to agree with Gin before reaching down and positioning himself against me. Slowly, he pushes in, and with a groan, utters, "This will be quick, you are so tight and warm. I will not last long."

It is tight and it pinches as he forces his length deeper. I didn't get a good look at his cock before this but it feels huge and I don't understand how he's supposed to fit. Mewling in pleasure and pain as he continues to make room for himself inside me.

He stops for a second and closes his eyes before he looks into mine. "Brace yourself, Sweetheart. This will hurt for a moment."

Tensing, my cunt squeezes down on his cock causing us both to moan before he thrusts the rest of the way in. Crying out at the pain of my innocence being broken, I can't stop the few tears from leaking out. Holding himself still, he gives me a chance to let the pain wash through me. And get used to his thick length lodged within.

It feels impossibly big. I don't understand how I even have the space for him in my small body, but the pain is already fading and I have the urge to move. So, I do. Rocking my hips a little, testing, and keen at how good he feels sliding inside me. My slick soaking him, making him glide so easily.

Tawson takes that as his cue and slides his length a short way out before pushing back in again. A rush of pleasure tingles through my body. He pulls out further this time and when he pushes back in it feels like the head of his cock brushes across an orgasmic button deep within.

"Goddess! What?" The shout is ripped from my throat, before he does it again, and again. Making me lose my mind.

His knot bumps against my opening. I had forgotten that Alpha's have knots. He already feels impossibly big, I have no idea how that is going to fit, too.

Grunting with effort as he fucks me, I shiver, clutching him. My legs hug his hips, urging him on. Another orgasm creeps up on me and I think he knows it.

"Hold it, Sweetheart. Don't cum yet," he pants out, his hands gripping my hips.

I have no clue how to stop it. But, I'll try because he hasn't been wrong yet.

Fucking me faster, he confesses, "Brace yourself, this is going to hurt but you will enjoy it." I have no idea what he's talking about but I tighten my legs on him anyways.

Tawson thrusts hard and shoves his knot against me. I don't think it will fit but in the next second it pops in and I scream.

I scream because it hurts, and also because the knot is now pushing, consistently, on that orgasm button and I cum. I cum harder than ever before and it doesn't feel like I will ever stop.

Along with his deep guttural groan, I can feel his seed splashing deep inside which urges me to tighten over his knot even more and I wail out my pleasure as he howls. I didn't realize how hot it was for a male to fill me. But, it is. It makes this feel a thousand times better knowing he could be breeding me right now.

Before I know what's happening there's a pinch of pain on my neck. Another climax bursts over me and I see stars.

Still cumming, my pussy constricts around his knot. Tawson wraps his arms around me and rolls to his back. The change in position lodges him even deeper, and he unleashes another burst of seed that has me wailing out another release.

I didn't notice when my males let go of my arms, but my body acts like it's made of jelly and I can't do anything other than lay across Tawson and loosely hug him. He still has his teeth lodged in my neck as he settles me on top of him.

When his teeth finally slide out of my skin, he proceeds to lick and clean the claiming mark. Each pass of his tongue over the bite forces shudders through me and I squeeze his knot again. It has a direct line to my clit and core and I wonder if it will always do that when he touches it?

Now that my climax has mostly settled I'm incredibly sleepy, murmuring into his neck, "That was nice. Thank you." He chuckles in reply and I realize how silly that sounded but I am too tired to say anything else so I leave it be.

"Sleep, my Omega. We will guard your rest. You are safe. You are *mine, ours,*" he says the last in a dark rumble that has shivers following me into sleep.

CH.14

Awareness comes to me slowly. I feel stiff and sore all over. The soreness reminds me of what I did last night and my face heats. Luckily, I'm tucked into Tawson's neck. As I come around fully into wakefulness I notice a strumming, happy vibration inside me, next to my heart. Actually, it feels like a string around my heart connecting me to...

Tawson! Oh! It's the bond.

I almost forgot about the claiming. It's fascinating being able to feel him, and his emotions. He's so happy, but he's also concerned and feeling incredibly possessive. I wonder what he feels from me? Does he know I'm awake now? I have so many questions to ask them. Since I didn't think I was an Omega, I did not learn much about them and how they work.

Saving my many questions for later, I tune in to their conversation. I feel sure that they wouldn't want me to panic or become scared by what they're talking about.

"Now that she's been marked by one of us her heat will come on faster. We need to get supplies and prepare because none of us will be leaving this nest until it is over," Rafe asserts, his voice laden with desire and longing.

Fen replies to him with a tone of anticipation, "We brought all of our stuff from our camp, we've stored it behind the bakery. We'll just need to make sure we have all the waterskins and jugs filled and brought up here."

"I will make a sign for her door saying the bakery is closed," Gin rumbles. His voice is so deep and gravelly I can feel the vibrations through Tawson, which makes me think Gin is still in the nest beside us.

"Bring our stuff inside," Tawson directs from below me. "With the bakery closed we can pile it in the front area until after. But, let's bring all of our clothing up here, I have a feeling she will want more of our stuff to line the nest as she gets closer to her heat."

Tawson continues, "Before we close ourselves in here with her, send another bird to the King, let him know we are indisposed and cannot continue the search. We have found our Omega and she needs us. Tell him to send another pack as soon as he can because we have scented the beast and it is only a matter of time before someone is killed or taken."

Hearing this has my heart speeding up at the thought of someone I know getting hurt. Tawson shifts around under me and his breath tickles my ear as he murmurs, "Sweetheart, I know you are awake. Please do not worry yourself about the beast. The King will send another pack to take care of it while we are busy taking care of you."

The way he says this, so calmly, and with such confidence, I realize he knew I was awake and wanted me to hear them.

Replying with a sleep laden voice, "But what about Dani and her family? I didn't get a chance to talk to her yesterday. No one was home and then we rushed back here because Gin scented the beast. Are you telling me I can't go to the market today? I can't go to her place to see if she's okay? But what if she's already hurt by the beast? She likes to roam the woods around here because of her Pixie side... What if she's been attacked?" My panic builds, but a rush of warmth and safety wrap around me and I realize it is Tawson sending me comfort through the bond. That will take a little getting used to but, I kind of like it, I like knowing he can feel me and respond to my emotions.

"There may not have been anyone home at your friends, but the place only scented of that family, not of the beast. The beast scent was faint which means it was likely still far from the village," Gin rasps from behind me.

Reaching over to him, I pat around until I find his arm and follow it to his hand. "Thank you, Gin. That does make me feel a little better."

"Does she wander far when she goes to the forest?" Gin questions, and I can hear the concern in his voice. "If she doesn't, she should be safe."

The concern I hear must be for me and not Dani, I get the feeling that Gin doesn't like too many people. I'm also pretty sure Gin would not like me being sad. I wonder if he would know what to do for a sad female? I mentally snort at the image of him panicking at my tears.

Responding to him with a smile in my voice, "I'm pretty sure she sticks close by. I know she particularly enjoys the woods behind my bakery, she's said something about a pond and waterfall before. I think this means there is still time for me to warn her to stay close to home." Mumbling the last bit to myself.

"Precious, it may be too dangerous for you to leave the nest right now..." Fen starts but

I cut him off before he can continue.

"Nope! No. I feel fine right now and I absolutely have to talk to Dani, and warn her. Also, I feel it is only right to let my best and only friend know that I have mates and am now in a pack... and that I am an Omega." Sitting up, I nod like this is a done deal, which it is.

Rolling off of Tawson to get out of bed, I feel all the muscles I used last night complain. A small groan escapes as I wiggle over Gin to the edge of the bed and he echoes me. My body stalls, did I hurt him? Or did he also pull a muscle helping Tawson fuck me into the bed last night?

Glancing up at him, he looks pained but okay, so I shrug and head to the bathroom. Once I'm finished I flash a smile at Rafe and Fen while snagging someone's shirt to throw on. It smells like Fen and fits me like a dress, which makes me chuckle.

Performing my morning routine, that includes drinking tea and making breakfast for all five of us. I move automatically, barely thinking about what I'm doing as I grab ingredients. When I start my morning baking, the light outside startles me. It is much later than I normally get up and my anxiety starts building. *How am I going to get everything ready on time? Oh no, oh shoot, what am I going to do? Will I be able to afford the tithe this month? How did I not notice the time?*

As the panic freezes me, Tawson sends warmth through the bond before he comes and hugs me from behind. Murmuring in my ear, "Sweetheart, we put out a sign last night that you would be closed for a few days. It's alright, you have no need to worry. We will take care of you."

Nodding my acquiescence, I know they will take care of me, they've been doing that since I met them. But I know it will not always be easy, I do have trouble asking for help so I will often try doing it all on my own.

While I am thinking about this I state firmly, "Since I know my scent will not change until the whole pack has claimed me, I understand that working the market will not be wise. But, I am determined to find Dani and let her know what is going on before we have to sequester ourselves for my heat." Leaning back into him with a sigh. "While everyone makes preparations, I am going out to find Dani, or at least her family, so she will be aware of the danger."

Feeling Tawson nod before he speaks, "Okay. But Fen and myself will be coming with you. There are more dangers to you than this beast. I know your town consists mostly of Betas, but due to the market there are many strangers around that are Alphas and I feel a bit... possessive of your scent. We will be with you to make sure no others think you are free for their attentions."

Tawson's focus has pink running all the way down my chest and I feel his appreciation through the bond before a growl rolls through me. This forces a gush of slick and ruins my panties.

"You need to stop doing that!" My hands fist at my sides as I stomp my foot in frustration. "I'm going to run out of clean underclothes and then what am I going to do? I can't go around with nothing under my skirts! Being an Omega is so messy. How in the world do they deal with this? Ugh!" By the end I'm just ranting in general. They all respond by rumbling with Rafe's loud laughter mixed in.

Rafe's laughter makes me irrationally angry, I throw him a disgruntled look and stomp up the stairs to change, yet again. He looks slightly chagrined, but mostly he looks smug and I want to slap that look off his face... Or kiss him. This wild influx of emotions is frustrating and I expect it to stop after my heat. I really hope they don't take my anger personally. I think they get it though because they haven't gotten annoyed with me yet.

I'm glad that Tawson chose Fen to come with us as I am still feeling a little salty towards Rafe right now. Hopefully that will change by the time I see him later. Although, my stomping feet on the way to Dani's place say otherwise.

My angry steps slow to a more leisurely pace, then I tip my head back and close my eyes. Basking in the warmth calms my irrational mood. I have a feeling that I won't get too many relaxing days with this pack of hooligans. No, that is untrue, they seem to be quite well behaved actually. I am the youngest of all of them and the one most likely to get into trouble. Even though I've never really been a troublemaker, Dani did tend to drag me along when she sought out some 'fun'. It was never my idea of a good time. I will miss her when they take me to their Keep. I wish I could take her with me, but I doubt she'd want to leave her parents.

Taking a deep breath I memorize the smells of my village. It has always smelled fresh, like the forest surrounding it, along with the scents of the villagers. Most of them smell inoffensive, except for Jeylo. He is awful, but he mostly sticks to the bar and his shack. And Jerrik of course, but he doesn't actually live here. I don't know why he comes here so often. He lives in what I would consider a castle but, in actuality, it's just the Lord's Keep. It's about half a day's travel from here and it seems like a hassle for him to make the trek so often.

I wonder if the pack's Keep is as large as the Lords. I've only seen it a few times when I was younger and accompanied Dani's family to deliver clothing orders for the Lord and his wife. It always seemed so grand. Even the gate to the courtyard looked elegant. Made from twisted metal, shaped into flowers, vines, and small creatures. I was always so intrigued by it, how in the world did someone craft metal into those shapes?

The courtyard was filled with flowers, bushes, and fruit trees that smelled sweet and fresh. Dani's parents always told me to keep an eye on her because she would always try to pick the fruit or take a flower, just Pixie things I guess. It was a game for me though, trying to keep her from getting into trouble while we were there.

They even had a fountain shaped like a mermaid, I found myself wondering if the Lord had ever met one. It was stone, but it looked so realistic it was awe inspiring. Water flowed out of the mermaid's mouth and down her chest to land in a beautiful pond. There were so many colorful fish, I wanted to sit and watch them for hours.

My musing about the Lord's Keep is cut short when I scent something strange. It almost smells like apple pie, and I really like apple pie. I don't even notice that I'm drifting towards the scent until Tawson snags me around the waist.

One second I'm walking and the next I'm in his arms and he's tucking my face into his neck. I fight him for a moment before I stop and realize what I'm doing.

Murmuring into his skin, "What is going on? Why..." I'm so confused, but his scent is very calming.

Fen probes urgently, "What do you smell, Precious?" He's tense, scanning the area, on high alert and I don't understand what's happening.

"It smells like apple pie. Why does it smell like apple pie? And why do I want it so badly?" Looking between the two males, I wait for someone to explain.

Tawson, with a heavy dose of concern and consternation, replies, "That is the scent of the beast we are hunting and it must be an Alpha or you wouldn't desire it so badly. But, it is hard to tell what its designation is, there's something wrong with it."

He has no reason to sound so concerned, now that I know what it is I'm not going to go looking for it. I do not have a death wish. Although, that scent is very alluring.

"Tawson, we have to take her back. The beast is getting closer to town if its scent is this strong." Fen continues scanning the area, one hand hovering over his sword, ready to pull it from his back.

"NO! I have to find Dani! I need to warn her. I can't just let her wander around the forest blindly when she could be in danger!" I clutch at Tawson's shirt as I cry out, pleading with both of my males.

Tawson sighs, a slight frown growing on his face. "We will go to your friend's home and see if anyone is there. The beast is not here yet, you are not in heat yet, and the two of us can take care of you if something does happen. I know you're worried, Fen, but the more stress she is under the longer her heat will take to get here. We will go there and then take her straight back to her nest."

Fen wants to argue, I can see the mulish set to his jaw, but he knows Tawson is right. "Fine. But I want it noted that I don't like this. I do not want anything to happen to my precious girl. But, you are correct that we can protect her." He looks so put out. A deep frown mars his face and a vein in his forehead pulses with aggravation. I feel badly that he is so stressed but I'm getting my way so I will keep my mouth shut.

Tapping Tawson on the shoulder, I want to be put down but he just shakes his head. "Point me in the right direction, Sweetness."

Sighing, I don't think I will win this argument so I point down the street. "Okay. We go to the end of this path and then turn right. We are almost there."

So much for enjoying the day. But, at least no one has attacked us, so I will take that as a win.

CH.15

Tawson lets me down to knock on Dani's door. We're quiet, listening for any sounds of life inside. But it is silent. The scent of apple pie is stronger here. I wonder how close the beast is to the village if I can smell it so intensely?

Looking up at Tawson and Fen anxiously, I fidget with my skirt. "Why isn't she here? What if something already happened to her? What if I'm too late? Oh Goddess, what if she's dead?" My panic builds and my hands flutter as I pepper them with questions.

Fen scoops me up and hugs me tight to his chest, purring to soothe me. "She is probably at the market with her family. Didn't you say she was a seamstress? Is her mother one too? Wouldn't they have a stall at the market?"

Right! "Right, they do have a stall

selling clothing and booking appointments for alterations. Her whole family usually goes. Dani does wander off because her attention span is as short as a gnat. But if she's helping her mom sell things she usually doesn't go far." Relaxing in his arms, I soften into him as my worry lessens minutely.

This explains why no one has been home two days in a row. I'm about to ask them to take me to the market when they both stiffen.

It takes me a moment but then I scent it. The smell of apples and spices have begun to permeate the air, to the point that it feels like I could face plant into a pie.

Opening my mouth to ask a question, Fen puts a finger to my lips, shushing me silently. I'm a little offended but I don't really know anything about tracking beasts or hunting anything so I keep my concerns to myself, for now.

Tawson slowly creeps to the side of the house to peer around the corner. Flinching back, he looks at Fen, lips pressed tightly together with a deep furrow between his brows. They are having a mental conversation but I still don't seem to have acquired any telepathy so I have no idea what's going on. Fen moves towards Tawson to look as well. I try to peek but he's holding me too tightly and I can't see past the edge of the house.

Wiggling I try to get Fen to put me down. If we're attacked I bet they could fight better without me in Fen's arms.

Reluctantly, he puts me down tugging my back tight to his body. This still gives me enough leeway to peek my head around the corner.

What I see has me as confused as Tawson. The creature just beyond the edge of the forest is very strange. It looks to be the size of a bear but it has the ears of a bunny rabbit and striped black and orange fur. The same fuzz down its legs, but the front feet transition to sharp looking talons like a hawk or something. Its back legs are that of a horse, hooves and all, with a short and skinny tail that ends with a puffy tuft of hair. When it turns its head I notice its muzzle is elongated like a wolf, along with some very sharp looking teeth. I have never in my life seen or heard of anything like this. It's almost like someone took parts of random animals and sewed them together to create this monster.

Peering up at Fen with wide eyes and questions bubbling up I frown when I notice he isn't paying me any attention. He has his gaze focused hard on the creature.

Looking back at it, I feel sad for the beast. I don't think it is natural. I think something dark created it and I wonder if it is in pain or if it functions just as well as any creature.

It has its nose down to the ground, snuffling like it is searching for something. Its long ears twitch and twist listening to the sounds of the forest and village. I wonder if it has a master, someone controlling the odd creation...

Looking back up at Fen to ask him something, he tenses while reaching for his sword.

Refocusing on the creature, I startle because it is staring straight at me. Squeaking out a quiet, "EEP," I backpedal into Fen, hard.

Picking me up, he places me in front of Tawson and steps around the corner with his sword up in a protective stance. Wings flaring out behind him blocking my view.

His skin changes, looking rougher and more solid. Shifting to allow his Gargoyle characteristics out more fully. There's no holding back my gasp of awe at the change. He's beautiful, regardless of the form he takes. The desire to touch him is strong but that will have to wait, we have a strange beast to deal with.

Tawson's hand on my shoulder keeps

me in place as he leans down to whisper in my ear, "Please stay between us. Your safety is paramount."

Nodding, I don't answer out loud, but I also find myself not very afraid. There's no sense of malice from the creature. *Why are they so worried?* Probably because they've been hunting this unknown beast for a while. But, I have a very strong feeling in my gut that there is something more that we cannot see yet.

Peering around Fen's wing, I take a moment to admire them. It seriously takes all of my focus to restrain myself from stroking him. *Goodness, I am distracted so easily*, I mentally roll my eyes. For now I won't distract him in case my gut feeling is wrong. The creature is still where I last saw it, staring at us. It hasn't made any aggressive moves.

When it spots me peeking around Fen, it whimpers and its ears droop, it looks sad.

Tugging lightly on Fen's wing, I marvel at the roughness and strength it must take to carry the weight of his stone body, and whisper urgently, "Fen, I think it is scared. Look at him! Put your sword away."

At the sound of my voice it whimpers again and flattens its body to the ground. It looks like a dog that has been bad trying to beg for forgiveness. Shuffling its body towards us, ears down, tail tucked, looking so pitiful.

"Precious, you don't know if this is a trick. We have been hunting a beast for weeks and this is the first sighting we have had." Fen looks back at Tawson. "This explains why the reports have been so confusing. This is like nothing I have seen before. There has to be black magic involved."

Tawson tenses even more against my back. "I think you're right. It definitely looks capable of killing someone, but it seems so... submissive. It must have a master pulling the strings." Rubbing a finger over his bottom lip as he frowns deeply, he continues, muttering to himself, "How in the world did I think its scent was that of an Alpha?"

The creature is still flat on the ground shuffling closer. I just want to pet it. It looks so sad, the urge to console him overwhelms me. So much so that my males will not like what I'm about to do.

"Hey there, sweet boy," I quickly step around Fen, dodging both their hands and head towards the creature while talking to it, "it's okay, we aren't going to hurt you. Shhh, shhh. It's alright, honey." At my words its ears perk up but it keeps itself on the ground. It even tucks its mouth under one... paw? Foot? Claw? I don't even know the right word for its appendage because it is such a mishmash of animals.

"What are you doing? Luella, get back here!" Tawson hisses, but doesn't make any sudden moves. Instead he advances slowly, doing his best not to startle the poor beast.

Ignoring him, I keep talking to the creature, "Oh hush. You poor baby. Look at you, you're a marvel. I've never seen anything as unique as you before! Are you going to let me pet one of your silky ears? They look so soft and inviting."

One of its ears perks straight up, as if saying here pet this one! Reaching forward slowly, keeping my movements steady and relaxed.

The moment I stroke its ear and marvel at how silky and amazingly soft the fur is, a flash of light blinds me. As I blink to clear the light from my eyes, I gasp and jerk back. There's an Elf curled up on the ground where the beast once stood.

Tawson scoops me up so quickly I barely have time to blink while Fen, still in his stone form, points his sword at the male's neck.

Staring, my eyebrows climb high on my forehead as my mouth drops open. He's naked... and blue, with skin the color of the sky and very pale blue hair. When he uncurls himself and looks up, his eyes are like rich pools of honey. All in all, he seems rather harmless.

Tawson sniffs the air around him, looking confused. "I swear your scent says Alpha but... you are not an Alpha, are you?"

With a sword at his throat his voice comes out shaky, "Hello. Uhhh, n-no, I'm a Beta... I think. Thank you for helping me. I've been stuck like that for a very long time and I don't really know who I am or where I am. All I know is that I am finally free of that voice." Shudders visibly wrack his body.

Fen and Tawson share a look before Tawson probes, "Do you know how that happened to you? How did you become... that?" Pausing for a moment, then with a hint of confusion Tawson continues, "What voice?"

The Elf clears his throat before speaking, "I... I don't really know? I don't remember much. All I know is a dark voice forcing me to move, kill, and kidnap, and when I didn't, it hurt me so badly." Wincing with remembered pain, his wide eyes waver with tears.

A closer look at his back shows faint lines. They appear to be scars and they cover the entire span from shoulder to hip.

"Oh, you poor thing! Fen give him your shirt, he has no clothes and it must be uncomfortable to sit on the ground like that." I start tugging on Fen's shirt trying to get it off him, but he's much too tall for me to be able to reach. Plus, he's still holding the sword to the man's throat.

"Precious, I..."

I cut Fen off. "Look at him! Does he look like he will be a danger to me? He's shivering, he's been through enough, if those scars tell me anything, and you look like you are twice his size. I doubt you need a sword to injure him." My voice is sharp and stern as I give him a pointed glare.

Sighing deeply before sheathing his sword, Fen strips off his shirt. There's a brief second where I wonder how he can take his shirt off even though his wings are in the way, but that isn't important right now. I'll have to remember to ask him later.

Dropping it on the man, Fen says, "Put it on. I do not need my Omega to see your cock." He's gruff and grumpy, reminding me of Gin.

Tawson's lips twitch before he gathers himself, finally putting me down. Holding out a hand to the man, Tawson tugs him upright once the stranger has donned the shirt. It hangs down to mid thigh on him, almost looking like a dress. He is very short, at least compared to my Alphas. Still taller than me, but only by an inch or two.

Looking shaky on his feet, the strangers

gaze flicks between all of us. "Thank you. Thank you for freeing me from that form." Full of emotion, he presses a fist to his heart.

"How did we free you?" Tawson squints at him, folding his arms across his chest.

"It was her. The moment she touched me I felt a weight lift and I was able to shift. I... I haven't been myself in... years. I think." He looks at me for a long moment before glancing at Fen and Tawson. "She must have a magical touch because I have been trying to shift for so long, but that voice always stops me. Everything it commanded, I had to do. I was stuck following horrible orders and..." The stranger cries great racking sobs, covering his face as he sinks back to the ground, curling in on himself.

When I move to hug him, Fen tugs me back and gives me a look that says 'W*hat do you think you're doing?*'

"Look at him!" I plead with my sad eyes. "He needs comfort! He has obviously been through something awful!" But my argument falls on deaf ears.

Instead of letting me go to the male, Tawson steps forward and puts a hand on his shoulder. "It's alright now, you're okay. Can you still hear the voice?" He is awful at comforting this stranger but it does slow the male's tears.

"No." Sniffling, the stranger looks up at Tawson. "My head is finally silent." The regret and pain on his face has something inside me hurting for him. What must he have gone through to end up like this? There's a strong need to console the injured and abandoned driving me, I've always felt the need to nurture and care for those around me. Especially after losing my parents but, this is fiercer than before I became an Omega.

Fen and Tawson share a look. "We should bring him with us back to the others. They need to be updated on the investigation. We are obviously looking for someone with incredible skills in black magic." Tawson's tone is threaded with agitation.

As we walk towards my bakery, I can't help considering the implications of this discovery. I know very little about black magic but what I am aware of is that it is forbidden to practice in our Kingdom. There have always been rumors about how it could twist the mind of the User and instead of them being the ones in charge the blackness consumes them and something else takes over. But, I don't know how true that is, because it's always been just a rumor. It's not like there are any Users in my village to ask, and even if there were, I'm pretty sure none of them would even consider speaking about it aloud. Hopefully, my males have more knowledge about this kind of thing.

Shivering even though it is warm, I glance up at Fen and Tawson. They both look tense. Even as Fen allows his skin to return from stone, his body is still rigid and his hand hovers near his weapon. Tawson has yet to remove his glare from the male and encourages him to walk in front of us. I guess they should be on edge, this is bad news.

CH.16

Everyone is gathered in my kitchen, staring at the blue Elf. Some with suspicion, some with curiosity and me? I am staring at him with sympathy because the poor male looks so lost and confused. He doesn't even know his own name! I wonder who did this to him... and why? Who is this dark voice that controlled him? I have so many questions but probably not as many as Tawson.

Before I will allow them to question the Elf, I tell everyone that I am going to make some food and one of them will fetch him some pants. He looks a little uncomfortable with only a shirt on. The thought of his maleness dangling in the breeze under the dress-like shirt forces a giggle out of me.

Unfortunately, this draws everyone's attention. Rafe smirks at me. "What, pray tell, is so funny, my Little Kitten?"

Clearing my throat, I try to wipe the smile off my face. "N-nothing. Nothing is funny. I-I must concentrate on this s-stew," stuttering, I try to think of something else to say so I don't have to admit where my mind wandered.

Rafe stalks towards me with a predatory look in his eye. "Now, now, Kitten. Lying to me is not very smart. Do you know what I do to punish liars?"

Slowly, I back around the island in the middle of the kitchen. Raising my hands as if to ward him off. "No one is lying! Nope. Not me. No need to think up any punishments. Totally unnecessary." Shaking my head like an idiot. There is no way he believes a word coming out of my mouth. I don't even believe what I'm saying.

I don't notice Fen behind me until I bump into him. Taking my wrists and holding them behind my back, Fen presents my chest as an offering to Rafe. Which he enjoys immensely if the look on his face is any indication.

With dark, mischievous eyes, Rafe stops in front of me, gently lifting my chin. "Little Kitten looks like she is caught in a trap. What do we do with trapped Little Kittens, Fen?"

My mind has gone hazy with desire.

Sweat trickles down my spine and a tightness builds in my core. These males are going to be the death of me. *How do they know the perfect method to create such chaos in my body?*

Fen rumbles a laugh behind me. "We get to play before having a tasty, little, snack." On the last word he licks up my neck and growls in my ear. My core flutters with desire. That sound wreaks havoc on me.

It seems like finally ridding myself of my innocence has made me lusty. One look from any of these males turns me on like a faucet and my cunt begins to leak the same too. Everything these males do has me wanting them more. I did not realize it would be like this. Then again, Dani was always looking for males to play with so I shouldn't be too surprised.

My hazy gaze flits around the room, looking for someone to save me from these two wicked beings. Unfortunately, I lock eyes with the only male in the room that isn't mine.

The stranger's pupils are blown wide and he's got both hands tugging on the bottom of the shirt. Is he nervous? Is he afraid for me? The words are waiting to leave my lips, to tell him I'm fine, when I notice that he isn't scared. He's hiding a hard cock under that strained fabric. Our display is affecting him strongly and a flush of embarrassment threaded with lust covers my face in a bright red.

Tawson stalks back in from getting clothing for the stranger, interrupting my stare off. He barks a laugh at my predicament.

"Sweetheart, you look a little ensnared." He leans against the wall with Gin before continuing, "I really do not want to intrude on your playtime, but we have a few important things to do before we can get back to Luella's pleasure."

"But, Tawson," Rafe huffs while pouting, "my Little Kitten was lying and I was about to have some fun with punishments!"

Fen releases me with a kiss on the side of my head, ignoring Rafe's whining to stir the stew.

A thoughtful look crosses Tawson's face. "After we deal with this little issue of the beast, you may continue with your punishment. We must set an example with our Omega early on if we do not want her to walk all over us." He's far too amused at my affronted glare.

Rolling my eyes in Tawson's direction, because that's just ridiculous. I do not need to be punished over having silly thoughts. Ignoring my males I gently question the Elf, "How are you doing? Overwhelmed yet? I bet it feels good to be in your own skin again, and to have clothing. I do think, since you can't remember your name, that we should come up with one for you. I can't keep calling you the blue Elf in my head. Or, I guess I could, but I think you might feel a little less lost if you had a name."

I think I added to his overwhelmed state because he is staring at me curiously but not saying anything. At least he has stopped crying, hopefully our playfulness is putting him at ease.

Gin grunts out a throaty chuckle and Rafe strolls over to us. "Don't mind her, Blue. Her mouth tends to get away from her occasionally. The best thing to do is just focus on the actual questions she has asked and ignore the rest." Rafe is laughing now because I elbowed him in the stomach, which ended up hurting my elbow instead. Sheesh, what is he made of? Rocks? No, wait, that's Fen. Rafe must have a lot of muscles to feel that hard. I mean, I have seen him without a shirt and it is quite a nice sight. I mentally shake my head, I really shouldn't let myself get so sidetracked.

Before we get into any kind of argument a soft, quiet voice cuts in. "Thank you. I am much better now that I am no longer stuck. All of this is incredibly overwhelming and I think I am in shock, but I am okay... I think." Taking a deep breath, he stares down at his feet, as if speaking in front of all of us was difficult for him.

Shouting excitedly, "THAT'S IT!" I jump up and down, startling everyone, myself included. "Sorry. I'm a little too enthusiastic sometimes. But why don't we call you Blue? If that's alright with you…"

Rafe lightheartedly nudges Blue. "Trust me kid, just smile and nod before she really gets rambling or we'll be here all night and I have some very important plans for her." Finishing with a playful leer directed at me.

"Sure… Blue is as good a name as any since I don't remember mine." Blue's voice is so soft it's almost inaudible.

"Okay." Tawson jumps in. "Perfect. We now have a name for our wayward beast. I have a few questions for you, Blue. Is that alright? We can talk as we have lunch and then we will put together a bedroll for you to rest." He quirks a brow at the stranger.

Blue stands a little taller when Tawson addresses him. It's like he can feel the dominant power coming off him. If anyone looked at our group from the outside they might assume that Gin, being the biggest, would be in charge. Either he does not want to bother being head Alpha, or size does not matter in regards to the amount of power an

Alpha has.

"Yes. I am happy to answer any questions you have. Though, I cannot guarantee answers. I do not think I remember enough to be very helpful." Blue's gaze shifts away from us, fixing to the floor as his cheeks redden with shame.

Tawson abruptly starts barking orders at everyone. "Gin, grab the extra chairs. Rafe help him carry in the additional table. Fen go upstairs and grab my bedroll, we will give that to Blue. Find space for him to sleep outside of the bedroom. Luella, Sweetheart, will you check the stew? Is it ready?" Tawson softens his voice when he speaks to me. I can tell that he cares deeply for me already, even though he hasn't known me long.

I flash a smile at Tawson, then direct my attention towards Blue. "Would you like to help me get bowls out for everyone?"

Shyly smiling at me, he nods. I point out where Blue can find the bowls and spoons while I stir the stew. Giving it a taste, I hum at the flavor, deciding it is done. Moving to swing the large pot off the fire, I grab a thickly woven pot holder to protect my hands. It's set up on a metal arm that swings which allows me to easily move my kettle or pots on and off the heat. Before I get a chance to actually move it,

Blue pauses beside me and gently rests a hand on my arm.

"May I get that for you? It seems like it will be quite heavy to move," Blue is so quiet as he speaks, I have to strain to hear him over the others. There's a light purple blush high on his cheeks, partially hidden by his hair.

"Sure!" I give him a bright grin. "Be careful because the arm gets very hot. Take this to protect your hands. I can't tell you how many times I have burned myself doing this."

A small smile peeks down at me from Blue's curtain of hair as he takes the potholder. Stepping back as he swings the pot off, I get distracted as Gin and Rafe carry in some chairs and a table.

Tawson mentioned something about extra chairs and tables but, where did they get these?

I must have said that last bit out loud because Rafe snorts. "Gin made these from some lumber he purchased at the market. He's quite handy, our Dragon." Clapping Gin on the shoulder, he walks past him to grab two more chairs from outside.

Gin grunts back before positioning the table beside mine and adding the chairs to it. Going over to Gin I lean against the new table and draw a finger over the new piece.

"When in the world did you have time to make these? Whoa, the craftsmanship on these are amazing! You, Sir, have a hidden talent!" If I wasn't watching him so closely I would have missed the darkening of his eyes when I said sir. But, the more important thing that I noticed was the slight reddening of the tips of his ears. That is absolutely adorable, I have to remember to compliment him more often because I do not want to be the only one blushing all the time.

Once we're all seated with our stew in front of us, Tawson begins questioning Blue. "Can you tell us what you were doing in the trees behind the house where we found you?"

Blue pales, setting his spoon down. "The... The voice steered me to this village and implanted the command to kill a specific scent and take another... I-It was the scent of iron and fire that I was to kill, and wild blueberries I was charged with taking. He never gave me names or pictures of the beings I was supposed to find. It was always a scent, and he didn't care if I killed more than that. He was actually happy the more I killed." Picking at his nails, he stares hard at his bowl of stew. The skin around Blue's eyes bunches with pain, his body visibly wracked with guilt. He must feel awful being forced to murder and having no say in where he could go. I couldn't even imagine being in that position.

Tawson looks at me next. "Do you know who in this village smells like iron and fire and wild blueberries?"

"Hmm... That sounds like the blacksmith and his wife."

"At least we won't have to go around sniffing all the villagers to find them." Tawson sighs, rubbing a hand over his face. Directing his attention to Rafe. "This afternoon you and Fen go to the market, see if you can find them. Gin you stay with Luella, protect her. I have more letters to send to the King and our Keep. Before doing that, I have more questions for you, Blue."

Gin looks incredibly smug about staying with me, I wonder if he thinks that means we're going to fool around... I mean, we probably will because who could turn down that slab of sexy male flesh? Now that I've gotten a taste of what sex is like, I think I've become rather partial to it. My thoughts make me snort a laugh, startling Rafe out of his pouting about leaving this afternoon.

"What is so funny about me leaving you this afternoon?" He directs a sullen look in my direction.

Fen, looking amused. "Well... Maybe it is a relief that you won't be here to 'punish' her for lying to you earlier?" Audibly gulping, I'd hoped they'd forgotten about that. Although, I can't say I'm not curious about what they're going to do to me, I have a feeling it's going to be fun though. My core gives an optimistic squeeze, excited at the prospect of some touching, while my mind drifts off thinking lusty thoughts.

As I'm considering all the fun things these males may introduce me to, I happen to catch movement in my periphery. Blue. *Oh. OH. I wonder what this poor male thinks of us? We're constantly bringing the conversation back to.. sex.* Mentally snorting at myself because I still can't even say sex in my mind without flushing, I really look at him. Blue looks more curious than awkward so that's good at least. He's still tugging at the bottom of the shirt, probably trying to hide his excitement. There's the slightest bit of purple on his cheeks exposing his embarrassment at all the sexual tension. But, he's trying to casually eat his stew while watching us. He's very cute. It almost feels like he belongs here, with us. *Hmmm... something to examine later.*

My contemplation is interrupted by Rafe's next words.

"Hmm... you could be right, Fen. Maybe we should get a quick punishment over with now before we leave, what do you think?" Rafe flicks his eyes to Tawson with a questioning look.

Tawson laughs and gives him a nod. Scrambling out of my chair, I take off running for the stairs. I don't know why I didn't head for the door, my brain is not functioning properly right now, too much adrenaline and desire coursing through me.

I don't even make it to the first step before strong arms band around my waist. I'm unceremoniously thrown over Rafe's shoulder as he takes the steps two at a time. Fen follows us with a dark smirk on his face. And I thought he was the nice one!

CH.17

Tossed into my nest and stripped, I lay there staring up at them with a smidge of trepidation and a lot of excitement. What is my punishment going to consist of? I mean, I know that it is normal to see males discipline their mates, so I have an idea. But, it is new to me and I can't help the anxiety building in my gut.

"Is this going to hurt?"

They smirk at each other before Fen nods and Rafe says, "It will hurt, but I promise you will enjoy what happens after... if you're a good girl."

My head swivels as I take a look around, as if I could find some way to escape. There is only one way out of this room and both their large bodies are blocking it. Plus they're much quicker than I am. I swear it's these short legs, it has nothing to do with the fact that I am allergic to running.

Rafe sits on the edge of the nest and hauls me over his lap. Squirming, I wiggle attempting to roll off of him, but it's no use. His arm is like a band of steel over me. He looks at Fen. "Hand or belt?"

Squealing in protest, I thrash harder. "No belt! That's... That's not..." trailing off because Rafe is laughing at me. Chuckles bounce me as his excitement pokes me in the side. He's enjoying this a little too much. I 'hmph' to show him how unimpressed I am.

"I think today, for a first offence, the hand is more appropriate," Fen muses. Trying to look up at him from my position, I can't because my hair is blocking my view. All I can see are his boots as he comes to stand near my head.

"Now, Kitten, if you can be a good girl and take this punishment without moving we will reward you with one orgasm each. Okay?" Rafe smooths a hand over my bum, which feels nice, but I have a feeling I am not going to like this. A spanking sounds so unpleasant.

Do I think this is fair? No. But do I want those orgasms? Yes, definitely. Can I handle this? Well, I won't know until he starts spanking me. But, honestly, a spanking makes me feel like a naughty child.

"I am a grown woman and I do not appreciate being treated like a child!" I shout towards the floor, trying to wiggle my way off Rafe.

"Precious." Fen squats by my head and lifts my hair so I can see him. "Women of all ages get spankings if they are bad. This is a way of making sure you will listen to us at all times, lying to us won't help keep you safe. I know you weren't lying about anything important, but we need to set a precedent for our relationship. This punishment is not only for lying to Rafe earlier, but also because you scared Tawson and myself. You ducked out from behind us to touch an unknown beast that could have killed you." He sounds so reasonable and the concern on his face has me feeling very badly.

When Fen puts it like that I almost feel like I deserve a punishment. What was I thinking?

Rafe adds, "Now that we have found you, we will not allow you to be hurt. But, you *have* to listen to us. We can't keep you safe if you run blindly into danger." His disappointment makes me feel even worse.

Letting out a deep sigh, because I know they aren't wrong that I blindly ran towards a known dangerous beast. But, to be fair, before they came here there was never any trouble.

"I'm sorry. I know that was stupid, but I was so drawn to Blue. This gut wrenching feeling told me that he needed me. I *had* to help him!" I try to explain.

"Good. I am glad you are sorry but you are still getting a punishment, otherwise the lesson won't stick," Rafe states. This is happening whether I like it or not. I'm just going to have to suck it up and deal with it. I nod to show my acquiescence.

Fen stands back to watch while Rafe tells me, "Keep your hands to yourself, or I will restrain you. Now I'm going to give you ten. You don't need to count, this time."

Closing my eyes, I wrap my hands around his ankle, bracing for the pain.

The first smack, I hear it a moment before feeling the sting. It isn't as bad as I thought it would be. So I exhale the breath I was holding. But, I relaxed a moment too soon because the second and third are harder. The fourth and fifth are lower, near my sit spots and that hurts so much that I can't hold back my squeak of pain. Six and seven are even worse since he goes over the same spots he already hit.

Holding tighter to his ankle, I'm resisting the urge to cup my behind. If I have to endure this pain I *want* my orgasms. Eight and nine are awful and I can't hold back the tears anymore, they trickle down to my hairline since I've let my head hang. Ten is the most painful, and I honestly feel very sorry for putting myself in danger. But I don't know that the threat of another punishment like this will stop me if it feels like the right thing to do.

I'm lifted and flipped over in Rafe's lap as he cuddles me tight to his chest. "It's over, okay? You're okay, Kitten. That wasn't so bad, hmm? All is forgiven now." He coos into my hair and gently wipes the tears off my face, kissing my forehead.

Fen is petting my hair whispering sweet and dirty things in my ear, "That was beautiful, Precious. Your ass is so lovely when it has a red blush to it. Makes me want to do very dirty things to you. It's such a biteable ass. Don't think I didn't notice the wetness gracing your lower lips. Shall we clean you up now, darling?" Who knew he could sound so sweet and so naughty at the same time?

My mind is whirling as I calm down and I'm stuck between shame and relief. It was as bad as I feared, the pain will linger for a while and I'm sure it'll remind me why it happened in the first place. But, at the same time, I'm so wet I'm dripping. Why did I like that? I swear pain has never been something I've enjoyed but... I think *this* kind of pain is different. I don't understand what's happening to my body. Is this because I'm an Omega or is it because I actually enjoy a bite to my pleasure?

Once I stop sniffling Rafe re-situates us in the nest so he's leaning back against the wall with me between his legs. Hooking my legs over his so I am open for Fen's gaze, my bottom scrapes roughly against his pants causing me to flinch. Fen's eyes darken and he licks his lips before kneeling on the bed.

My eyes lock with Fen's as Rafe nibbles on my ear, down my neck, and to my shoulder. Leaving a stinging sensation that he then kisses better. I am going to be covered in marks before I leave this room.

Fen is kissing and biting up my leg, making his way to my very wet core. Between the two of them I am feeling hot and uncomfortable. Letting out a whine of need, I desperately want Fen to touch me too. I need to cum. I need it very, very badly all of a sudden.

Both of them react to my whine with twin growls. My core squeezes hard over nothing in response and a gush of slick escapes me. Fen is there to lick it up off my thighs. When he makes it to my pussy he inhales deeply and lets out a groan. "You are the best thing I have ever tasted, touched, or scented. I could live off your slick, Precious." With those words he goes to work.

Fen licks both my lower lips clean, before making his way up to my clit. The moment he touches it I twitch.

"More!" I desperately cry out.

Licking all around my clit, he teases me with light touches before going back down and shoving his tongue as deep as he can get inside me. It's almost like Fen's trying to lick all the slick out of me, but the more he laps at me the more I produce.

When Fen finishes feasting on my slick, he kisses his way up to my clit. I know I am going to cum the moment he touches it. Which is exactly what happens, except he doesn't lick it like I anticipated. He sucks my clit into his mouth roughly and I scream out my orgasm. Twitching and writhing, the pleasure is so sharp that I absolutely gush. So much so that I am going to have to find new bed sheets because this whole nest is soaked in slick.

Fen doesn't stop sucking on my clit and it prolongs the orgasm to the point of pain. But it's a pleasurable pain. Reaching my hand down to push him away, Rafe grabs both my wrists in one hand stopping me. As he cages my wrists a thrill tickles through me and my stomach flips with nervous excitement. *Why do I like it when they hold me down?*

"No, no, no, Little Kitten. Take what we give you." Rafe's voice is so dark I almost don't recognize him. But, I like it. The cadence makes me shiver with need, or maybe because Fen is still torturing my clit.

Fen finally grants me some reprieve by licking all the slick off my thighs. He sits back with hooded eyes covered in my shiny release looking so pleased with himself.

I rake my eyes over Fen's gorgeous features, noticing a large bulge in his pants that makes my mouth water. But, he refuses to let me have what I so badly want. Instead he smirks while pulling me off Rafe and guiding me onto all fours. I shouldn't be surprised when Fen shackles my wrists to the bed.

He pulls me into a tender kiss and my slick tastes as sweet as honey on Fen's lips.

I'm so languid after that amount of rapture that I don't fight them maneuvering me wherever they want. Until I feel a hot breath over my reddened ass. Peeking over my shoulder at Rafe, he's staring at my cunt with a ravenous look. A nervous tremble runs through my body. Judging by the way Fen holds my arms down, I feel like Rafe is going to do something I may not like.

Before I have a chance to voice any objections, Rafe tongues me from my core right to my back hole. That was completely unexpected and a loud squeak escapes my throat. *Isn't that unsanitary?* But my thoughts are scattered when he does it again, touching my overly sensitive clit. My whole body twitches before Rafe tongues my ass again. The sensation is strange, I don't know how to feel about it and my body revolts automatically. My mates are not giving me a choice though. He licks around at first and then he slips his tongue inside my back hole, and... I don't hate it, but I feel like I should be protesting it.

"N-no, that is not... that's not sanitary, you shouldn't..." My objections are cut off when Fen kisses me, deeply. He licks into my mouth tasting every inch and battling my tongue. The kiss steals my breath away where I almost miss Rafe sliding a finger into my ass. Screeching, I try to move my hips away from the unfamiliar feeling, but he holds me still with an arm around my waist. Rafe forces me to take it as his finger stretches me.

It is a darkly pleasurable feeling that might actually make me cum. The foreign sensation shocks me so much I go still. Rafe takes advantage by sliding another finger inside. The stretch burns, but the minimal pain is counteracted by the insurmountable bliss. I am starting to really enjoy a little pain with my pleasure.

As Rafe plays with my ass, Fen strokes my breasts with one hand while restraining my wrists with the other. Each time he plucks at a nipple a jolt shoots straight down to my clit. Between the two of them another orgasm builds and it scares me because I should not be enjoying this so much!

Before long Rafe slides a third finger into my ass, really pushing my limits while he leans down and laps up the slick leaking out of me. It feels like too much and not enough, I don't know what I need. I rock into Rafe's movements desperately trying to find what my body craves.

Almost at the same time, Rafe slips down and bites my clit. I moan so loudly that I'm pretty sure anyone walking by can hear me.

Time stops as my ears ring, I can't breathe and my vision fades. A haze descends over my mind and warmth flushes through me. This experience is so far outside of what I know about intimacy, but I am so pleased that they know how to play my body like this.

Movement is a distant concept at the moment, I'm not sure I'll be able to get up. They have destroyed me with pleasure.

Regaining awareness, I find myself laying on top of Fen with him purring and petting my hair. Rafe is beside us stroking his hand down my back, murmuring sweet things to me, "My beautiful Omega. You are so sweet to us. We are so lucky to have found you and we will spoil you every day of our lives because you deserve it." He ends each sentence with a kiss somewhere on my back.

Drowsy and relaxed after that, I doze as thoughts trail through my mind. Punishments and pleasure are now a part of my life and while I enjoy it, these males certainly interfere with my independence. I have always been easy going, though, so I've let myself get swept away by their dominant ways. But every once in a while something inside me demands I resist and assert myself. It doesn't seem like I will win many arguments but the urge to rebel is there. There are two sides fighting one another inside me and I'm not sure which one is going to win. The stubborn part that wants to cling to my independence or the submissive part that desires to yield and allow them all to take over.

I've been on my own, having to deal with all the responsibilities of an adult for so long that it is almost a relief to let go and have someone else tell me what to do. But... not all the time. I have to cling to some of my autonomy, I don't want to lose who I am within their strong personalities.

Falling into a deeper sleep, I wake briefly when I'm shuffled from Fen onto someone else. It smells like Gin and my nose roots around finding where his scent is the strongest. Sighing, slumber claims me once again, leaving my conflicted thoughts for another time.

CH.18

Waking up to them having a discussion, again, is frustrating. Do they always have important conversations when I'm asleep? That's so unfair, what if I have things to contribute? Rude.

Still on top of Gin, my face is in his armpit. I'm surprised to find that it doesn't bother me all that much because his scent is so strong here and I love it.

"...Nothing... Not even a hint," Fen is saying, but I only catch bits of it. I'm not fully awake yet.

"Hmm... That is troubling. I don't think that Blue killed them yet because in a place this small I think we would have heard about it by now. There would have been warnings from the villagers and I bet they would close the market early. No vendors would want to stay if there was a chance they could be attacked," Tawson muses. I can picture him with a little furrow between his brows, arms crossed with one hand resting on his chin in contemplation.

"We did take a walk past the blacksmiths and we caught very faint hints of blueberries, amongst the strong Alpha scent of the blacksmith himself, but both were weak enough that I would assume the beings they belonged to had been gone for four days at least. Well before the market opened." Rafe this time, sounding sure with his guess. Which he should since he has a very good nose.

Sleepily, I blink my eyes up at Gin to find him already staring down at me. When he sees that I am a little more aware he smiles at me and rumbles a purr. I almost tell him to stop because their purrs relax me so much I could fall back asleep and I don't want to sleep, but I really enjoy the purr. So instead of telling him to stop I use his chest and push myself into a sitting position.

My movement gets everyone's attention, Tawson steps over to give me a quick kiss on the lips and a, "Good evening, sleepy head."

Fen and Rafe each take turns giving me a kiss and stepping back to continue their discussion with Tawson. Gin puts a hand on my cheek to bring my focus back to him so he can also give me a kiss. But his kiss is not quick and sweet, it is dirty and consuming. I can't get enough.

"Gin! Stop. We need to finish debriefing before we go back to pushing her into heat faster." Tawson gives Gin a look of regret before wiping it off his face for a more neutral look. "I spoke with Blue and got more information from him. Apparently, this voice wipes his memory routinely. The only reason he knows about being the one to make the kills in the other villages and towns is because he has overheard the voice ranting about 'getting closer to what he's looking for' and he's 'gathering power but it is going too slowly, he needs to start upgrading the kills to more powerful beings'. It sounds like he is following Blue along to his targets and he is stealing the magic from the bodies before they're fully dead. That could explain some of the strangeness of the corpses when we have looked at them." Tawson rubs his forehead and sighs heavily, sounding tired but also relieved at the prospect of new information.

Looking around at all of them, a smile plays at my lips. They're so big and muscular but that isn't all they are. I can truly see their kindness and integrity. Spending their lives protecting the Kingdom is a gallant purpose and I'm proud to be able to call them mine.

Bringing my focus back to Tawson. "So, from what Blue has said, this means the dark voice has to be near or in the village, because it sounds like they need to be close by to get what they want from the bodies and possibly needs to be close by in order to give Blue commands," I sum up.

Tawson looks pleased with my response. "Exactly what I was thinking, Sweetheart. Blue has not heard the voice since you somehow released him from his beastly form. I'm thinking there is something in the magic used to transform him into a Beast that allows this black magic to invade his mind. But being in Elf form blocks the connection. So, we have to keep an eye on Blue to see if any strangers approach him and for any possible shifting."

"Where is Blue now? Is he okay?" I inquire, sitting up taller, concern lacing my voice. I like him, I don't want him hurt or forced to murder anymore.

He's mine.

Whoa, *where did that thought come from?*

I'm interrupted from my strange musing by Rafe. "He is just getting his sleep area ready in the kitchen..." My sudden whine cuts him off.

He is *mine*, he should be here, in my nest with the rest of us. "No. I want him here. He should be here. He shouldn't be alone down there." Starting to get panicky, my hands grip at Gin's chest, I shake my head, as tears threaten to fall.

Lifted from Gin, I'm cradled in Tawson's arms. "Shhh. Sweetheart. Shhh... It's okay, we will get him up here. We will find space for him, don't worry." Hushing me, he softens his voice as he purrs to calm my distress, dropping kisses on my face.

Tawson looks over at Rafe, who's closest to the door. "Please inform Blue that he is going to sleep up here. Our Omega has claimed him." The last is said with a very serious note that I don't understand.

Rafe clomps down the stairs as Tawson sits on the bed beside Gin with me cradled in his lap. "Do you understand what it means to claim someone as an Omega?"

"N-no? I already told you that I don't know anything about being an Omega, I always thought I was a Beta, so why would I have read up on Omegas? Plus, they're super rare aren't they? Is it just Blue that I've claimed? Because that doesn't feel right. I need all of you here. If you're not here I don't think I could stop myself from panicking again. Oh Goddess, there's just so much I don't know! Why did this happen to me? Why me?" Anxiety has my words tumbling out in a rush and there is no stopping me.

"Not that I'm saying I wish you would have found a different Beta-turned-Omega, I think I would be rather unhappy if you were not with me. Just the idea of some other girl being near any of you makes me feel very rage-y, and that is not like me. I am not an angry person! Oh Goddess, these hormones are making me feel crazy!" Well, at least I haven't stopped being me. I was a little worried that parts of myself would change when I finished this transition into Omega. Although, it would have been nice to have a break from my erratic mouth.

Tawson holds me close while Fen rubs my back and Gin holds my feet in his lap.

"When an Omega claims someone, it is their way of putting together all the pieces they need to be healthy. They are really the ones in charge of building the pack. Since Omega's are so rare, there isn't a lot of information about this, but from what I understand it is their way of creating the best pack for themselves. In order for an Omega to be healthy and thrive, they need all the right partners." Tawson pauses for a moment to let this sink in.

"Apparently, Blue here has something

that you need to be happy. It could be any number of things, but I think it's because he has such a calming, quiet presence, compared to our loud bestial natures. Whatever it is, we all know that the Omega is truly the one in charge and if you say you need him, we will find a way to make that work." Dropping a kiss on my furrowed brow, he rubs my back.

It'll take me a moment to process this. It's... a lot. I don't feel in charge. I barely know what's happening to me. But, if I'm understanding him, this means I get to keep Blue and that has something inside me sighing in relief.

Rafe stands smirking just inside the doorway while Blue peeks into the bedroom with a wide-eyed stare.

Blue hesitantly steps around the doorway and picks his way over the bedrolls and clothing strewn across the floor until he is standing in front of me, hands clasped together.

"I understand not feeling in control of yourself," he relates, looking down. "But it will be okay. Uh, Luella. Especially with your pack here helping you. They are all awfully scary, but that just means they will be able to protect you better than anyone else could. Plus, they have been pretty nice to me considering I'm the murderer they've been looking for." With glistening eyes, he sniffles back the tears. Blue does not look like a murderer to me but... His beast form was frightening.

Even though he looked frightening as a beast, I was not afraid to touch him. *I wonder why?* Maybe it has something to do with being an Omega and claiming him?

Struggling out of Tawson's lap, I stand in front of Blue. He is only slightly taller than me, which is nice because I don't have to crane my neck to look at him. "Can... Can I give you a hug?" I ask hesitantly.

Paling, he swallows hard and glances at each of the Alphas in the room before stuttering, "I-I-I... C-Can't, you... You're Omega..."

Gin snorts a laugh, I toss a glare at him over my shoulder before refocusing on Blue. "I am an Omega, but I used to be a Beta. And sure, I have these big burly Alphas that I have claimed. But, I have also claimed you and you look like you need a hug. You have had a lot of shocks today, anyone would need a hug in your position."

Blue still looks apprehensive. "I-if you're sure no one is going to kill me for touching you, then, yes. Yes, I would like you to hug me, please?" Gosh, he's so timid and sweet. His fear and hesitance makes me want to bundle him up and squeeze him tight until he isn't scared anymore. I mean, how frightening it must be to not know who you are or where you came from.

Stepping into him, I wrap my arms around him tightly. It takes him a second before he does the same. The tension in his body slowly leaks out until wetness splashes against my neck and he lets out a quiet sob.

The poor male has been through so much and it isn't over yet.

Rafe steps up behind Blue and leans down to join our hug, same with Tawson and Fen at my back. Rafe makes a choked laugh and I glance up to see him pinching his lips shut as he contains his laughter. Glaring at Gin, I sigh when he joins our group hug.

Once he does it's like the dam breaks and poor Blue just cries his heart out until he's got me crying along with him. It takes a few minutes before he finally tapers off and in a congested voice mutters, "Thank you. I really needed that. I-it has been hard trying to wrap my mind around everything that has happened to me, and what I have done, unintentionally."

Humming, I nod in understanding. Rafe gently ushers us both towards my nest. The other three move aside so I can climb in and drag Blue along with me. He is still reluctant, like he doesn't think he should be doing this, but I am pretty determined to have my way. And I want to cuddle the poor beasty until he doesn't hurt so much.

When I've got us comfortable in the middle of the nest, I pop my head up to make sure my Alphas are still here. They are standing near the door having a quiet discussion. Gin is nodding like he's listening but he is staring longingly at me and the nest. I should probably listen to what they're talking about but I find that I don't care that much. Right now, there are more important matters. Like cuddling my Beta beasty and making him feel better.

Rearranging the pillows and blankets around Blue and myself, I make a wall on either side and then drape blankets over him. Slipping under the blanket, I cuddle tight to his side.

He tenses, trying to hide a grimace. "What's wrong? Do you not like comfortable things? Or is it me? Do you not want me?" My panic seeps back in.

Jerking, he stares at me wide eyed. "N-no! You are the most beautiful thing I have ever seen... I just... I don't feel worthy to be this close to you. Especially after knowing how awful I have acted as a beast. How do I deserve this?" Blue questions softly, looking scared and sad all at once.

"Nope! That is not how this works. Granted, I am still learning what it means to be an Omega. But, from what I understand, I decide who is in my pack and nest," I declare firmly. "Then again, I didn't really choose the Alphas... They found me and realized what I was and decided I would be their mate. Rafe even said I was going to be his mate when he first met me. So, I don't really know if I chose them or they sort of... crowded me until I realized I wanted them... Huh." Staring at the wall in thought, I wonder how this all happened so fast.

I mean... I was a Beta not even a full week ago. But, I don't think my instincts are wrong about them. They are very protective of me and I really like their scents. Everyone knows that if you like a scent that much it shows that you are highly compatible. I just hope this mysterious other brother, Alec, is as good as these males. There's a large part of me that longs to speak with Dani. She would help clear up my thoughts and guide me in my understanding of everything, she always had the right answers. With there being no sign of her or her family, all I can do is hope and pray that she is alright

When I finally stop getting lost in my aimless thoughts and refocus on Blue, he is smiling softly at me. "You are right. It is your choice of who you want in your pack, but don't I get a chance to say whether I want to be here or not?"

That thought freezes me in place. Am I forcing myself on him? Does he not want this? Is Blue only here because we saved him from killing again, and being stuck as the beast?

My alarm is thankfully cut off when he responds, "No, Beautiful Girl. No, I do want to be here with you. I may not remember who I was or anything about my life before becoming that beast, but you are the best thing to happen to me in a very long time." Wrapping his arms around me, Blue tugs me tight to his side. "Now, let's cuddle and nap together, okay?"

Even though I just woke up from a nap I feel tired again. I wonder if I've been so tired because of the changes my body is experiencing? That sounds likely. Plus, naps are the best.

CH.19

Covered in a layer of sweat when I wake up, I blearily look around. My stomach is cramping and my head feels fuzzy. Am I sick? I go to roll out of bed but I get tangled in the mess of blankets and arms. Rolling away from one body only to smack into another firm chest.

It smells like Gin, so I take a deep inhale and my stomach pangs again causing a whimper. Pushing lightly on Gin's chest, I mumble, "Need to pee. Too hot. Move!"

Chuckling, he scoops me up as he rolls out of bed. The movement is too quick and a little jarring and it makes my stomach dip. Tapping on him again. "Gin. I feel sick. I might puke, I need the bathroom quick. Please?"

Grunting, he carries me out the door and down the hallway into the bathroom before putting me on my feet again. Shooing him out the door before I pull the curtain across. I used to live alone and doors are expensive so I have never needed one before, but now if we stay here much longer I might have to ask Gin to craft one.

Once I'm finished doing my business and washing my hands, I splash water on my face. Sweat coats my whole body, my clothing clinging to my sticky skin. Why am I so warm? Maybe I'm getting sick... My thoughts are hazy and distracted as I step out of the bathroom.

"Ew! Were you listening to me pee? Gin, we need to have boundaries!" Wrinkling my nose I shriek. I'm pretty sure he would have stayed and watched me pee if I let him.

He grumbles so lowly I can't hear what he says but he picks me up again and takes me back to the bedroom.

Crawling back into the nest, I try to get comfortable but I can't. There's this nagging feeling that something isn't right. Looking over at Blue who is still napping lightly, I shake him awake.

"Huh? Wha?" he mumbles sleepily and cracks one eye open.

"You need to move, it isn't right. I need to fix this." Pushing at him until he sits up. Then I point at Gin and demand, "You, move him. I gotta fix this." Waving my arms wildly at the bed.

Gin is chortling loudly now but he steps forward grabbing Blue under both arms and hoists him out of the nest, putting him on his feet beside the bed. Blue is so confused and sleepy, he ends up leaning heavily on Gin.

Frantically, I start moving things around. As I come across the Alphas clothing I sniff each one of them before placing them in strategic locations. Crawling around I feel twinges wracking me with pain, and each time I get a cramp, slick leaks out of me. They slowly get worse and worse until I can't do anything other than curl up and cry.

"GET IN HERE, NOW!" My eyes widen and my mouth pops open at the way I'm ordering them around. I'm learning that I can be very bossy when it calls for it, especially when this strange sense of urgency has overtaken me.

They both climb in, one on either side of me, but it doesn't feel right. "Where are the rest of my Alphas?" I whimper at Gin.

Stroking the hair off my sweaty face. "They are coming, Little One. I promise. I will," pausing, he motions at Blue and himself, "*we* will help you. Don't worry."

Crying when I realize they aren't here yet. I don't know why I need them so badly.

One really big cramp curls my body. There's the feeling of something breaking inside me and a massive gush of slick flows out from my core.

"Oh! What? What is this? What's wrong with me? I've made such a mess," muttering angrily, I'm in pain and I think this is the most uncomfortable I have ever been in my life. My body feels foreign to me after years of knowing exactly who I am, but I don't get long to dwell on this as the cramps increase to blinding levels of pain.

When I look over at Gin, his eyes have shifted to that of his Dragon and his pupils are slowly swallowing the color of his eyes. He stares at me hungrily, rumbling a mix of a purr and a growl. Smoke steadily leaks out his nostrils as his Dragon makes himself known.

Every time Gin's Dragon pushes to the forefront, excitement thrills through me. He is such a dangerous being but all I see is need and longing. It's very alluring and all I want to do is cuddle up to him and stroke him, fuelling that desire.

The sound of his growl forces ripples through my stomach. It hurts even more and slick drips out of me at an alarming rate. Soon, all the liquid in my body will trickle out of my core, I'll be nothing but a dehydrated husk.

My thoughts are cut off by both Gin and

Blue striping quickly and tossing their clothes out of the nest. Which makes me angry but not enough to do anything except growl at them for throwing away good nesting material. The nest *must* have the scent of my mates!

Gin crawls into the nest and I get a good look at his cock as it sways with his movement, the heft of it pulling it down to bounce off his thighs. Any anger I had is quickly dissolved, only to be replaced with a fierce hunger. I knew it was going to be large but I didn't expect the ridges decorating it all the way to the knot.

My body is moving before I've even thought to. My hands grasp his cock tightly, like someone is going to take away my new toy, and lick the precum seeping from the tip.

Groaning in pleasure when I get a concentrated hit of him, I squeeze his cock tighter in my fists. His taste is so close to his scent that I suck him into my mouth frantically to try and get more. I'm feeling a bit feral.

It's his turn to groan. Wrapping my hair around one fist, he stares down at me. Gin's gaze is full of heat as he watches me try to take as much of his cock into my mouth as I can. Gagging when I'm not even a third of the way down, his cock taps the back of my throat.

Drooling down his length as I back off of him, I lick at the tip again trying to get more of his essence. When I move my hands experimentally up and down his shaft it causes more precum to drip. Sucking him back into my mouth, I use my saliva to slide my hands faster, thrilling at the feel of the ridges beneath my fingers. As I get down to the knot, I explore that swollen piece of him, moaning at the feel of it. Imagining how this will fit inside me.

Each time I pass over his knot he releases a grunt. He hasn't stopped his growly purr, which seems to be encouraging my slick to flow faster. A feminine energy fills me with each snarl and moan of enjoyment that I can draw from him.

As I continue to explore I vaguely hear Gin snarl at Blue. "Get down there and please her. She wants you in our pack so make her happy." When he releases a vicious snarl, I cramp and push one sticky hand into my stomach with a moan of pain.

"But I... I don't remember if I've done this before! What am I supposed to do?" Blue presses, panicking.

"Follow your instincts," Gin grunts out. He's so helpful to his pack-mates.

When I straighten to get back to sucking up Gin's taste, hands lightly smooth over my butt and thighs. Sighing with contentment, just being touched feels soothing and I want more. So, I look back at Blue and growl. A fuzzy feeling makes words difficult to form so I've resorted to inarticulate vocalizations instead.

Blue smiles shakily at me, which has me growling and frowning at him. Leaning in, he starts licking all the slick off my thighs getting closer to my core.

Now that Blue is finally doing as I want, I can focus on the cock in front of me. Mewling around the length in my mouth as my cunt is finally touched, I close my eyes to revel in these new sensations.

Gin growls deeply, forcing another harsh cramp.

Before I let go of Gin to grasp my stomach, Blue shoves his face in my pussy, frantically licking at my dripping core while his nose rubs against my back hole. I jerk in surprise, but don't actually try to get away. It feels… oddly nice.

His hands grip my cheeks hard enough to leave bruises, but I like it. Blue's enthusiasm surprises me, since he seems like such a shy male. I wonder if I taste good to him?

Gin tugs on my hair to refocus my attention on him. When I glance up, with my mouth wrapped around his tip, my hands squeezing and rubbing the rest of his ribbed member, he hisses.

"You look so depraved and I cannot get enough."

Whining around my mouthful. Blue has moved one hand to my clit and is circling it with slight pressure, while shoving his tongue deep into my core. It feels amazing, but I need more. I pull Gin out of my mouth.

"Knot? Please? I need you."

His growl is rough and my stomach ripples harder. It has me curling into myself. I'm so focused on trying to mitigate the pain that I barely notice them switching places.

"Yes, Beautiful," Gin's deep voice rumbles as large hands spread my cheeks apart. He places his thick tip at my opening, slowly pushing in. I keen with relief.

This.

This is what I need.

"Yes! More!" I cry out loudly.

A mouthwatering scent draws my focus in front of me. *Blue's cock*, I remind myself. He smells like apple pie and I could just eat him up. Blue's cock doesn't have any ribbing like Gin's, but it is much larger than his small frame would have suggested. The tip is leaking precum continuously, so I grab him and direct it to my mouth, lapping at it ravenously. It tastes so good I could do this all day. I will not need actual food if all of my mates taste so good.

Hissing at the stretch of Gin forcing his impressive girth in. Tawson felt huge but I'm pretty sure Gin is bigger and I'm not positive that he will fit. But, he continues making space for himself, with a chorus of grunts, growls, and deep groans that make me shiver with desire.

It feels like he should be all the way seated, but when I look back at him I see there is still so much to go. Opening my mouth, I start to speak, but I'm distracted when he pushes hard and a few more inches slide in, hitting something inside me that makes me jerk and moan loudly.

Muttering in a guttural tone, "That's it, Little One, squeeze my cock. Fuck, fuck. Shit, that's it."

Blue grabs my hair in both fists and directs my face back to him. I'm surprised by his forcefulness, but it's what I need. Gladly, I suck his length down like air, trying to take all of his cock. I couldn't with Gin because he was so long and thick, but Blue looks more manageable. I still gag before reaching the base but it feels easier to ignore it. Especially when Blue cries out, "Yes, yes, oh, Goddess. Please, Lu, don't stop!" It makes me feel powerful.

I am a moaning, writhing mess pinned in place by two cocks. Finally I feel Gin's knot bumping against my cunt and I try to push back on it. I need it inside me, now! But Blue won't let me off his dick to tell Gin that.

It doesn't matter anyways because Gin pulls back to the tip before shoving in hard, pushing me closer to orgasm.

The vibrations from my moans are going to force Blue to cum. I want that, I need his cum in my mouth. Starting to fuck my face, slowly, he is hesitant. Using my hair as handles, he holds me in place while finding his momentum. I think he is working up to match Gin's pace.

I am so wet, gushing slick all over Gin, that I can hear it when he forces his cock deep. It is a depraved, arousing sound. His knot bumping rhythmically against me. I keep trying to shove back when he pushes in, his knot slowly gaining ground. Until, Gin pulls out and pauses. He grunts at Blue. "You ready for this? When I force my knot in she will likely swallow you to the root."

Blue's response is a whimper and his cock jerks in my mouth, giving away his excitement.

Gin moves in and out a few more times, letting me feel him and all the ribbing along his length. It's amazing and I don't think I'll ever have enough. On the next push in, he forces that large knot inside. It feels too big, like I'm going to tear, and I cry out around the cock in my mouth, trying to protest even though I want it so badly. Instead of ripping me apart it pops in, lodging against that place inside me that forces an abrupt orgasm.

It also drives me forwards on Blue and I gag before swallowing the rest of his cock. My nose is rubbing the hair around the base of his member, and I can feel his groans vibrate through my throat. His cock twitches and hardens even more and then he's cumming. But I don't get to taste it since it is directed straight down to my stomach. I might pout about that later when I can think properly.

My scream of rapture is muffled due to the dick down my throat. Gin's knot swells even further, lengthening my orgasm. Or, is it causing multiple orgasms? It is hard to tell because the pleasure is overwhelming.

Gin's groan of satisfaction reverberates through my whole body. His release splashes inside my cunt, pushing me to clench down around him even harder. I need his cum, I need all of it. I am crazed by these desires.

Blue finally pulls out of my mouth, and I get a fleeting taste of him brushing across my tongue before he slumps back releasing my hair. With my mouth free I finally let my cries fill the air.

Gin leans over my back and brushes my hair off to one side. Spreading kisses along my neck and shoulder, he finds what he is looking for. Right under my ear, high up on my neck, he licks his spot before clamping his sharp teeth down.

Marking me, claiming me.

When the bond snaps into place I scream out in bliss, again. It is sharp and consuming and I think I may pass out from an overload of pleasure.

My body is limp under him as he tends to the new mark. He gently rolls us to our sides, keeping his mouth on the bite. Still tied to me with his knot, it occasionally forces another weak orgasm from me. Writhing, my cunt grips him periodically, and in response he releases more cum inside me. My belly is overfull. Reaching down, a small bulge forms where he continues to fill me.

Grabbing my hand, he brings it up to kiss the back. "Leave it, Little One. Every time you clench down on my knot I can't help giving you more cum. It is soothing the heat, it's good for you," he mutters smugly, satisfaction shining from his eyes.

Blue shifts until he is laying in front of me, leaving kisses all over my face. "Thank you, Luella. You are a Goddess. Thank you for including me, for wanting me in your pack."

There's no chance to reply because sleep is dragging me down. But I do hear Gin tell him, "When she has a chance she will bite you. Are you prepared for that?"

"You shouldn't let her, I am dangerous! What if the voice forces me to shift and kill again? I can't do that to her!" Blue is frightened. All I want to do is comfort him but exhaustion pulls me further into sleep. I hope I remember this when I come to.

CH.20

Waking up hot and wanting is not fun. Opening my eyes, I spy Blue sleeping next to me. Gin is behind me, his knot having softened and released while I was out. Feeling sticky, I smell heavily of Gin's cum. My mind is hazy but I can still think and it horrifies me a little that I want to roll around in the soiled bedding to get more of him on me. But I don't because I need a knot again, now. The urgency is pounding through my body and the cramps are back, full force. Squeezing my eyes shut, I curl around my stomach. When it relaxes for a moment I look around the room, hoping my other Alpha's are here but I don't see anyone. I don't know how long I was asleep.

Rolling over to Gin, I intend to wake him and demand his knot again but he is already awake and I can tell he is having a telepathic conversation. I have started to figure out the signs when they do this. A slight glazing of the eyes, and staring at nothing in particular.

While I am waiting for him to finish talking so I can demand he give me what I need, I hear footsteps coming up the stairs.

Rolling so quickly I disturb Blue from his sleep, I want to apologise, but I can't focus on that right now. I need my Alphas. I need more knots. It's their job to fix this, they caused it!

Rafe comes rushing into the room, already stripping his clothes off. "I am here for your pleasure, Little Kitten! What do you need?"

"Here, now! Knot!" Pointing at the nest. I am not very eloquent. Words are difficult for me in this haze of heat and pain.

Once Rafe is naked he leaps into the nest, making me squeal. But he doesn't squish me, he lands with his feet and hands bracing himself above me, smirking as usual.

But, I don't really care what he does right now as long as he gives me his knot. My eyes are pulled to his member like magnets. He is long, longer than Gin but not as thick. I reach for his hard twitching cock, but Rafe grabs both hands in one of his and pins them to the nest above my head.

"Nuh, uh. Let me."

"MINE!" I snarl at him. I didn't think I had it in me to snap at someone but, I have been learning a lot about myself since meeting these males.

He smiles, pure joy in the face of my anger. Before I say anything else embarrassing, Rafe reaches down with his free hand and shoves two fingers deep in my cunt, forcing a squeal of surprise.

"Oh good. Gin prepped you nicely for me!" Pulling his fingers out, he shoves them in my mouth. About to complain that it isn't what I need, but the flavor hits my tongue and my eyes roll back. The mix of my slick and Gin's cum is the most divine thing I have ever tasted. Sweetened cream over a cake flavored with tea and topped with strawberries. There's a lingering aftertaste of cinnamon that teases my tastebuds, bringing to mind comfort and strength, and a sweet warmth that caresses me. When he pulls them away from me I snarl again. But all he does is collect more and bring it to me. I frantically lick and suck at his fingers, trying to get all of it.

After he's done this a few times he nods at someone, but I don't have enough mental capacity to acknowledge that. My focus is purely on the ambrosia Rafe is feeding me. I think if I had been in my right mind I might have balked at this action... at least until I tasted it. It must be all the heat's fault that I'm acting like this? Right?

Someone's hands take over holding my arms above my head, I hazily look up into Fen's gorgeous face and smile. Chuckling, he leans down to peck me on the nose. Pouting when he doesn't kiss my lips, I want to taste him, too.

I'm distracted, which seems pretty easily done in this state, by Rafe rubbing the head of his shaft against my lower lips and clit. Each time he passes over my clit, sharp pleasure jolts through me. I try to grab him, but my arms are stuck so instead I settle for a growl.

"Stop teasing! Give me your fucking cock!" My lip curls, showing off my sharper canines as I make my demands.

Rafe's eyes light up, which is not what I intended. But it does get me what I want so I'm not too concerned. All I am truly preoccupied with is getting his knot in me.

As Rafe slides inside my tight, wet, heat, he wheezes out, "How the fuck did you last as long as you did, Gin? Goddess, she's so tight and warm. Fuck. I want to ruin you, Little Kitten." He looks into my glassy eyes with desire and adoration.

"I'm going to plow this sweet cunt so hard you're going to feel it for days." Leaning down, he nips and sucks at my breast. "I plan to leave bruises and marks all over your pretty body so everyone will know you're taken. You're *mine*." Switching to my other breast, repeating his actions, doing exactly what he said.

Rafe murmurs dirty, beautiful things to me while marking up my breasts. All the while he slowly pushes deeper and deeper until his knot stops him. Shifting my hips, I try to take that too, but he pulls back. The drag of his cock has my eyes rolling back in delight as I mewl, "Rafe."

He starts fucking into me violently, and I love it. Rolling my hips to match his frantic pace, moaning uncontrollably.

"Fuck, my sweet, naughty, Kitten. I'm gonna plant my seed so deep inside you. I'll be the first to breed this cunt. It'll be my pup. I can't wait to see you swell. I'm gonna keep you so sated on cock you won't be able to find any trouble. You'll be safely locked onto my knot." Rafe's mouth is filthy and I want what he does. I want his pup, or any of theirs. I want a part of them. Or, that could be the heat talking and I am completely delirious with pleasure. I'm cock-drunk.

Rafe's mouth runs non-stop because he can feel me gripping tightly around him every time he says something filthy.

I attack his mouth, tangling our tongues together, kissing him with all the ferocity and need rushing through me. My teeth sink into Rafe's bottom lip as he pulls away and he just smiles, kissing me again. I'm sure I'll be surprised at my behavior if I remember this when my heat is over. If my hands weren't held down, I'm sure he'd be decorated with scratches.

I am savage. Snarling, "Knot!" at him, demanding Rafe give me what will soothe the hungry beast inside me.

His smile turns wild and it delights me. I want him feral, I want him to lose control. I just want him.

Fucking me harder, I know he's going to give me his knot soon. I'm excited for that pinching, stretching pain of something so big being forced inside me. I'm getting addicted to that feeling and the deluge of pleasure that comes after it locks into place.

With little warning, he shoves his knot into me and I scream at the sensation. It is pure bliss. Fen releases my hands and my nails dig into Rafe's back. I'm so desperate to hold him close, like he will disappear if his knot isn't tying us together. Rafe will not escape me.

The rush of pleasure consumes me as he

hisses out his release. That feeling of getting stuffed full of cum has me moaning Rafe's name again. Managing to unhook my nails, he ignores my growls of protest, and kisses down my collar bone to my left breast. Licking a few places before he finds one that he likes and latches on, claiming me, leaving a perfect set of teeth marks around my nipple. The bite hurts and feels amazing all at once. Another orgasm burns through me. I clench around Rafe's knot forcing more cum out of him. I want it all.

Rafe rolls to his back, holding me tightly to him, before finally sliding his teeth out. Laving the punctures, he tends to the new mark. Each time he passes over it, I writhe with pleasure.

Once it feels like I have finally stopped clenching on his knot, I am sleepy again. But, before I am allowed to fall asleep someone is lifting me to sitting and tilting a waterskin to my mouth. Fighting them, I try to turn away, because that isn't the right taste but they are persistent. Finally, someone sighs and leans in to murmur in my ear.

"If you don't drink some water, I will not let you drink from my cock." It's Tawson, whispering in a dark voice. But it is successful because I am quickly sucking back some water, lest he change his mind. I need that. I need his cum, that will make everything better.

At last, I'm allowed to snuggle back into Rafe's chest. Nuzzling around until I'm comfortable, I sigh with happiness. Rafe strokes my back gently, leaving kisses on the top of my head. Happiness warms me through the bond. And I can feel how sated he is after fucking me nearly into unconsciousness.

Faintly, I hear someone ask, "Is she going to nap every time she gets a knot?" I think that was Blue.

"That is highly probable. With this being Luella's first heat and her being such a late bloomer, it is likely that her body is straining to adjust so quickly. The heat came on faster than I expected, but I am also glad it happened. Once it's over we can leave this village. We need to get her to our Keep and get word to the King about you." Tawson is always making plans, plus I can feel him through the bond. He's concerned, wary, excited, and extremely possessive, but he's curtailing that last one so his pack-mates can bond with me as well.

Waking up to unbelievable pleasure, is my new favorite thing. Fen is between my thighs slurping up the mess of slick and cum. My hands immediately fist his long red hair, tugging at him while I squirm, so close to an orgasm. I moan out his name, trying to ask... something, but I can't get my brain to think of words right now. Screaming, I see stars, when he sucks my clit into his mouth, forcing me over that cliff.

Sitting back he swipes a hand across his mouth and licks the slick off of it, all while staring at me with hungry eyes and a dangerous smirk. Fen has always seemed like the sweet one out of all of them, but right now he looks far from sweet and I want the beast lurking in his eyes.

Still panting, I'm limp after that wake up call. Fen slowly crawls up my body, leaving kisses everywhere he can reach. Once in a while he nips me, which forces me to focus on him and nothing else. He's demanding my attention without saying a word and it makes me a little crazy. I want his cock inside me, *now*.

When Fen reaches my face he kisses me, gently at first and then, slowly he consumes me. His movements get more and more dominant and I surrender to him. Fen licks into my mouth and I moan at the taste of him. Pushing forwards, I try to take control but he doesn't allow it. Backing off, he nips my lip before surging back in. Every time I try to take over, to get what I want, Fen backs off with another nip before continuing his domination over me. He does this until I relax and let him control the pace. When he's satisfied with my obedience Fen kisses over to my ear, nibbling along the lobe, making me shiver. Before mouthing along my neck, when he finds the spot I know he plans to claim as his he sucks harshly, leaving a mark as a space-holder.

So far, he has allowed my hands to roam across his body. Everywhere I can reach, I do, mapping out his muscles. I'm trying to reach his beautiful rear when he stops me. Lightly cuffing my wrists with both hands and locking them on either side of my head. I don't know why they all cage my hands. It's very frustrating. I just want to touch them.

"Eyes on me as I take you, Precious. I want to see every bit of pain and pleasure." Fen's voice is rough, and dark. I can practically feel the desire and dominance. He isn't using an Alpha bark, but it's close. I didn't realize this quiet, shy, delicious male had so much dominance in him.

I like it.

Staring into his fiercely beautiful eyes while he fits his cock to my opening, I shiver. The moment he starts pushing in, I close my eyes and revel in the feeling. But he stops, so I blink at him in confusion and chirp, "More?" It seems the further along my heat progresses the lower my vocabulary gets. I'm pretty sure when it gets far enough I will basically be a mindless fiend for sex and knots. I am not complaining though.

The moment my eyes meet his again, he continues pushing his cock into me. I didn't get a good look at him before he started this, but I'm pretty sure he's bigger than all of my other mates.

Every time I close my eyes in pleasure, he stops. So, I have to work hard to keep my eyes on him. I do not want him to stop. His cock is so thick, almost as thick as Rafe's knot and my muscles tremble as my body opens to him. The thought of how much bigger his knot is scares me and thrills me in equal measures.

Finally, he reaches the end of me, his knot teasing my entrance and his balls tapping on my ass. Fen rumbles, "Now, brace yourself." But I can't because he still has my wrists held down. All I can do is grip tightly over his cock and wait for him to wreck me.

Fen doesn't make me wait long. Just enough to have me feeling antsy. I need more knots. Pulling out almost as slowly as he pushed in, I squirm with impatience, trying to get more, trying to keep him inside me. Pausing with just the tip resting against my opening, Fen waits for my eyes to drift back to his. I didn't realize I was staring down, watching his cock slide out of me. It is arousing seeing something so large fit into my body.

When I make eye contact again he shoves in so hard I lose my breath for a moment, and then keen loudly. He stirs his hips before pulling out quicker, and then he's finding a rhythm and I can't stop the sounds he is forcing from me.

Every time I get close to my orgasm, Fen slows down until it fades. He does this until I am snarling, moaning, and acting like a feral little beast. Luckily, he has my hands pinned down, otherwise I'm sure he would be covered in scratches. As it is, I've gotten pretty close to latching my teeth into him. Fen is pretty good at avoiding that, and distracting me with his cock. Giving me a particularly hard thrust when I attempt to bite him.

Fen has started up a steady growl, as he fucks into me harder and harder, until finally he thrusts his knot straight in. I wasn't expecting it so suddenly, and since he hasn't let me cum yet, I explode with a shriek of pleasure. Literal stars flash behind my eyes, and I thrash until finally, I get my teeth into his chest right above his nipple. Latching on, I dig my teeth in deep, tasting his blood, my Omega brain saying we are punishing him for making us wait but also that he is a worthy Alpha and we must claim him.

He groans, deep and long, before biting me back in the spot he marked earlier. Fen's cock kicks inside me, spewing cum and filling me to bursting.

He starts cleaning and tending to his bite but I refuse to let go just yet. I need to make sure everyone knows this Alpha is mine. My scent will mark Fen deeply. My Omega brain is a wild animal while in heat.

When he rolls us so I'm resting on his chest, his knot shifts and lodges deeper. Closing my eyes, I mewl. Finally, I decide I can release my bite, before tending it. Licking him clean and making sure it's clearly visible. When I'm satisfied, I look at him, kiss him, and then snuggle in and immediately fall asleep. I know my Alphas will keep me safe.

CH.21

The days blur together and I'm only aware of very small bits and pieces of the rest of my heat. It's all limbs, knots and cum. Until finally, my heat is over. I know this because I can think clearly again.

I'm laying on top of someone, absolutely coated in cum and other bodily fluids. My neck aches from all the bites, same with the breast Rafe bit. I am also just plain sore from days of sex. My muscles are shaky and weak, I'm not sure if I'll be able to walk but I really need to pee.

Lifting my head, I peer around me, every single male is haphazardly strewn around the nest sleeping heavily. I must have worn them out, but I figured they would have fared better than me since there were five of them participating. Although, it seems like even that wasn't enough. I guess it will be a good thing that there's another member of their pack waiting for me at their Keep, before my next heat comes.

I really need to find some books on Omegas so I can learn more about what to expect from myself. Like, when is my next heat going to come? How often do Omegas get a heat? What kinds of instinctual behaviors will I find myself doing? I have so many questions and so little answers on what's next.

Movement out of the corner of my eye catches my attention, someone must have woken while I sat here contemplating my new life.

"Do you need some help, Lu?" A quiet, gentle, voice caresses me.

Blue sits near the outside edge of the nest, I whisper, "Yes, please. I have to pee and I really need a wash." We share a look and I laugh lightly at that. I'm a mess.

Standing, he stretches, giving me a great view of his body. I have to tell my cunt to quiet down when it gives a faint clench at the sight of his toned sleek body, I am in no condition for more sex. Honestly, how I can even want more right now is a major surprise to me. It must be an Omega thing.

With more strength than I expected Blue plucks me off of... I glance down, Gin's chest and has me wrap my legs around his waist. Carrying me out of the room and down the short hall to my bathroom before he places me on my feet.

Shooing him out, because I do not need Blue watching me use the privy. I know the curtain doesn't do much for the sound but at least he can't see me. When I'm done I pour some water from the jug I keep in here into a bowl and wash my hands and face. Afterwards, I realize that isn't enough. I desperately need a bath, so I poke my head out. Blue is leaning against the wall, arms crossed while deep in thought.

Clearing my throat to get his attention. "Uhh... Can you head down to the kitchen and put a full pot of water over the fire to heat? I need to wash... There's a tub out back that I drag in and leave beside the fire so I don't have to struggle filling it. Do you, uh, think you could drag that in for me, too? I'm just going to grab some clothes and I'll be right down." Watching me, a slight smile toying with the edge of his lips, amused at something.

"Can you make it back to the bedroom on your own?" Lifting an eyebrow in challenge, he drops his arms and takes a step towards me.

Blue is right to challenge me on that because I've been hanging on to the doorway for dear life, but I'm stubborn. I was going to crawl back to the bedroom when he went down the stairs.

Taking a shaky step towards him, my knees just won't hold me. Luckily, he knew this was going to happen so he catches me and hoists me up into his arms, heading back to the room so I can get clothes. I'm only pouting a little because Blue was right, but I feel like I'm losing all the independence I built up being on my own for so long. This is going to be a difficult transition and I know I'm going to have trouble asking for help.

When we get there, the Alphas have roused themselves and are sleepily peering around the room for something.

Rafe is the first to spot me and he scrambles out of the nest, stealing me from Blue. "Kitten! I was worried when I couldn't find you!" He is way too exuberant while I am this tired.

Giving Rafe a flat look, I drawl, "You can feel me through the bond."

"Well, yeah. But, that's just how you're feeling! We haven't tried to see if you can use the pack link yet. Oh! We should try that right now."

Too sleepy to understand what he's saying to me, I just point at my small closet hoping Rafe'll bring me over there so I can grab what I need. Blue has gone, and I think that sweet male is preparing my bath. I am so thankful he's here.

Rafe jiggles me a little to get my attention. "Little Kitten! What are you doing?" Now he's confused, frowning at me with a cute little wrinkle between his brows and a pout on his lips.

"Clothes, please. Then, bath." I don't have it in me to say more right now. I think I'm going to bathe and then nap again. I really wish I remembered everything that happened during my heat, because my body feels like I've been exercising, I shudder at the thought. Ugh, exercise is not something I choose to do. *Ever*.

Rafe brings me over to the closet and without putting me down he snags everything I point at before checking with me for his next instructions.

"Okay, now that we have clothes do you want help dressing?" Rafe quirks a brow, a smile teasing his lips as he stares at me.

Giving him a disgusted look, I curl my lip, because has he seen me? I am a mess of dried fluids and my hair is chaotic, like a pigel has tried to make a nest in it! I refuse to put on nice, clean, clothes without actually being clean myself.

"Ew, Rafe! Look at me! I need to wash so badly before I let any fabric touch me. It would probably just stick to me. Gross."

He lets out a loud howl of laughter. I'm glad my predicament amuses him. "But I like you smelling like all of us! You've never been more attractive to me. If I didn't think you needed some food and more rest I'd be fucking you against the wall already." Trying to hold on to his pout, he ruins it by smiling widely.

A flash of warmth rushes through me, centering on my core, causing slick to leak out. I hold back a groan because no, I can't actually be wanting sex right now, can I? *Nope! Not happening.*

I want to wash. "No, Rafe. Stop being sexy, and saying things that make me hot! Downstairs, now, please?" I'm firm with him but I still feel the need to ask politely.

He smiles all the way down the stairs and into the kitchen. Blue is dragging my heavy metal tub in from the back door and Rafe puts me down on one of the chairs to go help.

Admiring the flex and play of their muscles, I have to check if I'm drooling. My males are very attractive, and I have a feeling that I will be leaking slick all the time. Ugh, so unfair, how do Omegas live like this?

Rafe's back muscles glisten, he probably

also needs a bath after that fuck-fest. But, *oh*, that's such a nice view.

Losing myself watching them place it beside the fire and swing the heavy pot of water over it, I sigh. The sound of water splashing into the tub drags me out of my daydreaming and I struggle onto my feet so I can shuffle over to the shelves near the fire for my bar of soap and a cloth for washing.

"Rafe, can you grab another jug full of cold water from the well out back? The bath will need to be brought down to a safe temperature, although the heat might help melt all this off me..." Trailing off, I wonder if my little bar of soap will be enough to clean the layers of cum off my skin.

Rafe snorts before grabbing the jug and practically skipping out the door. Blue starts laughing at the look of disgust on my face.

"How can he have this much energy?" I huff at Blue. "It's almost like he didn't participate in... However long we were in that nest for. I feel wrecked! It's very unfair." I hmph and cross my arms. When I start listing to the side, Blue chuckles again and picks me up, nuzzles the side of my face and drops a sweet kiss on the corner of my mouth.

"It's probably because there were five of us to switch out and only one of you demanding knots, cocks and all the cum you could swallow," he comments, smiling at me flashing his dimples. *Why does he have be so cute*?

Staring him dead in the eye. "I do not want logic right now. How dare you make sense! I have earned my complaints!" Ruining my seriousness with giggles, I bury my head in his neck.

Wait. He smells clean and fresh. "Did you bathe already? How are you not covered in this mess too?"

"I stood out back at the well and washed myself before you woke up." He smiles down at me fondly. "I was, also, not the center of attention during that... What did you call it? Fuck-fest." Chuckling softly, he nuzzles me again. It's so nice to see the lightness in him, he's been somber since we found him and I wasn't sure how to make things better for him.

Shivering in sympathy, I have done that before. When I was too tired to drag the tub in. It is highly unpleasant but, in the mornings, it is a quick way to wake up. He must have been out there a while though because there are literal layers of fluid stuck to me.

"While I don't remember everything that happened, I do remember making demands for my Beta to give me his cock."

I smile affectionately at the memories. He always seemed so awed when I summoned him, and pushed whichever Alpha out of the way.

His ears turn red and he glances down shyly. Blue is so adorable. He mumbles something I can't hear and before I get the chance to ask what it was, Rafe comes back with the water for the tub.

I'm so excited to wash that I forget about asking him. As soon as the cool water is added I shove Rafe out of my way and slip into the tub with a groan of relief.

The heat soothes my muscles instantly, as well as softening the layers of spunk stuck to me. I grab the cloth and scrub a little, testing how easy it will be to clean.

It's still pretty stuck and I don't feel like scrubbing my skin off, so I just lean back, close my eyes and sigh. I'll soak for a bit before trying to scrub myself.

Quiet murmuring interrupts my peace, it sounds like the rest of the pack is awake and making their way down. I don't bother opening my eyes though because I am having some me time.

As I soak, almost falling asleep in the water, gentle hands gather my hair. Peeking an eye open I spy Fen soaking my messy locks before grabbing the soap and starting the long process of untangling it. Smiling, I sigh with happiness that I don't have to do it myself. I don't actually think I have enough strength in my arms anyways.

Relaxing into the feeling of him playing with my hair, sighing with bliss, I almost miss the second set of hands that start lathering up the cloth. Opening my eyes to Tawson lifting my leg out of the water to clean, I did not expect this kind of treatment. Is this an Alpha-Omega thing? Or is this how proper males treat their mates? Regardless, I am extremely grateful.

Smelling something delicious cooking, I have to ask, "Who's cooking? Wait, no not important, what is that delightful smell?" My stomach punctuates this with a loud grumble that everyone can hear, even through the water.

It's quiet for a moment, only the sound of sizzling breaking the silence, before I start giggling. Masculine chuckles join me after a moment, and everyone is smiling, relaxed after a long trial.

CH.22

Everyone scatters after we eat and Tawson carries me upstairs. "You know, I think my legs might never work again. What did you guys do to me?" I articulate my exhausted thoughts out loud.

Tawson huffs and smirks at my words. "Sweetheart. We only did what you asked us to do. Actually, you demanded and pushed us around until you got what you wanted. I did not expect that from you. You're so sweet and gentle, normally."

He's definitely poking fun at me but I don't fully remember what happened so I can't dispute it. Especially because the things I do remember have me believing him. I don't respond to his teasing, just cross my arms and pout.

When we get to the nest room Tawson sets me on the edge of the bed. "Do you have a travel pack? We need to get moving now that your heat is over. I am sorry that we have disrupted your life here so drastically, but I can't really feel bad because it means we got you and that is not something I will ever regret. I care for you so deeply already." The truth of his words ring through the bond. He cares deeply for me and it brings a tear to my eye. Aside from Dani, I haven't had anyone care for me like this since my parents.

Sniffling, I fight to keep the tears from falling before I'm wrapped up in his arms and cuddle tightly against his chest.

I peer up at Tawson, with watery eyes. "I didn't think I could fall for anyone, let alone a whole pack, so quickly. Honestly, before you found me I had zero interest in males. My focus was all on baking and surviving." Closing my eyes I nuzzle into his chest before continuing, "I am extremely sad to leave all I have worked for here but... I think I will be happier with the pack... as long as I can still bake at your home. I can still do that right?" Glancing up at him with big sad eyes, pleading with him to say yes.

With a warm smile, Tawson leans down to kiss my forehead, each eye, my nose and then leaves a lingering kiss on my lips. "Of course, Love. None of us would ever stand in the way of your happiness. We want you to be content in your new life, if that is baking... then we will be sure to get you any ingredients you desire." He's so warm and comforting. I figured my most serious male would be harder to get close to but... I think, along with the bond, that I've learned how caring and sweet he can be. I'm falling for him already. For all of them. These feelings make my heart warm. I'm so grateful that I met them. I've never been happier in my life.

I am very lucky, and those knots don't hurt either. Smiling through my tears, I squeeze him tightly. Until I feel him shaking. Glancing up at him again, I see him holding in a laugh.

Raising an eyebrow, I wait for him to explain. "Sweetheart, you said that out loud." Laughing deeply, Tawson crushes me into his chest. "I'm glad you enjoy the knots. I promise any of us will give you a knot whenever you need it." Smirking, he waggles his eyebrows at me.

A blush colors my cheeks and I hide my face in his armpit, mumbling out that I have a travel pack buried at the back of my closet.

Laughing Tawson drops me into the nest before sauntering over to dig it out. I don't know if I'll ever stop blushing.

Tawson packs up my entire wardrobe and my collection of trinkets while humming happily. I would not have pegged Mr. Serious

Alpha as someone who hums joyfully. But I'm enjoying learning things about my new pack.

Am I sad about leaving all of this? Yes. But I was getting frustrated with my life as it was. I was just complaining the other day that I felt stuck in a rut. I think I am ready for this change. I just wish I could find Dani before leaving, but I'm not sure if she'll be around. I've been out of commission for... I have no idea how long I was in heat for, a week?

Peering over at Tawson with a raised brow. "How... How long was my heat?" Uncertainty seeps out of my pores.

Tawson glances over at me and grimaces before answering, "It was about five days. The market has been over for three days already. Everyone who travelled here to sell has long since moved on to the next village."

I'm in shock to learn how much time has passed in a haze of pheromones and fucking. "Has... Has anyone come looking for me?" I ask quietly, thinking of Dani. No one else in this village really cares all that much about anyone outside of their families. Sure they've always been kind to me but I doubt any of them will miss me for more than my breakfast rolls.

"The first day we had the sign up saying you were closed, we had a rush of people asking for baked goods but after that no one knocked on the door. The only one any of us saw regularly, watching from afar, trying to hide in the shadows, was that Jerrik fool." His nostrils flare, as he grits his teeth and clenches his fists. The veins in his forearms pop and I completely understand his reaction. Jerrik is a jerk and a nuisance to everyone he comes into contact with.

Tawson goes back to packing as I think about the fact that Dani didn't bother coming by to check on me. We don't usually go more than a few days without seeing each other. The only thing I can think of, to explain why, is that she must have left town with her family to go somewhere. But, I have no idea where. As far as I know they don't have any family in the nearby villages. They do have a distant cousin in the neighboring kingdom of Telamaro, but I didn't think they even spoke to them though, let alone visit. Getting letters to another kingdom can be expensive because you need a User to send it to the Telamaro User in charge of incoming letters before they send them off through birds. All of this costs more money than any of the villagers have.

I'm getting frustrated at my own thoughts now. I just hope she's safe and alive. I wonder if I will ever see her again?

"Tawson?" My voice is hesitant as I catch his attention, "What... What do you think could have happened to Dani? She's my best friend. How could she just... disappear? You don't think the beast, uhh... Blue, got her before we found him... do you?" I chew my lip as my eyes drop to my lap, watching my fingers fidget with a loose thread.

Tawson's warm embrace surrounds me as he hauls me onto his lap. Nuzzling my head, he tips my chin up.

"I'm so sorry, Sweetheart! I know how important she is to you, and even if I didn't, I would care because you love her." He gives me a squeeze, letting me bury my head against his chest, "When I'd left you here with Gin and Blue, Fen, Rafe and I all did a thorough search. I'm sorry to tell you that we broke into Dani's home but I knew you would want some answers."

My head snaps up and I gape at the chagrin on his face. It's charming to see him so open. Tawson mirth overtakes the chagrin and he smirks at me.

"We locked up as best we could after we searched the place. There was a letter on the kitchen table addressed to the Lord. It stated that they decided to move and the home was now available. But it said nothing about where they've gone or why they suddenly decided to make such a drastic change. I'm so sorry."

Tawson truly seems pained on my behalf. It's very sweet that he wanted to help me find her so badly that he broke into Dani's home.

"After we get you to our home and know you are safe, I promise we will use all our resources to try and find her. You deserve the world, but if all you want is a bakery and your best friend I will do everything in my power to get that for you. I just want to see you happy." Tawson's words have tears glistening in my eyes. I've cried enough though so I sniffle and hold them back as I process this information.

"Thank you, Alpha. It sets my mind slightly at ease knowing she isn't dead. I really want to know why or how she could leave me without a word though. Something seems fishy about it all, doesn't it?" My brows crease as a frown mars my face. It's just another mystery on top of the whole black magic thing and I am in no condition to figure it out right now. Shaking my head, I try to clear the ominous feelings weighing me down.

With another tight hug and a few lingering kisses, Tawson puts me back on the bed as he returns to filling my bag.

It is early evening before my whole home is packed into a cart. Tawson has sent a bird to the Lord saying the bakery building is available for any newcomers.

I'm surprised we're leaving this late but it isn't my decision. Tawson has been looking more and more tense as the hours drag on. It is leaking through the bond putting everyone on edge.

I'm dropped onto the bench beside Fen, who is driving the cart. Blue is in the back with all our packs, and my entire home. The rest of the Alphas are on horses. Trying not to cry as we leave the only home I've ever known, I discreetly wipe tears off my cheeks.

Fen reaches an arm around me and tugs me tight to his side. His warmth, and scent, are comforting. He doesn't say a word, sensing that I am in no mood for any logic to make me feel better.

We are all quiet as I watch the village grow smaller and the trees loom taller above us. The cart rattles and bumps over the uneven dirt path, I'm grateful that they placed a cushion under me before we left.

The scent of the forest, deep and earthy, is soothing my emotions as we travel further into the woods. The sun going down casts long shadows, giving the forest an eerie and dangerous edge. But, I know I am safe with my Alphas.

We travel long into the growing darkness. Even after the sun has set and the moon casts faint light, we continue.

Leaning heavier into Fen, I fall into an uneasy slumber. But it is not deep enough to prevent me from overhearing their conversation.

Tawson starts, in his commanding voice, "Is she asleep?"

Fen shuffles around, jarring me a little as he looks down on me. "It seems so. She has not moved in quite some time, and there are these adorable little snores that tell me she is sleeping deeply enough." I can almost feel the smile from him.

Also, I do *not* snore. How rude.

"Good. I do not wish to stress her anymore than she needs to be. This move is enough for her to deal with." Tawson sounds relieved and uneasy at the same time. "Blue. We know you had been travelling in a, relatively, straight line but we are not sure where you originated. It could have been the first murder site or the voice could have sent you further to insure finding them would be more difficult. We just can't be sure. Do you have any ideas of where you were sent from? Any vague suspicion or impression would give us a starting point."

Blue shuffles around in the back, I feel the vibrations through the cart. "Hmm... I think-I... I am pretty sure I started my journey through the wilds near the Mikta Mountains. I have hazy recollections of darkness towering over me and the screech of Griffons." His voice is shaky as he tries to think of things that have been wiped from his mind.

Gin grunts, and it sounds like a question. It almost makes me smile, knowing he saves most of his talking for me. Since I am still 'asleep' I can't see who he directed that question at. But, a moment later Fen responds.

His voice rumbles through me since I am basically tucked into his lap. "Yes. We all know there is one area where the Griffons nest, but it doesn't mean it is near there. The Griffons do find places all along the mountains and that is miles and miles of area to search. Almost impossible unless we can convince the King to send all the teams to look," pausing, he sighs. "Gin, you could shift and fly above it. You would be able to cover so much more ground and possibly see things we would miss from the base of the mountains."

At this Gin growls in protest. But I don't understand why, doesn't he like flying? Does he not enjoy being his Dragon? I would love to see the world from up there. I wonder if I could convince him to take me for a ride?

My thoughts of Dragon riding are interrupted by Rafe. "Pfft, you know getting him to leave our mate for even a few minutes is going to be impossible. The new bond for any of us will make it difficult to be away from her. Tawson, what does it even matter? We are going to the Keep to settle our Omega into her new home. We will not be the ones initiating this search, it's going to get handed off as soon as we meet the new team being assigned." He sounds uncaring, but I think it is a front. I think he is concerned about me and about this danger we know very little about. Even I am concerned about it and I know very little of the world outside my village. They continue arguing as I fall into a deeper sleep.

Something chases me, something dark and huge. The darkness is like a wave that encompasses the sky making it near impossible to escape. I can hear screams that seem to echo from within, chills race across my body, warning me of my fate should I be caught. I run and run until my lungs scream and my legs want to give out, but I fight it. I don't want to be swallowed up. Where are my Alphas? Where is my pack? Why aren't they here to save me? I don't want to be alone anymore. I didn't realize how lonely I was until I met them and they wouldn't leave me be.

Jolting into wakefulness, I smack my forehead against someone's face. Crying out at the pain, how is their face so hard? "Owww. Why?" I am very eloquent first thing in the morning.

Laughter from more than one person sounds around me. "I'm sorry, Precious. You were having a nightmare and wouldn't wake up." Fen. That explains why his face is so hard. He is a Gargoyle, made of stone. Except he isn't in stone form so why in the world did that hurt so much?

I am cradled in his arms as he kisses across the lump on my head and murmurs his apologies into my hair.

I guess he can be forgiven, he was only trying to help. "It's okay, Stony. I forgive your face. I don't even remember what the dream was about... Something about screaming clouds and darkness? I dunno." Trailing off, I mumble about hard heads and darkness.

He huffs out a laugh and I squint up at him. "Stony? Is that my new name?"

Blushing when I realize what I said in my barely awake state. "Hmm... Yep. Yeah. Stony. Because, you know?" I stumble over an explanation before I give up. "Where are we?" I very subtly change the subject.

We made camp at some point. I must have been deeply asleep because I did not wake up once. The morning light is barely peeking through the thick forest, it is still fairly dark and I can see a bit of fog rolling through the trees. It's actually kind of beautiful.

Gin is cooking something over the open fire that smells juicy and delicious. Before I wander over to see if I can convince him to feed me, I need to pee. Wiggling to get Fen to let me up. When he doesn't I tell him if he doesn't let me go I will pee on him.

He releases me with a deep guffaw. I guess the threat of pee doesn't bother him all that much, I shrug as I wander towards a large oak.

Tawson calls after me, "Do not go far. There are dangers in the woods and I would not be pleased if you were injured." *Mr. Serious is at it again, in all his bossy glory*, I smile to myself.

Nodding my head, I continue to the tree I picked out. I am still half asleep as I do my business leaning against the tree. Sparkles start falling all around my head and I startle as a delighted smile grows. Stilling my movement so I don't mess on myself, I look up trying to find the source. Spotting a handful of tiny forest sprites buzzing around me.

After finishing what I'm doing, I focus my attention on them. Their little voices chime as they chatter at each other and me. Their language sounds like tiny bells. My smile widens as I reach up. I can't understand what they're saying because they are speaking their own language, but it is beautiful nonetheless. Stepping away from the tree I do a little spin, dancing with them. They get excited and sprinkle a rainbow of glitter onto my skin. What a magical way to wake up. Dani was always telling me the wonders of the forest, but I was such a homebody that I didn't pay her much heed.

They eventually get bored of dancing with me and fly off to do whatever it is sprites do, so I head back to camp. My stomach rumbles loudly as I make a straight line to Gin, hoping he will feed me.

Before I make it to him Rafe stops me. He spins me around looking at the beautiful sparkles the sprites decorated me with. I smile at him as he barks out a laugh. "How do you find trouble so quickly, Little Kitten?"

"No trouble! They just came for a dance before heading on their way. It was magical, Rafe! And look! I'm so pretty now." Smiling widely at him, I do a little shimmy to make all the sparkles glitter in the early morning light.

Leaning down he kisses me silly. Licking at my lips until I open for him on a gasp. Rafe winds one arm around my lower back and one hand on my neck before leaning me back into a dip. My hands clutch at his shirt, hanging on tightly, although I know he won't drop me. The kiss steals my breath as our tongues mesh together. Rafe tastes so delicious, warm caramel melting on my tongue with a hint of salt to really bring out the flavor. It brings to mind sweet comfort and perfect autumn days, wrapped in a cozy blanket. It's so good I can't help but whimper.

When he sets me back on my feet I'm breathless and panting, staring up at him hungrily. The kiss has me feeling tingly and warm, even though the air is cool. But instead of doing anything else, he whistles a little tune as he wanders off to help Blue and Tawson repack our bedrolls. How dare he tease me like this and then just stroll off without a care in the world while I stand here wet and wanting. Propping my hands on my hips, I scowl after him before a chuckle escapes and I shake my head. Rafe always knows how to make me laugh.

I'm off kilter as I make my way to Gin, who sits there with fire burning in his eyes. He enjoyed watching Rafe kiss me.

Tugging me onto his lap when I'm close enough, he feeds me bites of meat. I don't protest or fight to feed myself because it is far too early for me to deal with these males.

CH.23

After everyone has eaten there's just a few things left to pack. Rafe asks me if I'd like to wash, he found a creek nearby we can use. The water will be cold but I'm eager to be clean.

He reaches a hand out for me, but before I get the chance to take it Gin picks me up and grunts at Rafe. I guess Rafe understood what that grunt means because he holds both hands up and steps back muttering, "Okay, sheesh! You have to share. Rude, Dragon..." He stalks off complaining loudly about 'sharing is caring', and 'he must have a head full of rocks'. I hide my giggle in Gin's neck.

The smugness wafting off him, has me barking out a laugh, as he stomps through the trees towards the sound of trickling water. I mention once that I could walk, but he just gave me a look and I knew that wasn't going to happen. Instead I rest my head against him, enjoying his scent and the peacefulness of the forest.

When we get to the small creek he strips me immediately, dropping all my clothes in a heap by some rocks. I don't fight it, he's seen me nude already and I quite enjoy how they look at me. It's a little surprising how comfortable I've grown in such a short amount of time but it feels right. Plus, I think I may have an easy time coaxing him into some fun before we head out again. I am voracious for them, and their cocks.

Ever since that first time with Tawson, it's like they opened the gates and released a beast intent on gratification any moment she can. I would like to feel Gins' big, ridged, Dragon cock inside me again.

Quickly, he strips off his own clothes as I wander into the water. It isn't deep but I'll be able to splash water on all the places that really need some freshness.

Glancing at him over my shoulder, I try for a coy look, but feel like I'm failing because he stomps into the water beside me and cups water in his hands to splash on me. I squeal at the frigid temperature and squint angrily at him. Gin chuckles and does it again, smiling at my outrage. Splashing him back seems like the right thing to do, so I scoop up some water and toss it at his chest, laughing at the shock on his face.

"Is this really what you want right now?" Gin's mouth twists into a sly smirk as he reaches down and cups his stiffness.

Oh, he plays dirty. Obviously, I'd much rather play with his cock so I let the water flow through my fingers and drop my hands.

"Good girl," Gin's low rumble tingles through to my core, "now, hold still so I can clean you before I make you all dirty." Fire burns in his eyes as he tends to me.

It's nice to have him wash me, especially because I get to feel his hands all over my body. It's beautiful foreplay. I was only going to clean my privates and my pits but he runs his hands all over me.

When he passes over my nipples again, I can't help the small moan that escapes. A deep rumble vibrates from his chest as he shifts from washing to stroking.

Taking his time roaming over my breasts, he maps the skin and plucks at my hard buds. Each time he pinches a little harder, almost like he's testing to see how much pain I'll enjoy. So far, I haven't disliked any of it.

Gin's hot breath tickles my neck before he rumbles in my ear, "Feeling needy, my

Little One?" Even the sound of his deep voice thrumming through me causes a groan. My core drips slick, readying for his huge cock.

But it seems like he wants to take his time because he concentrates harder on my nipples. Mouthing down my neck, over his mark. The moment he touches it my knees give out from the jolt of pleasure that thrills through my body. Gin knew that was going to happen because he catches me easily and lays me down on our pile of clothes.

Now that he's above me, he switches from hands to mouth. Licking and biting my breasts leaving red marks all over. I worry that the same jolt of pleasure will happen when he touches Rafe's bite but it is a fairly mild reaction compared to his own. Pleasure still tingles through me but nothing so shocking.

Biting a nipple, Gin pulls, enjoying the way I squirm and grab his hair trying to stop him. But, I end up holding him there as the pain morphs into pleasure and I whimper with need.

I want his cock inside me. I need something thick and hard to grip.

"Gin," my husky voice pleads, "Alpha, please. I feel so empty." Pleasure rushes through me at his groan.

Releasing my nipple, he looks up at me

with mischief in his eyes and moves to do the same to the other one. A litany of whines and quiet *please, please, please's,* are set loose as I beg my mate for more.

Soothing the pain with his tongue before he slowly, so slowly, moves down my stomach. Kissing and biting until he gets to my belly button then he licks into it making me laugh.

"It tickles!" I smile down at him, seeing satisfaction in Gin's eyes.

Continuing his path down, Gin licks into the hollow of my hips. Wiggling, I try to force his attention to my leaking core. But instead of going where I want he starts mouthing his way down my right leg.

"Please? I need you!" I make a frustrated sound getting his attention.

Smirking at me, Gin goes back to what he was doing. Ignoring my pleas for him to touch me where I need it most. I can't believe I've become such a wanton thing.

My Dragon goes all the way down to my toes before switching to the other foot and oh, so slowly, making his way back up. I'm practically sobbing by the time he kisses my hip bones because I'm so desperate for attention on my clit and my cunt.

I worry that Gin's going to bypass it altogether, and I let out a loud sigh of relief when I feel him exhale heavily on my wet lips.

"You are the most exquisite thing I have ever set eyes on. And I have lived a very long time." Gin glances up at me, and I inhale sharply at the literal fire in his eyes. "You are mine, and I will never let you go," he rumbles lowly, it almost sounds like there's a bit of his Dragon in his tone, as smoke seeps from his mouth and nostrils. It creates the impression that he speaks with dual voices as his Dragon pushes to be noticed. The thought, and sound, has a potent desire rush down my spine.

I don't care about anything except getting him to touch me so I nod rapidly. "Yours! Please!"

Finally, *finally*, he lowers his head and licks my clit. I'm so wound up at this point, I don't think it will take much more for me to cum.

"No!" I cry out as Gin moves off before the tension snaps. How dare he stop me right on the edge! A snarl escapes my throat at the fierce need.

But he doesn't go far, he licks up the mess of slick I've smeared all over my thighs and then into my cunt, catching more. I don't know if I will ever stop leaking around them.

When he licks into my cunt, it feels like he's shifted his tongue because it's so much longer and I think it's forked. Gin glances up at me and our eyes meet as he pulls his tongue out to flicker and stroke my clit. The forked tip almost wraps around my nub and my vision grows hazy before I moan loudly, not caring if anyone can hear me.

I start begging again, because he isn't letting me cum. Every time I get so close, Gin slows down and moves on to somewhere less stimulating. I growl and whine trying to coax him back to my clit.

Grabbing two fistfuls of hair I pull my mate's head up so he looks at me before pleading,

"Please, Gin, please, I need your cock. I need it more than air. Please!" I look a mess of sweat and tears from all the teasing and his stubborn look softens as he moves up to kiss me.

Tasting myself on him, I enjoy it, licking into his mouth as much as he'll let me. Gasping when he plunges his cock deep inside me abruptly. But I revel in the pleasurable pain of my walls stretching around his ample size.

"Yes! Oh! Oh! Please!" Begging, I moan and I'm not sure of the words coming out of my mouth. They don't matter anyways.

Leaning back, he changes the angle inside me. His ridges pressing tightly to something delicious. On his first full stroke I cum, tightening around him, making him fight for every inch as he fucks me through it.

When I can finally open my eyes I see Gin gritting his teeth, fighting off his own orgasm trying to make this last longer. I had forgotten how good his cock felt inside me and every time his ridges bump that sweet spot in me I can't help the way my core ripples around him.

Wrapping one arm under me, he lifts my hips up so he can thrust faster, deeper. I'm a moaning thrashing mess under him and I love it. I don't realize I'm chanting 'knot' under my breath, matching his strokes until he growls out,

"I'll give you my knot, Little One. I'm going to fill you and plug you tight, keeping all my seed inside you. Breeding you." His last words are said in such a dark tone I shiver. I can't tell if it's out of fear or delight.

Gin is close, his cock getting harder and thicker. On his next thrust he slows down, and works the knot in steadily. My cunt stretches around my Dragon's massive size and I almost tell him to stop, but I want this so I clench my jaw and keen.

His groan of pleasure when it finally pops in, locking into place feels right. Cumming hard, my vision whites out, and my mewls echo through the trees. I can feel his seed release, he rocks each spurt deep inside me.

When Gin picks me up to readjust us into a more comfortable position, it shifts the knot forcing another orgasm from me. Whining through it because I'm over sensitive and doubt I could do it again without passing out. This is very different from when I was in heat. I'm more responsive now.

Cuddling me tightly, my mate places kisses on my head and inhales my scent.

"Such a good girl. Letting me breed you. Fucking my Little One full. Gonna do it again and again until you catch, and then I'll fuck you some more because I can't get enough of you."

At Gin's words, my cheeks redden and I squirm with happiness. Except, when I wiggle it shifts the knot compelling another orgasm.

"No more. I can't cum anymore." I fall limply against him as I mutter breathlessly.

Gin chuckles lightly and simply says, "Okay."

By the time we make it back to the others, it's late morning. I needed another wash after that romp.

Tawson is looking extra grumpy. "We don't have time to fool around. We need to keep moving, Gin. You know this." He glares harshly.

I go to defend him but Gin shushes me and grunts out a '*sorry*', before plopping me in the cart beside Fen.

Fen looks down at me with a smirk and a twinkle in his eye, I'm pretty sure he would have done the same thing. Dropping a kiss on my head, he snaps the reins, sending the horses forward.

Relaxed after my time with Gin, I lean back and enjoy the sounds of the forest. The birds chirping, the small animals burrowing and climbing trees, and the bugs, and sprites, buzzing around. It's so magical and peaceful, it makes me wonder why I didn't spend more time in the forest with Dani when I was younger. She's a Pixie, so it made sense to me that she craved the trees and plants. But, with me being a human, I didn't think I would get as much out of it as her so I didn't bother as often, even though she invited me every time.

I hope I see her again. I hope she's safe, and with us taking Blue, the beast, the village should be safe. Especially the blacksmith and his wife, since they were the targets.

Tawson and Gin are discussing

something but they're far enough ahead that I can't make out any words. Rafe is trailing us, I guess to protect our rear. I know there are dangers in the forest, but aren't most animals smart enough to avoid travelers tramping through, making noise?

Boredom drags a sigh out of me, earning a lifted brow from Fen. I smile and shrug, turning to face the back of the cart. It's a good idea to spend this time getting to know Blue a little better. Tawson said it would be about ten days for us to get to the mountain pass and another fourteen to get to their Keep on the other side. We shouldn't have to camp out too often, there are plenty of villages and Inn's to stay at on our path.

Just as I open my mouth to ask Blue a question, I'm jolted in my precarious perch and teeter over into Fen. The cart has stopped abruptly. Peering around I notice the rest of them have spread out and look on edge. Rafe has his sword out and his head cocked like he's listening to something.

Fen tugs on me until I'm seated properly again and as I open my mouth to ask him what's wrong he slaps a hand over my face. I give him an aggrieved look, but then I hear it too.

CH.24

oughing, barking sounds, echo through the trees. Whatever it is, it's drawing closer. There are terrifying noises that don't sound like any animals I've ever heard before. And it seems like there's more than one.

If we're quiet enough will they pass us by? Is this some pack of aggressive animals and we've trespassed on their land? My thoughts stall for a moment and a shiver of fear crawls down my spine, maybe they are mutant beasts like Blue... Maybe he isn't the only one evil has created.

With wide eyes I glance up at Fen, trying to convey my thoughts with a look. I wish I could use their pack link. Didn't they claim me? Shouldn't I have been brought in already? Ugh, this is frustrating!

The noises grow closer, and the closer they get the more horrid the sounds are. It's as if I can feel claws raking down my back, death echoing in those howls.

My morbid thoughts are interrupted by the cart shaking and the sounds of thrashing from the back.

Blue! Turning to look, he's red faced and sweating. Prominent veins bulging on his forehead, as if he's fighting an invisible foe. Blue's skin almost looks like it's bubbling in places as hair grows and recedes. He's fighting a shift!

Scrambling away from Fen and into the back, I need to get to Blue, need to help somehow. Fen tries to grab me to keep me beside him but I move too quickly. Something deep inside me telling me I *can* help him.

I know I'm making too much noise, but I don't think those creatures need sound to find us. They must have a way to track us that we are unaware of. Frantically, I shove bags and boxes out of my way in my mad rush to get to Blue.

The moment I reach out and touch him, he falls quiet, panting from exertion. Keeping my hand on him, I brush the hair off his sweaty forehead. He lays there clammy and exhausted from the stress of fighting his own body.

Looking at me with wide fearful eyes, he clasps our hands together. "Lu, I'm afraid.

I don't want to hurt anyone. I can't hear the voice but... every time those creatures growled I could feel my beast trying to force its way out. It wanted... no, it *needed* to go to them." He shivers with dread. "I think they are like me, I think they're beasts created through black magic. And... I think... I think they're hunting us." Gulping heavily, terror shivers through both of us as we make eye contact.

Peering over at Fen, I hope he heard us. His eyes are slightly glazed, he's talking to the others, *good*. He must be explaining what Blue just said.

It seems like my hand on him is the only thing keeping him from shifting. I have no idea why, or how I'm able to help him. Maybe it's an Omega thing? Or a pack thing? But... it doesn't feel like it. It's almost like I can feel this soothing rush flow from my hand to him. Maybe... maybe I am not *just* anything...

The first time I saw him I had this insane urge to go to him. Like, everything would be alright as long as I could touch him. And I was right, I fixed him... or, at least I gave him the ability to switch back to his two legged form. But, I guess I have to stay in contact with him now, until we can get rid of the creatures hunting us.

Wildly searching for the rest of my

mates, I don't see anyone. It's almost like they've melted into the trees and disappeared. I should have realized a while ago that they weren't actually merchants. I feel silly thinking of it now.

It's silent, no birds or animals making any noise, not even the bugs. Everything knows to hide. A feeling of malevolence creeps over the woods. The beasts must be close.

A loud coughing bark echoes around us, it's so close now. Trying to slow my racing heart, I listen for anything to tell me where they are but it's silent as a tomb.

Just then, a huge fireball ignites to the right of us. A scream of pain that couldn't come from anything except an animal, sounds all around. Was that one of my guys attacking them? Or are they trying to scare us?

A shock of bright light and something that looks like electricity moves on our left, another screech of pain and then silence. I blink my eyes to clear the spots of light from my vision.

We must be surrounded, but the others are keeping them from the cart. I'm thankful for that, but I am also scared for them. I do not wish to lose any of my males. I've only just found them!

When I look behind the cart again,

trying to spot Rafe, a large, dark shape darts from shadow to shadow. It almost blends into the darkness cast by the massive trees, but I can see it has stripes of red all over its body.

My hands grow clammy. Terror pumps through my veins as panic raises chills over my body. With my mind racing, I try to push down my fears. If I let myself I could easily fall into this hysteria and become a hindrance to my mates trying to protect us. I can't let that happen. We all need to survive this, I don't think I could be whole without them. Giving myself a second, I squeeze my eyes shut and send up a prayer to the Goddess asking for protection.

Opening my eyes, I shiver in the mild breeze as my focus darts around trying to spot the beast. I'm afraid that Rafe has been injured or killed if something has gotten this close to us. Curling up beside Blue, I hug him tight to me. Hoping it will keep him in this form, and for comfort. I can't let myself fall apart until this is over.

The brindled shape emerges from the shadows and glances at us before disappearing again. How is it doing that? Is it just observing? Is it learning us? I wish I could speak to my males, I hope to the Goddess they are still alive. I need them, I bite my lip to keep all my whimpers inside.

Before my thoughts can grow more morbid, a shape detaches from the base of a large Ducha tree and launches itself at the bushes to our right. Thunderous battle sounds echo through the air.

What in the world did I just witness?

That beast was huge, at least as tall as me. It moved on all fours like an animal but its face looked like that of a being, or closer to that of a tree dweller. A type of animal that has a humanish face but is covered in fur. They do not speak words, their vocals are limited to screeches or hoots.

What was even more troubling was that it had the body of a bear, but the limbs and tail of a reptile. Its ears were bat-like, large and swivelled constantly like it could use them to pinpoint prey.

Figures tumble from the bush, both looking bloody and injured. The brindled beast is reminiscent of a dog, but much, much, bigger. It snarls at the monstrosity and... it looks like magma is leaking from the red stripes across its body. Each step it takes sizzles and burns the ground. Leaving charcoal footprints in the dirt.

The monster, now favoring it's back leg, clashes with the dog. However, when it comes into contact with the magma, it releases an ear-piercing cry. Pieces of skin melt away, the scent of burning flesh sickens me. The dog clings to it, ripping chunks off but, I don't look away. What if it comes for us next?

The bear-like beast thuds to the ground, no longer making noise. When the dog's head swivels in my direction, its brilliant orange eyes meet mine. I know them. It's Rafe!

This must be his shifted form! Awe has my mouth dropping open. He's the biggest Shifter I've ever seen. *So, this is what a hellhound looks like? I think I like it.* The dangerous air he exudes tickles my insides. Excitement at how hazardous and capable my mate is builds up and I have to choke down an unlady-like squeal. The urge to pet him is very strong but I remind myself that I just witnessed Rafe melting that bear creature by being close to it, so that's probably not a great idea. He barely had to do anything. Although, the fierceness in his movements as he took it down so quickly was telling. The confidence I have in my safety grows ever stronger knowing I have such a fearless protector. This isn't even including my other mates, who must be equally as dangerous.

I'm so thankful he's alive that I start crying. After suppressing my emotions throughout this experience it was unavoidable that this would happen.

Leaning down into Blue, I bury my face in his chest, trying to keep myself silent. I don't want to draw in anymore beasts. He wraps himself around me tightly and I can feel him shaking.

I have never been more afraid in my life and I just want my pack to come back to me. It takes me a moment, but I realize that even though the forest is still silent, the malevolent feeling has dissipated. I hope that means we're safe for now.

Part of me wonders if I could have helped these creatures like I did Blue. But, I didn't have any urges to go out there and touch them. No, these creatures spelled death or worse for me if I had tried.

The sounds of bones cracking and reforming come from behind the cart. Pulling away from Blue's chest, I spot a very nude Rafe shifting. I immediately stare at his cock and it distracts me from my tears as a blush creeps down my chest. It takes effort to suppress the flutter in my stomach trying to tell me that now is a great time to allow lust to consume me. The stress has gotten to me because I should not be watching his member when we all almost died, and I still don't know where Tawson and Gin are.

Rafe walks over and gently wipes a few

stray tears off my cheeks before leaning down to kiss me. It's a sweet kiss, just a press of lips together, a way to let me know he's here and he's okay.

"It's all right now, Little Kitten. You are safe and the danger has passed." Brushing my hair back, he looks me over, like he needs to reassure himself that I'm uninjured.

Rafe peers over my head, and I turn to see Fen slowly letting the stone fade from his skin. It is amazing to see the change.

"Fen? Are you okay? I was so busy watching Rafe fight... that thing," - I gesture at the poor disfigured beast - "that I didn't notice any other attackers. Are Tawson and Gin...?" Trailing off, uncertain I want to know if I've lost one of them. I know I would have felt it through the bond but I'm not thinking straight right now.

"No, no, they are perfectly fine. They're just checking the perimeter around us in case there are more hiding," Fen reassures me. He sounds so calm and relaxed, his expression soft and composed.

I let out a long sigh and lean against Blue again. My body feels limp after my muscles relax, I don't know if I can handle this kind of stress regularly.

"Blue? Do you think if I let go, you'll

be okay?" Voice shaking with uncertainty, my eyes glisten with tears, ready to fall. I take a deep breath and attempt to gather myself. Having three of my mates here for support gives me the strength I need to regain my composure.

Patting my hand resting against his bare arm, Blue sighs. "There's only one way to know. Ever since you touched me and it stopped I haven't felt anything except exhausted from fighting it."

Nodding, unable to form any more words, I slowly pull my hand off and sit up so I'm no longer touching him. When nothing happens. I release the breath I was holding and collapse against him again. Thank the Goddess I somehow stopped the shift. I couldn't bear losing him.

I startle, almost falling off the cart, when Tawson and Gin appear on opposite sides of me, both reaching for me. Tawson moves just a little faster and pulls me tight to him. After a moment he places my feet on the ground and starts checking me over, inspecting for injuries. I try telling him I'm fine but Tawson is very insistent.

Gin does the same when he makes his way over. They are very silly, but I can't say I don't appreciate the care.

When I try to see if they are hurt, Gin and Tawson dismiss me. Absolute fury takes over so quickly I barely have time to recognize the feeling. How dare they dismiss my need to ensure they're okay. I stomp my foot in frustration, crossing my arms and level an indignant glare at them. Why can't they let me make sure they're okay, too? Don't they know I worry for them?

"What is wrong with you two? How dare you dismiss my concerns so easily! I am your *mate*. I deserve to make sure my idiot males will survive -" Their chuckles cut off my angry tirade infuriating me even more.

"Sweetheart, we're fine. Even if we had gotten injured we would have been healed already." Tawson looks at me like I'm the cutest thing he's ever seen and it only adds to my ire. Gin's smile has grown to an actual grin and if I wasn't so mad I would swoon at how handsome it makes him.

Just as I open my mouth to blast them with my fury, gentle arms gather my close. The scent of buttery, flakey pastry and baked apples soothes my anger as Blue nuzzles my face.

"Lu, while I agree that they were being unnecessarily dismissive, I understand their rush. We don't really want to hang around here. *I* don't want to be here any longer than necessary in case more are on their way." Blue's sweet voice mostly calms me but a thread of hurt still lingers.

"Tawson, Gin, I know we don't want to stay here but this is your mate! How could you treat her so callously? Even if it was unintended, she is our *Center*! Luella deserves your patience and consideration no matter the circumstances." Every single male stares at Blue with shock and approval. While my feelings are hurt from their insensitivity, Blue standing up for me and being the voice of reason warms my heart and lessens the pain.

"I'm sorry Luella, that was unacceptable behavior on our part. But, Blue is right and we should not tarry here long. We don't know if there are more." Tawson crouches down in front of me as he apologizes, kissing my hand. "When we are somewhere safer you can check us over as long as you'd like, I promise."

"Can you sense anything? Do you think there are more on their way?" Tawson eyes the exhausted male cuddled up to me.

Blue shakes his head, lips pressed tightly together. "No. I thought I was the only one... But these, I think they were working together and communicating somehow. I know that something they did almost caused me to shift and join them but Lu here saved me from that."

Looking at me gratefully, he gives me a shaky smile.

Tawson nods, his jaw rigid as he rolls his neck as he stands. "Rafe did you notice anything about the one you killed? You got closer than either of us." He motions at Gin and himself. "Our innate magic works better from afar and... the bodies ended up fairly obliterated."

Rafe shakes his head before pausing. "Well... It's a little hard to tell since they are not natural creatures but... come here and look at this." Waving us all over, he crouches down beside the beast.

With a grateful kiss on Blue's cheek I step away from him intending to see what Rafe is pointing at. But, Gin drops his heavy hands on my shoulders, keeping me close to him. He leans down, his large frame almost engulfing me as he nuzzles my hair.

"I'm sorry, Little One. I did not mean to hurt you." With his apology and his warmth encompassing me I soften. I know he would not intentionall hurt my feelings but it did hurt. It is far too difficult to stay angry with him though. I can feel how much he cares and I don't enjoy being mad.

He won't let me get any nearer to the bear-like beast than the back of the cart but I can see what Rafe is pointing at.

It looks like a brand, or a rune, burned into the underside of its belly. "It was giving off a black mist before I killed it. I think it was what allowed whomever to control them. Did you notice this on the other ones?" Rafe questions Tawson.

Tawson doesn't answer, he just grunts angrily and shakes his head. "No, and there was nothing left of our kills. Cut the rune out so we can bring it with us. There are texts in our library that may help us identify that rune. If nothing comes up there, we can bring it to the College of Users and get a Master to look at it."

Turning away from the disgusting sight of Rafe cutting the skin off the dead beast, I climb back into the cart, Fen following behind me.

"How much longer till we get to the next village?" Leaning heavily against Fen, I peer up at him with sad, tired eyes as I yawn.

Sighing he wraps an arm around me. "We have a long way to go, Precious. But, if we get moving now we should make it to an Inn before dark."

That is reassuring, although the thought of being on the road for weeks while we travel to their home gives me anxiety. Hearing those coughing barks and growls will give me nightmares for a long time. I rather dislike feeling as if we are prey huddling in the dark hoping we won't be seen.

Needing a distraction from my unhealthy thoughts, I snuggle closer to Fen's side and urge him to explain something.

"Fen? What is the College of Users?"

"In the capital city, Varough, there are many places of learning. One for Users, Hunters, Knights, etcetera, and then there's the Library. Anyone can go to one of these Colleges, or Guilds, and become an apprentice, if you've got the skill and the drive to do it. The College of Users is specifically for beings who have innate abilities with magic. They learn how far their abilities reach and, if they're skilled enough, they can eventually become a Master User. They are fairly rare because not many beings have enough innate ability to Use all schools of magic." He's gone into lecture mode and it is the perfect distraction from the awful thoughts circling in my head.

"The schools of magic are; fire, earth, water, air, and spirit. There isn't as much known about the school of spirit compared to the rest of them, but it does seem to touch on things to do with the body and mind. It's actually quite fascinating," Fen continues to drone on about the College of Users and it's enough to have me falling into a fitful sleep against him. I wish I could Use magic, it would give me some comfort to know I could protect myself and my males against attack. Although, after watching Rafe take down that monster, I am reassured slightly by the fact that he is rather dangerous on his own. And I bet the others are equally as fierce.

CH.25

We manage to reach the Inn in Gisham before dark, but it was close. I sense eyes watching me from all around, even though I'm pretty sure there's nothing there. There's this vague foreboding unsettling me, I predict that I'm going to be anxious for most of this journey.

Experiencing the terror of those creatures attacking us in the forest has left me unnerved. How many more of them are there? Were they hunting a scent? It didn't seem like they needed sound to find us. I'm afraid they were hunting either Blue or myself, because that one monster was heading straight for the cart. The beast barely even noticed Rafe's hound stalking from behind, which must be how Rafe was able to defeat it so easily. I think that's the main reason he was able to take it down so easily. These creatures do not seem very intelligent, I bet they follow the orders they're given exactly as they're given. That could bode well for us if we're attacked again.

I would like to believe we are done dealing with black magic monsters but something inside me is screaming a warning to be waryl. A shiver shudders through my body and I wrap my arms around myself. Going with my mates is the right thing to do but, I am afraid of what is out there, waiting in the darkness.

Standing by the doorway to the stables, I watch the guys unpack what we will need for the night while a young stable boy tends to the horses. Fen tosses him a coin, the young lad's wide gap-toothed smile has me grinning. It's heartwarming seeing such simple joy, I miss the simplicity of my bakery. But, I don't think I would trade my males for that life back. When we get to their Keep and I get settled, my mates will help me get back to what I love. Nerves flutter in my belly like tiny sprites when I think about the mate waiting for me. *Alec.* Will he like me? Is he as handsome as Tawson? Is he kind? Each little sprite unsettling my stomach is a different worry about this mysterious mate.

Goosebumps rush down the back of my neck to my arms, and shivers steal across my body as I turn to face the growing darkness. Long shadows stretch like fingers over the ground until the light of the Inn chases them away, the warmth and sounds from inside are welcoming. Bugs chirp and animals rustle the leaves as they go about their lives.

Remembering the absolute silence before the attack, I'm happy to have the bustling sounds of life. The Inn faces out towards the thick eerie forest and I will never look at it the same. Wandering out a little ways, I look out at the bustling village.

Gisham is a little bigger than Pekayan, and it feels busier. Even with the evening light waning, the village is still buzzing with activity. Instead of the market that I am used to, there are storefronts lining the main roadway. It is made of hard packed dirt with wagon ruts and the occasional hole. All of the houses branch off and it looks like most of the merchants live above their shops, like I did.

Meandering further from the stables, I peek in the open front door of the nearest store. It appears to be an alchemist's shop with jars filled with ingredients lining the walls. There's a counter in front of a doorway, covered by cloth. It is likely blocking the way to the store owner's home. On the left of the counter there are a few tubs that contain strange ingredients, they smell pungent and ripe. Wrinkling my nose with distaste, I step away.

All of the stores seem to have a similar layout, but different stock, of course. The clang of the blacksmith's hammer adds to the sounds of the village as they work into the night. Interesting items displayed at the trader's storefront entice customers to come in and spend their money.

"Fen, look! They have pastries." Stopping, I look back, realizing I've wandered further than I meant to. I didn't even tell them where I was going, I honestly didn't intend to go this far. It's just so interesting to see the differences from my village.

I'd gone with Dani and her family once or twice to the Lord's Keep, which was only a half day's walk from our village, but it is so different. I never imagined beings would want to live this close to each other. Your neighbors would be intimately involved in everything that happened in your life, living like this. But, I guess beings have a diverse range of preferences. Just because I don't think I'd like it doesn't mean the beings living here feel the same.

Walking back towards the Inn, I'm not paying attention to where I'm going when I bump into two large bodies coming out of one of the stores. I literally run into one of them, nearly falling on my ass. Stumbling, the male grabs my arm to steady me. It was like walking into the side of a house!

"Ooof! Oh! I'm so sorry. I must not have been looking where I was going," Apologizing, I hold my hands out as if I injured the large male with my slight frame.

Taking a second, I really look at who I've carelessly walked into and note two nearly identical hulking Orcs. They tower over me, at least seven feet, they're both bald with pointed ears decorated with jangling metal piercings. The Orcs don't wear anything except a loin-cloth, leather sandals and leather straps over their chest to hold weapons and sacks, so I am able to see the swirling designs across their bodies.

It's really quite beautiful, and if I wasn't afraid I'd get eaten I would ask to study them more closely. Their skin tone is classic for Orcs, a ruddy greenish color, that makes the black of the tattoos stand out. Fading sunlight darkens their eyes like inky pools, giving them a menacing air. Besides the Orcs' tattoos, their tusks are the most interesting feature. I'm fascinated by them, the ivory tusks reach up from the bottom jaw to just above the top lip. The one on the right, that I didn't run into, has embossed metal bands wrapped around the ivory. I wonder if that's just for decoration or if it's a status thing in their culture?

I'm interrupted from my perusal by the Orc I ran into.

Huffing, he frowns down at me from his considerable height, but he doesn't say anything. The stranger's stare has me shrinking in on myself, afraid I've insulted him.

His friend, on the other hand, flashes a leering grin that highlights his tusks, as if it will entice me.

"Well, hello there, Wee Lassie. Where might you be off to in such a rush? How abouts you come for a drink and get to know the both of us. The Pink Pony Inn has a delicious stew and excellent ale." The Orc's accent is strange and charming, even though my nerves do not allow me to truly appreciate it.

Before this moment, I had not realized that I am not very good with strangers. It's odd how I was so comfortable selling goods in my booth at the market but faced with these intimidating males my body has frozen. Possibly because most of my customers were beings I'd seen every day, or every month.

My mouth is so, completely, unprepared to give this Orc a response that I stutter out nonsense and shuffle back a few steps. My intention was to say no thank you but the silent, gruff one still has a firm hold of my arm, halting my retreat.

He drags me closer, so I'm situated in between them, and I catch their scents. They must be brothers, because they smell so similar it's difficult to tell them apart. The silent one smells like peaches and cream, while the chatty one smells like peaches and honey. Both sweet, and kind of make me hungry, but I thought being bitten and claimed would have changed that? Shouldn't I not find other Alphas scents alluring? When someone is claimed doesn't their scent change so that all others will know they are taken?

Confused, I'm frozen in shock. "Uh...Um... N-no t-thank you. I have a pack and I r-really need to get back to them," I finally manage to stutter out a coherent sentence.

The Orc's glance at one another before the silent one, still clutching my arm gently, starts herding me towards the Inn completely ignoring what I said.

The chatty one walks alongside me remarking, "Your scent is still sweet as can be, so either your pack is incomplete or they are not doing a very good job taking care of you. Don't worry, Shortcake, we can look after you." No longer leering, he must sense my discomfort. The brazen Orc attempts a pleasant grin, but it appears fierce instead, putting me even more on edge. My stress levels have almost reached the breaking point.

I'm shivering, from fear and from the cool night air that snuck up on me while I was wandering around. Why did I wander away from my pack? I have to realize I am not in my home village anymore and I don't know any of these beings, plus it is not safe! What if more of those monsters attack?

What was I thinking?

How have my males not noticed I was gone yet? My fear and frustration are mounting, but I am too afraid of what they will do if I don't comply. They are so much larger than me, they could easily hurt me.

As my frustrated thoughts circle around in my head, I hear a very welcome voice.

"Let go. She is *mine*." Gruff and to the point, Gin releases a predatory snarl as he charges towards me and my unwanted friends. The only reason he stops is his fear of injuring me in the process.

But, the chatty one steps in front of me giving Gin the opening he needed and he slams his fist into the Orc's face. Being as solid as he is, Chatty barely moves. Swiping a hand under his nose the Orc laughs as he flings the blood away.

"I like you. That's how you protect your

Omega!" Brazenness and joy threads through the Orc's words, confusing me. Why is he laughing after being hit in the face? What is *wrong* with this male?

The silent Orc does not let me go, tucking me close to his body, like he's trying to protect me. Which is silly because Gin is one of my Alphas and he is not. Maybe he's just trying to make sure I don't get in the middle of this altercation.

"Alright my friend, while I'm happy tae throw some fists, I figure you may want her back more." The Orc's voice, while rough and lyrical with his strange accent, is calm. "We found this wee beauty wandering through town all alone. She looked lost and cold so we decided she could use a couple of friends."

Gin releases a loud, angry, growl before he responds, through clenched teeth, "That is *my Omega*."

At his words Chatty steps forward with a sigh, "Ya speak the truth, I scented her on you. Brynd let the lass go to her Alpha."

The silent one gently tilts my chin up so he can look into my eyes. A terrifyingly possessive growl echoes through the street, Gin is not happy that another male has his hands on me. But, it almost feels like the Orc is asking me if this is what I want.

Nodding slowly, I feel a little sad that I won't get the chance to learn about them. The brothers actually seem pretty decent, they didn't hurt me or steal off with me. I think they were legitimately trying to help someone who seemed lost and out of place. They are just... very large and frightening so it makes them seem unapproachable.

Releasing me with a nod, his eyes look a little dejected at saying goodbye to me so I whisper, quiet enough that I hope only he can hear me, "Thank you for being kind, if a little scary." With a small smile at him, I turn and scamper over to Gin.

Immediately, he lifts me into his arms and leans down to sniff my hair, I guess checking for any scents of discomfort or pain. When Gin's satisfied with what he finds he grunts, glares at the Orcs and stomps back to the Inn.

I peer over his shoulder at the Orc brothers. Brynd, the silent one, is staring at me longingly while making hand signs to his brother. The chatty one is watching Brynd's hands move before looking up at me and mouthing something I don't catch. Giving them both a smile, I tuck my face into Gin's neck and steal his warmth, it really is chilly out now. I'm going to need warmer clothing soon.

When we reach the others at a table in the corner of the Inn's bar, everyone seems a little on edge. I worry while I was foolishly wandering that something else happened. Did they catch wind of more beasts?

It isn't until Gin sits with me firmly planted on his lap, with everyone staring at me, I get a wave of disapproval radiating through the bond with them. Realizing that, maybe, it was me wandering off without telling anyone that has them all on edge.

That is confirmed when Tawson growls in a dark, angry tone, "Luella, you cannot just wander off without one of us. You could have been hurt or taken! Your scent has not yet changed because we have another pack member that is not here. I don't know how often you ventured out of your village but not every place is safe, in fact most places are highly unsafe especially for an Omega. There are too many vagrants and thieves looking for opportunities and you, with your delectable scent and beauty would sell for a large amount. I need you safe, *we* need you safe. Please. Please do not wander without us."

Tawson is so angry, but it is out of fear for me that his voice shakes. My stomach sinks as I realize the worry and stress my absence caused. I am not used to the way things work in a relationship, but I thought they were with me. I've grown so comfortable and feel so safe in their presence that I just assumed they were around.

Looking down, ashamed for causing them all grief I pick at my nails. In a meek voice I respond, "I'm sorry. I didn't really mean to go far... I didn't actually mean to go anywhere, I just... I needed a distraction from the anxiety and I figured looking at the differences from my home would help and then all of a sudden I was far down the road and it was dark and I was about to make my way back here when I literally ran into an Orc."

Taking a deep breath, I continue to blurt out my impromptu adventure. "They were brothers and they looked terrifying but they were actually rather kind, if a lot intimidating. They didn't try to sniff me or take me or anything.

"They were actually bringing me here because apparently the stew is delicious and they make the best ale. One of them didn't talk at all and the other wouldn't stop talking, I think to make up for his brother being silent. But they actually smelled rather nice and behaved fairly politely towards me once they realized I was scared. They even tried to protect me from Gin when he came to find me," I ramble it all out, quickly. My cheeks flame with embarrassment and I decide to hide in Gin's neck again.

One of them chokes back laughter and then a *thwack* sound, like someone smacked them. My guess is Rafe was laughing and Fen or Tawson slapped him on the back of the head.

It's silent for a moment as they all absorb the mass amount of information I just dumped on them before Tawson responds, "Love. Beautiful. Take a deep breath for me, okay?" Gentling his voice, I hear a purr laced through the words. "Everything is okay. I just... you can't go off alone. The thought of something happening to you is painful for me. We are going to eat something, because it's been a long and tiring day and then when we get to our room Rafe is going to punish you."

Rafe splutters, "What! Me? Why me? I don't want to..." *Thwack.*

"No. It's happening and you're doing it. Use the strap. This is a lesson I want to become ingrained in your head, Luella." Tawson barks at Rafe before responding to my squeak of dismay at the thought of a strap being taken to my bottom. I also know he is being very serious when he uses my name instead of the nicknames he's given me.

"B-but I am sorry for wandering and I already promised not to do it again!" I try to argue. "And where were you? There's so many of you, why didn't anyone see me wander off? It's your fault for making me feel so safe around you! I've never really been the adventurous type. You all just make me feel protected and secure enough that it encourages me to see the world around me!" My voice shakes as I allow my anger to surface.

It's not all my fault and they have to see that. I've had one spanking before and it was with Rafe's hand. It felt painful enough, I can't imagine what a strap will feel like. If they don't understand my side of this, I'm going to be awfully sorry to have wandered off.

My mates grow quiet and a very solemn Blue speaks up, "You're right, the fault is not yours alone. But, we were all shaken after the attack and I think nerves are running high right now." Our Beta glances around meeting each of our eyes before he continues, "We were all focused on unpacking and getting some warm food that no one noticed your interest in the village. But, Luella, you are more important than all of us and we each need you in different ways. Please, please stay with us." He looks down at his lap, whispering the last sentence as he loses his nerve.

The clinking of bowls being dropped on the table interrupts our tense silence. Righting myself in Gins lap, I reach for a bowl of stew. Not realizing how hungry I was until I smelled the roasted veggies and meat.

Before my hands can wrap around the bowl nearest to me, one of Gin's hands pulls my back tight to his chest before snagging my intended bowl. Making a noise of frustration, I huff at him. I'm hungry and I'm stressing about the punishment I'm soon to receive. I don't want to fight about anything else.

He doesn't relinquish the bowl, instead brings a spoonful to my lips. I consider being stubborn and demanding Gin let me feed myself, but I'm in enough trouble as it is. So, I open my mouth and moan at the taste. It really is delicious, those Orcs weren't lying about this being a good place for food. I'm not much for the taste of ale, I find it much too bitter. What can I say? I have a sweet tooth.

The whole meal is tense, for me at least. All I can think about is the upcoming punishment. I don't think I deserve it, but I also wish they wouldn't make me wait. Waiting and worrying is worse, I think, but I may change my mind after getting the strap.

They chat about the beasts, the attack and our long journey. I'm only half listening, until I catch Fen asking Blue about what happened to him during the attack.

"Did you hear that voice in your head? Is that why you were shifting? Or was it involuntary, because of the nearness of black magic in the other creatures? What did you feel when Luella touched you? I'm trying to figure out what's going on and how we can help you the next time this happens, because I doubt that was the last attack we will see," Fen fires questions off rapidly, not waiting for Blue to respond. It's almost like he's thinking out loud.

Blue, a small smile toying at the corners of his lips, waits patiently for Fen to finish speaking. "I'm going to try to answer all your questions in order, but bear with me because I'm not sure I'll remember them all."

Chuckling quietly, he sets his spoon down and folds his hands on his lap. "No, there was no voice in my head. The shift felt like it was being forced on me and I was fighting it with all I had, because I feared if I did shift, I would turn on all of you and I couldn't live with myself if I hurt anyone... again.

"It almost felt like the barks and growls were commands from the dark creatures, trying to force my shift. They were calling me, pulling me to them. But, the moment Luella touched me, skin to skin, everything stopped. It was like the whole world stood still and I could finally breathe again." Blue sighs and flicks his eyes to me before meeting Fen's gaze. I shrink in my seat as I realize the implications of my wandering.

"Her touch soothed the beastly part of me, the unnatural creature that I am... I-I don't think I should stray far from her until we figure out a way to stop the black magic from affecting me." Fear and pain linger in Blue's voice. Shaking a little as he talks about the shift being forced. I can't imagine the horror of not being in control of my own body.

All my mates are focused on this discussion, knowing the more information we have on those beasts the better prepared we will be the next time they find us.

It is pretty important information that I should have thought of. I'm angry at myself for wandering off now because what if he needed me, and I wasn't here? Ugh! Now I feel like I do deserve to be punished for failing Blue.

Quiet for the remainder of the meal, I tune out of the rest of their discussion. Busy berating myself for not thinking, I wait for my punishment.

CH.26

Rafe stole me from Gin as we all headed up to the room, and I can't help but smile at Gin's grumble. He's such a grumpy male and I'm so fond of him, of all of them, already. I didn't think feelings of adoration developed this quickly, I guess I've been lacking this kind of attention for a good portion of my life. It's a little overwhelming for someone so unused to intimacy.

The room feels small with everyone crammed into it. It's just a basic square room, a single medium sized bed with a couple pillows, and a small table by the window. I'm a little surprised they didn't get more than one room. I quietly inquire about it.

Tawson replies, "We felt it was not safe to split up," pausing, he eyes me, "and no one wanted to sleep in a room without you."

Tawson's words have my mouth

twisting into a small smile. But, my face drops when I remember my punishment. I'm uneasy as I trail my gaze over Rafe's features. Is everyone staying to watch my punishment? I don't like the thought of everyone watching me cry from a thrashing.

Before I get the chance to ask, Rafe strips me faster than I can blink. One moment I'm nude in front of my pack, the next Rafe pushes my chest into the mattress with my ass on display.

Whimpering, "Please." Not really knowing if I'm pleading for him to spank me or not. All I know is that I'm afraid and feeling guilty.

Rafe shushes me with a gentle kiss on my head. "Tawson, pass me the strap? Little Kitten, if you can behave and stay still for your ten strikes I will reward you with pleasure, deal?"

Squeezing my eyes shut, I grip the bedding hard. "I-I'll try," I whisper, bracing myself.

Rafe pets my back, soothing me a little. "Relax, Kitten. It will hurt less if you aren't tense, alright?"

Nodding, I take a deep breath. I can do this, I am brave. And I deserve this punishment. How could I have forgotten that *my* touch saved Blue from being taken? Also, who knows if those black magic creatures were there for Blue, the pack or me. Shame has me hiding my face in the blankets as I squeeze my eyes shut. Tears threaten to fall but I resist them. The more I think about it, the more I realize how stupid it was for me to wander off without checking that someone was with me.

As I'm exhaling, consciously telling my muscles to relax he strikes.

Thwap!

"Oh! Oh! Ow!" Crying out, my feet dance in place, trying to mitigate the sting.

Rafe smooths a hand over the welt, and the moment I stop moving he snaps it against me two more times. Attempting to hold still, I squeeze my eyes shut, fighting my tears. It stings so badly.

Four, five, six, he strikes quickly in succession. Rafe grabs my hands when I try to reach back. I'm not sure what I was going to do because touching the welts reignites the hurt which Rafe demonstrates by rubbing a hand over the criss-crossing marks.

"Shhh, be still. You're almost done. Relax, you have earned this. The pain will remind you to stay close to us next time you think of wandering off," Cooing at me, he tries to be reassuring.

As Rafe quickly snaps through the last four, I sob, unable to stop my tears. Salty lines leave tracks down my cheeks as I finally let go of the guilt.

Rafe picks me up and cuddles me in his lap. Gently brushing my hair back, softly saying sweet things, "My brave, beautiful Omega took her discipline so well. You're such a good girl, staying still just for me."

My butt stings and burns as it rubs against his trousers, causing more tears to fall. I should have stayed in the stable, I should have grabbed someone if I was so curious. I shou... my self admonishment is cut off by a kiss.

Rafe tastes my salty tears as he licks my lips. He doesn't seem to care though, even licking up the tear tracks over my cheeks. Rafe smiles softly at the question in my eyes.

"Kitten, every part of you is delicious. I will always be here to love you and care for you. Even if you disobey, you know I will punish and then comfort you. Do you want pleasure now? You were a good girl for me, I know the first time getting the strap is much worse when you're unsure what to expect."

Nodding, I kiss along his chin, everywhere I can reach and whisper into his ear,

"Please."

Rafe snakes a hand down to my clit and brushes alongside it, teasing me with faint pressure. His finger swipes over it and then back to circling around. Each time my mate touches that little nub I twitch, the pleasure feeling sharper after the pain from my strapping.

My face is tucked into his neck and I'm chanting a litany of 'please' and 'more', desperate for something that feels good after the guilt and pain. Moving lower, he spears me with two fingers, forcing a groan out.

Hooking his fingers inside me, Rafe massages back and forth, igniting a fire in me. His thumb taps on my clit with every down stroke. Slick pours from me, soaking his pants as well as the bed.

"There's my dirty Kitten," murmuring sultry things into my hair as I writhe on his lap. "Soaking my pants, trying to get me to take off my clothes, hmm? All you have to do is ask, Love. First, I need you to be my good girl and cum for me. Cover my hand in your slick, claim me with your scent." My mate revels in the honey he urges from my body, nibbling on my neck as he turns me to mush.

"One day I'm going to make you cum so many times I'll be able to bathe in it. You're so wet after getting the strap, did you like it more than you want me to know? Hmm? We might have to find reasons for some punishments if you enjoy it so much." Every word he says has me squirming, the filth that comes out of his mouth embarrasses and turns me on in equal measures. I can picture him bathing in my slick and the thought of my scent so thoroughly coating him has me gushing and my core tightening. An orgasm hovers right on the edge.

I need something to push me over. Whimpering and moaning into his neck as I clutch at his shirt, not sure if I'm even saying words. Licking his neck, the potent taste of warm salted caramel makes my eyes roll back. I'm moving my hips, riding his hand as he fucks me with his fingers. Slipping a third one into me, the feeling of more, of tightness, in my cunt makes me lose it. Crying out into his neck, the orgasm has my vision going white.

The scent of caramel cookies surrounds me, bathing me in desire. Rafe, fucking me with his hand continues to murmur filthy, delicious things in my ear. A feeling of need rushes through my entire body. My instincts roar to the front of my mind. Relaxing into them, I allow my primal urges to drive my movements.

Scrambling over him, I find impressive strength filling my muscles allowing me to push him back onto the bed. Clawing his clothes off, I vaguely note trails of blood and feel an odd pressure at my fingertips. My mind is too far gone into the primal instincts of my Omega that I cannot pay attention to that.

When his clothes are in shreds and I can reach his cock, I immediately sink down, taking him deep. I bounce on Rafe's hardness a few times before pushing harder for his knot to pop inside me.

Groaning, as if he's in pain, Rafe clutches my hips in a bruising grip. I don't care if he leaves bruises, I love when my mates mark me. Rocking my hips, I grind his knot inside me. It pushes against that sweet spot forcing another orgasm. I twitch and rub on him, fucking him through it to prolong the sensations.

Leaning down, I mouth along Rafe's chest, stopping to bite at his nipple. The corners of my lips twitch into a smile when he laughs it the sensation. I make my way up, following his scent to where it's the strongest before sinking my sharpened teeth into him.

"Fuck! Fuck, fuck, fuck! You little minx." Moaning loudly, he swears as he cums, filling me. His knot growing bigger, plugging me tightly. Wrapping his arms around me, Rafe rolls us, tucking me under his body.

"I am going to fuck you so full of seed,

you will not leave this Inn without my pup growing inside you," Snarling into my ear, he grinds up into me delighting at my cries.

The sound of that has me tightening on him, mewling as I cum again. My teeth are still locked into his skin and he isn't trying to get away. Rafe rocks his hips, grinding and rolling to prolong my orgasm. Closing my eyes, I moan into his skin, before finally relenting and letting go. My tongue cleans the bite mark that claims him as mine. Other females will know Rafe is taken. A smug feeling has my lips curling, this is *my* mate and no one can take him from me.

Rafe is still fucking into me half an hour later. I'm so tired, but I can't stop cumming. He's made sure of that by growling and rolling his hips like a beast. Rafe has cum so many times my stomach feels bloated. Evidence of his pleasure leaks past his knot, proving just how overfilled I am.

Rafe climaxes again before rolling onto his back, snuggling me tight to his chest.

"Sleep, Little Kitten." Rafe nuzzles my head as he murmurs into my hair, "my good girl."

I fall asleep on him, listening to his praise.

When I wake, Rafe is still knotted within me. I don't know how long I've been asleep for, but if his knot hasn't gone down it can't have been long.

He rocks his hips a little and cums again with a quiet groan.

"Stop that! You can't hog her all to yourself, Rafe," someone whispers angrily.

His smugness radiates through the bond. "Shouldn't have assigned me to punish her then, hmm?"

More than one of them scoffs. Someone else chuckles. I had forgotten they were all here, watching my punishment and then seeing me go a little feral on Rafe.

My cheeks burn, the blush spreading down my chest. Rafe leans in close to my ear. "I know you're awake."

Blinking sleepily at him, I try to sit up. "How long was I asleep?" I groan and cup my cum bloated belly. "How much seed have you stuffed in me? Why hasn't your knot gone down?"

Gin growls angrily, forcing me to clench over Rafe's knot, and we both moan.

Fen laughs, pure amusement on his face,

"He has been hogging you all night, Precious. I am thoroughly impressed with his stamina. I am honestly surprised he has any seed left in his balls." Chuckles echo around the room.

Rafe groans out, "Yeah, I think I'm all out now. I can even feel the knot softening a little. Although, Gin, if you growl like that again I will not be held responsible for my knot getting hard again."

Instead of a growl, I can feel the glare Gin levels at him. I hide my smile in Rafe's chest.

When the knot softens enough, his cock slips out of me in a deluge of cum and slick. "Oh! Oh no! Look at what you've done, Rafe!" I reach down, trying to stuff my finger into my cunt to stop the stream of cum. Not realizing my instincts are in control of me, telling me to keep it inside so I will not leave here without a pup in me.

When I recognize this feeling I pull my hands up. The scent of us mixed together hits my nose and I stuff my fingers in my mouth. Sucking and licking them clean, we taste so good together.

My eyes are closed as I suck the taste off myself and I hear more than one groan of pain.

"Rafe, you bastard. Hogged her all night, and now we'll be riding out with hard cocks. Do you know how difficult it is to ride with a hard cock? I hate you right now," Fen grumbles.

Blinking my eyes open, one sweep of the room tells me everyone is awake and the bags are already packed. I peer down at myself, wondering if I'll be able to take a bath before we leave. A warm wash would be nice, plus I'm pretty sure I'll be leaking cum for the whole day.

Glancing over, Tawson is busy finding clean clothes for me.

"Tawson?" I call softly, "is there time for me to wash? Is there a bath here or could we get a bowl of warm water and a cloth? I am kind of a mess."

I must look as bad as I think because he's holding back laughter. Getting up, Tawson stalks towards me.

"I've already requested a tub and hot water to be sent up here." He kisses me, no fear or disgust at tasting Rafe on my lips.

Leaning into him, I revel in his attention. When Tawson pulls back all I can do is blink owlishly at him. My brain has not yet woken for the day, and these males make my thoughts all fuzzy. Their scents affect me so strongly, or maybe it's the bond and feeling their affection and desire for me.

Tawson steps back and looks over at Fen and Blue. "Can I trust the two of you to help her bathe, without getting distracted?" He smirks knowingly. "Blue, I think you will have to be the voice of reason here."

"Hey! I know we need to get moving, I won't get distracted and fuck her for the next six hours like Rafe." Fen scoffs. He is so offended, his nose wrinkles as his lips purse, it's quite funny.

Trying to hide my laughter, I cover my mouth but once it sneaks out and I get going I can't seem to stop. Rafe joins me, snickering as he wipes a wet cloth over himself, cleaning the smears of us off him. My laughter trails off as my eyes follow the cloth in Rafe's hand from his abs to his cock. I'm hypnotized by it. Dick-matized? I'm pretty sure I heard Dani say that once...

I'm distracted from my staring contest with his cock when Blue steps in front of me.

"Here, Lu. Let's wrap this around you while the staff bring in the tub, hey?" he says softly, while using the gross sticky blanket to cover my nakedness.

Blue must see the affronted look on my face because he whispers faintly, for just me, "Not that I don't enjoy the view, because I desperately want to run my hands and mouth all over your body. But, and I think I speak for everyone, we can't have strangers looking at what belongs to us." It's the most possessive thing that I've heard come out of his mouth and it warms me up inside.

CH.27

Sitting beside me, Blue doesn't seem to mind the sticky mess. We watch the others start grabbing all our bags as the staff bring in the tub and water to fill it. It must have cost my mates a lot to afford this kind of luxury. Then again, I haven't ever stayed at an Inn before so who knows if this is normal treatment for their visitors.

Being a Beta, surrounded by a bunch of Alpha's and an Omega, Blue could be overlooked easily. But, I think he's really settling into this life that I've dragged him into. I mean, if he didn't want to be a part of our pack we wouldn't make him. Although, my inner Omega might have something to say about that. Just the thought of him leaving has something angry writhing inside me.

It can't be easy for Blue to try and find out who he is when he can't remember anything of what his life was like before he was messed with. Blue's generally pretty quiet, but I think that's because he prefers to observe. At least he doesn't seem afraid to speak up when he feels the need to, Blue is really coming into his own and gaining confidence within the pack. I am glad he's with us. Blue feels like mine, and I really need to bite him, and claim him for my pack.

When the staff finish, our pack-mates head out behind them. Tawson stops at the door, looking back at us.

"Try not to take too long, we need to get on the road. I want to make it to the next town as fast as possible." The concern in his voice is telling. Tawson's probably thinking of the attack, just like I am.

It sends a shiver down my spine.

Fen nods solemnly, Blue echoing him and then Tawson's out the door closing it behind him.

Wiggling out of my sticky blanket cocoon, I slip off the bed. I don't expect my legs to nearly give out on me when I stand. Stumbling, I squeeze my eyes closed as I prepare myself for the fall. A sigh of relief escapes me when Blue catches me. I know I'm clumsy on a normal day but this is a bit much. *What are these males doing to me?*

"Whoa! What happened to me?" I wail, my body feeling like I've fought a few rounds with an Ogre or something. More cum slips out of me as gravity tries to pull me to the ground. When Fen chuckles I blink open my eyes, my brows rising as I remember he stayed to help. Blue's chest shakes with his silent laughter.

"That is what happens when you let Rafe go all Alpha on you. All night," Fen remarks, still chuckling at my predicament.

Blue cuddles me tight to his chest, nuzzling my face as he carries me to the tub. I growl out, "Well, then... I just won't let him do this again..." My words fade away, knowing I'm lying.

Blue gently lowers me into the hot water and my sigh hisses out as it immediately soothes my sore muscles. But the moment my backside touches the water, I remember my strapped ass and screech at the pain. "Ow! Ow, ow, ow."

Fen kneels beside the tub, a wash rag and soap in hand and hums. "Well, with pain like that it should be easy for you to remember to stick near us, hmm?"

The fiercest scowl I can muster creeps over my face, I'm far too tired and sore to deal with his sass right now. I want to smack that look off his face. Fen is supposed to be the sweet one! But, it is true, the pain in my ass will be a decent reminder not to put myself in stupid situations.

At the look on my face he sighs. "Oh, Precious. I am sorry you got a punishment, but I worry about what could happen to you if you're not within my sight. You may be a claimed Omega, but you don't scent of it, yet. Luckily, we know you won't get another heat for three months, and we should be at our Keep well before that." His eyes are full of anxiety and he glances down at his hands as they wring the cloth. "I am worried about our journey though. We don't know if or when another attack might happen. I think I may drive myself mad thinking through all the possibilities of you getting hurt or taken from me."

Sighing, I am also worried about the same things. They let me sit and get lost in thought as they get to work washing me.

Blue concentrates on the mess of my hair, using a cup to pour water over me while trying to untangle it. It's very relaxing as he pulls the soap through it.

Fen, meanwhile, is having a lovely time soaping and scrubbing my chest. Eventually, he makes it to the rest of me, but he seems to drift back to my breasts whenever he can. I hide my smile at his antics.

When I'm clean I know I'll have to stand, but the thought of putting weight on my legs has me heaving out a tired sigh. Hopefully, I have rested enough to regain my strength. I stand there as my mates towel me off and quickly dress me. It's a relief to let them because, even though I slept, I am still exhausted. Probably from getting knotted all night, it is not a good way to get a decent sleep. But I will likely do it again, I can't lie to myself.

As we ride out of Gisham, I can't help but look back. Trying to see if the two Orc brothers are around. I don't know why I'm still thinking of them. They made an impression on me and I might have liked them, once I got to know them. Maybe they'll find me again some day.

We will be traveling hard for the next two days. The trees start to thin a little as we leave Gisham. It's more open, allowing the sunlight to shine through brilliantly onto the forest floor. It feels bright and cheerful, even though we're all on edge.

The hours pass slowly with very little excitement. We spend the time chatting about inconsequential things, until we camp at night. There's always two of them on watch duty. They never let me take a turn, and I'm not truly upset about it since I doubt I'd be able to stay awake.

My mind wanders as we travel. Looking back on my quiet life before my Alpha's, I know now how lonely I was. Dani was always around but it isn't the same as having my pack. I love Dani as if she's a sister, but a sister is no partner. The difference is jarring and it almost hurts at the realization. How could I have been so happy in my sad, solitary life? Why was I okay with settling alone? Did I think that having no partner, or mate, was really the best way to live? I'm so thankful my Alpha's found me and decided I was going to be theirs.

I do wonder what has happened to Dani. I miss her more than anything, though I will never regret leaving with my pack. Tawson said he will help me find her when we reach their Keep, and I will hold him to it. All I can do is hope and pray that she is safe.

My thoughts wander as the hours pass and even though I'm bored I can appreciate the scenery. I'm thankful that there have been no signs of more black magic beasts.

Each night, I crawl into a bedroll with one of them for warmth, cuddles and some cock. They've created a monster, I'm finding myself so turned on all the time. And since they caused this, they better take care of it.

None of them turn me down, and the others enjoy watching as I lose my mind every time I'm knotted. My pack all very much enjoy teasing me to the point of madness, waiting for me to growl and snarl for them to '*stick their fucking dick inside me already*'. My mates love when I demand and beg for them.

Gin and Rafe tend to be rougher, more primal; while Fen, Tawson, and Blue vary. They can be gentle and sweet while making love to me, or my mates can push me around and fuck me until my eyes cross. I enjoy all of it. I haven't found something I won't do yet. Although, every time one of my males plays with my back hole, I get squirmy and uncomfortable. That isn't supposed to be for sex, is it? I vaguely remember Dani saying something about the incredible dark and twisted orgasms she got from that, but it sounds wrong. My males don't listen to my protests about that kind of exploration mainly because they can clearly see me dripping from the pleasure.

The second night we camp I cuddle close to Blue since I feel kind of disconnected from him and I want to bridge that gap. I haven't gotten to know him as much as the others, mainly because he doesn't really know who he is. We chat quietly. I already know he's a bit shy but incredibly sweet and caring. It's hard to reconcile that he's the same beast who murdered people, but black magic is not something to joke about.

Blue will never initiate sex, he's much too timid and uncertain in his abilities and his place with me. So, I take things into my own hands. Literally.

Pulling my dress off, I don't have any underclothes that I can find, I think one of them has been stealing them so I'm left bare under my dresses and skirts. Blue watches me with wide, stunned eyes as I move closer to him.

My lust for him drives my Omega urges to the forefront, making me bold. Blue is *my Beta* and I'm going to make sure that everyone knows it.

"Take your clothes off, Beasty, I want to slide my slick pussy down your cock and milk it for everything you've got." I nudge him with a whisper.

His breathing speeds up, lips slightly parted, and a flush steals across his cheeks before he quickly strips himself. While Blue is smaller than the Alpha's he's no less attractive to me. I actually find him adorable as he rushes to comply with my desires. It's nice that I get to be in charge with him, for now at least.

Snuggling close to him, I rub my soft nude body against his. His cock bumping against me, smearing pre-cum, already hard and dripping for me. Blue's mouthwatering scent intensifies as he leaks pre-cum. His hardness is a slightly darker blue than the rest of him and all I want to do is shove that dark blue cock in my mouth and suck him down. His apple pie scent brings up thoughts of rolling out flakey, buttery pie crust and spices mixed in with juicy apples. Goddess, I'm going to devour this male. I don't know what he can see on my face but Blue's gaze shows a wild hunger for me.

Finding his confidence, he wraps a gentle hand around my neck to pull me in for a soft, licking kiss. Surprise at his dominant move has me gasp out a quiet noise of pleasure. My breathy sighs escape between each kiss, thoroughly enjoying his tenderness.

I'm completely enamored by Blue's soft lips, but then his warm touch draws my attention as he palms my chest. Stopping to pinch and pluck at my nipples, Blue smiles at my squeaks of pain, knowing I enjoy that bite.

One hand continues caressing my breasts while the other slips down to my wetness. I'm leaking a lot of slick. Gathering some on his fingers, Blue brings it to his mouth. Watching in rapt fascination as he tastes me, I enjoy his groan of delight.

"I may not remember much, but you are the best thing I have ever tasted in my life. I could live off your slick," murmuring into my lips, he lets me taste myself on his tongue.

At my shiver, he smiles and runs his fingers through my wetness again. This time Blue drags the slick up to my clit, slipping over and around my nub. Twitching a little at the intensity, I keep as still as I can, enjoying his touch.

Blue's mouth wanders, nibbling my neck, and my eyes roll back. I'm always reactive when my mates do that, it feels so good. Especially, when they touch their own bonding marks.

As his fingers play with my clit, Blue watches my face, adjusting the pressure and pace depending on how loudly I moan. When he's got me right on the edge of an orgasm Blue pulls away from my clit and a whimper slips out. He smiles knowingly at me. I did not expect this shy, sweet, Beta to have a teasing side to him. Maybe there is a beast inside him afterall, one that has nothing to do with black magic.

I love and hate the delayed gratification. But he doesn't make me wait too long. His fingers slip down into my slit, deeper and deeper until he discovers that spot that drives me insane. Blue slides his finger over it watching me twitch and mewl, stopping the moment I'm about to fall over that cliff.

"Please, Beasty! Please make me cum. I need it so bad. Cock? Please let me have your cock." Whining, I plead with him, not making much sense. It seems as if the more desperate I am, the less brain power I have. Starting to ramble, beg and snarl, I try everything to get my way.

Blue's lips twist into a devious smile against my own and he kisses me hard before moving his fingers back to my clit.

I'm turned into a whimpering sweaty mess as he goes back and forth between my clit and my sweet spot, without letting me cum over and over again.

Finally, he rolls us so he's on top. Slipping his fingers out, he guides his cock to my dripping cunt. He doesn't push inside right away but bumps his tip into my clit, watching me jerk and twitch. Until, I've had enough. I want my Beta, right fucking now! Lunging at him, I snap my teeth high on his neck marking him as mine. The moment I do he shoves his cock fully into me.

Moaning into the bite, I'm not ready to let go. But, that doesn't seem to bother him at all. He starts fucking into me hard, and rough. Loving it, I release the bite to yell out,

"Yes! Fuck! Yes, Beasty. More!" Before

licking it as much as I can with the way he's fucking me.

Sitting up, Blue wraps his hands under my hips to change the angle. The moment he pushes into me like this it forces a scream out and I cum. His tip rubs over that spot continuously and I think my brain has melted out my ears.

His balls slap into my ass on each stroke adding to the sensations thrilling through my body. Without a knot he can get so deep. My hands grab at him trying to bring him closer, but Blue resists with a groan. On my next orgasm he stills as deep as he can get and floods me with his release. My body writhing in bliss.

Both panting, Blue leans down letting me wrap my arms around him, and kisses me hard.

"You are my Omega. I will care for you for the rest of my life. I intend to make sure you are happy and safe, for as long as I live," he whispers into my lips, so serious.

My eyes water at the sentiment, strong feelings I'm not ready to name thrill through me as I stare into his eyes.

"I want to do the same for you. You're my Beta, my mate, a surprise I wasn't expecting, but will cherish forever." It's such a tender moment, I will remember claiming Blue

because he was a marvel that stole a piece of my
soul.

CH.28

We tiredly arrive at Doebra after three days of travelling. I didn't realize how far it was from Gisham. Apparently, Doebra is slightly further South than Gisham but Tawson didn't like us being out in the open. He is apprehensive about the possibility of another attack, even though it was fairly quiet on this last leg of travel. We were all on edge.

This time when they're unpacking and stabling the horses, Blue holds my hand. They must have had a discussion when I was sleeping, again, about how to keep me from wandering. Honestly, after the punishment I got, I doubt I will forget and roam far from them again. Plus, I really didn't like disappointing them. It has made me a little more mindful of my surroundings. I'm changing so much from the person I was a month ago, for the better I think. I feel stronger and braver. I'm starting to realize that I am very special to my mates and it's an addictive feeling.

Since Blue has a hold of my hand, I feel safe in allowing my eyes to drift over this new village. It is smaller than Gisham and Pekayan. All I can see from here is a small farm with a few sheep and goats, no blacksmith or anything that looks like a trader. I wonder if they have a market that pops up once a month like my village does?

Late afternoon sun blinds me, but the slowly waning daylight casts long shadows off the homes. I catch movement out of the corner of my eye near the furthest building, but when I look I don't see anything. It must have been an animal, I shrug off the feeling of eyes on me. I'm just unsettled because of the attack days ago.

I'm actually surprised that this town has an Inn, but I guess travellers stop here pretty often if they're doing the market circuit. Not all merchants want to sleep outside.

Tawson leads the way into the tavern. Gin comes up behind Blue and myself, placing a guiding hand on my lower back. They're all working hard to keep me in the middle of our group. They are serious about not letting me wander off again, and about my safety. I'm pleased they are taking this seriously but I'm still a little irked that they lost me in the first place. There's so many of them, how could every single one of them take their eyes off me? I catch Rafe staring at my ass. *All. The. Time.*

We make our way to one of the empty tables, this place is pretty dead, only a few locals sitting near the bar drinking. Once we are seated, a bar maid drops off some ale and asks if we want food. My stomach rumbles in answer, making her laugh cheekily at me.

"Aye, lass. I'll just bring a plate out for everyone then, hmm?" She gets a round of nods before heading into the kitchen. The smell of roasting meat and vegetables makes my mouth water.

Gin huffs a laugh at me as he leans back in his chair. The creaking of the wood catches my attention and I worry that it will not hold his size.

"What? I'm hungry! The dried meat and hard bread we eat on the road is not very filling and you know it!" I point a finger at him, squealing a laugh when he nips at it.

I've learned Gin doesn't talk much, unless it's just the two of us. He's the strong silent type, who prefers to deal with others by growling and scowling. When we're alone though, he speaks to me in his deep, velvety voice, knowing I adore the way he sounds. It makes me feel special that Gin saves his voice for me alone. Unless he has something really important to say to the group, but then he usually uses the pack link.

I'm still frustrated and confused about why I haven't been able to use it. I would absolutely love to be able to talk to them through the link. Although... Would that be too much? They might find me annoying if I could speak into their minds all the time. I'm sure I wouldn't abuse the priviledge... Okay, I would definitely use it far too often. But, I mean, how *cool* is it to be able to do that? The novelty would wear off eventually and then it would be fine. I just worry that they might not like me as much if they could hear my nervous rambling.

My eyes flick around the table, from male to male. Fen and Blue are leaning on the table towards each other quietly discussing something about research. Rafe is slouched in his chair tapping his fingers on the table in a rhythm that I know will start to annoy Gin very soon. My lip twitches with the need to smile at that, Rafe has zero ability to sit still and it's amusing to see how long it takes him before he has to get up and find some sort of trouble.

My gaze rakes over Tawson, sitting so

properly with his arms crossed as he frowns at the few patrons in here. My decision to distract him from his fretting happens before I've even finished the thought.

"Tawson, since you claimed me for your pack, shouldn't I be able to talk with you? In your head, I mean," I ask, interrupting an argument that's about to start between Rafe and Gin. The rest of the males have paused to watch them in amusement.

Tawson looks thoughtful before he answers, "Hmm... You're right, it should have been enough with my bite alone. Especially now that everyone has claimed you." He looks at Fen. "Do you think it's because Alec hasn't bitten her yet? Or could there be something else interfering with the link?"

Fen turns towards Tawson, stroking his chin as he contemplates the question. "Well... I do have a few theories. I really wish I had access to our library. I'm sure I could find some information to support my theory but, it is probably because Alec isn't here. Or, more likely, it's because of what she is, which I also don't know yet."

Choking on the gulp of water I was drinking. Sputtering, I practically yell, "WHAT DO YOU MEAN, WHAT I AM? I'm human!" I've always been human, haven't I? Although, now that I think back I vaguely remember Gin mentioning something about me not being human. I had far too much going on to focus on that at the time, though.

Gin pats me on the back, in support or to help me cough the water out of my lungs, I'm not sure which.

Blue takes my hand and gives me a squeeze before bravely speaking up, "Umm... Well... No one said anything after it happened, so I wasn't completely sure of what I actually saw but... in Gisham, when Rafe was, uh... teasing you with his hand and you got a little feral, you... sort of... changed?" pausing, eyes wide, he shrugs like he's not sure how to go about explaining this. "Do you remember how you got his clothes off so quickly? Or were you too far gone by then? Did anybody else see claws on her hands? Or am I crazy?" His voice is shaky and unsure as his gaze bounces from Alpha to Alpha, searching for recognition.

Gin grunts, sits back in his chair and crosses his arms before looking around at everyone and then focusing on Blue.

"I saw them. Was surprised. Curious." He does not say anything else.

Gin really only seems to talk in full sentences to me. I snort a laugh, even though I'm feeling a little scared. Did my hands change into claws? How is that even possible? *I. Am. Human.*

But... I always thought I was a Beta and that turned out to be wrong. So maybe it's true.

Rafe just looks confused, I assume he didn't notice them because he was almost as feral as I was. Tawson leans over, putting his elbows on the table and clasping his hands together, a thoughtful quirk of his brow as he studies my hands like they'll become claws just because he wills it.

"I was not watching her hands, I had a much better view. So I did not notice how his clothing turned to shreds. I had assumed it was Rafe ripping them." Tawson shrugs, seeming unconcerned but I'm starting to know my head Alpha and I'm pretty sure this news is troubling him.

We all look at Fen, waiting for him to speak. It seems like he did see them because he is the one who mentioned I might not be human.

With a sigh, he nods. "Yes, I did see them. I was a little distracted so I did not observe them as I might have liked to. My nude, feral mate is highly arousing to watch when she demands her pleasure from us." His eyes flash to me with a dark, hungry look. "Precious, when we get to our room I would like to work with you to try and bring them out. Without you needing to go feral."

Gulping, I dart my eyes around at each of them. "I-I don't know if I can. I didn't even notice it last time. What if you all just hallucinated it? I swear, it's never happened before and if it did actually happen, it was probably a fluke. Plus, I don't know if I want claws! What if they pop out when I don't mean to and I hurt one of you! What if I am some other kind of being and it's really dangerous? What if I shift, or whatever, and I lose my mind? I can't..." my panicked words are cut off when Gin claps a hand over my mouth.

Leaning down close to my ear, his breath tickles me as he mutters, "Don't worry, Little One. It doesn't matter what you are because I am a Dragon. Top of the food chain. Whatever you are will bow to me." The way he whispers in my ear has me closing my eyes against the instant arousal it provokes. Goosebumps shiver down my spine, straight to my core. I squeeze my thighs together to prevent my slick from leaking out onto my dress and the chair, but it's no use. I'm a mess. I really need to find out who's been stealing my underwear. Omega's really shouldn't ever go around pantiless.

Gin inhales deeply, still by my ear, before grinning all sharp teeth and menacingly attractive. "Mmm... That's my Little One.

Getting ready to take this thick Dragon cock up your cunt?"

He's still speaking, so quietly that I don't think anyone else can hear him. The rest of them are in a deep discussion about what I could possibly be. Meanwhile, I'm sitting here trying not to lunge at Gin and fuck him in front of the few beings in here.

We're all interrupted by plates of food being dropped on the table. The barmaid gives the guys a look and focuses on Gin. As she opens her mouth to say something, probably ask him for sex, I glare at her and snarl,

"Mine!"

I'm not thinking anymore. I'm all instinct and reaction. Standing on my chair so I have room to move, I toss myself at her. Hands come around me and snatch me out of the air. Gin holds me tight to his chest as he roars with laughter.

Everyone stops to stare at him. I don't think they've ever heard him laugh out loud before because the look on their faces is pure shock.

The barmaid has gone very pale and holds her hands up as she slowly backs away. "I- I'm s-sorry! I d-didn't know!"

She escapes to the kitchen and stays

there, probably avoiding the crazy Omega. I'm pretty sure if I see her again I'm going to gouge her eyes out, or something equally as painful so she knows not to proposition taken males ever again.

I'm still snarling and fighting Gin's hold on me, but it is like being held by solid rock. I don't think I'd ever be strong enough to get away unless he allowed it.

Vaguely, I overhear Fen exclaiming, "She did it again! Look, her hands have changed to.. are those paws? I'm surprised Gin has any skin left."

When what he said registers, I calm down and glance at my hands. Yep, those are paws. Light brown furry paws with some deadly looking claws! They are quite pretty actually, short brown fur, a little bit of beige-y white near some of the 'fingers'. Admiring the deadly looking claws I tilt my hands this way and that to get a better look before I catch sight of what I've done. I've shredded Gin's shirt and his shoulders.

"Oh Goddess! Gin, I'm so sorry. I can't believe I hurt you! Oh, no. Oh, no. *Why did I do that?* I'm a nice person! I don't lunge at females! I don't attack people! *What is wrong with me?*" I cry out at the sight of blood.

My hands have slowly reverted back to

normal as I wail at Gin, apologizing for causing him pain.

He just laughs again and nuzzles me, giving me an adoring look. "I'm alright, Little One. I promise, it did not hurt. Look, look closely," Gin gently guides my head to his shoulder, showing me how quickly he heals, "the wounds have already closed and I have other shirts." His purr starts up, relaxing me into a melted puddle of Omega.

Leaning into his chest where I can feel the vibrations the strongest, I let the sound wash over me, calming my anger and aggression.

I startle with a jerk, teetering on Gin's lap when I look up and see Fen right beside me, leaning close to observe my paws.

"I'm glad I got the chance to see them again. They look like a type of cat's paw. I wonder if you have latent Shifter genes in you. They were probably activated by one or all of us mating you. It can happen sometimes with Shifters. There's something in their saliva that can cause this." Fen sounds like he's lecturing a classroom on Shifter genetics. I wonder if he's a scholar... Giving myself a mental shake, feeling my cheeks heat, I should spend more time talking to my males, getting to know them better instead of fucking them. I have gotten a little obsessive over their knots, and cocks. Which is quite funny to me since I came from zero intimacy to an overabundance.

"Absolutely fascinating! I've read about this but never seen it in person before. It is actually quite rare, mostly because Omegas are rare and Alpha-Beta pairings are decently uncommon. Or if they do happen they tend to be the same type of being," Fen continues, but he's just staring blankly at my hands as he speaks. I actually think he's talking more to himself than any of us now.

Interrupting his musings, I tug on his shirt to encourage his focus, "Fen? Are you a scholar? Because I've never met anyone that seems to know so much about everything like you do. You're really smart. Does this mean I'm going to shift into a cat? Am I going to get even smaller than I already am? Aw... I'm already so tiny compared to any of you, except Blue. I'm only a little shorter than you." Glancing at Blue, I smile warmly as I give him a sheepish look, "Thank you."

Blue chuckles quietly at this and nods while Fen responds to my mad rambling. "I *am* a scholar! I read as many books as I can get my hands on, research is my specialty. I can't wait to show you my library at the Keep. It has books on almost anything you could think of and probably some you wouldn't. I'm not completely sure if you will shift fully. Not all the cases I've read about shift fully, some only get a partial shift. Ears, tails, claws and sometimes teeth. There's probably less than ten percent that actually gain a full animal. It's really an interesting phenomenon and I'm excited to study your progression with this. It seems like strong anger or rage triggers it. That may change as you get used to it and eventually you might be able to control it..." he's cut off in his ruminations.

"Yes, it's all very interesting. And Fen, you will keep track of this, correct? I am pleased that she will have a way to protect herself if we do experience any more attacks. But, Sweetheart, you can't go around attacking females that are attracted to us. We will always turn anyone down because you are our heart. Our Center. Plus, once you have bitten all of us it will discourage any interest," Tawson says, giving me a heated look.

I know I haven't bitten everyone yet, but I will. *They are mine*! My pack, and I am possessive of them. I didn't realize I had it in me, but I also haven't had any experience with males until they came along. Plus, these Omega instincts are no joke. I am so much more aggressive than I've ever been. It's a little strange for me to experience these drastic changes. But, I am adaptable. I will be strong, because this is my life now. I no longer feel stuck in that rut of sameness. I didn't expect so much excitement in my life but hey, beggars can't be choosers.

CH.29

The rest of the night is quiet compared to dinner. We share a room again, no one wanting to be far from me, and I don't want that either. My instincts demand they stay close, needing their scents for comfort and safety.

I behaved myself, so there were no exciting, painful or lusty punishments. It was a night for cuddles and just enoying each others company, it made for an excellent night. We slept, woke early and left at first light. It is a four or five day journey to Havish and, barring any attacks, it should be a relatively nice ride. The trees grow further apart the closer we get, on the other side of Havish is grass and farmlands. It is nice being able to see so much more, but it also puts everyone on high alert. The more open it is, the less cover we have from any attacks. Tawson also mentioned that bandits and thieves tend to frequent the roads, looking for easy coin.

I'm in the cart with Fen, Blue's in the back. Gin trailing behind us this time, with Rafe and Tawson leading our little group.

Relaxing, I lean my head back to enjoy the sunshine on my face. Warming me from the chilly morning air. That feeling of eyes creeping up on me again. Looking around I try to figure out where it's coming from.

Peering back at Gin, I see a shadow slip behind a tree in the distance. Sitting up straighter, my body tenses.

Fen bumps my shoulder to get my attention. "What's wrong, Precious?"

"I don't know... I thought I saw something... it was probably just a critter scared of the noises from our group. Something skittered into a tree," I utter, slowly, hesitantly. Trying not to cause concern because it doesn't feel malicious, just curious, whatever it is. Taking a second to think *'how do I know it isn't malicious?'*, I mentally shrug.

The feeling passes and I relax back into sunning myself, thinking about my paws. It shouldn't be surprising to me that I have some sort of cat in me. I've always enjoyed sunning myself. Sitting outside every morning to catch the early rays, while I drank my tea. I wonder what other signs there were of my latent heritage? Dani did catch me chasing butterflies once or twice... But that's just fun! It isn't cat-like, is it?

Eventually, I drift off and nap, curled up against Fen's leg. Using him as a pillow. He's much more comfortable than the bench, even with the cushion.

The sound of horses clomping closer to the cart and the scent of wildflowers, a gentle sweetness bringing to mind a beautiful sunny day lounging in a meadow by a softly flowing stream alerts me to Tawson's presence. As the wind changes it brings me the scent of salted caramel and my mouth instantly waters for a taste as Rafe rides near.

"Do any of you scent that? It's faint but it could be someone tracking us," Tawson questions sharply, with no small amount of concern.

"I thought I caught something in the wind but it was so faint I figured it was either an animal running away from us or a traveller long past," Rafe replies, taking deep breaths trying to scent the air.

Fen hums thoughtfully. "It's much too difficult to catch anything with the wind blowing our scents behind us. If someone is following we'll never know it unless we can see them, or the wind changes. But, I think if it was something to worry about they wouldn't be so sneaky about it. Thieves and bandits are more of the 'rush in and stab' type versus the 'sneak around and try not to be seen' type. Honestly, most criminals aren't that bright." His thigh shivers under my head. "I also don't think it's any of those black magic beasts. They were loud and I'm pretty sure Blue would sense them like before. Plus, I don't feel any oppressive darkness, do you?"

Tawson grunts, and I can hear the anger and caution in his tone when he speaks again, "No. You are correct Fen. Just, keep your eyes and nose on alert. I don't want anything to happen to them." I'm pretty sure he's pointing at me and Blue. We are the weakest of the pack. Although, Blue would be pretty formidable in his beast form if he could control himself.

Tawson and Rafe continue discussing possible dangers as they ride ahead. Fen hums, petting my hair as he thinks. And I fall into a deeper sleep, trying not to let their words worry me too much.

The next two days go by smoothly, if a little boring. No attacks, no more strange scents in the air and no other problems. I spend some time chatting with each of my males, getting to know my pack better. When my backside gets sore from sitting in the cart for so long, I plead with Tawson to let me ride with one of them.

Relenting eventually, he decides it will be him I ride with. Sitting in front of him, practically on his lap, I take the opportunity to tease him. Making sure that, with the rocking of the horse, I rub back onto his cock and forwards onto the front of the saddle. I end up teasing myself as much as him and he gets me back by sticking his hand under my skirt and shoving his fingers into my cunt. But he doesn't let me cum, Tawson just holds them there, keeping me on the edge. We eventually need to take a break to fuck because we're both so worked up. I'm pretty sure everyone knew what we'd been doing because they all snicker as we rush off into the woods for a break to 'relieve' ourselves.

I'm pleasantly surprised that I was able to get Mr. Serious to relax his vigilance for some silly fun. I do think he enjoyed himself immensely, although he wouldn't knot me, because Tawson didn't want to take that much time off our journey. Knowing he's concerned about attacks, I think it's my job to make sure he takes time to de-stress.

I take turns riding with everyone, doing the same bit of teasing. And why not? They're my pack and they started me down this path of constant arousal so it's their job to tend to me when I'm needy.

No one complains, although I can feel Tawson's eye twitch every time someone says we need to stop to relieve ourselves. He knows, we all know, I don't know why we don't just call it what it is. A sex break.

On our fourth day, travelling to Havish, Tawson says we might make it by nightfall. I'm excited at the prospect of an actual bath. I don't really mind sleeping in the woods with my pack. I end up sleeping on top of someone, fucked and knotted into exhaustion, which is quite comfortable. But the lack of hygiene is bothersome.

I'm back in the cart with Fen, staring off into the woods, not really looking at anything in particular when I notice something moving. It looks rather large and it's darting from tree to tree, trying to stay in the shadows. It's got to be some sort of large animal hunting something. I am surprised that it would come so close to travellers. Most animals know to avoid beings, since they tend to get eaten. It doesn't really matter what game we hunt, food is food when you're on the road and a hot meal sounds so much better than travel rations.

Watching it for a while, it eventually disappears deeper into the trees. This area is very open and it must not enjoy the fact that hiding spots are few and far between.

Leaning back, I watch the sky for a while, observing the sun slowly setting. I hope that means we're close to Havish and a bath. I look for Tawson, it's his turn riding in the back, and see him a fair distance away.

"Fen, do you think we're almost at Havish? It's starting to get dark and Tawson thought we might make it if we moved fast enough," I question, not able to hide the hopeful note in my voice.

He chuckles lightly. "Looking forward to an actual bed? Or warm food?"

"Neither, although, both do sound really good. I'm excited for a hot bath! No more cold creeks, or streams, and doing a light wash. I need to soak all this travel dust out of my hair," - clearing my throat with embarrassment - "and all this slick off my thighs. When I find out who stole all of my underclothes, I'm going to kick them in the shin." I cross my arms and frown, my nose wrinkling slightly. It really is inconvenient to travel without them. At least I found my breast bands, I can't imagine the pain I'd feel after a day of bouncing around on horseback or in the cart. I shudder a little at the thought.

When I turn to look at him again, he's

got a funny look on his face. "Fen? You okay? Don't worry we should be there soon and then you can take a bath with me, if there's room. You look like you need to relax." I pat his thigh in understanding.

Fen chokes out a strangled laugh. "Hmm... Yep, yeah, a bath with you sounds like exactly what I need." Glancing up, he checks the sun, then looks back at Tawson, whose green skin almost shimmers in the slowly setting light, with a frown before getting that glazed look of telepathy, then he relaxes and continues, "And we should be there in a few more hours. It'll be darker than we would have liked, for travelling, but we'd rather get there late than camp out in the open."

I sigh, we're so close. These last few hours of travel, especially in the dark, are going to be difficult, I think. Everything gets very tense at night. Understanding that the chance of an attack is exponentially higher in the dark since thieves, bandits, and possibly those beasts do tend to feel more comfortable moving in the darkness. With the trees thinning there's more cover at night to hide them from prying eyes. But, unless they have a User to help, it is almost impossible to hide their scent.

I don't bother making conversation with anyone, I know they need to listen to the sounds of the wilderness. Trying to stay alert for strange noises, I'm finding my mind wandering to those Orc brothers again. I wonder what they would have done if Gin hadn't found me before they got me to the Inn. They didn't feel malicious, they honestly felt like they were trying to do something nice. I'm very curious about the silent brother, Brynd. That Orc was gentle with me while keeping me close and he smelled very nice. I could definitely come up with a pastry that tastes like him... peaches and cream.

It can be difficult to find cream though, unless there's a farm nearby or you own some goats. One of the couples in my old village used to sell me their goat milk. They knew I'd put it to good use and they always enjoyed purchasing the things I'd make with it, plus they got a discount for providing me with necessary ingredients.

This is the longest I've ever gone without baking something. Travelling isn't very favorable for baking. Although, if I had the right ingredients I could make flatbread. I bet that would go nicely with some of the critters Rafe and Gin have hunted for us.

By the time my thoughts have wound themselves up in circles, thinking of everything that's happened I note how dark it's gotten. We must be close now.

Spying lights up ahead, I sigh. That's got to be Havish. Turning, I whisper to Fen, "Is that it? Are we there?" Tugging on his sleeve a little, I make sure he's listening.

Leaning down, he drops a kiss on my head before answering, "Yep, I think that's it. I'm glad we made it with no trouble. It is much later than I'd hoped but, it's better than trying to set up camp now."

Tawson rides closer as we make our way into town. Rafe and Gin are already at the Inn, talking to the stable boy and organizing stalls and storage for the cart and horses. I am very lucky that they allowed me to take all of my things. I know travelling would have been faster if I didn't have so many crates of stuff.

Blue hops off the back and comes around to help me out, keeping hold of my hand. Following me as I go to stand at the entrance looking out at the village. It's bigger than Doebra, but not by much since it's hard to see anything in the dark. The only lights I can see, aside from the ones from the Inn, are small lanterns in the homes scattered about.

I find the shape of their homes to be strange. They're so different from the other places we've stayed. They look more dome shaped than steepled. I wonder if this is better when it rains and snows. I'm curious enough that I might ask Fen about it, if I remember.

Before long, Blue is tugging me to the Inn. We follow the others, Gin coming up behind me. I've noticed he tends to stick close when he can. More so than the others. I think his Dragon is pushing him to be near me.

We watch as Tawson pays for a room and food to be brought up. The Inn is quiet, since it's so late, but there are a few drunks wavering in their seats. They look like they shouldn't be allowed to drink anymore. The lingering aroma of stew in the air has my stomach growling. We didn't stop for dinner, but I did snack on some dried meat. It wasn't enough to satisfy me, so I'm glad Tawson thought to request some food.

All I want to do right now is eat and sleep. Hopefully, I'll be able to bathe tomorrow before we leave.

Gin takes my other hand, and I'm penned between Blue and him as they lead me up the stairs to our room. *It's a tight fit, as usual,* I snort out a laugh at my immature sense of humor shaking my head when my mates look at me funny. It's become common for us all to cram into one room. I can't remember whose turn it is to sleep with me on the bed. I have offered to sleep on the floor in a bedroll but none of my males were having that.

Gin and Blue undress me tenderly, stroking my skin as they bare me to the room. A knock on the door pulls me from my sleepy state. Gin stands in front of me, blocking the view, so the owner doesn't see me nude. As the innkeeper leaves, the smell of stew drifts over to me and I try to push Gin out of my way. Chuckling lightly as he goes to pick me up, Tawson beats him to it.

My lead Alpha tosses a smirk at Gin. "It's my turn. You've been hogging her for every meal."

A muffled growl sounds as Tawson sits on a chair with me in his lap. He starts feeding me the stew, and I'm too tired to protest that I *can* feed myself. My arms are going to forget how to bring food to my mouth if they constantly feed me like this!

The clatter of bowls lets me know the rest of my pack are grabbing food as well, but I'm too exhausted to focus on anything but my own stew. My eyelids droop lower and lower as I try to focus on the spoon being brought to my mouth. Eventually, my eyes shut and I miss the next spoonful that Tawson feeds me. I end up with stew smeared over my cheek and a few drops onto my chest and a muffled snort makes my eyes twitch open.

Rafe has both hands clamped over his

mouth as he tries to hold in his laughter. Gin slaps the back of his head with a grunt, but turns an amused smile my way. Tawson sets the spoon down and spins me around so I'm facing him.

"Let me get that," leaning down, Tawson licks the food off my cheek, pausing to drop a sweet kiss on my lips, "Just a little more, Sweetheart, and then you can go to bed." With an arm behind my back he bends over my chest and slicks his tongue over the drips that have decorated me. Now I'm turned on *and* exhausted, but I make an effort to ignore that. I really need some sleep. It isn't long before bedrolls are being laid out and Tawson is tucking me in before undressing himself.

I'm mostly asleep by the time he gathers me close and I revel in the fresh, clean scent of Tawson. The natural, wild smell of an untouched forest in the heat of summer and the soothing cool spray of a small creek settle me after a long day of traveling. The bed dips on my other side and the delectable scent of tea and cinnamon rolls over me as Gin cuddles close to my front, with Tawson at my back. I'm so warm and safe when I drift off fully, smiling to myself at the way my life has changed.

CH.30

Waking to a mouth on my cunt, is my new favorite thing. I'm already moaning and whining for whoever it is to let me cum. One of my mates must have been at this for a while. Reaching for them, I plan to grab handfuls of hair and direct them where I want but my hands are caged by someone holding them down above me.

Blinking my eyes open to Gin leaning over me, watching my expression as he gives me a toothy smile. My attention is drawn to Tawson's green eyes looking up at me as he shoves his tongue deep inside, catching all the slick dripping out of me. The sight has me shuddering with need, adding to the tightness building in my core.

"Please, please, please. I need to cum, please!" I whimper softly.

Tawson replaces his tongue with three

fingers, smirking as he pushes me into a whirlwind of pleasure. The abrupt stretch, mixed with his tongue flicking my clit is more than I can handle and I scream out,

"Yes!" and cum hard, shaking through the pleasure. Gin holds my hands down, while Tawson holds my hip with his free hand, keeping me as still as possible between them.

While I'm recovering , Tawson slips his fingers from my pussy and trails them down to my rear. Teasing me, spreading my juices all over before slowly pushing one finger into my ass. I squeal and buck my hips trying to stop him, even though I've learned that I really do enjoy this dark pleasure. I feel like I'm supposed to fight it, it's not supposed to be used for this! But, I like the dark, twisted orgasms that make me blind and deaf to everything else. It's like nothing I've ever experienced.

Gin bites and tugs on my nipples, distracting me so I hardly notice as Tawson adds a second finger to my ass. The pinch from Gin's teeth has a direct line to my core and every time he bites and tugs on them I jolt as it electrifies me. Awash in sensation, I can't stop the mewling cries from escaping.

By the time my nipples feel puffy and raw from Gin's playing, Tawson has three fingers in my ass, stretching me out gloriously.

Tawson throws Gin a nod then removes his fingers, leaving me devoid of the fullness I desire. A whine slips out at the empty feeling. They jostle me as they change positions, Gin is now lying down and Tawson turns me to face Gin, dropping me directly onto his hard cock.

"Fuck!" I shout at the sudden intrusion over his massive ribbed member.

Gin groans and tugs me down, kissing me stupid. I don't realize he's distracting me again until Tawson moves against my body. *What is he doing back there?* When he presses the tip against my ass, I try to lean back, intending to stop him, because I do not think I can fit both of them inside me!

"Shhh, easy Sweetheart." Tawson croons, stroking a hand down my back, "trust me, *us*, we'll take care of you."

Gin holds me against his chest cuffing my hands behind my back as Tawson slowly works his oiled cock into my ass. My raw nipples drag against the coarse hairs on Gin's chest making my head spin as all I experience too many sensations at once. But I can't lie to myself, I love this.

"You were made for us." Gin's voice is ragged as my cunt grows tighter with two cocks stretching me, "such a good girl, stretching for our cocks."

Squealing, I protest, "You're too big, Tawson! I can't fit both of you! That just isn't possible, look at the size of your cock!" Nothing I say deters him and it adds to the hedonistic pleasure of the moment.

Tawson keeps pushing until the head of his cock pops in past that tight ring of muscle. Closing my eyes against the pinch and burn of him stretching me, I whimper at the fullness. He doesn't move, letting me adjust, while Gin groans at the extra pressure against him.

Tawson's cock in my ass morphs from painful to a twisted kind of rapture. He pushes forward slowly, testing my limits as he slides in deeper. My squeals have turned to keening moans, I'm unable to hold them in. I didn't want them to know that I was enjoying this.

Tawson stills, his hips flush against my ass. He's embedded and I'm so stuffed that I'm sure my body is going to split in two. Tears flow from my eyes, an overabundance of sensation that I don't know how to handle. It's too much and I cum, I didn't even know it was building, I'm screaming and clenching tightly on both of them causing them to growl at the feeling.

When I finally settle limply on Gin's chest, they start moving. As Tawson pulls out, Gin pushes in, and they continue this rhythm, driving me mad. They pick up speed and I can feel them rubbing against each other through that thin piece of skin. Another climax builds rapidly and pushes me over the edge. I hold my breath as wave after wave of pleasure radiates through me. I'll never be able to walk again after this. Is it possible to die from too many orgasms? *I don't know how long I can take this.*

My head swims and my vision blurs, I might black out from too much bliss. Tawson slides a hand up my side, stroking gently over my breast before grabbing my shoulder. Using the leverage to fuck into me harder. Leaning my head against Gin's shoulder so I can see Tawson's beautiful lean body flex as he works all of us towards an explosive ending. His teal braids are damp with sweat and tangled against his neck and the fierce, glazed look in his eyes makes me clench over both of them. Tawson stills and releases a grunt as he cums, reaching down to knead his knot. I'm glad he didn't try to shove *that* into my ass. His knuckles brush against Gin's knot, compelling a curse from him. Gin fucks up into me a little faster.

I have enough coherency to reach up and grab Tawson's arm bringing it to my mouth. My Omega instincts are in the driver's seat now.

These Alpha's are worthy.

Biting into his wrist hard, I taste his blood on my tongue and revel in it. Tawson howls in reaction, jetting more seed into me. I pull my teeth out of his wrist to lick and clean it, feeling rather smug about it.

"I'm going to knot her, so you'd better prepare or pull out." Gin snarls at Tawson. The veins in his neck pulsing as he strains to hold back.

Tawson chuckles and grunts as he looses another splash of cum into me. It's too much and it leaks out and down to cover Gin's knot.

Tawson's cock stops kicking inside me and he slowly pulls back, slipping out. I fuss at the open feeling, but as soon as he's out Gin shoves his knot into my cunt and my eyes roll back into my head. I relinquish Tawson's arm and snap my teeth into the closest part of Gin I can reach, which happens to be his very muscular chest. My hands claw over his thick frame, so much bigger than any of my other mates, leaving thin pink lines.

The Omega inside is thrilled anytime I leave marks on my mates. Every time I see the scratches or bites I'm left with a feeling of pride. *This must be why they always look so damn smug as they leave bruises and teeth marks all over me.*

The orgasm is explosive and that's it. I'm

done. I black out from the intensity, it's too much pleasure for my body to handle. I don't know how they expect me to function after this.

I'm not out for long. When I come around, Gin is still knot deep inside me and my teeth are still lodged in his chest. Shooting ribbons of cum, he fills me. A hiss slips out, I'm so sensitive from the countless orgasms they gave me. I don't even bother trying to sit up, letting my head loll against Gin and lick at my claiming mark.

Gin lazily pets my back and ass. Long, soothing strokes, helping my body come down from the high. Nuzzling his nose into the side of my face, Gin drops kisses everywhere he can reach.

"You back with us, Little One? Did we work you too hard?" The smugness in his tone makes me roll my eyes, but I can't resist smiling at my mate. Gin's so pleased with himself for turning me into this mess.

Groaning out a garbled reply, I don't bother lifting my face from his chest. I don't think I said any actual words. His laughter bounces me causing his knot to shift inside me. I squeeze my eyes shut as my body convulses with another orgasm.

"No more. Please! I can't cum anymore.

You've killed me. I'm done. That's it. No more sexy stuff." Managing to lift my head, I grumble the words out, hoping everyone can hear me.

A chorus of laughter is the only response. Good. That means they all know this pussy is closed for business.

I'm slowly regaining the ability to function, enough that I can think again and make demands, but movement is still far out of my reach.

"How do you expect me to ride like this? Do you understand what you've done? I can't move!" I wail out my complaints as Gin cuddles me against his hard body, "You know what? I'm going to cuddle with Blue in the back of the cart and share his bedroll tonight. The rest of you are on a time out! Ugh, someone better be finding me a hot bath." The desire to cross my arms and pout is strong but that would require movement.

"Aww, Kitten! I didn't do anything wrong!" Rafe grouses, but he's trying very hard not to smile. The big jerk. The longer I keep eye contact the harder it is to prevent my laughter from slipping out.

Rafe's lips tremble before breaking out into a massive grin. His loud guffaw echoes around the small room and I can't fight it any longer. My giggles join him as Rafe makes his way over to me.

"You might not have done this to me... this time. But, you laughed!" My words squeak out in between chuckles. I know all my protests are futile, I'm definitely going to be pawing at one of them for a knot later. Honestly, I can't help it! My mates make it so good.

Tawson comes over, brushing my hair off my face so I can see him smiling down at me fondly. There's an emotion, a softening of the seriousness that he always presents, gentleness shining down on me, as he maintains eye contact. I'm not ready to acknowledge that feeling yet.

"The bath will be brought up here and ready by the time this beast has finished knotting you." Tawson ksses me soundly before returning to whatever he was doing, probably packing.

It feels like hours pass as I wait for Gin's knot to go down. I'm hungry and sticky and I desperately need a bath. When he finally shrinks enough to release me, Gin slips out unbothered by the rush of cum and slick that covers him.

Catching me glancing down at the mess, he quirks an eyebrow. "I'm going to enjoy a bath as soon as you're clean." Gin shuffles me up enough to kiss the tip of my nose before handing me off to another mate.

These guys toss me around like I don't have legs that work, *they probably won't work right now anyways*. Huffing, I snuggle into Fen's chest as he carries me over to the tub I hadn't even noticed arrived.

Between Fen and Blue, they get me washed quickly before helping me dress. Gin steps into the tub, glancing down at the tiny space. He's far too big for any regular tub. *I wonder how he bathes at home?* The tub must be massive to fit his bulk.

Gin looks ridiculous, the small tub comes up to his calves and appears as if he's standing in a foot bath. With an irritated sigh he scrunches down into the tiny space. The wood makes a creaking noise and everyone stops to watch. Holding my breath, as if that will help the integrity of the tub, I ogle my largest male squishing himself down. Gin's knees are pressed tightly against his chest as he uses a cup to scoop and dump water over himself. Growls rumble out of him steadily as he carefully cleans himself in the cooling water. One wrong move and I swear that thing is going to burst apart.

I'm too busy watching Gin to be of any help packing, although I'm pretty sure it's all done. Once Gin's washed, he carefully maneuvers himself up without breaking the thing. The rest of the pack each take a turn, not bothered by the cooling water. I shiver thinking about it.

After checking out of the Inn, Fen and Gin take our bags to the cart and ready the horses. The rest of us sit in the dining area, quickly grabbing a bowl of porridge for breakfast before setting out. It's going to be about two days until we reach the cabin at the base of the mountains.

Fen told me it was built by a group years ago. Travellers kept complaining about the treacherous journey through the mountains without a safe place to rest.

We'll be taking Peril's Pass. It sounds pretty alarming and is the only well-known path to the other side. Making the trek through the snowy peaks is hazardous for anyone. I'm impressed that merchants make the trip fairly often, but they always hire mercenaries to protect them. There are many dangerous creatures who call the mountains home.

Peril's Pass is fraught with danger. There's often a threat of rock falls as well as the weather changing quicker than you can blink. My deadly mates should be enough to ensure our pack's safety, especially Gin. I mean, he's a Dragon, basically the top of the food chain. We *will* be okay.

Trees become scarce, replaced by brush and low bushes the further we travel. It's interesting to me because I come from such a thickly forested part of Saforia. I've never seen the land like this; so open. It's unsettling.

However, observing the various wildlife in their homes is an enlightening experience. There are lots of little mammals that burrow and it's pretty cute watching them. When they see us coming they let out adorable squeaks, warning the others. Then they scatter, diving into their little underground homes or up into the trees.

We've been on the road a while and my body is exceedingly sore from the vigorous sex this morning but I can't stop the smile that graces my face as I think about the fact that I've claimed and bitten all of my mates now. I still can't use the pack link to mentally speak to my males, but I can feel our bond humming. They're all there and as I close my eyes I can see the strands reaching from me to each one of them. When I feel that bond, a soft warm sensation fills me with joy.

Tawson calls a halt for a break and lunch. We don't bother moving off the road since we haven't seen any other travellers since Gisham.

Getting out of the cart, I stretch with a groan. Travelling is harder than I thought, and I'm not even doing any of the work. Blue hands out bread and cheese since he has yet to leave the cart.

Taking my portion, I walk a few steps away to work the tingles out of my legs. A fluffy little critter catches my eye and I slowly head in its direction wanting to get a better look.

The openness of the land here is unnerving. But, it's also kind of pretty. Blue skies feel endless as they stretch into the horizon. Sunlight kisses my skin as I tilt my head back and close my eyes, enjoying its warmth. While the sun is nice, the weather has started to cool and the cold has never been something I've enjoyed. I hate being cold.

Every snowy season I hid in my bakery, staying warm and cozy. My kitchen unfailingly grew hot with the fire and ovens going. It was perfect for me. Dani complained about it being too warm for her, but she's also the weird one who liked to frolic in the snow.

Dani constantly tried to get me to join her, I'd last maybe ten minutes before I was too cold to do anything except shiver. I wonder if my aversion to the cold has something to do with whatever latent Shifter I am? Or maybe it has something to do with being an Omega... I do really enjoy lots of blankets, pillows and soft things. That doesn't really scream '*I enjoy the cold*'.

An alarming screech interrupts my thoughts on the approaching cold season. My head snaps towards the noise. Another loud cry breaks the silence, sounding familiar, full of malice and pain. *Oh Goddess!* I know that sound, those malformed beasts! My feet are moving before the thoughts have finished forming and I run for Blue. I need to help him!

They can't have him!

I'd hoped there weren't any more of them, but it seems our luck isn't that great.

CH.31

Fen glares in the direction of the beasts while shifting to stone. He draws a large sword and growls something to the hound beside him. Rafe's hellhound snarls in response, hackles raised as magma drips from his cracked skin and maw. Gin produces two axes bigger than my head, I have no idea where he's been hiding them. Tawson unsheathes his sword, eyes glowing a bright green as a crackling aura surrounds his body.

My feet pound into the ground as I race to the cart. Fear tangles in my gut, but I force it down. I can't think of that right now, Blue is the only thing that matters. The black magic *will not* take him from me.

Blue is *mine*!

I'm surprised to find him sitting and bracing for the forced change, but nothing is happening. "Blue! Are you okay? Is it affecting you?" Huffing out, my breath wheezes from running so hard. I didn't realize how far I'd drifted from my pack, I really need to stop doing that. I swear I thought I'd learned my lesson.

A screech rings out around us, joined by a coughing growl and the sound of wings. I can't hear the sounds of footsteps yet, so they can't be that close. Yet, the noises from these beasts echo as if they're right beside us.

Reaching for Blue's hand, he pulls back with a shake of his head. "Wait, Lu. Wait and look! It's not affecting me anymore. How?" He's looking at his hands in awe.

Before I get the chance to answer, hideous cries reverberate through the open spaces. The sounds are almost deafening, there has to be more beasts than last time. The black magic User must have sent double the amount after his last attack failed. Shivering, a prickle of unease creeps down my spine. We're heavily outnumbered.

The Alphas spread out around us, forming a perimeter to protect me and Blue. Paws thud against the ground, intensifying the fear. It feels as if they're heading straight for us. The creatures are close and my heart races in time with the sound.

A blur of movement to the left of us

catches my eye. With it being so open here I have a clear view of how many beasts are coming for us. It terrifies me, because that is far too many for us to fight. We're going to die here and I am not ready to leave this life. I want more time to love my pack and I still need to meet my last Alpha. I have so many recipes I need to try and I haven't seen my new home yet! I haven't even had the chance to tell my pack I love them. I've been avoiding it because it feels too big.

The first line of beasts crash into a snarling, angry Gargoyle and a Hellhound. Rafe and Fen demolish them faster than I expected. But, there's so many more. The monsters climb over the bodies of their fallen, not caring one bit.

Regardless of how inappropriate the moment, my core clenches at their ruthlessness. *Why do I find their violence so attractive?* Shaking my head to refocus on the danger, my eyes dart around the carnage.

A group of beasts break off and circle around as they attempt to avoid Rafe's flames and Fen's impenetrable form. Gin smirks as he joins the fight, battle axes raised. For a moment I'm completely awestruck, Gin stands about five feet taller with huge bulky muscles. Light reflects off his skin revealing black and blue scales. Brilliant slitted yellow eyes scene the oncoming threat, tracking prey like a reptile.

My mouth drops open, Gin has a tail! Deadly spikes trail down Gin's spine from neck to the tip of his tail, ending in a mace-like club. The larger barbs at the end appear to drip a caustic fluid. I'm proven correct when he slams it into the side of one of the beasts and the destructive liquid immediately eats away at the creature. The beast shrieks so loud I have to cover my ears, the pain filled cries make me flinch. I can't watch anymore, the excruciating screams are torturous and tears brim in my eyes. I do not enjoy the death of these monsters, but it's them or us, and I prefer we come out of this alive.

That was disgusting but effective. Gin has taken on a group of ten on his own, faring better than I would have thought against these beasts.

Tawson is our last line of defence against the hoard of beasts coming for us. Glancing back at us, he shouts,

"Luella, Blue, climb up a tree. Get out of their range while we fight. I need to focus and not worry about you two." Turning away, that crackling aura around him explodes as a line of beasts crash into it. The creatures shake and shudder as flashes of light impale their bodies, leaving smoking carcasses on the ground. The next wave meets his sword as his aura seems to recharge.

My chin dips in understanding, I won't fare well in a fight. I have zero experience with weapons, plus I'm dwarfed by even the smallest beast here. Blue takes my hand and drags me out of the cart to the nearest climbable tree. It is not close and I'm wheezing for air by the time we reach it. The widespread trees make me long for the dense forests of home.

Blue surprises me with his strength as he lifts me above his head and shoves me at the lowest branch. Quickly, I wiggle myself up and climb a few more limbs for good measure. Some of these beasts are very large and I want to be well out of their reach.

When I look down to see if Blue has followed, he's gone. Searching through the branches, I finally spot Blue. But something is wrong, my gut twists with unease.

No!

Blue's shifting. Why would he do this? The black magic will take him from me.

"BLUE!... PLEASE!" My voice screeches out for him as tears stream down my cheeks.

I'm losing him.

As I struggle to climb back down, Blue's

eyes meet mine, a rueful smile plastered on his face stops me in my tracks.

"Don't worry, it isn't them. I have control over myself again." And then he's gone, into his beastly form, joining the fight.

Clinging to the trunk of the tree, I sob. Terror ravages my body and it takes all my effort to keep my balance. My pack is risking everything to keep me safe, but there's so many monsters. What happens if one of them... I don't know what I'll do if I lose any of my mates. They have become so important to me in such a short amount of time.

Fear and panic almost distract me from the shaking, shuddering motions. I almost lose my balance as a particularly hard jerk jostles my precarious perch. Grasping harder, I look wildly around. Something that looks like a bear crossed with a raccoon and deer has found my tree. I did *not* count on one of these creatures being able to climb. Why didn't we think of this? These are monstrous creations constructed from many creatures!

Climbing higher, I'm not thinking, just letting the panic take hold. My breaths come in fast, sweat trickles down my spine, and my clammy hands make it harder to hold onto the rough bark.

The screech of an eagle leaves my ears

ringing, forcing my attention to the sky. Another dark creature is heading straight for me. It looks like a Griffon, but there's something wrong with it. Its eyes are completely white and its body appears rotted.

I scream as it swoops in and grabs my arm and shoulder, digging its talons in and easily puncturing my skin. Thrashing, I struggle trying to get away. But it grabs my side with its other clawed foot and lifts me out of the tree.

"NO! GIN, FEN! HELP ME!" I shriek for my winged mates, hoping they will come for me. But, when I catch a glimpse of the fight below, all of my males are being swarmed by beasts. Blood and bodies litter the clearing, but my mates are still upright.

Tawson wields his sword with one hand and focuses beams of electricity at the creatures as he slashes through them. He's clutching his side with the other hand as blood seeps through his fingers.

Rage burns in Tawson's eyes when he catches sight of me disappearing into the sky. Trees and vines burst from the ground to aid them, slaughtering large groups of the beasts. But, it seems never ending, one wave goes down and another takes its place. My mates are far outnumbered. I don't know how they will survive this.

Hearing my cries, Gin's face twists with despair. The moment he looks away from the fight, another beast leaps at him, trying to take him to the ground. But Gin grabs its neck with clawed hands and rips into its spine. As he tosses the body away another one attacks, keeping him busy so he can't shift fully into his Dragon.

Fen is buried under a mountain of beasts trying to claw through his stone skin. It isn't effective, but they are preventing him from coming after me. I lose sight of them as the rotted Griffon carries me far from my mates.

Tears track down my face, blurring my vision. Blood soaks into my dress as my wounds throb from the pressure. It feels as though the claws are going to tear straight through my body every time the Griffon flaps its wings. My hair clings to the blood and sweat covering my neck. The absence of my males leaves an aching hole in my heart, the emotional pain joining the physical, and I'm left with hopelessness.

As the Griffon climbs higher into the sky the temperature grows colder. My body, already stressed from the blood loss and talons digging in, starts to shiver violently. The world, already blurred from my tears, slowly turns black.

◆ ◆ ◆

Pain erupts throughout my body when I hit something hard, only briefly rousing from the darkness.

I waver in and out of unconsciousness. When I do wake briefly, my eyes refuse to open and my body won't budge when I try to move. I am trapped. Beings shuffle around me as footsteps echo. Confusion flashes through my mind. *Why is it echoing?* A pinch on my arm makes me flinch minutely, my body too heavy to actually move. *What are they doing to me?*

Muffled conversation sounds far away until a dark, angry, voice screams. My ears pop as noise filters in clearly.

"GIVE IT TO ME! GIVE ME HER BLOOD! I need to check it. I must know. Must know. This is the one I can feel it. Yes. Yes. Yes. She is perfect. The markers are here! Excellent. Cage her and do not heal her wounds. We want her weak. Weak. Weak." The voice trails off into a cackle that ends in a hacking wet cough. The madness is obvious, even without being able to see the male.

It isn't long before I'm out again. The angry voice's words echoing in my ears as blackness takes me. *Did they take my blood? Is that what that pinch was? Why am I perfect?*

What is going on?

It must be hours later, maybe even days, when I finally blink my eyes open. Confusion and pain is my entire world right now. There is no part of my body that doesn't hurt. Deep puncture wounds from the Griffon's talons cover my right shoulder. Checking my side, my dress is ripped up, and the injuries there look bad. They are still sluggishly bleeding, but it is slowing. The yellow and white puss weeping from the wounds concerns me the most.

Taking stock of the rest of my injuries, bruises and scrapes decorate my entire body. My left side is damaged almost worse than the right, I'm guessing I was dropped onto that side. At least I'm alive.

Closing my eyes, trying to focus through the pain to find my bonds, a sigh escapes. They're still there. Mentally reaching out to touch one of them, a flash of anger, fear and pain strikes me and somehow I know it's from Tawson. Repeating the same with each bond, the need to check that my mates truly are still alive drives my actions. Each of them have a range of emotions from fury and agitation to discomfort and worry. As my males feel me touching their bond, flashes of reassurance hit me, which then changes to rage when they sense my agony.

Sighing with relief, I back off the bonds for now, needing my focus on trying to get out of here. Hope clings to me, my mates will be able to find me. The thought of never seeing them again gives me the determination to get up, and push past my pain. I am more than just a nobody. I am their mate and I need them.

Eyeing the space around me, I gape as I take in my surroundings. There is a large cage encircling me, the bars appear to have been pulled up from the stone underneath me, obviously made from magic. It's fairly dark, but a faint glow clings to the walls. I'm uncertain what it is exactly. A curiosity that I would normally be fascinated with, but right now it is just a relief to have some light. The dripping of water echoes through the space. Stalactites and stalagmites decorate the ceiling and floor. That along with the strange glow on the walls tells me it is likely that I'm in a cave.

The griffon must have brought me to the mountains where they roost. I can't see the entrance to the cave so I must be deep inside. Even if I get out of this cage, escaping the cave could prove more difficult. I have a feeling the tunnels snake through the mountains like a labyrinth.

Glancing up, I sigh. The cage bars go fairly high but there is no roof. If I can climb out of here I may have a small chance to escape with my life.

Pausing, my eyes unfocus as I wonder why I'm alive. I thought those dark creatures were sent to kill, not capture. And what was with the rotting griffon? Fear strikes sharply, immobilizing me momentarily.

There must be a Necromancer!...

Oh Goddess, I'm in so much trouble. I've heard of them, and nothing good. Was it him that took my blood? Was that an infection induced nightmare or was that real?

Supposedly, Necromancers had been killed off in the last great war. They tried to take over control of Saforia with an army of the dead. But, the last King we had was able to defeat them, I don't remember how though.

Taking a deep breath, I let it out slowly to calm my nerves. Nope, I will not let the fear take over. I may be weak and unable to fight, but I am not ready to give up. I have to get back to my pack. I have to tell them how much I love them. It can't end like this!

It's a struggle to get to my feet, my right side throbbing. When I put pressure on my left leg it gives a little, most likely injured when the griffon dropped me. It doesn't help that my right side aches and my head feels fuzzy when I stand. I'm a mess of injuries, but I can't let that stop me from trying. I can't just give up. This mantra repeats in my mind over and over.

Limping over to the bars, I clutch them tightly. I'm pretty small, maybe I can squeeze through them. I can fit my arm out and my shoulder, but my breasts catch and my head is too big to fit. Sighing in frustration, I peer up at the top of the bars. I guess I'll have to climb.

As I contemplate how to climb up, faint footsteps echo in the distance. Immediately my body sinks back down. I don't want whoever this is to know I have the strength to stand. Being underestimated is my greatest asset right now. I really should go back to the spot I had woken in, but it would take far too much energy.

As the steps grow closer, chills drive down my spine. I don't want to deal with this. I stop my maudlin thoughts, now is *not* the time for crying.

"Hmmm... I'm surprised you're awake. You're weak, you should not have been able to wake up so soon." Craning my head back so I can see the male speaking to me, I wince at the pain of moving. Instead of the disgust and fear that wants to play across my face, I grimace and hope that's all he can see. The male is short, around Blue's height and plain. Everything about him is ordinary. Trimmed brown hair, brown eyes, and a slim build. I would easily overlook him in a crowd. The stranger could have been in the market and I'd have never known.

Shrugging in response, I wince again because that was stupid. My shoulders both ache like someone tried to rip my arms off.

"Nevertheless, I came to check how our favorite new captive is doing." Chuckling, his eyes bright with intrigue. "Nothing to say to me? Hmm... you are definitely a strange one. Every other Omega we've taken would not shut up. Always wailing and screaming, ugh. Awful. I can at least appreciate your silence. But, it won't last long." He smirks at me, darkness brimming on his face.

This is not the dark voice I remember from my waking nightmare. Who is he? I wonder if he's the one in charge of the beasts and collecting magic off the corpses. He could have been in my village following Blue before I saved him.

I don't dare make a sound, regardless of how many questions are on the tip of my tongue. I doubt this male will be of any help, he's enjoying my misery far too much. The malice in the stranger's eyes gives him away. Evil lives inside him and all it wants is to make me hurt. I memorize his features from his neatly cut hair, the gold hoops in his left ear, his pale skin, to the malicious smirk twisting his lips and the tiny freckles decorating his stubby nose. Tawson will want this information when I see him again.

His scrutinizing eyes linger on me while remaining silent, the cruelty in his gaze almost cutting. A finger taps on his chin as if contemplating what to do next, then he turns abruptly and marches out. I lay there long after his footsteps have gone, barely breathing. If he caught me trying to get out, it would only spell bad things for me. Closing my eyes, I exhale heavily. My hand rubs at my forehead, trying to massage away the headache. Just a few more minutes and then I'll get up.

All my muscles feel stiff when I attempt to drag myself up. I must have accidentally fallen asleep, which is only going to make my escape more difficult. Using the bars for stability, I pull myself to my feet and attempt to stretch out the kinks.

Climbing without cross bars will be challenging and I'm not sure I can do this. Ignoring my injuries I take a deep breath, I've got to try though.

My left hand reaches up, taking a firm grip of the stone bar. Grabbing on with my other hand, I pull while using my feet to brace against the base. Instead of climbing, blinding pain forces me to slide back down.

Kicking off my shoes, I think it may be easier without them... leaving them at the edge of the bars so I can reach them from the other side. If I get out, I'm going to need them.

Now, with bare feet I have a better grip of the stone. My side and shoulder ache with screaming pain and my arms shake as I slowly pull myself up. Managing a few feet before the agony in my punctured shoulder burns so badly my arm goes limp. I cling with my other hand and feet, trying to slide down slowly. My hand slips and I collapse in a heap at the base of the bars, groaning in anguish before passing out.

I don't think I lost consciousness for too long. Nothing seems to have changed.

Squeezing my eyes tight, I fight against tears of defeat. Clenching my fists, trying to ignore the agonizing pain in my right shoulder, I get angry. *This is stupid! How could this have happened? And why me? What does this black magic User want with me? What did he mean by the right markers?* I choke down my scream of rage, when I feel a tingle spread through my fingers and hands.

Claws form at my fingertips. I forgot! I forgot I had claws. Ugh, I'm so stupid. Keeping the feeling of rage in my mind, I return to the bars and dig my claws into the stone. Yes! I can do this. Even with my right arm not working properly and my left screaming in pain, I can do this.

It's slow going and I have to restrain my screams as I drag myself up the bars of stone. It feels like hours pass as I climb. I'm barely cognizant of my feet, I've grown claws there too making the climb a little easier.

I'm surprised no one has come to check on me since that male. But, maybe they assume I'll be too weak to do anything since I'm just an Omega? Or maybe they just don't think I could escape this. Honestly, without my claws I wouldn't be getting out of here.

Once at the top, I shimmy my legs through the bars and twist my upper body around so I slide down the outside of the cage. It's hard, so hard, and my injuries are making this feel near impossible. Sweat dampens my hair and trickles down my spine, but I ignore it. My muscles are screaming and as I start to slide down, my right arm gives out again and I cling as hard as I can with my left. But, I've lost my rage to the pain and my claws retract, my hands and feet revert back to normal. Closing my eyes, I brace myself. This is going to hurt, my muscles relax as I fall backwards.

The drop feels like it takes forever and

yet, also feels like it happens in a second. I'm sweating, crying and holding back any noise.

Arms band around me and pluck me out of the air. I can't hold back my keening, because there isn't one part of my body that doesn't hurt. The momentum from my fall being interrupted by strong arms is another sort of agony. I am thankful that I didn't hit the hard ground again though. That would not have helped.

A voice I recognize exclaims, "Oi, Wee One. Y'er lucky we followed you. I'm not sure you'd 've gotten out of here on your own."

Shocked, my eyes fly open, the scent finally registering. Peaches and cream, peaches and honey. Looking up into Brynd's dark eyes, I mutter, "Oh! Thank the Goddess." Catching the shocked look on his face before darkness closes in.

CH.32

My body being jostled wakes me from my unintended sleep. Firm rough hands hold me gently, but tightly against their chest. Inhaling the scent of peaches and cream brings comfort and thoughts of a hot summer day, juicy peaches and light fluffy cream slide down my throat. The taste is exquisite and it surrounds me in a cocoon of warmth, all I want to do is burrow in deep and stay here. The scent is familiar but my brain just can't place it.

"Shhh!" Someone whispers, harshly, "I scent about fifteen rotted things to the right. Hopefully, there is another way out, because I can't fight them all on my own and you need to protect her." It sounds like the chatty Orc I met in Gisham.

What are they doing here? Where am I? Why does my body hurt so bad? I have too many questions and as I swim out of the darkness of sleep the aches throughout my body grow more insistent. I'm too confused and in too much pain to understand what's happening.

My anxiety spikes as I open my eyes to blackness so dark I fear I'm blind. Blinking away the sleep lingering in my vision, I calm slightly when I pick up a faint glow along the walls and ceiling. I must be within the cave still. Vague outlines of stalactites cast ominous shadows along the rough and rocky walls. Tunnels branch off in too many directions from where we've stopped.

Brynd, the silent Orc brother, watches me closely. His brow scrunches, facial features laced with concern. It's as if he's asking *'Are you okay?'* and I'm not certain how to answer because I'm not completely sure what's happening. I'm flustered and in agony and I have no idea where we are.

He must see the confusion on my face because he gives me a sympathetic smile before shaking his head, like he's not sure why he asked that. It's pretty obvious I'm not okay.

Glancing down, I take stock of my body, spotting the tears in my dress and the puss leaking from large punctures in my side. My shoulder has the same wounds, while my legs are covered in bruises and my left side looks black and purple, it's possible something is broken. No wonder I hurt so much.

The more I wake up the more I remember. My pack! Oh Goddess, the attack! I quickly check my bonds, *oh, thank you Goddess* they're still there. I can sense they're not too badly injured, but there is a chaotic mix of panic, concern, anger and fear. When they notice me touching the bonds there's a clamour, all of them trying to see if I'm alright at once. It is almost too much for me, my head starts aching again and I squint my eyes shut.

My mates must have felt it when I passed out. Testing out my ability to use the bonds, I push love and serenity at them, attempting to calm them down. It takes a while but eventually works. A rush of affection from all of them fills me with warmth before I muffle the connection. I need to focus on getting out of this cave and why the Orc brothers are here.

Refocusing on Brynd, I open my mouth to ask him what the fuck is going on but he covers my mouth with one giant hand. My eyes narrow and I shoot him a glare for almost smothering with his pillow sized hand, but Brynd shakes his head before nodding over at his brother.

My eyes widen when I smell rotting

flesh and hear creatures close by. A chill of fear slithers over me and I'm thankful for his giant hand, the thought of even breathing too loudly scares me. The putrid scent of death makes me gag. It's so strong, stronger than the single griffon I'd met. There must be hundreds of decaying beasts. Chatty peers around a bend in the tunnel before flattening himself against the wall and motions us to do the same.

Brynd squishes me between him and the rocky wall. The sounds of footsteps and claws clicking against the stony ground echo around us. I can't tell which direction they're going, but if the look on Chatty's face is any indication, they're coming straight for us.

My palms sweat as my body tenses with a fear so strong it makes my heart thump wildly against my chest. I bury my face in Brynd's neck, trying to hide. I'm not made for this, I can't fight! What the hell have I gotten myself into? A few tears squeeze out and I know he can feel it. Brynd clutches me tighter in an attempt to give me comfort.

These creatures are going to find us, there's nowhere to hide! As the footsteps grow closer, I hold my breath, my eyes darting around over Brynd's shoulder so fast my brain doesn't have time to register anything.

Catching the other Orc brother's lips

moving, like he's muttering to himself, I frown in confusion. Chatty's eyes are closed and he lifts one hand moving it in a strange pattern. I almost gasp aloud, but choke it down because I don't want to be the reason we got caught.

Chatty's a User! I've never met one before, this is incredible! But... What in the world was a User doing in Gisham? And why are they following me? Me, of all people? I'm no one. A nobody from a tiny village at the far edge of our kingdom. There is nothing truly interesting about me, except... I am an Omega now. That is intriguing to many, especially Alpha's. Plus, whatever shifter blood that runs in my veins.

I rest my forehead against Brynd and try to breath shallowly, I can only hope his brother is capable of hiding us from these beasts... I'll save grilling them for when we're out of here, because I *will* be getting some answers.

The glow of a torch flickers off the cave walls telling me how close we are to our demise. Numerous shadows creep into view like a menacing nightmare, there's so many monsters heading our way. I can't tear my eyes away from my imminent murder. I think I'd rather watch my death coming for me, if there's a chance at survival, I'm going to grab onto it and cling for dear life. Hiding from danger is my first reaction but thoughts of my mates and the surge of love through the bond gives me the strength to face what's coming.

The group of monsters round the corner, so close to Brynd's brother. But, they don't even glance at him! They walk right past him, filling the tunnel with horrifying creatures. These monsters appear to be a variety of Shifters and animals sewn together seamlessly and animated into living beings. If this is a Necromancer, how are they using living beings to make these? How is Blue not the walking dead? I have too many questions about what the fuck is going on here, and why didn't they kill me?

Pungent decay permeates the air, the scent has me fighting a gag. The creatures are definitely dead and reanimated. Not all of them are like that though, I wonder why some of them are rotting and the others look fine? I hold my breath, tucking my nose into Brynd's neck in an effort to hide the sound of my shallow breathing. Worry threads through me, what if the spell only hides us from sight and not from sound?

There's so many of them, it feels like it takes hours for them to march past us but in reality it's probably only a few minutes.

As the light of their torches fade and the sound of their echoing steps grows quieter, I finally take a deep breath, sighing as I let it out. The tension leaks from my body as I wilt into Brynd. His arms give me a sense of safety, not as good as my mates, but still eases my anxiety. We need to get the fuck out of here, I peer up at him before glancing over at his brother.

I motion Brynd towards his brother, so I don't have to speak loudly, in case there are more beasts nearby. I'm surprised at how quietly he can move as he steps closer to his brother.

"How the fuck do we get out of here?" I whisper sharply, hoping to the Goddess that they know the way. Before I let him answer I ask, exasperated, "And what in the world is your name? I can't keep calling you Chatty or Brynd's brother. I mean I could but..." my anxious words cut off by a hand over my mouth.

I glare at Chatty, holding back his laughter. Brynd's body shakes as he silently chuckles at my word vomit and I work to hide my wince at being jarred from his amusement.

"Shh.. Wee One. Let's not call attention to ourselves, hmm? I don't relish wasting more magic and energy on hiding from those things again. I'd rather save it for when we're really in need, eh?" He smiles at me fondly before bowing. "Let me introduce myself properly.

The name's Brenth, User, Orc, and fabulous dancer."

The last bit has me biting back a laugh. Nodding, I try to repeat my question but his hand is still over my mouth. I lick it, if he's going to cover my mouth he's going to get slobbered.

Pulling his hand away quickly, he looks at it and then me in shock before covering his own mouth as if to hold back his guffaw. I'm quite pleased with myself for surprising him. This has been a welcome distraction from the agony and terror.

Once he has himself under control he makes some strange hand signs at me, or Brynd. I'm confused, is he casting another spell? But Brenth nods before looking at me next and whispering, "Alright, Wee One. Let's get the fuck out of here, eh?"

I'll take that as a yes, they know how to escape this maze of horrors. I exhale with relief but remember that we may have some distance to cover before I can actually relax. I'm just happy that I'm not on my own. Those hours, or days, in that stone cage, alone in the dark were terrifying enough.

With Brenth leading the way, taking his time to check around corners before waving us on, we proceed through the tunnels. Brynd trying not to jostle me as we move. I doubt we could move very quickly if I were hobbling after them, my side and leg are killing me. I'm concerned about the puss leaking from the wounds the griffon left on me.

We take too many turns to count and I start to wonder if they actually know how to get out of here. Three separate times we've had to hide behind stalagmites or duck into emptyish rooms to avoid more creatures marching through the tunnels. Anxiety coils my muscles tight, every movement aches, and it is not helping my wounds.

We have one extremely close call when a group of ten rotted griffons march past our hiding spot and one of them stops. It lifts its humongous disgusting head to sniff around, turning sharply left and right before stepping closer to us.

Clenching my jaw shut to prevent my teeth from chattering, a cold sweat gathers on my forehead. I don't think I can sustain this state much longer. My wounds are getting to me, I've lost too much blood and I definitely have a serious infection sapping my strength.

As the griffon gets closer to our hiding spot, Brenth starts up his magic barrier to hide us. None of us want to have to battle in these close quarters, especially because it is likely the sounds will call other beasts. We just can't fight them all off, not if we want to survive.

It is tense as we wait for this thing to leave us be. Eventually it snorts and shakes its head before trotting after its brethren, leaving us to deflate as we all sink to the ground.

Brenth wipes sweat off his brow before he glances at Brynd and then myself with pinched lips and a desperate look in his eye. "Lass, I dunno if we'll make it out today. We might have to find a room we can barricade ourselves into so I can rest. My magic stores are running low and I don't know how many more times I can hide us before fighting is our only option."

My eyes are wide and I'm shaking my head before he's even stopped speaking. "No. No. No. We need to get out now!" Panicking, my heart races so fast I'm sure I'm going to pass out again and my stomach rolls with nausea and fear. "No, Brenth. They did something to me when I was mostly unconscious... I couldn't move or open my eyes but I heard them. They took my blood and did something to it. This voice... this mad voice hissed something about having the right markers. If they notice me gone they will not let us leave easily." I'm shaking so hard I don't know how Brynd is still able to hold on to me.

Both of them are staring at me wide eyed. It's silent for long minutes as they process what I've just said.

"Okay. Okay, Wee One. We'll find the exit. I know it's close, but it seems the closer we get the more beasts we encounter. This will not be a simple escape." Brenth sighs heavily, swiping more sweat off his brow. He mutters a few swears under his breath before standing.

CH.33

It must be hours later that we come upon a cavernous room. Even with the lit torches, the room is still fairly dark but, on the far side, sunlight shines like a beacon of hope. We're almost out of here. I want to cry with relief, instead I just clutch tightly to Brynd and exhale shakily.

Brenth waves us back against the wall, not letting us enter. I hear noises after a few silent beats. Strange squawks, chittering and growls echo from the room beyond. The brothers flatten themselves against the wall, Brenth muttering, casting a spell. Hopefully he has enough to conceal us again. I want to wail at the thought of us being so damn close to the exit with yet another obstacle blocking our freedom.

We wait, all of us holding our breath. Listening for the noises to either come closer to us or further away. When it sounds like neither, we shuffle a little closer to the doorway. I try to peek over Brenth to see what's happening, but he's very tall and I'm still tucked close to Brynd. I manage to catch a few glimpses of the cavern beyond.

There's a group of animals, not the creatures formed out of black magic but actual, whole, animals. They could be Shifters but I'm not sure how to tell unless I see them shift. They're all standing in the center of the room, inside a salt circle. None of those animals would normally be caught in the same room but they're all just standing, docile, making the occasional noise. Almost, like they've been hypnotized.

None of us move. I think the brothers are almost as afraid as I am. Letting myself sink back into Brynd again, I try to give my aching body a rest. The strain of sitting up and looking into the room too much for me.

The animal noises cut off abruptly and, if I hadn't been looking at Brenth I would have missed him jerk back slightly in shock. He steps back, as quietly as he can and flattens himself against the wall no longer watching the room.

Looking pale, he swallows heavily as he wipes his palms on his pants. Whatever he saw must have been bad because, so far, he's only shown me good humor and strength.

Bringing a trembling hand up he puts one finger to his mouth, silently telling us to be quiet. Like we aren't already trying not to even breathe, lest we get caught.

The sound of chanting starts and slowly grows louder, a deep male voice. It sounds awfully similar to the mad, dark voice that I heard earlier. I wonder if it is the Necromancer turning those animals into more monstrosities. But, then, I hear the sound of chains and the cries of many beings. The wails of 'help', 'don't do this', and 'please, have mercy', sound through the cavern and into the passage we're hiding in.

The scent of rot permeates the air making my eyes water at the stench. The thought of all those beings dying or transformed into beasts hurts my soul and I can't do a thing to stop it. I doubt the brothers are strong enough on their own either, otherwise, I'm sure they would have done something other than hide.

Closing my eyes as the chanting continues, I try to block out the noises but it's no use. The cries of the chained beings turn to screams of pain, echoing loudly off the rocky wall. The sounds of animals screeching clashes with the shrieks of beings until everything goes silent. A single tear escapes as I huddle into Brynd, hating myself a little for just letting this happen but knowing there is absolutely nothing I can do. I wish my mates were here. They would know what to do. The pack is trained for this, they would be able to kill this unholy nightmare, I hope. Thoughts of my males momentarily distract me from the horrors in the next room.

We wait until the clinking of the chains falls silent and the sound of someone muttering and cursing draws further from us. Brenth shuffles closer to the doorway and scans the cavern. He holds a hand up to stop us from moving any closer, someone must still be in there.

"Git. To the barracks. You will be called upon when needed." Another voice snarls, but it isn't the same being who was chanting. My stomach flips when I hear the male speak, the same bland sneer taunted me in my cage. He sounds bitter and angry and I pray the Goddess will help conceal us.

The tromping of many feet exit the cavern, luckily not using the same tunnel we're currently in. After a moment of silence, a single set of footsteps reverberates through the room and tunnel. I can't tell which direction they're going until Brenth tenses and reaches for a sword strapped across his back.

Shit, are we going to get caught? Is Brenth strong enough to fight whoever this is? I don't think this is the Necromancer. My gut tells me that this male is the black magic User and I do not think we can fight him.

I thought Brenth cast a spell to conceal us? Is it not working anymore? I can't handle the stress of this. I just want my nest, my bakery and my pack. I don't want to be here anymore, I hold back my sniffles, letting tears fall freely onto Brynd's chest.

The footsteps grow closer before they stop, right at the entrance to our tunnel. Looking up, I catch sight of the male. I didn't hear his name nor the Necromancers. But he is so plain, it is hard to imagine he is the same male that gives off an air of malice. You can almost feel the darkness wafting off him. I can only wonder about his motives for aiding with something so horrible.

He sniffs the air, and I hope he cannot smell us. Squeezing my eyes shut I pray. I pray that he won't find us. I pray that we will get out of this. We're so close. I just need him to leave.

I can't catch his scent over Brynds, since my nose is mostly tucked into his chest. I don't know if I really want to know what he smells like either. He's helping someone so foul he must smell just as bad as those rotting things the Necromancer has created.

I guess Brenth's spell is working because he shrugs and walks away from where we're standing. Brenth watches him, probably to note when he exits the cavern.

When his footsteps can no longer be heard, Brenth waves us a little closer before stepping into the cavern.

I gape in disgust. The salt circle is gone and the ground is covered in blood and other things that I don't really want to think about.

Brynd blocks my vision with a hand. Trying to prevent me from seeing the horrors that were performed here. I pat his hand in appreciation, because I really did not need to see that. Nudging him away from my face I keep myself from looking down again. He moves his hand reluctantly, as he continues walking towards the sunlight.

I hadn't seen much when I peeked in before the whole black magic, Necromancy, animals and beings being smushed together thing. But now that I have the chance, I spy shelves carved into the rocky walls. Jars filled with strange and gruesome things, eyeballs, fingers, brains. Manacles hang from the walls and chains dangle from the ceiling. I do not want to know why, I'm sure it's for some horrific purpose that would add to the nightmares I'm already going to have. A long wooden table near one of the other tunnels sits littered with different knives and tools. Deciding that I'd really rather not look at anything else, I close my eyes. This place is filled with atrocities.

The three of us are as silent as possible as we creep across the room. And by silent I mean neither of their footsteps are making any sounds and I'm curious if Brenth is using magic to silence them. I thought he was running low?

I'm listening hard for any noise to indicate the Necromancer or anyone else is coming back but everything is quiet, thankfully.

Beyond the exit of the cave, the sun slowly rises over the Mikta Mountains casting a warm yellow glow over the land below. One final tear creeps down my face. I wasn't sure we would make it out of there. For a while I was sure we would be caught. The Orcs would be killed and I would be thrown back into that cage. I really don't want to know what they had planned for me. Shuddering, I squeeze my eyes shut attempting to wash the chilling thoughts from my mind.

I had guessed the griffon had taken me to the mountains, but I couldn't be sure until now. We take a moment to gather our bearings near the cave opening. My shoulders droop as I inhale the crisp morning air, thankful I can no longer smell the decay that infested those tunnels. The most persistent concern now is how the hell we're getting down.

We're high above the sparse tree line, and the view is awe inspiring. The area below doesn't appear familiar, not that I'd be able to tell anyways. The trees eventually give way to grassy hills on the right, and to the left a village similar to Gisham lies far in the distance. Mountains obscure the sightlines making it difficult to determine our location. Honestly, all I really want is to get away from the Necromancer's hideout and back to my mates.

My eyes flick up to Brynd, but when I attempt to speak, his large hand silences me again. Squinting at him in irritation, disgruntled by his method of muffling me, I let out a silent curse before I relent. We might be out but we're not away from this place yet. We don't want to draw any attention to ourselves. We're still too close. Without knowing when my captors will return, it would be best to put some distance between us and them. A shudder runs through me as I wince at the thought of more beasts coming after me. I've had enough of them to last a lifetime.

CH.34

B renth makes more hand signs at Brynd, who bobs his head in return. Then, we're off, following Brenth down the path away from the cave.

It would be convenient if Brenth knew some healing magic. This whole thing would suck so much worse if we went through all of that just for me to die from a stupid infection. But, I'll wait until we're away from here before bringing it up. I'd hate for them to have rescued me for nothing.

The narrow, uneven path slows us down. Eventually, the path just ends and we pause for a moment.

Brenth whispers, "This is going to get challenging. Wee One, how strong do you feel? We're gonna need ya to hang on to Brynd's back like a pack so he has his hands free for climbing." He grimaces at my various injuries before shaking his head.

Wincing in response, I mutter. "Yeeeaaahhh," Stretching out the word, "um, I'm pretty bad off, I think the puncture wounds are infected. But I swear if you can get me off this mountain I'll hang on to him for dear life. I'd rather chance falling off a mountain than go back to that place." Snapping my mouth closed, rambling isn't the best idea right now.

Quirking his lip a little, he gives me the briefest of smiles. "Hmm... Brynd? You got enough juice to heal her a little so she won't fall?"

Brynd gives a silent affirmation before setting me down. I wobble, my legs not holding my weight very well. Reaching out blindly, I try to grab anything to steady myself. Warm hands grasp my shoulders bracing me. Exhaling slowly, I lean back into Brenth, thankful that they're here. I whisper a quick 'thanks' before peering up at Brynd.

I should have realized that, with them being brothers, they'd both be Users. Brynd gives me a thumbs up before I see his mouth move, no sound coming out, and he makes a motion with both hands towards me.

Bracing for the buzz of magic, my muscles tense, but I don't feel anything. I hadn't planned on closing my eyes, but I blink them open in confusion when nothing happens. The moment my eyes open, a tugging sensation pulls on the deepest wounds followed by white hot pain. It's as if the toxins are being extracted from my body. The lacerations slowly stitch back together. My jaw clenches so tight I fear my teeth will crack. Tears stream down my cheeks freely, but I refuse to make a single sound. I didn't think being healed would be so painful, but there's no way I'm going to make any noise and get us caught. Horrified, I gape down at my side as the griffon's claw slowly backs out of my flesh. Fresh blood and puss dribbles out, soaking into my torn dress, slowing and scabbing right before my eyes. Awe helps dull the pain as I watch the gash seal and the claw drop to the ground. The knitting sensation stops when scabs fully cover the wounds.

Brynd is sweating and his normally moss green skin is now more of an olive tone. Concern laces my brows at how pale he's grown, did he overdo it? I want to shout at him for hurting himself to help me. I could have waited!

Although I feel much stronger than I did, my left leg is still bruised and aching but I don't care about that. I struggle to my feet and throw my arms around his waist... Well, with my short stature it's more like his hips, then I whisper a litany of '*Thank you's*'. Squeezing as tight as my arms can, I try to show him how grateful I am for what he's done for me.

His arms come around me in a gentle hug, being careful of all the other injuries littering my body.

"Alright, alright, you two." Brenth chuckles softly, "we should get moving, I want to be much further from this place before we stop and figure out where exactly we are."

Nodding against Brynd, I'm hesitant to meet his gaze. "How am I supposed to get to your back? It'll be like climbing a mountain, which I'm not sure I'm any good at, since I've never tried..." I trail off muttering to myself about mountainous Orcs and not being able to jump that high.

Brynd's body shakes with silent laughter. I shake my head and avert my eyes while hiding a smile. I guess I am feeling better since I started rambling again.

I have to choke back a shriek of surprise when Brenth picks me up and places me on Brynd's back. My arms wrap around his neck and my legs as far as they can around Brynd's ribs, which isn't far because he's a very large Orc.

"A little warning would have been nice!" I snap at Brenth in a hushed whisper when I've got myself settled.

He just smiles jovially. "Sorry, Wee One. You must admit, It was quite entertaining." Brenth's smile drops as he scans the area. "Let's get the fuck out of here. Follow my path, I'll guide us off this blasted mountain and to safer ground."

He contemplates the drop, I assume to figure out the best place to start climbing down, then gingerly swings himself over the edge. *Did he just jump off the mountain!?* I suck in a harsh breath as Brynd does the same. But, calm slightly when I realize there's a narrow ledge and we're not going to fall to our death.

I'm impressed with their ability to move so nimbly, they're such large males that it took me by surprise.

We follow Brenth down the mountainside. Eventually, I close my eyes against the nausea at the thought of us falling. My anxiety spikes and I have to open them again, because it was much worse not being able to see where we're going. Each time we drop down my stomach does a flip, thinking this is it, we're going to die. But, I'm surprised every time he finds a foothold.

Clinging to Brynd, I loosen my grip when I feel him cough at the pressure. The heat of him beneath my body, the way his shoulders flex under my grasp and the muscles bulging in his biceps as he works hard to keep us from death all culminate in my arousal. My mind wanders and I can't help but admire his strength, I never realized how attractive arms could be.

When the perfume of my slick unfurls around us I focus my attention down for a distraction. *No getting turned on while death may be imminent,* I lecture myself. Also, these males aren't my pack! What is wrong with me?

Brynd is panting and sweating from the strain of climbing down a mountain. I worry, for a moment, that he's getting tired but he proves me wrong.

Brenth finds a ledge for us all to fit on and makes some hand signs while announcing, "We're going to take a short break here. Sit down, breathe and drink some water." Helping me off Brynd's back Brenth sets me down in between them, handing me a waterskin.

Icy water burns against the dryness in my throat as I take a long drink. My eyes widen when I realize I haven't had anything to eat or drink since I'd been with my pack. I have no idea how long ago I was taken. Luckily, the anxiety of this climb is holding my hunger at bay.

Thinking of my mates, I check my

bonds. As soon as I open myself to them, they all clamour for my attention and it instantly makes my head ache. Thrusting that down the bonds, I try to get my males to quiet themselves.

One by one each bond dampens until it's just Tawson pushing worry and fear down the bond at me. I attempt to tell him I'm okay, I'm safe. Not being able to connect through their telepathic link really sucks. It would be so much easier if I could just use words to explain what's going on. Instead I push tranquility, and love back at him, trying to explain that I am ok. That I miss my mates. I push those feelings at each male, so they know I'm thinking of them. Tawson returns with a questioning feeling, and I have no idea what he's trying to ask.

Grunting in frustration, I try to think of how to tell them I'm lost but okay.

Brenth looks at me with a raised brow as he takes a swig from his waterskin. "What's wrong, Wee Lassie?"

"It's my pack. I'm trying to figure out how to tell them I'm okay, but I have no idea where we are and no idea how to get back to them." Weariness dragging my shoulders down, my body curls in on itself.

"Aye, tis a challenge to do without words, Love. But, don't worry too much. They can use the bond to figure out which direction you're in so they'll come across us eventually. You can do the same. We are going to do what we can to help you." He pats my head gently, probably afraid of knocking me off the mountain with his massive mitt.

Another hand pats my leg in sympathy, and I glance over at Brynd, giving him a grateful smile as I lean into his side before looking back at Brenth. "I don't know how to thank you both for finding me and getting me out of there," pausing, I squint my eyes in suspicion. "How did you know where to find me? It's not like that place is easily accessible or common knowledge."

He has the grace to look sheepish, and a blush tints his cheeks yellow. "Ahh... well... ya see... When we met you in Gisham I may have placed a magical tracker on you... If you hadn't noticed, we're scent compatible and it isn't as common as you'd think. We just wanted a chance to talk to ya." He's so bashful, it's actually very cute.

It takes me a second to process what he actually said. When it sinks in I look at both of them in shock. "Wait, what? No... Really? Hmm... I just thought you guys both smelled nice and that meant, generally, that you were not bad males, or beings that wouldn't hurt me... Isn't that part of the reason we have developed such an enhanced sense of smell? To know who to avoid and who would make good, strong, mates? Or was I taught wrong? I mean, my small village doesn't have a schoolhouse or anything, the children are all taught by their parents, or the villagers who deigned to pay any attention to the orphan in their midst. I mean..." I shove my hair off my face, irritated as it falls in my eyes, "When I think about it, it's actually highly likely that I wasn't taught all the right things. Considering we're such a small village, at the most Southern point of Saforia, so far from the Crown and the big city, the knowledge could be wrong. I know we got a lot of merchants..." My scattered thoughts are cut off by Brynd's hand, again. But I'm not upset this time. I was lost in thought, incoherently muttering since my mind and body are overly exhausted from this traumatic experience.

Brenth no longer seems bashful, he's holding his stomach trying to keep himself from roaring in laughter. Brenth wheezes as he tears up, he's working so hard to contain himself. They've figured out that my mouth just kind of... does whatever it wants and I have very little control over it. At least I haven't said anything comparing their *size* to their ginormous hands and feet, but it's early days and I'm sure my mouth will get away from me soon enough.

Wiping his eyes when he's done laughing, Brenth gives me a fond look. "Aye. You are correct about the scents that smell nice to you, or at least aren't offensive, meaning the being will likely not harm you. But, the ones that smell so good it makes your mouth water, or other things." He gives me a cheeky wink, and my cheeks flush. "Those are the ones that are compatible with ya. The ones that would likely make good mates. I'm sure the Researchers in the capital have more concrete information in their Libraries, but this is really all we need to know."

Nodding that I heard him, I stare off into the distance while I think about this. All of my mates, current ones anyways, smell so good I have the urge to roll around in their clothes and make sure their scents are all over me. I do get that feeling around these two but maybe not as strongly. Could that be because I'd already been bitten and claimed by the time I met them? Or is it because, while we are compatible we would make better friends than mates?

Turning to ask Brenth this, he cuts me off as my mouth opens. "We need to keep moving. I promise we'll answer your questions later. When we're somewhere a little safer than this." He gets to his feet with a stretch, drawing my eyes to his beefy chest and rippling abs.

Brynd wraps an arm around me and

picks me up as he stands. I look over my shoulder at his chest too, wondering how it would feel under my hands, my tongue... I shake my head to clear the dirty thoughts from my mind. For one; *they are not your mates*, and secondly; *we are still in danger, stop ogling the sexy Orcs and focus on getting the hell out of here*, I tell myself, hoping my perfume hasn't wafted up to them.

Okay, maybe I don't see them as just friends...

Brenth smirks at me as his hands lift me to Brynd's back, holding on just a second too long before letting go. Nope, I did not hide my perusal of their forms very well. I just don't think I have it in me to suppress that part of me, not now that the Omega inside me has been awoken. She demands so many things that had never crossed my mind before.

It's definitely been a learning curve, and I don't think I'll ever figure it all out. Some of it is just instinct and that scares me a little because I do some things before I even think about it. Like, biting my mates. I didn't know Omegas bit their mates back. No idea that it was required to ensure the claiming was completed, but that's what it felt like when I bit each of them in turn. No one can take them from me now, metaphysically, at least.

As we start the harrowing process of descending, again, I think about what Brenth said. I should be able to use the bond to determine the direction of my mates. When I look inwards and focus on the bonds, their emotions clamour for my attention. I try to examine them without actually touching them, but nothing happens. Instead, I attempt something different. It's almost like unfocusing my eyes but internally... To visualize the bonds but not get stuck in the enthusiastic feelings from my mates. As I do, a strange sensation builds. I have the strongest urge to go right... to the east and down a little. The distance sends a pang of sadness straight to my heart. I miss them. But, I believe these Orc brothers will do as promised, and get me back to my mates.

CH.35

It took all day to climb down off the mountain and my arms and legs are shaking with exhaustion from hanging off Brynd like a backpack. Night blankets the land by the time their feet touch the ground. Looking up at the cliff face we just scaled, it feels like it should have taken much longer. But these two are seriously tall and extremely agile, they made it look easy. I'm placed on my feet as we all take a short break after that descent. But, Brynd doesn't appear any more exerted than Brenth, even though he's been carrying my extra weight.

That's more than I can say for myself, and I didn't do any climbing. My arms and legs are exhausted from clinging to him so tightly. The stress of everything is getting to me. I'm way more tired than I should be. Then again, there's still some heavy bruising and my leg hurts so much more after keeping such a firm grip all day. My injuries require a healer, but I doubt there's any nearby. *Which direction was that town?* On top of that, my mates call to me. Now that I know which direction they're in, a driving need pulls me towards them.

"I know it's dark and we don't know exactly where we are, but we should get further away from here. I have an itch on the back of my neck, like someone is watching, and I'd like to be as far from here as possible tonight," Brenth states, no longer whispering but subdued. It has been an exhausting, trying day. I mean, who knows how long we were wandering through the tunnels before we'd found the way out. It could have been days but without light, there was no way to tell.

We've paused at the base of the mountains, the moonlight just bright enough to make out the lightly treed space around us. My agreement is quick to follow Brenth's statement, with a nod my eyes flick up to Brynd. He's sporting a serious, but thoughtful look on his face as he makes a few hand signs to Brenth. Watching as they motion back and forth, I think it must be a silent language. I've never seen anything like it before, but it makes sense a visual language would exist for those who couldn't speak or hear.

I'm jolted out of my tired musings, releasing a squawk of surprise and flail my arms, smacking into a hard chest as I'm suddenly scooped up into strong arms. They must have finished their conversation while I was lost in thought again.

My eyes fly up, expecting Brynd, but I'm surprised to note Brenth carries me this time.

"A little warning would have been nice!" I hiss at him, before all the questions I have bubble out of me, "Do you guys have a secret hand language? Is Brynd not able to talk? Can he hear me?"

Brenth struggles to hold back a smile, staring down at me with amusement shining from his eyes.

"It isn't really a secret language," his chuckle is soft and full of mirth, "it is called sign language. It's taught in the capital, there are more mute beings than you'd expect. Brynd was born without a voice, we have no idea why. But our clan did not want a defective Orc and tried to kill him when it was discovered. Luckily, our parents did not wish him dead, yet they did not want to lose their standing in the clan either. So, they took him to an orphanage in Varough. I did not wish to part from my twin so I went with him. I was furious that they would treat someone this way and wanted no part of them. I'm still angry with our parents for abandoning him, but it is what it is."

He shrugs his big shoulders, the delight he'd expressed at my uncontrollable mouth has disappeared and sadness pulls his lips into a frown. Brenth heaves a big sigh, looking away as he collects himself.

Giving his head a shake as if to throw off glum thoughts, Brenth continues, "he can hear, there has never been any problems with his ears, but sometimes we prefer to sign. Especially when we're doing something or going somewhere we shouldn't. It's quite useful when we need to be quiet, like when we're rescuing a damsel from a Necromancer." He cocks an eyebrow, his teasing smile returning full force as he glances down at me.

I'm in awe of the both of them, but also so angry at their clan. How could someone decide to murder a child just because they can't speak? How dare they! The anger builds within me and my hands tingle, a sign they've formed claws again. Hanging on to that anger, I stare at my hands, enjoying the feeling this time. Enjoying the fact that I have some form of defence, a powerful feeling for someone who's never really had any strength.

A sharp intake of breath from above startles me and I lose it. A sigh gusts out as my hands revert back to normal.

"Lass, did I just see your hands shift?

Are you a sweet little shifter? Those looked like kitten paws, how adorable." Brenth smiles widely at my frown.

"I am not a sweet little kitten. I am fierce!" My statement is ruined with a snort of laughter. I wave my hands in front of me, clearing my laughter away, as I get a hold of myself. "Okay, okay, I'm not really fierce. I can't seem to shift any more than my hands and feet. So I don't really know if I am a cat shifter, but I get claws when I'm extremely angry."

A 'hmm' is his only response as he looks at me consideringly. Shrugging, I return to our original conversation.

"How did you learn the sign language? Can you teach me too? I think it would be very useful to know, especially if I ever have to sneak around again. You're both Users, too? I saw you do magic and Brynd healed my infection and some of the wounds." I attempt to limit my questions, but my never ending curiosity makes it extremely difficult.

Brenth holds eye contact with Brynd for a moment before answering me, "Tawny, a woman who helps out at the orphanage, taught us. She noticed him trying to use rudimentary hand gestures and figured out he couldn't speak, offering to teach us if we'd be willing to help her out by cleaning her yard and doing other things for her. I think she knew we would refuse otherwise, because no one does anything for free. She eventually became a sort of... mother figure for us." He pauses, staring up at the sky with a fond smile before continuing,

"Tawny's a human Beta who lives alone, helping out at the orphanage because she was lonely and wanted children. She eventually adopted my brother and me as her own. When Tawny realized we had an innate talent for magic, she helped us get into the User's college." Brenth speaks so fondly of his mother, the real one who actually cared for them both. It makes me wish I could meet her and thank her for being such a good woman.

Yawning, I lean into his chest, tucking my nose into his shoulder. "She sounds amazing, Brenth. I'd love to meet her someday. I have a million more questions for you but I'm so tired. Would you mind if I slept a little? I'm not very helpful with travelling, since my leg is still damaged." My eyes grow heavy and his face blurs as my lids slowly close. "Also, did I say my mates feel like they are that way?" I point to the right towards the mountains a little.

"Sleep, Wee One. We'll travel for a while yet. I'll wake you when we make camp. And don't worry, we'll head towards your mates. I have some questions for them." His chest rumbles into a soft purr under me. A feeling of comfort and safety washes over me as I fall into a fitful sleep.

My body is overly hot. The two large bodies on either side of me give off a ton of heat. Taking a moment to assess my injuries, I run my hand over all the bruises and cuts I can remember. My left leg, hip, and shoulder are still badly bruised from being dropped, but thank the Goddess the puncture wounds are no longer infected and bleeding. They're scabbed over and healing well. Still hurting, but I can definitely move better now. My whole body is still exceedingly sore. My stomach swims with nausea, but I figure it is due to the pain. I used so many muscles I didn't even know I had, to climb out of that stupid cage. I'm pretty impressed with myself.

Rolling to my back, I take in both brothers' forms. Brenth snoozes heavily, nowhere near as deadly and frightening when his face relaxes in sleep. My eyes meet Brynd's dark ones, he's already looking down at me, his lips quirked into an amused smile.

It's still dark out, so I must not have been asleep for long. "Morning? Or... evening?" Pausing, my cheeks warm. "I mean, hello. Yep, that's better. Have you gotten any rest? Or are you on watch right now? I know you can't tell me but I'm gonna talk at you anyways, okay?" I stop to breathe, taking in Brynd's silent laughter as I sleepily ramble at him,

"I feel like I need to get all my thoughts out because I've been through something, ya know? This is not how my life is supposed to go. I was never the type to crave adventure and travelling. The best way to spend an evening is making a blanket fort, eating something tasty that I've whipped up and cuddling by a fire! Not... being kidnapped by frightening beasts, finding out Necromancers are still around, and thrown in a cage deep in the mountains. This experience is going to give me nightmares for the rest of my life." Faltering, I suck in a deep breath, looking around our little camp. My eyes are drawn to the roaring fire calling to me like a moth to the flame.

"Can we move over to the fire? I don't want to wake Brenth. He looks like he needs the rest. Both of you worked hard to get me out of that hell and you guys deserve a break." Flicking a shaky smile at Brynd, my nerves are soothed when he smiles and bobs his head.

Plucking Brenth's arm off my waist, Brynd tugs me closer toward his chest. I did not expect Brenth to be a huge cuddler, once I'm free of him, Brynd scoops me up like a doll and gingerly places me on a rock near the fire.

Plunking himself down on another rock, Brynd leans to the side and pulls a pack onto his lap. How did I not notice they had a pack with them? Did they have it the whole time in the cave? Nope, what am I thinking? Of course they did, where else would it have come from... we're in the middle of nowhere!

He pulls out an already skinned and prepped Burrel, it's a small, chunky and fluffy critter that lives in burrows at the base of trees and eats the nuts that fall off of them. They do make a tasty dinner, they have lots of fatty meat on them. But, they are small so I doubt one will feed both of us. Brynd is a lot bigger than me.

Once it's propped over the flame, the scent of roasting meat permeates the air and my mouth begins to water, I can't remember the last time I ate. *How many days has it been since I was taken? How many days did it take to get out of there?*

Zoning out, staring at the roasting meat, I jump and start slipping off my rock when Brynd pokes me in the side, forcing out a giggle as I flail trying to catch myself. I thump onto the ground and toss a disgruntled scowl at Brynd, hiding my wince of pain.

"Listen mister!" Brynd's face lights up with delight at my reaction so I give him the meanest stare I can and inform him, "There will be no tickling, you hear me?" Wagging a finger at him, I clamber back onto the rock, trying to channel Tawson's serious demeanor. Which, I don't think it works because he laughs silently at me.

Throwing my hands up in frustration, I groan, that never seems to work. I bet I look as angry as a kitten. Exhaling heavily, my shoulders slump as I'm reminded of Rafe. He would have said something humorous and had everyone laughing. I miss his bright presence.

Finally, Brynd gets a hold of himself, swiping a tear off his face and pats me on the head. I glare and purse my lips, but he just smiles at me and points at the roasting meat. I think he is asking if I want it crispier. I mean, who doesn't love it when the outside is crispy and the inside is full of juicy meat? I give him a decisive nod. "A little longer and it'll be perfect. I wish I had ingredients so I could show you guys my appreciation with baked goods." Huffing sadly, I miss my bakery... and my pack.

Brynd surprises me by plucking me off my rock and tucking me into his lap before he grabs the roasted meat. I may have let out a mewl of surprise, definitely supporting my angry kitten theory. Rolling my eyes at myself, I shake my head and smile.

He starts pulling pieces off the meat and I gasp. "Wait! What are you doing? Don't burn yourself! You have to let it cool first! I thought you guys were well used to travelling?" I'm shocked when he doesn't act like it hurts at all to touch burning hot meat.

He quirks an eyebrow at me and I realize this must be an Orc thing. They are known to have incredibly tough skin so I guess he barely feels the heat.

"I can't eat that yet, it's too hot for my tender skin. Us humans... or, shit. I'm not fully human! I wonder if shifting would have healed me if I'd been able to shift fully... But all I've been able to do is get claws to come out." I muse, noting Brynd staring at me with a question plastered on his face.

Right. He missed my conversation with Brenth yesterday as he scouted ahead. "Oh, um.. yeah, so... Like a week ago or maybe it was only a few days." Waving my hands as if to clear that away, I continue. "We noticed that strong emotions, mainly anger, make my hands shift to paws and claws. My mates think I have Shifter blood in me. They believe mating may have triggered or forced the latent genes to activate. A barmaid tried flirting with one of my mates in front of me, and if they hadn't caught me, I was going to claw her eyes out so she couldn't look at them anymore... These

Omega instincts are no joke!" My eyes scan his face for any traces of judgement, I can't help but fidget with the skirt of my dress as I wait for Brynd's reaction.

He starts chuckling silently again, but his heated stare sends a rush of warmth through me. But it's the prideful look in Brynd's eyes that have me inhaling sharply. *Well, okay then.* I don't think my crazy actions are a turn off for him.

Brynd brings the savory meat to my mouth and pauses, waiting for me to accept his offering. For a moment I'm hesitant, but then my body takes over and closes the distance. My mouth parts, taking small delicate bites. Our eyes lock, and it's like I'm in some sort of trance. Are my instincts pushing me to accept an Alpha's care?

Brynd takes his time feeding me, until I shake my head. I'm quite full now, exhaustion creeping over me again.

I watch with fascination as he eats the rest of it, bones and all. Warmth grows in my stomach as he licks his fingers, I'm mesmerised by his movements. My eyes trail down the line of his throat as he swallows, down to his strong chest. Brynd's rippling with muscles and it's not like I'm unused to seeing it. Maybe it's the rich mossy green of his skin, stretched tight over his abs as he bends over to rummage in his pack. I've never been more thankful that Orc's don't seem to wear shirts.

Shaking myself out of these lusty thoughts I refocus on the fire and try to think about boring facts instead. Okay, right, Orcs have very strong teeth and the ability to digest pretty much anything. They're mostly carnivores, eating very little vegetables. Until we find a town, meat will be fine for me, but eventually I'm going to need something green to supplement my diet.

Tossing the roasting stick into the fire, Brynd wipes his hands off on a rag he pulls out of the pack before handing me a waterskin. I drink deeply, feeling parched after the salty meat. Without thinking too hard about it, I cuddle in close to him and close my eyes. Briefly, I consider fighting my attraction to these males, but my instincts already scream *mine*. I will need to speak to my pack before actually allowing anything intimate to happen.

Falling asleep to him stroking my hair, I find it very soothing. My sore body relaxes into Brynd's hold. I wonder if that's the cat in me that likes being petted, or if that's the Omega. Maybe it's a combination of both? Either way I fall asleep, warm, comfortable and full. I couldn't ask for more right now, with the exception of my mates.

◆ ◆ ◆

A rocking motion slowly drags me from my slumber. Not quite ready to open my eyes, I bask in the warm sunlight beating down on me and the calming movement of being carried. Taking a deep breath, inhaling the sweet scent of peaches and cream, I know Brynd is the one carrying me.

Rolling my head upwards, I study his face. He's not looking at me, and his face is tense and alert. This has my heart jumping, afraid those beasts have come to take me back. But I don't see anything except Brenth's back ahead of us.

I start to ask what's going on but a hand covers my mouth gently. Brynd shakes his head no when our eyes meet. I guess that means there is trouble nearby.

Listening hard, I attempt to figure out what put them both on alert. But, my dull human-ish hearing can't catch anything except the sounds of birdsong and buzzing. The wildlife around us would be silent if there was a visible threat.

The brothers' footsteps are soundless as they creep through the brush and sparse trees, keeping the mountains on our right side as they travel.

I'm surprised how fast and quiet they move. It isn't the first time I've wondered if they use magic to help them remain silent.

CH.36

We travel this way for hours. Quiet, tense and vigilant. But, nothing happens. There are no attacks, no other beings, and no angry wildlife.

Eventually, Brynd's muscles relax as he lets out a relieved breath. Brenth's eyes meet his brother's and they have a silent conversation before he explains what's going on.

"Sorry 'bout that, Wee One. I scented something dark in the air and wanted to get as far from it as possible. I have no wish to tangle with those things and I'd like to keep you safe with us."

My whole body slumps, relieved. I'm surprised I didn't think to scent the air. I'm so used to being a Beta human that I've forgotten I have better senses now. *At least I have protective bodyguards*, I muse as my eyes drink in Brenth's large muscled form. The mossy green skin covered in intricate black tattoos, the tusks giving them a deadly air and the comfort they've shown me all culminate in my attempts to deny how attractive I find them.

"I know you said you both have had training with magic, but I get the feeling you have much more experience than you're letting on. Either as a hunter or a warrior, I'm guessing, or am I wrong?" I ask curiously, sitting up straighter.

Brynd snorts, while Brenth smothers a laugh. "Aye. You've got it, lass. We have gotten as much training in as many different fields as we could find. So, we've had both hunter and fighter training, as well as assassin, thievery, blacksmith and crafting. Honestly, being in the capital made it fairly easy to find someone to teach us. Survival became second nature and we wanted to be prepared for anything." Brenth speaks as if all of that training was truly easy for them. But, having seen what it takes to be a hunter or a blacksmith, I can only imagine the difficulties they've faced throughout their lives.

My wide eyes shift from Brenth's face back to Brynd's, who's got a cheeky smile beaming at me. "Whoa. No wonder the both of you can walk with such silent footsteps. Assassin training?" Astonishment fills me. Their dedication to learning is truly admirable.

"So you've both apprenticed with all of those? What about cooking? Because, sure it's great to know how to fight and kill others, but food is way more important if you ask me." I think about the Burrel Brynd fed me last night and realize it was definitely seasoned. It would have been bland otherwise. They must know how to cook, being hunters too.

"Yep. Hunting and cooking go hand in hand, Love. But we never did learn any baking. You really need a full kitchen for that kind of thing... and patience, which we don't have, at least for that sort of thing anyways." He turns to wink at me.

"Hmph! Baking does not need a full kitchen. If I had the right ingredients I would whip up a tasty flatbread over the fire!" I cross my arms, a frown puckering my brow. I'm offended by his view of bakers but I guess it does take a lot of patience though, how many times a day did I have to wait for the breads to rise? But I always filled the time with making other things, so it never felt like I was waiting.

"Now, now, Wee Lass! I meant no offence. I'm looking forward to the day you bake me something. Neither of us are built for spending a full day in the kitchen. But, I would if I got to spend the day with a beauty such as yourself." Aaand I'm blushing again. Time to change the subject.

"Any ideas where we are? I don't recognize anything, and there's much less of a forest here than I'm used to. It's very open, except for the looming mountain beside us." I glance around, curiously.

"I think we've exited the mountains on the other side. Closer to the capital, but I haven't figured out where we came out yet. I couldn't spot the coastline from where we emerged so it's hard to pinpoint our location. Although, if we go by the feel of your bonds, I think we're currently heading for Peril's Pass. I have an inkling that your mates are making their way through the pass, following the bond. Which would put us somewhere just below Banell and the rolling hills," Brenth observes.

I'm confused by the name but I think I get the idea. We've somehow made it through the mountains bypassing the 'only' path through. I just knew there had to be more than one pass, but I hadn't thought much about it before being thrown into this nightmare.

I take a moment to look into my bonds, to ensure we're going the right way. I want my mates back. I need the comfort of Fen's hugs, the safety of Gin's embrace, Rafe's goofy personality, Tawson's protectiveness and leadership, and of course Blue. My Beta. My sweet male who just enjoys being near me.

Remembering the attack, I recall him controlling his own shift without being summoned back to the dark. I wonder if the black mage released him? But, I doubt someone with evil intentions would just release something they created. How did Blue gain his freedom? Especially without me touching him... Something to figure out when I'm back with them.

I can sense everyone is okay through the bonds but there's also concern and fury bubbling along our connection. Every once in a while I'll send a feeling of tranquility and affection, just to make sure they know I'm thinking of them.

I'm really glad I have these two here to look after me. I'm a strong enough person to be able to admit I likely would have died on my own, or worse. I just hope my mates don't attack first and ask questions later.

When we make camp again that night. Brynd goes off to hunt while Brenth leads me to a shallow stream. I shoo him away so I can undress and wash, but he refuses to leave me alone. With furrowed brows and a shake of his head Brenth mutters about protecting silly Omega's.

"There are too many dangers around. I would not forgive myself if you were injured or taken again. I have seen a nude female before. It isn't like it will drive me insane with lust." Although he ruins that statement by adjusting himself. "I'm no animal, Wee One. I promise you, I am here for your safety. Sure, I may gaze at you, but I will not ravish you without enthusiastic consent." Winking at me as he licks a tusk suggestively.

A shiver of arousal flutters through me unexpectedly. I tell myself that he is not one of my mates, this is inappropriate. But my pack is not yet complete so, maybe they really do belong to me. My arousal perfumes the air even as I try to talk myself out of it.

Groaning when he catches a whiff of my desire. "Just bathe, Wee Beauty. I will protect you and nothing else." Brenth's brow pinches as he scrubs a hand down his face.

Relenting, I'm desperate for a bath so I quickly strip off my dirty dress and sit in the shallow water. I have no soap so a rinse will have to do. In order to scrub off all the grime, I grab a handful of small rocks and use them to scour my skin. The roughness of the stones feels like it's taking a layer of skin off but I don't care how much it hurts. I urgently need to get the feeling of dried blood off my body, and the icky feeling of darkness that cave left on me. The scrubbing leaves pink lines in its wake but fade slowly in the cold water.

Brenth is true to his word, keeping a vigilant eye on the space around us and only glancing at my form a few times.

When I've finished washing, I stare in disgust at the dress before deciding to wash it. Dragging the dirty fabric into the water, I scrub the dress against the rocks along the bottom. I manage to get most of the dirt out, all that is left are the stains from my blood and the tears in the side. Not much I can do about that until I can find some thread and a needle. I'm no seamstress, but I do know how to patch a hole.

When I'm finished I step out and squeeze as much water out of the fabric as I can. A large green hand plucks it from me and does a much better job wringing it out.

Taking that time to squeeze out my hair, I try to swipe the water off my body. I sincerely hope I will dry quickly. The air cools as the sun sets, and soon I will freeze if my dress does not dry quickly. I did not think this through. Sometimes I feel very dense...

Brenth's eyes narrow on my shivering silhouette in the fading light and he sighs deeply. "Ach, you couldn't wait to wash the dress till tomorrow? Ya can't wear it now. It's unfortunate that neither Brynd nor myself wears shirts. Let's get a fire going to dry you and the dress." He waves me to follow. Which I do, bare and shivering. My arms cross over my chest and my thighs press tightly together in a sad attempt to hide my nudity.

I should be more self-conscious about being naked, but I think I'm so tired and hungry that I've gone past caring. First I try to prevent Brenth from seeing me bare and now I'm awkwardly marching beside him trying to pretend I don't care.

When we get back to our small campsite, Brynd has a fire going and a bunch of rabbits and burrels roasting. The smell has my mouth watering as soon as it hits me. I'm focused on the food and fire, barely glancing at Brynd to thank him. But I note the desire in Brynd's eyes as he catches sight of my nude, wet form. Choosing to ignore this development, I look away and bite my lip to hold in my nervous laughter.

Wandering over, I sit on one of the two rocks Brynd must have placed close to the fire but before my butt touches the seat, I'm lifted and plopped onto Brenth's lap with a squeak.

I stutter out a refusal, "Oh! Uh... Um... N-no thank you... Uhhh, I-I'm kind of naked a-and I'm getting you wet." Stopping, I try to swallow down the embarrassment when I realize how that sounded. "W-wait! No! T-that's not what I meant! I-I'm wet from washing, n-not from anything else... Oh my Goddess, someone please shut me up! Why are you letting me embarrass myself like this?" I turn a glare on both of them, my cheeks burning.

Crossing my arms tighter, squishing my chest, I watch the two idiots howl at my ridiculous rambling. "Ugh! You are both terrible! Why don't you wear shirts, huh? Then I could wear one like a dress and I could stop being so embarrassed! Instead, I'm stuck sitting here, nude and wet in front of you when the only ones who've ever seen me like this are my mates. Then again, you both smell amazing... maybe you guys will join my pack? Argh! This is something I should talk to my pack about isn't it? I can't just make these decisions because my instincts are saying 'Mmm, yummy. Bite them and ride them both into the sunset'. Being an Omega is annoying and stupid and I miss the simplicity of being a Beta!" My shouts finally run out of steam and I end up just pouting.

I'm staring into the fire, trying very hard not to look at either of them after my irrational and angry tirade, mortified at everything I said. Brynd starts signing out of the corner of my eye, more curious than angry now, I glower up at Brenth and demand to know what he said.

It's Brenth's turn to look abashed, his cheeks turning an adorable yellow with his blush. He clears his throat. "Hmm... well... Yes, so, he... no, we want to know if your pack would be likely to accept us? You smell as tantalizing to us as we do to you and when you barreled into my chest I knew I had to see if we were compatible as mates. My brother and I want a family and we were willing to settle for a nice Beta that fit with both of us, but we haven't met one yet. Most did not like that Brynd can't speak and thought it would be too difficult to learn... and then you literally crashed into us and the moment you touched him, and me, felt like everything we'd been searching for." Silence rings out as I digest his words.

The brothers remain quiet while I work through my thoughts. Would they fit in with my guys? Well... they're very strong and capable. These Orcs have magic and know how to use it to protect me. The brothers have saved me once already and who knows if I'll be needing more saving in the future. *I seriously hope not.*

My guys accepted Blue very easily because I wanted him in my nest and to participate in my heat. It feels like my mates all accept what my instincts desire. If they're saying these two belong with me, my mates would likely accept them, too.

Although, Gin was pretty possessive when he came to find me and saw these two touching me. But, he is a Dragon and they do tend to exhibit hoarding behaviours. He would learn to like them, especially if they brought me back to him. I feel like Tawson would be the one to take the longest, not because he would deny my instincts, but because he'd have to figure out if they would follow him as head Alpha. I think that kind of leadership role is chosen when the pack first forms... or it's solely based off their dominance level. I'm not totally sure since this isn't something I thought I'd ever have to deal with.

My mates and the Orcs would probably have to do the whole macho, Alpha, posturing bullshit. Which I don't totally understand, couldn't they just talk it out instead of punching each other? Whatever, the point is that yes I do think these two would fit with us. I like them. They're kind to me. They are funny and fun to be around, as well as respectful. I think I'll enjoy learning how to sign so I can have secret conversations with Brynd.

The more I think about it, the more I want them. My instincts, when I listen to them, are telling me I need them.

I've been lost in thought for so long I didn't notice food being pulled from the fire. It's only when the smell of roast meat hits my nose that I refocus. Brenth is holding food up to my lips. Automatically, I open my mouth, my instincts completely taking over while I was busy thinking.

Moaning at the succulent taste of meat seasoned with unknown herbs, my eyes shut as I embrace happiness.

"Oh my Goddess! How are you so good at this? Where do you even find the herbs for this? You don't carry around herbs in your pack do you?" I mutter, smacking my lips together after I swallow that delicious bite.

Brenth's laughter shakes his body and mine. I curl in on myself, my face shutting down all the pleasure I was revelling in. The need to hide the way my body jiggles has my face burning with mortification. The warmth from the Orc behind me almost made me forget I was nude.

When I peer over, Brynd is smiling widely at me and it soothes the shame that flashed through me. None of my mates have ever disliked anything about me and I don't actually think these Orc's are any different. They've already said they want the chance to join my pack and I don't think they would have done that if they didn't want *me*.

"It was something we learned when we apprenticed as hunters. They taught us what plants to look for while we hunt. There are many herbs to be found in the wild that really take the meat to a different level. Brynd has a much better eye for the herbs, though," Brenth answers for both of them.

"I'd ask for you to teach me but honestly, I don't see myself ever hunting. Some of these herbs might be nice in a dinner roll though…" Trailing off, I contemplate how I might incorporate them into something savoury. Oh! I could make an herb-y, cheese bread that would taste amazing with these roast meats, or a thick stew. I hope there are goats at the Keep… or maybe I can get my mates to buy me some? I'll need goats if I want to make cheese.

I zone out as Brenth continues to feed me. Vaguely, I hear him tell his brother something but I'm not paying attention. It isn't until the food is gone and I'm full and sleepy that I remember I'm naked. I shiver as a cool breeze whips through our little camp.

"Uhhh, guys, is my dress dry yet? It's pretty dark and even though the fire, and you, are warm the wind is picking up and I'm really feeling the chill." I peer up at Brenth but it's Brynd that gets up to fetch my dress.

I didn't see Brynd hang it on a large stick near the other side of the fire so it would dry quicker when we got back from bathing. But as he hands it to me, warmth radiates from the fabric. I hug it close to my face, relishing the heat.

Hopping off Brenth, I quickly pull my dress on, already missing his heat on my back. But, the toasty cloth feels really nice on my body and I sigh with pleasure. Exhaustion hits me fast and I stumble unexpectedly. Although, I should have since I was tired before we even got back from the stream, I'm surprised I didn't fall sooner.

Brynd catches me and gives me a look. I'm getting pretty good at interpreting what he's saying. This one is full of frustration. *'You should have said you were tired! Brenth is readying the bedroll and you're going to snuggle tight in between us, okay?'*.

I've discerned that he is truly quite sweet and just wants to protect me, even from myself. I swear if he mentions spanking me for not saying I'm tired, I know he'll get along well with my mates. They're all about spanking me for silly things. But, I can't say I haven't enjoyed them. Sure, it hurts but they always make me feel really good afterwards so I can accept it. Plus, it does help me think twice about doing something stupid... maybe.

The fire is still burning as I cuddle in between their large, hard, bodies. I'm warm, fed, and safe, and my inner Omega is crying out. Telling me to take these two before someone else does. I never said my instincts made perfect sense, but they haven't truly led me wrong yet.

CH.37

I don't know how I always sleep through them waking, packing up and starting to move, but it happens every time I fall asleep. My body is draped over Brenth's arms as he carries me through the increasingly thinner trees. We've almost completely left the forest. Grassy plains, sparse shrubs and large rocks await us as we travel on.

"Any idea how far we are from the pass? Or is the plan to just keep walking until we come across it?" I query through a yawn.

"I think I have an idea of where we are now, so I can hazard a guess that we're about two days from the pass. Once we curve around this jutting part of the mountains we'll likely be able to see the pathway since the grasslands range from here to Seabell. If we head north to Banell, the city of Elves, the terrain shifts from rolling grassy hills to desert. I've heard it's quite a beautiful place, although they are suspicious of everyone and do not permit travelers. I think you'd enjoy visiting if they'd allow it, I've heard that it's quite beautiful." Brenth explains, as I let my gaze wander over the oddly skinny trees.

He continues, "But, I'd advise we not venture there until you've reunited with your pack. The more we can avoid other Alpha's the better. You'll need to speak with your Alphas to see if they might be agreeable to us joining your pack. And hopefully allow us to claim you. Your scent needs to change before you attract more compatible Alphas, or you may end up with a much larger pack than you'd like." Brenth lets out a hoot of laughter, as if the thought of me attracting more Alphas is so hilarious.

Giving him a deadpan look, I sigh heavily and roll my eyes. "I did not even know I was an Omega before those sweet idiots strolled into my village. I had zero plans of attracting any males, let alone an entire pack of massive, dominant ones that like to tell me what to do! I've survived twenty seven years on my own, thank you very much. I know how to survive..." I trail off grumbling about dominant males, spankings, and having my whole life uprooted.

Working hard to ignore the way his body shakes with laughter, I cross my arms and look around, trying to spot Brynd. Usually he's the one who carries me. I don't mind Brenth, except when he's inferring that it's my fault I'm drowning in males.

Maybe I do prefer when Brynd carries me, he's much more gentle, and I'm learning his sign language, which is a very fun distraction from all my worries.

"Ahhh, lass. I did not mean to touch on such a sensitive subject. I did not know you were such a late bloomer, it's quite rare for a latent Omega. The latest I've heard of an Omega emerging is twenty, so you must have had a rather rude shock when it happened, hmm? Did you have no warning? Yer Mam or Da say anything about it?" Brenth truly sounds repentant. Like he didn't mean to upset me.

But what he asked has my shoulders slumping and sadness permeate my body instead of grumpiness. With another sigh, I uncross my arms before answering, figuring I owe these two my history if I have plans to add them into my pack.

"Where's Brynd? I don't want to repeat this story twice, so I'd like to wait until he's here too."

Tucking his arm under my ass, Brenth shifts me to one side, freeing up his other one to let out a piercing whistle. It startles me so badly I almost chuck myself out of his hold. He quickly readjusts me so I'm secure again, in one arm.

"Brynd is scouting ahead, making sure we're not heading into danger," he explains, pointing in front of us at something large moving across the open space.

These plains are unsettling, I'm not used to being able to see so far in either direction. I feel vulnerable, like something could easily swoop down and steal me away again... that is one fear that will follow me into old age.

It's only a few moments before Brynd is with us again. I'm surprisingly happy to see him, I wave and beam at him.

"Brynd! I missed you when I woke. Although, your brother sure can entertain," My sarcastic remark huffs out as I smile.

Leaning in, ignoring his brother, he kisses the corner of my mouth, stunning me. I enjoy it, it is just unexpected since neither of them have made any moves on me, even when my Omega perfume wafted around us displaying my naughty thoughts.

Brynd glances at his brother with a question on his face. "Our future Omega has a story to tell."

Taking a deep breath to fortify myself,

I start. "Even though it happened so long ago, the pain of losing my parents has never diminished. It just gets a little easier to bear over time. I was around fifteen, or so, when they both got sick. Our village was too small to have any Users and we couldn't afford to bring one in."

My shoulders curl in, and I fight the tears wanting to fall. To distract myself I pick at a loose thread on my ripped dress until I've regained control before continuing, "They died quickly, the sickness taking many before it moved on. Fortunately, I had my friend, Dani, and her family to help me. I lived mostly on my own, even at fifteen, but I spent a lot of time at Dani's home. They fed me and did what they could to care for me.

"Figuring out how to feed myself and earn money was vital for survival. Baking allowed me to support myself and live on my own all while doing something I loved." I allow a small smile as I wistfully think of my old bakery. It was such an accomplishment for me and I'll forever be proud of what I created.

My face falls as my thoughts return to my parents, "So, if they did say anything, I don't remember it. I had no idea about my latent Omega genes. Our village is small and made up mostly of Betas. There is only the blacksmith that's an Alpha, and I honestly had no clue his wife was an Omega. I think they're hiding, possibly to prevent her from attracting more Alphas if her scent hasn't changed." My brows furrow as I think about it. *Did my parents know that I would present? Is that why they lived there?*

"Why would they be hiding her or you?" Brenth asks, curiosity bright in his eyes.

I tell them my theory, thinking that maybe my parents knew I was going to present as an Omega so they tried to hide me too. Brynd is observing me intently, a curious look in his eye, I can't help but wonder what's going through his head. Brenth's brows have risen so high they seem to be merging with his scalp,

"Well, that is a theory I've heard bandied about in the capitol so it isn't too surprising. I bet there are many small villages with hidden Omega's... curious indeed. Tell me lass, how did ya meet yer pack, being as hidden as you were?"

"When I met my Alphas I thought they were merchants that had travelled there for our monthly market. But it turns out, that was a cover." A silly smile crossed my face as I reminisce about my first meeting with them. "My mates work for the Crown and were investigating mysterious deaths across Southern Saforia. The trail led them to my village, where they hoped to capture the beast responsible and prevent more carnage. We actually ran into the beast by accident. It had been snuffling around in the forest behind Dani's house and I'd been drawn to it." I'm stopped by a gentle hand on my shoulder. Brynd has moved in close, his brow puckered as his lips tip down. I don't need him to speak to understand that he's concerned for me. Brynd's worry brings a smile to my face, it's well in the past but it's cute that he wants to protect me.

I pat his hand before and murmur that it all worked out before I go on, "I instinctively knew I had to touch the beast, and when I did, it forced him to shift back into an Elf. We discovered black magic was responsible for his monstrous actions. The Elf had been stolen and controlled by a dark voice commanding his beast form. But, my touch seemed to prevent him from shifting and kept the black magic at bay." Pushing the hair out of my face, I tell them about Blue with a fond smile.

Brenth looks thoughtful, rubbing his chin, and Brynd just looks curious about my past. "I guess it's common for parents to hide their Omega children, giving them a chance to grow up before Alphas start hounding them. I'm not surprised a single Alpha-Omega pairing would hide to prevent growing their pack. Some beings just don't want to deal with that many dominant personalities. This is why I always say it's important for packs to have at least one Beta! They're the level headed ones who balance out the aggression in Alphas. Plus, Beta's are excellent at soothing Omegas."

"Huh. I did not know that about Betas, that makes sense though. I have a craving to be near Blue all the time and the Alphas took to him very quickly. I think part of that was because he was so vulnerable and scared when we first found him. As we travelled, Blue's personality came out more and more. The black magic had an effect on Blue's memories, he has no recollection of his past. He's learning who he is and who he wants to be now that he's free of the cursed darkness," I muse, tapping a finger on my lips as I contemplate this..

Our trek into the grasslands continues with us casually getting to know each other better. I'm pleased to find these two have a strict moral compass that makes my body tingle, and they're quite attractive, which doesn't hurt. I'm pretty sure I'll be adding the brothers to my pack once I am reunited with my mates. I can only hope my males will accept them as easily as they accepted Blue.

Brenth said that we'll likely make it to the pass in two days. They haven't sensed any dangers or followers which allows us to relax slightly. Although, I'm pretty sure these two will always be vigilant when traversing the wilds. They have enough experience to know not to let their guard down with possible threats around.

Just talking about the dangers has a chill race down my spine. I don't know if I'll ever get used to the openness of the plains. The lack of trees is disturbing, but the sun feels amazing warming my skin. At least until midday when the temperature is at its warmest, then I feel like I'm melting. It's pretty gross how much I can sweat.

Luckily, these two well trained hunters know how to find water sources, which gives me the chance to bathe in the fading light. Most of the time one of the brothers carries me, but I do take some time to walk. The various plants within the tall grass intrigue me, and I can't help marvelling at the little grassland critters, I'm so accustomed to the animals that live in the forest back home.

It's been a difficult, but quiet trek. My injuries, though partially healed, ache with each step. The jarring motion while being toted around has stabbing pains radiating from the wounds. I work hard to keep my whimpers in, I don't want to slow us down even more.

We arrive at Peril's Pass around the time Brenth predicted. The mountains loom above us, casting dark ominous shadows. I'm glad I didn't have to take that path. But, at the same time, I would not want to traverse the cave system again.

"Lass," Brenth snags my attention as we make camp, "I'm going to fill the waterskins. I won't be far. Stay here, Brynd is going to hunt our dinner."

We settle down near the dark gash in the mountains so we can watch for my pack. My job is to tend the fire while the Orcs busy themselves. I've been checking the bond constantly to make sure they're not already on this side of the mountains. They feel relatively quiet today, subdued and tired. I poke at Tawsons bond a little, trying to get a reaction from him.

Tawson responds with amusement and curiosity. I bet he's wondering why I'm poking him. I return anticipation and impatience, hoping he understands to hurry up and get through the mountains. Tawson's warmth spreads through our connection. I can tell he's still tired but our little exchange seems to have given him a boost of energy.

Deciding to do the same for all of my bonds, I prod at Rafe. He conveys joy and impatience, just like me, I know he can't wait to be reunited. Fen issues curiosity, fondness and warmth. My sweetest Alpha, always curious about everything, especially me.

Gin, the grumpy old man that he is, relays irritation and a need so strong my core instantly heats. I throw my annoyance at him, hoping he understands it's not fair to make me wet from so far away knowing I can't do anything about it. And what does he do? Gin returns smugness and laughter. I'm going to get him back for that.

And then there's my Blue. He projects a shy wash of concern and a burst of happiness. Goddess, I just want to cuddle him so hard. He needs me and he's still so far away, it has tears threatening to fall. I try to hide it from them but, of course, they're so deeply entrenched in me that they can all feel it. After our exchange my mates have a bit more pep and move faster towards me. But, they are still so far away.

Brynd returns from a hunt and I quiet the bonds to reduce distractions. He carries a few rabbits, burrels and some sort of bird.

My lips tip up as Brynd joins me near the fire. "Are you going to cook them all right now? Do you need help preparing them? I've never skinned or gutted anything, since I always purchased my meat already prepared, but it might be good for me to learn."

Brynd returns my smile with one of his

own. He places the animals down at his feet and begins signing slowly. They've both been teaching me the basics, it's challenging but I'm starting to figure it out.

"You pluck, I cut". He keeps it very simple for me, knowing I don't have a large vocabulary yet.

Bobbing my head, I grab the bird. This bird is so strange compared to the ones in my forest. Its three toed feet are similar, however the body is much more plump. The feathers are an interesting mix of browns and greens, likely to camouflage in the tall grass. I'm sure it will cook up nicely.

Getting to work plucking the feathers out, I prepare it to be gutted and then roasted. A small leather pouch near Brynd draws my attention, green leaves poke out the top. It must be herbs he gathered while hunting, I'm sure it will add amazing flavors to the meat.

We work in comfortable silence. Once in a while I poke at the fire or add another log to keep it going. It's been some time since I saw Brenth, twisting my body around my eyes scan the open plains hoping to spot him.

"Brynd, when did you last see Brenth? It's been a while since he went to get water. Do you think he's okay?" I bite my lip, anxiety threading through me at the thought of him in trouble. My fists clench in frustration, we don't have a bond, which means *I can't check to see if he's alrigh*t.

Brynd glances around, lifts his nose to the air to take a few sniffs, before answering, *"No danger, smell. He..."* He makes a sign I don't understand and I shrug and shake my head. Huffing out a breath, he mimes something narrow and then walks his fingers down the middle.

I brighten. "Oh! You think he went to check the entrance to the pass?" He nods, but he has a wary look on his face.

My smile dims. "The pass is pretty dangerous isn't it? But wouldn't the entrance be less so? Arg! I hope he isn't doing anything stupid," then, in a smaller voice, "I hope my pack is okay. I'm sure I'd feel it through the bond if they were hurt, but I think they would try to hide that from me." He pats me on the back in sympathy before we get back to work with less enthusiasm, both of us worried for Brenth and my mates.

CH.38

The sun begins to set by the time we've finished preparing all the meat. Brynd keeps a few unskinned rabbits off to the side.

"Smoke meat, last long," Brynd signs. It's smart to smoke the meat, turning it into jerky. It's the best way to have decent food for a long journey.

Our meat roasts over the fire by the time darkness blankets the plains. Brenth is still not back and I'm very concerned for him. Brynd is as well, he keeps glancing towards the dark slash separating the mountains.

The pass entrance is barely visible from camp. The brothers did not want to be too close in case of lurking danger. The realization that Brenth has gone into the pass has my heart racing and my palms sweating. I'm going to yell at him so bad for this, how dare he make me worry. This must be why my mates spanked me for wandering off alone. *I wonder if Brenth would allow me to spank him?* The thought has me cackling. Brynd quirks an eyebrow, a smile twitching at the corner of his lips.

Snorting, I inform him, "After my mates found me with you two in Gisham I got a pretty hard spanking for worrying them and I was just thinking, I wonder if Brenth would submit to a spanking from me." A smile splits his face as he roars with laughter, silently.

"Big funny, want see. Not happen." Wiping a tear off his face, Brynd shakes his head. I agree, Brenth would not allow it. But the visual has me giggling as I prod the fire. It's a nice break from the tension.

By the time my meat is half gone, footsteps shuffle in the grass. I perk up hoping it's Brenth, and not something dangerous.

A familiar voice calls out, "It's just me, don't stab me!" Brenth chortles like what he said was so funny.

I am not amused though. When he finally steps into the light from our fire, his face falls when he spots the disappointment and irritation in my eyes.

"I'm sorry, Wee One! I just wanted to scout the pass and make sure there weren't any dangers lingering around," he mutters sheepishly.

"You could have at least let us know before you disappeared for hours," I level a glare on him, crossing my arms and wrinkling my nose.

"Aye, I should have. But I knew you were safe, Brynd wasn't far. And I didn't think I'd be gone so long." Brenth gives me puppy eyes, pleading with me not to be angry with him. It's hard to keep up my anger when he looks so sad.

I notice dark blue staining his arms and pants. My frown deepens, "What is that? Why are you blue?"

Glancing at the stains, he curses, "Uhh, I took care of a few Grimps, as all. I thought I got it all in the stream..."

"is that their blood? I did not know some creatures bled a different color. I wonder why?" The last part I add quietly, knowing that Fen would likely have an answer for me. I feel kind of bad for snapping at him, knowing he put himself in danger to try and help my mates.

"Aye, their blood is blue. There are some creatures out there that bleed all sorts of colours. I've seen many of them as a hunter," Brenth explains, "any chance ya saved me some meat?" He pleads, hands up in supplication.

Feeling mischievous, I give him a sly

look. "Hmm... Nope I don't think we did save you any." I'm still not even halfway through the burrel and there's another rabbit and bird roasting over the fire.

Out of the corner of my eye I spot Brynd smiling at me while he eats his share, not helping his brother in the least.

"But... There's so much food roasting, you can't possibly eat it all! I know how much you can eat, Wee Lass." Moving closer to me, he stares at the food in my hand with hunger.

"Food is for Orcs who use their big boy words," My tone comes out mocking as I hold back my laughter.

"Don't be like that, Lass!" Brenth exaggerates his pout as he continues to stalk closer.

Realizing his proximity, I decide the best way to save my meal is by running. But Brenth snatches me mid step and I giggle wildly.

Sitting down with me on his lap, he takes the burrel from my hands. As I try to protest, Brenth tears a chunk of meat off, placing it gently between my lips. His soft smile has me instantly forgiving him, Brenth really is quite the sweetheart. I'm glad he can make me laugh, after the horrors I've been through, I need it.

He only grabs food for himself once I've waved him off, not able to stuff anymore into my belly. I feel so much better now that he's back, safe.

Brynd signs something at him, but I don't have the energy nor brain power to decipher it right now.

I'm drifting off as Brenth replies, "No signs of anyone having been through the pass since we made the journey. I don't think her pack has made it this far. I hope to the Goddess that they are safe. It would kill me to see her sadness if she lost any of them." Brenth cuddles me closer to him.

"Can you set out the bedroll? She's already asleep and I don't want to put her down. I know she sleeps better between us, and I think she needs the comfort of both of us right now." His deep voice is soothing to me, pushing me deeper into my slumber.

A screeching, bone chilling cry jars me into wakefulness. Jumping to my feet, as my heart pounds, I search wildly around for the source.

The sky is still dark and the fire has almost burned itself out, so I know I can't have been asleep long. Frantically scanning the area for the brothers, I don't see them anywhere. Panic chokes my vocal chords as I try to find a weapon of some sort.

How could they have left me alone? I thought they wanted to protect me... Unless, they're out there hunting whatever made that sound. That's more feasible than being left as monster food.

I grab a burning chunk off the fire, hoping I won't have to use it. Without trees for cover, there aren't many places to hide. We chose this spot because the grouping of bushy plants helps conceal the camp and it's not far from the creek. Crouching down and keeping the brush to my back, I ready the burning log and wait.

Silence stretches between each breath. Not even the wildlife dares to make a peep, for fear they will be the ones eaten.

Why did those Orc's leave me alone? A loud thud sounds in the distance, followed by an animalistic scream of pain. My muscles tense so hard it irritates my injuries.

I can only hope that wasn't one of my companions getting injured.

Listening hard, I hold my breath as my body shakes. The sound of something thrashing around in the long grass has me choke back a scream. There's a wet *thwack* and silence rings out around me. I hope that it was my Orcs taking care of the threat, but I fear I'm alone and vulnerable.

Footsteps rustle the grass dragging something heavy. The sound intensifies, letting me know whatever it is comes my way. My body shakes violently as I grip my weapon tighter, but the fear leaves me fumbling. A familiar silhouette forms in the fading firelight, a sigh of relief gusts from me and I almost collapse.

"Oh, thank the Goddess you're alive, Brynd! I was so scared when I woke alone to that sound. Where's Brenth, is he okay? Are there more monsters out there?" I rapidly fire questions at him, anxious to know they're both alright.

Giving me a look that says *give me a second, I'm a little busy*, he continues to drag the corpse towards the fire.

While waiting for Brynd to respond, I use my weapon to rearrange the logs on the fire, making sure there's enough airflow to encourage the flames.

My eyes shift to Brynd when he drops whatever he brought back with him. He's covered in blood, so it's hard to tell if he's injured anywhere. Grabbing one of the waterskins and a rag, I wipe the gore off of him, checking for wounds as I go. Brynd is surprisingly patient with my frantic hands, and luckily, I don't find any cuts or even bruises on him.

The tension in my shoulders ease now that I know Brynd is okay. However, it comes right back when I realized what was dragged into camp. Throwing my hands over my mouth, I bite back a scream. I should be used to seeing these abominations by now.

It seems like the Necromancer's creatures have found us. Straining my ears, I don't hear other growls or barks. Wildlife slowly resumes its song, an indication that the danger has passed.

For now.

A tug on my sleeve draws my attention to Brynd. He signs, *"Scout, look, scent, creature. Return soon."*

The rest of my anxiety drains away at those words, leaving me feeling exhausted. Stumbling as I make my way back to the bedroll, I practically collapse in the blankets. This lethargy feels like more than just the relief of not being eaten, but I just can't focus on that right now. Brynd's brow puckers and worry shines from his eyes as he watches me weakly flop down.

The sound of fingers snapping gains my

attention as I burrow into the blankets. My head turns towards him and Brynd gestures to a rock, then to his eyes and points out to the darkness. He's going to stay here and keep a lookout. A tired nod is the only response I can muster, as I try to cocoon myself in an attempt to feel safe. I miss my pack.

Regardless of how tired I am, I can't fall back asleep. Tossing and turning, my mind is too overwhelmed to offer me any actual rest. What if there's something else out there? Brenth is alone and exposed, my only solace is knowing how many skills he's mastered. I can only pray he is safe.

None of this is helping with the distance from my mates, my heart hurts with their absence. *What if they're attacked again? They better make it back to me in one piece.* I roll over until I can stare at Brynd, keeping him in my line of sight eases some of my fear.

Dawn creeps in by the time Brenth returns to camp. Darker mossy tones under his eyes show the depth of his exhaustion. The way his brows draw together demonstrates his worry. I sit up in my blanket cocoon when he steps close to the fire, drawing his gaze to mine.

Brenth barks out a rough laugh and shakes his head at me, smiling ruefully. "You are the most adorable, angry looking little thing." His face sobers. "I am glad you're alright. I was worried you'd be frightened if you woke alone, but I needed to draw it away from our camp. I'm sorry, lass, don't be cross with me."

My brows furrow and my mouth twists. "I was frightened when I woke to that horrible screeching. But, when I couldn't find either of you, I grabbed a weapon and crouched down near the brush. And I am cross with you! Don't make me worry that you will be eaten or too injured to get back to us." Pointing a finger at him, I flail in my cocoon and topple over as I try to maintain my stern demeanor. I'm not actually angry with him, but Brenth needs to know he's not allowed to die on me.

Smiling again, he leans down to pick me up, blanket and all. "I know you don't have experience out here, so I worried. We had to lure the beast away and kill it. The creature was mighty hard to draw out though, it was very intent on you." Inner eyebrows raised and lips pursed, he looks more concerned than I've ever seen him. "We may not be able to stay out here another night. I'm sorry, Wee One. Unless y'er Alphas get through the pass by midday, we must move until we can find better cover." Giving me an apologetic look, he holds his breath as he awaits my response.

Sighing, I snuggle deeper into my

cocoon before answering, "That was the one thing I kept thinking. There's not enough coverage here, it's too open, too easy for an attack. I want so badly to wait here for them, but I'm afraid doing that will get us all killed or kidnapped again..." I sniffle, and blink back a tear, not wanting to let it out right now. I need to be strong. If I give in right now, I'll lose it. It feels like it's been weeks since I've seen my mates and I miss them so much.

Brenth pets me, soothing my ruffled emotions. "We will give them until midday, unless there's another attack. We're closer to Banell, but I know the Elves don't like strangers in their midst so they may not accept us in their village. We can always head for Seabell, it's a large seaside town, easy for us to get lost in the crowds and hide. It would likely also have the ingredients I'll need to brew a cloaking potion for ya."

"How many days to Banell and Seabell? If Banell is closer, wouldn't it make more sense to go there? I wonder if Blue is from there? I honestly haven't seen any Elves aside from him, but I'm also from a very small village." I probe before my attention diverts to musing aloud.

His finger on my chin draws my gaze back to his. "Banell is only about three and a half days from here, while Seabell is approximately eight... It's much further and it's all open grasslands so there wouldn't be much cover until we got there. But, like I said, the Elves don't usually allow strangers into their villages. So, we'd be taking a chance either way."

Inhaling, I take a moment to think it over. I don't enjoy the thought of such a long walk in the open to get to Seabell. But, regardless of how exciting it would be to meet more Elves and maybe ask them about Blue, the possibility of arriving just to be turned away concerns me.

"I think... I think it might be worth it to go to Banell and speak with the Elves. Maybe I could convince them to help us if I tell them about Blue, the Necromancer and those horrible beasts. We could at least try asking for horses or supplies." I look at both of them to see what they think about my suggestion.

Brynd nods at me when I catch his eye, and I think that means he's with me.

Pursing his lips, Brenth responds slowly. "Well... You do make a good argument... And, the hills give a little more cover than the walk to Seabell... Alright, we'll head for Banell if your mates don't get here by midday."

Brenth is still frowning as he looks around. Sighing he asks his brother, "Are you good to stay up and keep watch? I really need to get some sleep and I think this feisty little thing could use some more, too."

It isn't long before Brenth wraps himself around me and we both fall back asleep, leaving our worries for tomorrow.

CH. 39

Warmth beats down on my closed eyes. My body refuses to move as I bask in the sunshine heating me in the cocoon of blankets I've wrapped around myself. It takes a moment before I can understand why the sun is shining so brightly. My eyes pop open to the blinding light and I jacknife into a sitting position. The blankets are so tangled around me that it takes some serious flailing and embarrassing struggles to free my arms. I shade my eyes to see past the brightness and for once I haven't slept through the Orcs packing up and moving on. We're still in our camp and it's got to be about midday.

Yawning, I stretch, squeaking as I move and chuckles almost startle me into toppling over. My head whips around to find Brenth eyeing me with amusement, his lips pinched together in an effort to prevent more laughter. I do my best to ignore him until I've fully woken myself. I bet he's watched every stupid thing I've done since waking up. *Ugh, why am I so awkward? I thought I'd matured past this.*

I feel as tired as I did before Brenth cuddled me back to sleep last night. I wonder if I'm getting sick? Or it could be that this 'adventure' has been a bit much. The stress must be getting to me.

My stomach grumbles, telling me it's past breakfast. It's been rare in my life that I've had the chance to sleep in so long, but this current nightmare has not allowed regular sleep.

Brenth sits by the fire, keeping it going as he fails to contain his laughter anymore. It must be the disgruntled look on my face or it could be the messy hair taking on a life of its own.

"You are such an adorable little thing. All messy and grumpy in the morning." Brenth smiles fondly at my scowl.

"You have too much..." I wave a hand vaguely at him. "I'm too tired for all that." Slowly, I drag myself out of the blankets and get to my feet.

Before I even ask, he's holding out a skewer of meat for me. It's probably cold by now, but I know it'll taste great anyways.

The moment I step within arms reach Brenth hauls me onto his lap. I don't bother fighting it because; one – he's much more comfortable than a rock. And two – I feel too off to be annoyed.

He doesn't let me take the skewer. Slowly he feeds it to me, piece by piece. I just open my mouth and accept it, like a little baby bird. I mentally shrug, telling myself this is totally normal behavior. I mean, my Alphas do this too. It must be an Alpha thing, providing for your Omega or potential mate.

When I'm done, he eats the rest. I'm finally awake enough to think. "Is Brynd scouting? Have there been any more hints of those abominations? Any other creatures lurking around us? What about my pack? Any sight of them from the pass?" I basically interrogate him.

"Wow, Okay, let's see. Yes, he's out scouting and doing a little hunting along the way, it'll be good to have for later. No, nothing that either of us has seen. I even cast a small spell checking for black magics and all it showed me was the dead beast we buried last night. Nothing lurking, no animals we can't handle, and no, I'm sorry, Wee One, we haven't spotted any movement from the pass. It could be they're just taking their time, being safe."

Sighing, he gives me a disquieted look. "We're going to have to move. We can't stay here and wait for more beasts to attack us in the open. Your pack knows how to find you, following the bond. They will come to us when we find somewhere safe to hole up, okay?" He's so patient with me, I want to squeeze him tight and plant kisses all over his face in appreciation. But I don't, because I am determined to do this right and make sure my pack is okay with them first.

I'm staring at the dark slash in the mountains, where I know my mates will eventually emerge. I know. I *know,* we have to get moving, but the thought of going further away from where they are, makes my stomach hurt. I want to go to them, but I know that's stupid. The black magic comes from the mountains, and if those creatures are truly hunting me, it's best to put as much distance as possible between us. I just... I miss them.

I miss Rafe's silliness and Fen's quiet comfort. Gin's safety and warmth, and his grumpiness. Blue's soothing presence and Tawson, my steadfast Alpha. Stoic and confident, he always had a plan, Tawson would know what to do. He would probably agree with finding somewhere safer for me. Knowing how Tawson would handle the situation helps me realize we've already stayed here too long.

Looking up at Brenth, determination straightening my shoulders, I sit up taller and nod decisively. "Let's get packed up. We should move as soon as Brynd gets back."

He doesn't say anything, just bobs his head in agreement and the tension around his eyes relaxes. Brenth was worried I would fight him on this. I'm glad I could lessen his stress a little, I don't think this is really what they were looking for when they followed me.

Maybe I should apologize for dragging the brothers into my mess, but I actually think Brenth is having fun protecting and teasing me. I bet they both enjoy being able to utilize the many skills.

We pack up camp quickly. I'm kicking dirt over the fire when Brynd strolls over. He signs something to Brenth, reporting on what he observed. I catch the words *'Scent, clear, no move'* he didn't sense or see anything. It makes me sad because that means my pack isn't here yet, but I'm also happy because there's no trace of any more monsters.

"Okay, let's move." Brenth puts the pack on, bedrolls tied tightly to it and tips his head at his brother. "Wee One, Brynd is carrying ya. I want to get as far as we can today and y'er tiny legs can't move as fast as us." I've noticed his accent gets stronger the more stressed he gets. It's interesting. I wonder where they're from, I've never heard anyone with that accent before.

The skin around my eyes crinkle with suppressed humor before I snort out a laugh. "That's because you're both giants compared to me!" They respond by shaking their heads and tossing me wry smiles.

I meet Brynd's grasp willingly and he tucks me into the crook of one arm. Sitting on him like a queen, I cross my arms and toss a glower over my shoulder at Brenth. Humph. I'm trying to hold back my laughter though, because I truly do walk so slow compared to their massive strides. Also, I kind of like being close to them.

The day grows hot as we walk through the grass. The cloudless sky gives us no reprieve. We try to conserve the water, but I'm sweating almost as much as they are and I'm not even walking. Our path runs parallel to a stream, allowing us to stop frequently. As the heat increases, I swear the blistering sun threatens to dry up the shallow stream.

The sun dips behind the mountainous backdrop, but my Orcs are determined to get me out of here. Brenth pushes us on into the coming darkness, wanting to get further from where we were attacked.

My sightlines vanish as darkness encompasses the grassy plains. Only when we can no longer see our path do we stop and make camp. Brenth builds a very small fire to give us some light and a place to roast our meal. The exhaustion from the heat has us finishing our food quickly. Brynd and I curl together on the bedroll while Brenth takes first watch. He's not willing to leave us vulnerable.

Brenth wakes me early in the morning, they must have switched places while I slept. He hands me some food and to my surprise Brenth doesn't feed me. *Have I grown so used to all these Alpha's feeding me that when they don't it feels like a rejection?* I shake off these strange thoughts and stuff food in my face quickly, now is not the time to throw a hissy fit just because I had to feed myself.

After eating, camp is disassembled and we're on the move, this time Brenth carries me.

I still feel off. I'm too tired and my body is achy. It's most likely the bruises causing my discomfort since Brynd healed the worst injuries.

The next two days pass in a similar manner. It's quiet, except for the noise of wildlife, and I swear it gets hotter the closer we get to the rolling hills in the distance.

The landscape changes around me. The grass grows sparse and the plants shift from lush bushes to spiky plants. The dirt beneath our feet grows coarse, turning into sand. I've seen a few reptilian critters, skittering from rock to rock and some insects that make me shudder in disgust. Anything with more than four legs repulses me.

Eventually the little stream we've been following turns off to the east, but we continue north, to Banell.

On the third day as we eat our breakfast I can no longer contain my whines.

"It's been three days, Brenth!" I widen my eyes and push my lip out into a pout, "it's so hot here and there's no shade to be seen. How much longer?"

Brenth chews his reptilian breakfast, swallowing his bite before responding, "Lass," He gives me a patient smile, "it's not long now. We should make it there before the sun sets.

We're fully inside what Brenth calls a desert, which gets hot as soon as the sun rises and freezes when it sets. The sandy ground and rocky hills are strange to me, as are the unfamiliar animals. I don't think I like deserts. I miss the shade of trees and the green of the plants around me. The dull beige desert is broken up by the occasional brown or bland greenish-brown plant.

The terrain grows more strenuous as we trek up and down the hills, slowing our pace significantly. I feel bad that they've had to take turns carrying me, but I would slow us down so much more if I had to walk. The sand is hard to travel through, their feet sinking in on each step.

Instead of stopping for a midday meal, we eat jerky while pushing forward to Banell. Our water runs low as does our energy, but we have to keep going.

The air cools with the facing sun by the time we spy a large fence, the top carved into spikes. It looks decidedly unfriendly, and I'm very concerned they will turn us away. We need supplies if we're going to get out of this wicked place.

Brynd places me on my feet as we stop in front of the gate. I don't see any beings or any handles to open it.

Brenth steps forward and knocks, yelling out, "Hail! We are weary travellers looking for a safe place to bed down, a warm meal and some water. Please, can you aid us?" That's the most proper I've ever heard him sound. Usually he truly embodies what we all think when we hear the word 'Orc', gruff, foul-mouthed and brutish.

I'm staring at the top of the gate and fence, it's the only reason I see someone peeking over the top. A glimpse of red hair, pointed ears and luminescent blue eyes appear before they duck down again.

A strong feminine voice shouts back, "Orcs and a small human? Strange travelling companions, no? We do not allow strangers into our village. You Orcs should know that."

I don't give Brenth a chance to answer. I beg, "Please! We're in desperate need of water and food... And... I have questions. One of my mates is an Elf and he can't remember where he's from. I was hoping someone here would recognize him if I described him. Maybe he has family here?" I started strong but my voice grows wobbly as I talk about one of my mates.

Her head peeks over the fence again, looking straight at me this time. I give them my best pleading look, big innocent eyes, hand pressed together raised up and a hunch in my shoulders. Hoping I can sway them to help us.

"Where is this mate of yours? Why is he not with you?" She questions suspiciously.

"I was kidnapped from my mates." I heave out a sigh. "I was lucky that these two saved me. They have been helping me to get back to them, but we were attacked again while camped near Peril's Pass, so we had to move." I try not to let myself ramble, as I usually would. This is not the time to get carried away.

We hear indistinct murmurs from beyond the gate, several voices blending together as they discuss our plight. I'm hoping, praying to the Goddess, that they allow us entry. I feel so exposed out here, and I'm so tired. I'm starting to think there is something more wrong with me. We desperately need to rest somewhere that feels safe. I don't know if that's here, but I can hope.

It feels like they make us wait hours, but it's probably only a few minutes. I'm anxiously shifting from foot to foot, picking at my torn dress and chewing my lip. The fence these beings built is honestly pretty impressive, especially because there are no trees in sight. It's also got to be at least ten feet tall, it towers over both my Orcs who are easily seven feet. The Elves must have had to travel pretty far to find enough wood. It spans miles in either direction from the gate. I can just barely see where it turns, the corners having large spikes decorating the edge, giving it an ominous appearance.

A nudge to my ribs interrupts my runaway thoughts, my anxiety getting the best of me again. Jumping, I stumble unsteadily grabbing Brynd's arm for stability, before jerking my head up towards the gate. There is a small vertical slit opening up at about six feet. Taking a tentative step forwards, I can only hope no one is going to shoot an arrow out of it.

I jerk back when a pair of brilliant yellow eyes appear and stare down at me.

"What is your name?" A deep, husky, male voice questions. Not the female we'd been talking to before.

I stutter a little, "Um... Uh... Me? Right. I-I'm Luella Bakken, of Pekayan... I'm a baker..." Mumbling the last bit, I don't think they care what my profession is.

The eyes narrow a little before the male speaks again, "Hmm... Luella, the baker. What are these Orcs to you?"

"M-my friends. Uhh... Probably going to be my mates at some point... T-they smell nice?" I'm so startled by the question that I kind of blurt out that I like their smell. I almost turn around and tell the brothers I can't go in there now, I've already made a fool of myself. But, I suck in a deep breath and ignore my burning face.

The male chuckles lightly, his laugh deep and raspy, reminding me of Gin. "Your potential Alphas, hmm? Does that mean you're an unbonded Omega? We might take you in for that alone."

Both brothers step up to either side of me, Brenth placing an arm around my shoulders while his brother tucks me close to his side with an arm around my waist. They practically engulf me in their large forms, trying to protect me from these Elves.

I don't mind that they stepped up but I need to make something clear. "No. I am claimed. But my pack isn't finished yet, which is why my scent hasn't fully changed. But like I said before, I was kidnapped from my pack, which includes an Elf we saved from some truly black magic. So... Don't go getting any ideas, kay?" I tried so hard to sound tough and commanding but that's just not who I am. I ended up asking instead of telling and sounding so soft while I said it. Ugh. I annoy myself some days.

Tilting my head, I brush my hair away from my neck and tug the top of my dress down a bit to show off Rafe's bite. I may have pulled it a little far though and flashed a bit too much of my chest. The eyes widen in surprise before they return to a flat stare.

Yellow eyes clears his throat before speaking, "Yes, well. So, I can see. Give us a moment." Then the little door closes and we're left standing in the cooling darkness.

My shivering prompts Brynd to pick me

up and cuddle me into his chest. I snuggle in tight, enjoying the warmth he gives off. If I sneak an extra sniff or two of his scent, no one can really blame me. I'm stressed and exhausted and I will take my comfort when I can.

They don't keep us waiting long. The big gate pulls open slowly. I think all three of us are a little shocked that they're actually letting us in. I fully expected them to turn us away, maybe chuck an extra waterskin and some food over the fence so they don't feel bad.

We move to step into their village but before we can, a line of Elven warriors block our path with spears. My body tenses, thinking this is it, they're going to murder us instead of sending us away. But nothing happens, aside from a few warriors moving aside and allowing someone to step in front.

A male Elf stands before us at about six feet tall. Beautiful reddish-brown skin compliments his yellow eyes. This must be who I spoke with at the gate. Glossy white waist length hair is collected into hundreds of tiny braids and gathered into a large band. His elongated ears come to a point at the top with piercings lining the edge, but Blue's ears are much shorter than this Elf's. *I wonder if Blue is only half Elf.*

Wearing beige leather trousers, sandals and no shirt, his body is decorated in metal jewellery. Bronze metal cuffs wrap around his biceps and forearms. Numerous necklaces hang, some appearing as if they're decorated with bones. His plump lips seem so kissable, yet his harsh jawline adds a more masculine touch. He's beautiful.

We gape at one another, taking in each other's presence. Brenth coughs to get my attention, snapping me out of my trance. I blush, of course, and wave a little hello. I want to take it back as soon as I've done it, but it's much too late. Yellow eyes laughs, it makes him appear much younger and less severe.

"You are very refreshing, Little Bit. Welcome to Banell." Sweeping his arm out as he turns sideways, the warriors move back to open a path.

CH.40

My jaw drops at the sight before me. I expected a village in this wasteland of sand and heat to be the same, but it's so green. An oasis in the middle of the desert.

The village has been constructed around a vast lake. Exotic trees, bushes, flowers, and other plants surround the lake giving the space color and life. I don't see any houses, only a few permanent stalls for merchants. I'm stunned as I see a door at the base of one of the thick, squat trees open, letting a woman and child step out. Scanning the base of every tree, I spot doors that blend in with the bark.

"This place is amazing! How? How is everything so green and alive when it feels dead out there?" I wave faintly behind me, a baffled expression taking over my face.

Most of the warriors and the yellow eyed male laugh at my inelegant question. But, it's his dark, husky voice that answers me, "We are Elven. Nature is one with us. And, thank you." He bows his head with a sly smile directed at me, eyes crinkled in the corners.

"Come. I'll show you where you will stay tonight." Turning abruptly, he walks off, without checking that we're following.

Following our Elven guide with Brynd still carrying me, gives me the opportunity to continue gaping at the surrounding beauty.

I don't pay attention to where we're going, lost in thoughts of this place and the Elves. We stop at one of the tree houses and our nameless guide waves us in ahead of him. A few warriors follow behind us, but they stay at the door as we're shown into a comfortable living space. Instead of chairs, cushions line a rug on the floor, adding some color to the brown of the wooden walls.

A hearth separates the kitchen and living spaces. It includes a small table, wash basin, small counter tops and a few cupboards. It's cozy, but the cooking space leaves much to be desired. A set of stairs opposite us probably leads up to the sleeping space and privy.

Our guide invites us to sit on the cushions as he seats himself.

"My name is Zenik, my father is the Chief of this village. I have some questions for you." His attention is directed at me, mostly ignoring my Orcish bodyguards. Zenik does flick a glance at each brother before coming back to rest on me.

I take a deep breath, trying to build my courage. This Elf is very intimidating. Finally catching his scent, it's spicy, almost making me sneeze, he smells of ginger and mead. A little sweetness to offset the sharpness.

"I guess you're wondering about the Elf I mentioned?" I ask, my shoulders rising as I hunch a little. This male is unnerving, and I can't quite figure out why.

"Mmm... Yes, I am very interested to know about this Elf you have claimed. But, I'd also like to know more of you, Omega. You are aware your designation is rare, are you not? And with your scent unchanged, you will attract many and not all good." Smiling shrewdly, his eyes squint in a scrutinizing manner.

An involuntary shiver rushes through me, his smile sets me on edge. My instincts tell me to watch how much I say. Glancing up at Brenth, I catch his fierce frown at Zenik before looking back at me. He shrugs, as if to say *It's up to you.*

Sighing before focusing back on the Elf, if I want their help I guess I should explain everything. "I'm going to start at the beginning. I used to be a Beta, until a month or so ago..." I go on to explain how I learned I was Omega and that I know very little of my designation. I detail how we came across Blue, watching Zeniks face carefully. He pales and narrows his eyes, fists clenching as he listens to my story. When I get to my kidnapping and injuries Zenik stops me.

"You are currently injured?" He asks, shifting forward as concern takes over his face.

"Well, Brynd healed the worst of it, but we needed to conserve his energy and magic in case we were attacked again. I still have some nasty bruising and possibly cracked ribs but I'm okay, I think... These two haven't let me walk much, so I've been able to rest and allow my body to start healing," I clarify, thinking of the heavy feeling that has been bothering me the last few days. I wonder if I am more injured than I thought?

Standing abruptly, Zenik quickly strides to the door then proceeds to speak to the warriors waiting outside, returning once he's finished. He was too quiet for me to hear anything, but the pleased look on Brynd's face indicates something positive. I guess his hearing is much better than my own.

Peering over at Zenik, I open my mouth to ask what's happening but there's a knock at the door. All of us look towards the sound.

"*Enter,*" Zenik shouts, and an elderly Elf shuffles inside.

The newcomer is not too much taller than I am. Braided grey hair reaches his waist. It must be an Elven thing... He's also sporting a bushy grey beard, it makes him look a lot less imposing than the warriors. His pale orange eyes catch my attention as he focuses directly on me.

Zenik stands and bows to him, surprising me. Isn't he the Chief's son? Shouldn't it be the other way around? Should we get up and bow?

I go to stand but the elderly Elf stops me. "No, young Omega. Please, relax. I am Healer Wick, I am simply here to tend to your wounds. If you wouldn't mind showing me where?" His voice is strong for how slight he looks.

I fidget in place, nerves make my hands shake. Since the bruises take up my entire left side I need to remove my dress. Blushing, I glance at all the males in the room.

"Umm... I need to remove my dress to show you all of the injuries... Is... Do you, maybe, have a less ruined piece of clothing I may change into? And... Um... Could you all maybe turn around or something?" Struggling through my requests, I feel awkward and timid, not wanting everyone to see my naked body. It felt different when I was travelling with the brothers and bathing in streams, but I do not wish for Zenik to see me like that. My instincts tell me he is not a potential Alpha.

Zenik flushes a deep red before muttering about going to get me some clothing and quickly leaves. The brothers tell me they're going to check upstairs to see about our sleeping arrangements.

Now alone with the healer, I quickly strip off my tattered dress, leaving me completely bare. I hold the dress in front of myself, attempting to hide my nudity but leave the injuries visible. I've been through a lot in the last... however long it's been since I've been with my mates and it shows.

Healer Wick tsks as he looks over the deep black and purple bruising on my left side. Taking note of the healed puncture wounds in my shoulder and side on the right.

"Oh, dear. You have been through some difficulties, eh?" He tsks as his eyes come to rest on my face. "Will you be comfortable if I place my hands on you? I need to feel the wounds to check how bad they are inside."

Scrunching my face in confusion, I

do not have much, or any, experience with healers.

"What? How can you see the injuries inside me?" I pale and back up a few steps. "You're not going to cut me open are you? Oh Goddess, I don't think I need any healing. I'm fine, this will all heal, I'm sure of it." My fear is heavy, and tears leak from my eyes as everything finally hits me. I miss feeling safe, even though I was bored in my old life, I miss it. I did not have to worry about injuries, infections, kidnappings or anything else that's happened to me.

Crumpling to the floor as sobs choke me, I clutch tightly to the ragged fabric. The healer rushes to my side, startling me, before he kneels down and cuddles me tightly.

Cooing soft words into my hair and rocking me gently. "It's all right, Dear One, you are safe here. No one will hurt you. Shh, shh, it's okay. Let it all out, you've had quite the trying time, hmm?"

Stroking my hair, he hums softly. His touch comes across as comfortable and safe. The hug feels like what I vaguely remember from my father, comforting and familial. Even his scent is soothing to me, herbs and incense, not quite as good as one of my Alphas though. He smells exactly how I assumed a healer would.

When my sobs taper off and I feel like I'm wrung out, he places me carefully on one of the cushions. "I'm sorry, Dear One. It's alright, I am happy to be a shoulder to cry on. It's a large part of being a healer." Smiling gently at me, Wick softly pats my shoulder.

I give him a watery laugh, sniffling. "I'm actually surprised that I haven't really broken down before this. I miss my mates and I've been so scared. Trying to be strong is so much harder than I thought."

"I have a feeling that your inner strength will only grow from here. But, I'm just an old male, a little addled from too many years of inhaling medicinal plants and whatnot." Huffing out a shaky laugh, I know he's trying to make me feel better. "Now, let me get a look at those bruises."

Nodding, I shift so my left side is facing him. Gently, the healer places his hands on each bruise, spending a few moments with his eyes closed and humming as he touches each one. Tingles surge where our skin touches, but it doesn't hurt, he's very careful not to press on them.

He motions for me to switch sides and he does the same to each scab on the right side. Spending a little more time with these. He frowns as he touches each one.

"Where did these come from? I sense much blackness, an ichor, in these. Most of the actual injury is healed, these scabs will soon turn to new skin and scar deeply. But I am most concerned about the darkness invading them. It is almost like an infection, festering in the punctures. As though it is growing and attacking your body. It has already started to a small degree, spreading slowly from the wounds." Looking at me with knitted brows, he purses his lips, sounding worried.

Every word he says has me paling further and feeling sick to my stomach. Oh Goddess, please tell me I'm not going to turn into one of those beasts? This must be why I've been feeling so tired and unwell.

I recount my story to the healer, sparing no detail about the terrible creatures. My hands fidget frantically, dizziness washing over me as panic hits me. "I'm not going to change am I? I don't want to rot like that thing or turn into one of those abominations..." The tears begin anew.

He quickly hugs me again, the pressure of his arms soothing me. "No, Dear One. I will not allow you to be infected by this darkness. Let me call your Orcs to comfort you, I must go prepare the healing tent. We are going to flush your body of this evil and make you whole again. Is that okay, young one?"

Getting a hold of myself, I take deep breaths. The thought of the brothers comforting me helps relax my alarm.

Wick releases me and stands, shuffling his way to the door, poking his head out briefly before returning with a bundle of cloth.

"Dear One, there is a bathing chamber upstairs. We have magic on our homes that enables you to fill the tub with hot water from there. Take this, go clean yourself and then cuddle with your Orcs while I prepare."

He's kind but there's a thread of steel in his tone. Wick is determined to help me, and that alone has tears threatening to fall again. I haven't felt this kind of care and concern since my parents died. This Elf reminds me of a kindly grandfather.

I hold back my tears and throw myself at him for another hug. Muttering thank-you's into his chest. Wick squeezes me gently before disengaging. He places the new clothing in my arms, giving me one last smile before waving me towards the stairs and slips out.

I find the brothers laying in the bedding. It is not a raised platform like I am used to, but a sunken pit filled with plentiful blankets and pillows. The sleeping space looks so inviting, but I should clean myself first.

When the Orcs see the redness around my eyes and nose, they both get such a fierce look on their faces. The way their brows draw down and the scowl that twists their lips around their tusks is frightening and appealing all at once. Brynd even bares his teeth and I swear the silent vibration from his growl shoots straight to my core. Mentally shaking my head, I scold myself. *These Orcs are not your mates. Stop that!*

"Where is the healer? I'm going to kill him for making you cry," Brenth grits out through a clenched jaw. His hands are fisted so tightly his knuckles turn white. He looks furious and I can't fight my attraction towards them both but I will ignore the wetness seeping from my cunt until I see my mates again.

My cheeks flame as I rush to soothe his anger, "No! No, he didn't hurt me! Everything that has happened... sort of hit me all at once and I broke down. Healer Wick was very kind, like I imagine a grandfather would be. He comforted me and then checked my wounds... finding dark ichor festering deep inside the punctures... he seemed very concerned about it. He sent me up here to bathe and cuddle with you both while he goes to prepare something that will flush it from my system." All the words tumble out so quickly, some of them run together making my tongue trip, but I think the brothers understand because they both relax.

Brynd reaches me first, scooping me up and holding me tight to his chest. He drops a kiss on my forehead, and my face flushes again. He's very sweet, for a large scary Orc warrior.

Brenth lets out a gusty sigh relaxing his fists. "Fair enough, Wee One. Let us show you their fancy bathing room! It's quite the marvel. I've never seen anything like it!" His eyes brighten and his face transforms with the smile he beams at me. "Who knew magic could be used in such a way... I wonder if they'd teach me how to do it?" He mumbles to himself.

They both take me to the tub, showing me the knobs that make water whoosh into the tub. One is cold and the other hot. As the tub fills, they show me a basket full of soaps and liquids that I've never heard of before, but they all smell so good. The first smile I've had in a while crosses my face as Brynd opens each one letting me smell them until I find one I like. The large silent brother is so gentle with me as he brushes my hair back, softly running his finger down my cheek. The heated look he gives me does not help my resolve to wait for my mates, but I'm stronger than that and they deserve better too.

Brenth hums and leans in to kiss my cheek. "Och, there she is. The wee beauty that stole my attention from the moment she crashed into us." He smiles down at me so affectionately, I can't help but return the feeling.

These two have done so much for me. I want them, I want to touch them and love them like I do my pack. But, I don't feel right doing anything with them until my mates are with me again. No matter how lusty I'm feeling. I have some self control.

I don't feel shy around them anymore, they've seen my nude form enough times while I bathed in the wilderness. Quickly, I shuck the ruined dress, hoping there are panties in the bundle of clothing Healer Wick gave me. It's been a while since I had a pair.

Sighing with relief as I sink into the hot water, I enjoy the soothing sensation on my muscles. Brynd kneels beside the tub and lifts a wash rag and a bar of soap, silently asking if he can clean me. I nod, excitement electrifying me. I'm looking forward to having his hands all over my body, even though it won't lead anywhere.

Brenth asks if he can do my hair and a pleased smile crosses my lips. Being pampered feels amazing.

Relaxing into the tub, the brothers work their hands over me. Closing my eyes, I lean into the feeling. Fingers running through my hair and over my achy muscles forces out breathy moans as I allow these Orcs to care for me. I feel like a princess just sitting here letting someone else do all the work. It's so soothing I can no longer fight my exhaustion and I welcome sleep.

I wake very briefly when strong arms lift me out of the tub. Another set of hands dry me with a large piece of fabric. They even dress me in panties and a nightgown. It isn't long before I'm falling back to sleep cuddled between their large, warm bodies.

CH.41

Hushed conversation filters through the room, waking me from a deep sleep. Someone else must be in the room because a low voice responds to Brenth. My head rests on his chest, his whispered voice rumbling in my ear. Brynd cuddles close to my back, purring silently in his chest. The vibration soothes all my worries. I'm not quite ready to get up and face my problems, everything feels simple when laying in bed. It's easier to pretend those headaches don't exist.

But, it's not my lucky day. The conversation quiets a moment before a large hand strokes my hair, down my back and pats my ass. I jump in surprise, releasing a squeak at that. Disoriented but awake, I'm confused. My bleary eyes try to understand where I am but nothing looks familiar. It takes me a minute before I can focus.

My voice is muffled from the chest I speak into. "Wha... maa...fuuu...?"

Laughter is my only answer. Sitting up, with wild hair and eyes that are barely open, I repeat, "What. The. Fuck?"

More laughter. I glare at Zenik, who's standing near the door and then over at Brynd who holds his hands up as if he's innocent.

Brenth sits up and the movement shakes me a little, helping me wake up even more. Brenth hides a smile at my leveled glare. In response, I cross my arms and pout about being awake.

"Och! Don't give me that look, Wee Lassie! I argued for you to be left to rest." Brenths voice is a little rough from sleep as he denies his involvement, tugging me more firmly onto his lap.

Awake now, I turn my frown back towards Zenik. "Why do I have to be awake?"

His face softens as he uncrosses his arms. "Healer Wick has everything ready for you. You're fine in the sleeping gown, you'll likely have to remove it anyways. Maybe put on a breast band and panties, if you're uncomfortable showing anything? I'll wait downstairs, don't take too long, Wick gets crabby. Although, I think he would soften just for you, Omega." Zenik's yellow gaze considers me a moment before turning and disappearing down the stairs.

I ask Brenth where the rest of the clothes got to last night before climbing off him. Slipping a breast band on under the gown before I use the privy, wash my face and clean my teeth. The brothers are ready by the time I walk out of the bathroom.

Heading for the stairs before either one of them has the chance to pick me up, I take my time going down each step. Even without my injuries I'm quite clumsy. A fall would be extremely unpleasant.

Zenik and an older Elf wait on the cushions in the living space, there's a wooden platter containing steaming bundles in the middle of the seating arrangement. Whatever it is smells so good. My mouth waters as I wander over to join them.

"Good morning," I say quietly to Zenik, and introduce myself to the other male. "Hello. I am Luella," pausing, I can't remember if I gave them my name yesterday. "Thank you for allowing us entry. For granting us safety."

The older man's gaze rakes over me, studying me. "I am Chief Zarren. Welcome to my village." He tosses a quick glower towards the Orcs, if I hadn't been watching him I would have missed it. "Be sure not to cause trouble, outsiders often misunderstand our ways. Once you are healed we will give you supplies and you must be on your way. The only reason you were allowed in, is because you are Omega and it is cruel to allow one so precious as you to suffer."

My gut screams at me not to trust him. There is a sinister air about this Elf that makes my stomach twist and nausea build. My inner Omega can sense something bad about Zarren and I'm inclined to trust this feeling. He does not want us here, or he does not want my Orcs here. Zarren probably wouldn't allow me to leave if I wasn't already accompanied by the brothers.

"Thank you." I try to hide my dislike by giving him a short bow of my head, "We are grateful you have allowed us sanctuary in our time of need." Keeping my eyes down to conceal my true feelings.

"You are something special." Zarren makes a brief noise of delight in his throat, "You already know your place, you would not require much training to be the perfect Omega."

Is he insinuating that I should be meek and submissive? I resist the desire to curl my lip at his words. I mean, I can be with my mates, sometimes... But, I have a strong stubborn streak that most Alpha's wouldn't tolerate. I just need to hold my tongue until we can get out of here. Zenik seemed kind and understanding yesterday, but if he's anything like this male I would not want to spend any more time with him than required.

The room is speechless after his unsavory statement. A quick peek at my Orcs shows how hard they are fighting the urge to smash this male into the ground. Brynd's fists tremble with his tension and Brenth is taking deep breaths in order to contain the fury he'd like to spew. Zarren seems oblivious to the tension, but as I study him out of the corner of my eye I spot the twitch of his lips as he surveys the room. I don't know what his goal is, but my gut is telling me to get the hell out of here as fast as possible.

Zenik breaks the uncomfortable silence, "Please have a seat, we have brought breakfast." He shifts his gaze towards me. "You will need to eat before we take you to Healer Wick. You will need your strength for the healing."

Nodding, I sit. The brothers join me on either side. I feel safer between them, a buffer from the shrewd stare of the Chief.

The meal is uncomfortable and silent, but at least the food tastes good. It is different to what I'm used to but I'm enjoying the new flavors and I allow myself a few moments to consider what kind of pastries I could make with some of these ingredients. My mind will never stop thinking up new flavor combinations.

We eat our fill before they lead us out to the Healer's space. Staying close, between Brenth and Brynd, I need the feeling of security from them. Ever since I met the Chief my belly feels twisted and uneasy. It's screaming at me that this male is dangerous and I should get far away from him.

I don't even bother looking around at their village this time. I just want this over with so we can leave.

Quickly checking my bonds, my mates feel closer, I think they are through the mountains. I'm giddy, excited to see them and scent them again. It has been far too long since I've been able to touch my males. Stroking each bond, I push excitement and happiness to them, receiving the same in return.

When we arrive at the Healers, I swiftly close out of the bonds, not wanting them to feel any of my pain when the healing starts. I know how much it can hurt.

Healer Wick gives me a hasty, almost imperceptible, smile before greeting the Chief.

"We are ready to heal and drain the

darkness. Everything has been set up inside."
We all go to step forward but Wick holds out
a hand. "No, I am sorry, but only the Omega. I
cannot have any other auras in the circle while
I heal her."

Taking my hand, he leads me away from
my Orcs. Unease sits heavy in my gut, but he
does not allow the Chief or Zenik in either,
which helps ease my discomfort. Sneaking one
last glance at my Orcs as I disappear through
the doorway, they sport similar expressions of
apprehension.

A hazy smoke fills the chamber and a
medicinal scent permeates the air. There's a
circle of salt laid out with a reed mat in the
center. Wick directs me to lay on the mat after
I disrobe.

Strangely, I feel comfortable with him.
He has no desire for my body and he only wants
to help. A feeling of lightheadedness washes
over me as my thoughts grow foggy.

"W-why is it so hard to... um..." I blow
out a harsh breath and squeeze my eyes shut
before blinking rapidly, "why can't I think?"

Wick gives me a weak smile, his eyes
not quite meeting mine. "It is to help with the
extraction of darkness. I need you relaxed and
susceptible to my magics," he explains.

A strange look passes over his face

before he whispers so quietly I could have imagined it, "I'm sorry. I will do what I can to bring you back after this."

Nodding sleepily, I lay my head back, waiting for him to begin. My eyes shut as he starts chanting in Elvish. It is such a beautiful language, the sounds soothing all my worries. I don't even twitch when he smears an odd smelling paste on my bruises and over the healing puncture wounds.

As he continues my mind grows heavier and heavier. Even with my eyes closed I see a swirl of color, it's quite beautiful. I want to reach out and touch them but my arms are leaden.

A sucking sensation startles me, like something is being pulled from my insides, but I can't move. The ache in my side begins to twinge and throb as tears flow freely down my face. My mouth twitches, needing to open, to cry out, but my muscles no longer work. It doesn't stop no matter how hard I try to speak or move, or do anything. I'm trapped in a circle of pain.

As the harsh sucking sensation grows more painful, the chanting increases to a deafening volume. The pressure releases me and I'm able to scream at the sharp, cutting feeling. It feels like something inside me was sliced away. Even once things calm, I'm still unable to move my arms or open my eyes. There is a brief feeling of heaviness that seems to settle over my mind, but it's too difficult to focus on it.

The sensation of my injuries being healed warms my body, but does not hurt like it did when... someone healed me... When that is over, I heave a sigh of relief as I feel my body come back to me. First in my toes, then fingers, then I'm able to blink my eyes open. My vision is blurry as I take in the room, trying to understand where I am and what's happening.

A kindly face peers down at me and I smile at him.

"Hello. I'm Luella. Is this your home? Where am I?"

The elderly male frowns down at me, holding out a hand to help me sit up. "Luella, Omega, do you remember coming here?"

Considering the male and the room around me, I'm confused. My thoughts are jagged and difficult to piece together. Brief flashes of different faces flicker through my mind. Rough, green skin and tusks sharpen in my mind and I brighten.

"Oh! Yes! My..." cradling my head in my hands, I feel nauseous as a sharp pain slices through my mind, "No, I-I can't remember. I came here with someone... right? Why do I feel like I'm missing other faces? It hurts trying to bring up the memories. Why am I so sad that I can't remember them? I can feel them... in here." I tap my chest over my heart.

He leads me over to a low table and helps me to sit on one of the cushions then takes a seat beside me.

Leaning in closely he whispers, "Those missing faces are your mates and your Orc guardians. You are an Omega. I have just healed you. I pulled a great darkness from your soul, it is a traumatizing process. The memory loss you're experiencing is something else... But, it will all come back to you in time, I promise. For now you need much rest. Please, drink this and I will fetch your guardians." He hands me a clay mug with an herb-y smelling concoction.

Scrunching my nose as my lip curls at the smell. He laughs jovially, patting me on the shoulder. "I know it tastes awful but it will help your body heal faster."

Sipping it slowly, I try not to spit it out after every taste, it is truly disgusting. I watch him as he walks to the door and pokes his head out.

There's quiet murmuring and then raised voices. The healer sounds harsh and angry before someone is shoved inside, knocking into him.

The man that was shoved inside looks a little familiar but I cannot place him. He looks at the healer apologetically before coming to sit beside me.

"Hello, Luella. Do you remember me?" His face looks kind but he won't meet my gaze. He grimaces and all I feel is confused.

Frowning at him I try to bring up his name but fail. "I'm sorry, I'm having difficulty remembering things at the moment. Please, remind me of your name?"

"I am Zenik. The Chief of this village is my father. I am here to aid you back to your home for rest. After a difficult healing like this you will need to sleep for at least a day or so." The male peers into my mug and, seeing it mostly empty, helps me to my feet.

As soon as my legs straighten, I wobble, my head feeling stuffed full of cotton. Dizzy and disoriented I try to take a step and fall. Strong arms catch me lifting me to a hard chest.

Tucking my face into his neck, inhaling a spicy scent. My nose twitches while holding back a sneeze, Zenik is far too pungent for my liking.

He chuckles lightly. "I will carry you

back, I would not wish for you to injure yourself so quickly after being healed."

Making a noise of agreement, I very quickly fall asleep in his arms as he carries me away from the hazy room. The fresh air is nice but not enough to rouse me from my healing sleep. I don't even think to ask him about my mates or the Orc guardians.

CH.42

It must be days later when my consciousness surfaces. My rumbling stomach seems to be what woke me. Alone in a large sunken, pillow filled nest, I roll to untangle myself from my cocoon of blankets.

My face lands in one of the pillows and a puff of the most delicious scent surrounds me, peaches and cream. A shudder works its way through me and I don't move for a few deep lungfuls, revelling in the smell. I struggle to free my arms in order to bring the pillow with me as I turn onto my back.

My head lands on a fluffy blanket and another mouthwatering scent fills the air around me. Peaches and honey. My core clenches and slick leaks out of me. Sighing, I close my eyes and relax into these rich succulent scents.

Finally getting to my feet I peer around

the room. My bladder is shouting at me and I need to relieve myself, badly. Finding what I'm looking for, I head to the privy, thinking about those scents. *Why do they smell so familiar...?*

Doing my business, I clean myself up, trying to conjure the faces associated with those smells, because I know them. Those scents are important to me, I just can't remember how or why.

A chill winds through my body upon finding a delicate, yellow dress on the edge of the bed. Someone came into *my* room! My lip curls and a snarl escapes me, my Omega is furious at the gall of them to encroach on my space without consent. The dress is much shorter than I prefer but there's nothing else to wear, so I pull it on after tossing the sleeping gown to the floor.

An Alpha had the nerve to scent mark it! The smell is okay but it does not make slick leak from my core. Why was given a scented garment? It feels... rude and presumptuous.

Once I'm at the bottom of the steps, a sense of familiarity washes over me, I know I've been here before. I curiously eye the two males in the living space.

Giving the two males a quizzical look, I make my way through the room to sit. They are similar, except one appears slightly older. Their ears give them away as Elves. The males greet me with a smile and I return it with a clumsy curtsy, feeling very silly. This is a foreign feeling, I'm sure I've never done that before.

"Hello. Do I know you?" I question as I drop down on the cushion across from them.

The older one gives me a satisfied grin, slapping the younger one on the back. "I am Chief Zarren and this is my son Zenik. We have taken you into our village, you were in need of food and water. You'd been wandering the desert outside our walls for some time before you came across us. We have graciously taken care of you and given you a home. You are to stay with us, living in our village with my son as your mate."

Confused, my brow furrows and an uneasy feeling warns me to keep my guard up. I do not remember any of this. Needing assistance sounds familiar, why do I get the feeling I wasn't alone? Was someone with me when I came here? My brows scrunch together and I try hard to recall. I get a brief flash of green skin and tusks before it's gone again.

"I... I do not remember how I got here. I'm sorry. I do not remember being mated to you, Zenik." Zenik's face twists with contempt, but it's directed at his father. "Are we... mates? I thought I was a Beta?..."

As I speak, a dull aching pain thrums as brief thoughts flash through my head. I remember baking things... a market? Four large males and one slightly smaller. He needs me, they need me. Why am I here? I am not meant to live here. I'm certain of this, but the throbbing pain intensifies as I try to recall my past.

Bringing my hands up, I clutch my head and whimper at the pain. Arms circle around me and I'm lifted onto a lap and cuddled close. Zenik smells exactly like the spicy scent on my dress.

Taking the comfort where I can, I don't fight his hold. I'm determined to bring forth my memories, regardless of the difficulty. I am very stubborn when I want to be.

"Shh... Omega, it's all right. Just relax, you do not need to remember right now. All will be well." Zenik rocks me gently on his lap, stroking my hair and humming softly.

I quiet in his embrace and when I can open my eyes, concern shines back at me. My eyes are drawn to his leering smug father. His stare makes me feel slimy and I avoid it by tucking my face back into Zenik's chest.

Zarren's grating tone scratches my ears when he speaks, "Good. Comfort her, feed her and then take her upstairs and mark her." He orders harshly. My body tenses as the words sink in. I do not want that. I may not find Zenik offensive, but I do not wish for him as a mate. I already have mates...

Wait a second... I have mates! I remember. But all their details are fuzzy, like looking through a frosted window. Reaching up to my neck, I pretend to massage the muscles at the sides and back, feeling for bite scars. The Chief's unsavory presence gives me chills and my gut tells me to conceal any personal information. His presence feels menacing and dark. Finding the scars, I sigh with relief.

They are real!

I just need to get those memories to come back to me. Frustration bubbles, the desire to just *know* what I'm missing hounds me, but I don't know how to fix this.

I continue to hide from Zarren's view until the door slams, indicating his exit. Zenik waits a beat before uttering softly,

"He's gone now. I know what he said but I have no wish to force myself upon any lass. Please, eat and I will try to explain things. I know you will be confused and have trouble remembering things."

Staring [1]into his eyes, watching for some sign or indication that he's being truthful, I frown. My Omega is tense but thankful that he has no plans to force a bond, but how does he know I can't remember things? I scramble off his lap to my own cushion.

"How do you know my mind is foggy? What did you do to me? Why can I recall green skin and tusks when everyone I have seen so far has been Elven?" Firing questions at him in rapid succession, I don't give him a chance to answer me. "I think I already have mates. I do not mean to offend, but I do not desire you as a mate. I am sorry. You seem like you would make a good friend though. I bet Dani would like you. Oh Goddess! Dani! I-I know... She's a friend... I think?" There's a feeling of urgency to find her whenever she crosses my mind. Is she lost? Am I lost?

Taking a moment to breathe. My mouth seems to remember who I am. The rest of me just needs to catch up. I wonder if I just keep asking questions, the rest will come back to me...

Zenik's muffled laughter distracts me from my racing thoughts. When he sees me staring, his amusement falls.

"I'm sorry, Luella. My father runs this village with an iron fist, it is suicide to disobey him. But... I cannot condone what he is doing to you. You're an Omega! The laws regarding Omegas are meant to keep you safe from being taken against your will." He sighs deeply, like the world rests on his shoulders.

"I will not mark you. I will do what I can to protect you from his wrath. Wick and I will try to help your memory return, but I cannot guarantee anything. This is strange magic and I don't fully understand it." He scrubs a hand down his face as exhaustion pulls his shoulders down.

"But... Why? What does he have to gain by forcing me?" Confused and frustrated I scowl at him. Being an Omega sounds pretty stupid.

"Do you not know how rare Omega's are? Your designation is the only one who can reliably give Alpha's true children. If an Alpha breeds an Omega they will always have Alpha or Omega children. Usually Betas only have Beta children. Although, my research suggests Omegas taken by force have trouble breeding at all. It has something to do with the stress levels, forced Omegas end up becoming barren. The research said it is a protection mechanism that has evolved to try and prevent forced bonding."

My mouth drops open in shock at the information. "Being an Omega sounds stupid.

Who cares if you can only breed Beta's? We're all beings! It doesn't matter what your designation is. Ugh." I groan as I massage my temples. My head aches as I attempt to force memories to the surface.

Zenik shakes his head and sighs heavily. "It is not something that has ever bothered me but... I think there is something wrong with my father and I do not know how to help him." He brings his head up and forces a weak smile. "Eat, then get some more rest. You are still healing. I will try to keep my father away from you."

Patting my shoulder, Zenik gets to his feet. I watch curiously as he composes himself. It's fascinating how he puts on a mask of indifference. It must be required to deal with his father. Nothing about this situation is trustworthy, I'm going to need to stay on guard while I'm here.

Harsh yelling interrupts my restless sleep and I shoot upright. My heart pounds and I grasp my chest as fear courses through me.

Thudding footsteps coming up the stairs has my tension ratcheting up. Blinking sleep out of my eyes, I'm literally ripped out of the blankets and jerked into a hard body. The scent is so strong, my eyes water as I try to figure out what's happening.

The male who grabbed me leans in close and runs his nose along my neck. Shivers of disgust tremble through my body. I try to lean away from the touch, but as soon as I do the male wraps a hand around my throat, squeezing just enough to cut off most of my air.

Panic has me reacting before I can think. Wheezing, I claw at the hand, my eyes bulging as dizziness slows my movements.

The male shakes me violently before he leans in to whisper, "If you move again I will be forced to punish you harshly. Do as I say and you will be fine, pretty little Omega."

All I can do is nod frantically and try not to pass out. Finally, he eases his hold and I noisily suck in air. My body weakly leans back into him. Even though I despise his touch, it's the only thing keeping me upright.

As my vision clears, Zenik stares at us in horror from the doorway.

"Father! What are you doing? I told you she needed more rest before I could mark and claim her. This is not helping!" He waves a hand in my direction, concern wrinkling his brow as he watches me gasp for air.

"Shut up, boy. You're weak and

incompetent. You can't handle an Omega. I don't know what I was thinking. Go play with your warriors and plan drills and hunts." The male behind me sneers at him, clutching at my throat again. He doesn't cut off my air but my eyes go wide with dread as he continues, voice dark and full of lust,

"I have an Omega to claim."

My heart aches and my mouth goes dry. My limbs feel heavy and I have no idea how to escape this. I do not want this angry male. Zarren smells wrong and my instincts are insistenting that bad things will happen if I do not get away from him.

Zarren shifts his hand from the front of my throat to the back of my neck with a painful grip. Bruises are inevitable. I'm shoved forwards, almost tripping over my feet as he marches me out and down the stairs. As we pass Zenik I give him a pleading look. He slumps against the wall and looks away, avoiding the abuse. What a weak, shitty Alpha. Who does that? Who ignores this kind of cruelty?

Feeling betrayed, I choke back a cry. Wasn't he just saying he would try to keep his father away from me? How can he let this happen?

Zarren doesn't slow or let me speak. As

we pass through the front door, Elven warriors line the path. My attempts to catch their attention are futile, they carefully keep their eyes away from me. When Zarren notices what I'm doing his grip grows punishing and I have to swallow a whimper of pain.

Leaning in, Zarren sneers at me, his foul breath turning my stomach "No one will help you. You are mine now. So you'd better start behaving or you will not enjoy the consequences." His leveled smirk has fingers of dread scraping down my insides.

I attempt to swallow my terror, but my throat feels like it's closing up. The weight of his threats settles on my chest, suffocating me. Dizziness overwhelms me as my world narrows down to his grip on my neck. What am I going to do? I need to get away from him before he tries anything. There is no way I could live with myself if he claimed me. I don't think I'd want to. Zarren would be inside me, all the time. Forced to feel his sick emotions and endure awful things at his hands. Shaking my head as he continues to march me through the village, I try to calm my mind so I can think of a way out of this.

My hysterical thoughts are interrupted.

"Sir. There's a problem at the cells. The... uh, prisoners are causing a scene. The villagers are getting restless and unhappy." The pale faced warrior swallows repeatedly, eyes shifting around nervously.

"And why haven't you dealt with it?" Zarren grates out, squeezing my neck until I wince and curl in on myself. I guess I'm not allowed to look at anything.

"A crowd is building and they are not happy. They are demanding to speak with you, Chief." His voice is unsteady and I can almost smell the pungent aroma of fear wafting off him.

"*Vell. VELL!* Fine. Bring me the collar and leash." Zarren snaps at someone. The heat of his rage has me sweating and fidgeting. I try to step away from his anger without him noticing, which is impossible as he's still got an excruciating grip on my neck.

Moments later the warrior returns and hands something to Zarren. I don't look up, afraid he will hurt me.The leather collar wraps around my throat. I whimper in response to the unfamiliar feeling. The attached leash is passed off to the large warrior beside him.

"Take her to the room I had prepared. Tie the leash to the bars overhead and lock the door behind you. Keep a guard on the door at all times. She is not to be given any opportunities to escape." His voice is low and grinding. I swear I can feel malice and darkness hovering around him.

This is bad.

CH.43

The room I'm shoved into is horrifying. There are bars lining the ceiling. My 'leash' is tied tightly to a ring that slides along the bars. There's no way for me to reach it and there is nothing in here that I can use to cut through the leather.

It's practically barren. A small bedding area, consisting of a few blankets and a single pillow. There's a bucket in the far corner and I shudder to think about having to use it. My tether allows me enough movement to reach the bucket and the bedding, it stops short of the door. If I stretch my fingertips are still inches away. This windowless prison is a nightmare.

I jump at a loud *thunk.* It must be the guard latching the bolt, locking me inside. Dread settles heavily on my shoulders and my breaths grow shallow, the air feels thick and difficult to inhale.

Standing in the centre of the room shaking, I close my eyes and mentally count down from ten. It's a decent effort to slow my gasping and try to regain control of my panic.

Okay, Luella, you are not stupid. You can get out of this. Just breathe and think.

When my heart finally stops racing and the tremors in my hands settle, I open my eyes. My hands trace the collar in search of a latch or tie. But I can't find anything. Confused, I frantically explore around and around. All I can feel is a perfect, unmarred circle of leather encasing my throat. The leash is wrapped around it in a loop with no discernible connection.

What the fuck?

How? It must be magic, squeezing my eyes shut I exhale slowly. *Do not panic. No more panic.*

My eyes shoot open as a strange thought strikes me. I need to get angry. Anger will help... Somehow... But I can't remember how or why. A searing pain cripples me, and I collapse to the hard floor cradling my head.

Okay, I take a deep breath, I forgot that trying to remember anything hurts. I know this but I need to do it anyway. No one else is going to get me out of this.

Taking a deep breath I think about all the things that infuriate me since I woke up from the healing.

- No memory of my mates
- Being told some stranger is going to claim me
- Being hauled out of bed and choked
- Placed in a collar and locked in a windowless prison
- The thought of Zarren forcing me to mate him

Fury flows through me, down to my hands and my feet. Tingles spread over my body, but I don't let it distract me. Something is happening and it feels kind of good. All of a sudden fur sprouts and claws spring out of the fluffy paws that have overtaken my human hands. My feet follow and then everything pauses. When I look inside myself it almost seems as though there's something blocking me. I should be able to shift into... I can't see it but I know I have a beast inside me.

And she wants out.

Badly.

I shake my head to refocus because that's not my concern at the moment. I need to get out. I flex my claws, extending and sheathing them, testing out my ability to control them. Once I've got a handle on it, I bring my sharp talons up and easily slice through the leather leash. I'm a little more careful as I slip a single claw between my neck and the collar. Once the leather slips free, I stretch my neck and sigh in relief. Tipping my head back I take a deep breath, fortifying myself for what's next.

I hang on tightly to my anger because I need my weapons available. I position myself behind the door and sink into a crouch. Opening my mouth, I let out the loudest Omega whine I can produce. Alpha's have difficulty ignoring an Omega in distress and I plan to use anything I can to my benefit.

Only a few seconds pass before the door swings open. The Elf takes one step inside and I lunge for his ankle, clawing through it. As he falls I wrap the dirty blanket around his head, muffling his cries and any attempt to bark me into submission. I refuse to lay down and accept this, no one will stop me.

I am *not* weak.

The guard reaches for his head and I snarl, "If you alert anyone to my escape I will kill you instead of leaving you in my prison." My voice trembles, but I know he can hear the desperation in my tone because he stops trying to move.

Instead of responding, he reaches down to his bloody ankle, puts pressure on the injury and lays still.

"Good. Stay here. If you want to live you will tell no one what happened. Say you were knocked out, I don't care. But do not let them know I am on my own. Do you understand?" Practically hissing at him, I wait until his blanket wrapped head nods once. Snagging the key from his belt, I slip around the partially open door and lock him in.

Taking a moment to gather myself, I lean against the door and release a shaky exhale. My claws have receded with my anxiety, but I know how to get them back if I need them. Standing tall, I push off the door determined to make my escape.

Now to figure out how to escape this house. I don't think I'm in a treehouse like the ones in the village. Since the dungeon is constructed from stone, it's probably similar to a Lord's manor. Quietly, I stalk through the hallways, listening carefully for any sounds.

Anytime I hear voices coming I slip into the closest room and hold my breath, waiting for them to pass by. I must be underground, I haven't come across any windows yet, and the air feels oppressive and stale.

By the time I make it to the stairs

my body trembles with apprehension. There's nowhere to hide in this hallway and it seems like this is the only door out. So, when I hear two male voices arguing quietly as the door opens, I have to bite my lip to prevent any sounds from escaping. All out of options, I close my eyes and let infuriating thoughts flow through my mind.

As the tell-tale tingles rush through me, Zenik and Wick stumble to a stop mid-step as I hiss angrily at them.

"Omega! You're alright? Oh, thank the Goddess. I was so worried for you." Zenik steps forward as if he will touch me but I am not having that. I can't trust him. He allowed his repulsive father to take me and cage me. That is not okay.

Zenik jumps back as I swipe at him, hands up with wide, surprised eyes. Wick breaks the tension by laughing into his hands, trying to silence his amusement. He joins Zenik with his hands up when I turn to him, a glare on my face and claws raised.

"Please, Luella. We are here to get you out. I promise. We have come to rescue you, but it seems you are much stronger than anyone could have guessed." Wick soothes, hushing his voice.

Zenik adds, "Yes, I swear. I tried to stop

my father, but he's out of control. I fear only his death will stop him. Please, I didn't mean for any of this to happen." His eyes cast downward, shoulders slumping as he brings his hands in front of him to plead with me.

The longer they speak the calmer I become. My fury wanes and the claws recede. "Fine. But... Can you fix my head? Every time I try to remember something, daggers strike agony in my brain. And I know there are things I *have* to remember." I glare at them both, baring my teeth and holding my head up high. There is no time to process events or allow weakness to stop me.

Wick is nodding before I've finished my demands. "Yes, come with us. Please. I had to brew a counter potion to help you regain your memories, but it takes time and... I'm sorry. I'm sorry there wasn't more I could do to stop this from happening." He pleads while glancing away to hide the sheen of tears in his eyes. I believe him.

I approve of his apology and I will give him a modicum of trust.

"Fine. Is the way out clear?" I clip out, my harsh stare focusing on Wick. I am not ready to accept an apology from Zenik. I do not know why, but something inside me tells me to make him grovel. He is not a worthy Alpha and I am glad my inner Omega does not desire him.

Wick nods and reaches for my hand, pausing when I flinch away from his touch. "Sorry. Follow me, and please, stay between us. We will try to hide you if we encounter anyone."

They lead me out and, surprisingly, we do not encounter any other guards. *Where are they and why hasn't Zarren come to check on me?* I am glad, but also, highly suspicious.

I'll save my questions for a more convenient time. Exhaustion weighs me down now that adrenaline isn't driving me and I trudge after them. Our small group moves quietly out of the manor and down a heavily treed and overgrown path, it is silent. The absence of sounds, bugs, animals and Elves, unnerves me. There's a foreboding feeling nagging at the back of my mind. Something bad is coming. They lead me to the healer's home and quickly usher me inside.

Slumping down onto a cushion, I level an arctic glare on Zenik. "How are you going to fix me? How are you going to fix this village? Your father isn't the only problem. He has enough warriors at his disposal, to make this rescue and escape dangerous. How are you going to get me out of this village? I can't stay here, it isn't safe."

Before Zenik can reply, Wick shuffles over with a steaming cup of violet liquid. It smells awful and he laughs when I sneer in disgust.

"It tastes as bad as it smells, I'm sorry. But, if you drink this it will help clear your memory. You will sleep for a short while as it works. When you wake up everything should be back to normal." Placing the cup in my hands with a grimace, he wipes his sweaty palms on his robes.

"Let's get this over with, then." I say on a sigh. Staring into the liquid, a giddy feeling of hope tickles through my stomach before I tip back the cup quickly. If either of them lied to me about this I will wake up and hurt them. I have claws and I know how to use them.

CH.44

Rage wakes me from the healing sleep and I feel ready for a fight. My thoughts clear while taking in my surroundings, thankfully I'm still on the cushion by the low table. Anger simmers in my blood when my eyes land on Zenik sitting across from me.

"What. The. Fuck." The scowl I level on him could cut down lesser men. "I'm going to kill your father and burn this fucking village to the ground. One of my mates is a Dragon, I'll have you know, and he's possessive, protective and *very* hot tempered. He'd probably do it just because your father thought about taking me for himself."

"Shit!" Zenik pales as he struggles to swallow. "One of your mates? How many mates do you have?"

"I have five. But, I'm pretty sure I'll be adding my Orcs to our pack as soon as we're reunited. There's a Dragon, a Hellhound, a Gargoyle, a Summer Fae and an Elf who'd been turned into a freaky monster through black magic." I tick them off on my hand "Blue is a mix of a wolf, hawk, rabbit, horse and lion. He's quite beastly and vicious, I've seen him tear other creatures apart faster than I can blink, and he's the Beta in my pack." Sighing as the fight drains out of me, I miss them so much.

Gently, I prod my bonds, hoping that they weren't damaged by whatever was done to me to make me forget. They feel fine but it's almost like there's a veil draped over each connection. I need some time to figure out how to remove it, but that will have to happen after I find my Orcs and get the fuck out of here. I'm not much for swearing but these days it feels more appropriate to toss in a 'fuck' here and there.

When I refocus on Zenik and Wick they're both very pale. Zenik's hands are shaking slightly. I wonder if he's going to pass out? But he surprises me by jumping to his feet and pacing around the room, hands running through his hair.

"Fuck. Fuck. Fuck. Your mates are the Kings elite squad. I was slightly worried about forcing you before, knowing you had mates out there. But now that I know it's *them*, I'm afraid my whole village will be razed to the ground.

Shit. Fuck. My father really can't seem to see past his greed." Continuing to pace, he mutters to himself about being murdered and fried.

Clearing my throat, I attempt to get his attention but he's far too panicked to hear me. I grab a cushion and chuck it at his face.

Nailing him right in the forehead, I crow my victory. Arms up and waving as I do a little jiggle in my seat. He stops and stares at me, like I'm the crazy one.

"You need to calm the fuck down. Last I checked, my mates had just made it through the mountain pass and were headed in my direction. So you probably have another day or two until they get here. My advice is to gather my Orcs and quietly get us out of the village so we can go meet my mates, away from here," I tell him sternly, attempting to channel Tawson, but I'm not sure if I'm pulling it off. At least he looks like he's listening.

Zenik winces at the mention of my Orcs. "Right. About that... the Orcs have been imprisoned so we could separate you from them and work the magic needed to befuddle your mind."

Fury builds again and my face flushes as my fists clench and unclench with the desire to punch him. Gritting my teeth I snarl,

"Those are *my* Orcs. *Mine*! How..." I'm

cut off by Wick gently placing a hand on my fist. Attempting to soothe my rage. I twitch but manage not to pull away. Wick had no choice and he has shown me that he is on my side. I'm still angry with Zenik and I don't know if I can trust him.

"I am sorry for the part I played in this, I did not agree with Chief Zarren about taking you forcefully. But if I disagreed he likely would have sent me to be caged until he felt I could be trusted again… or he may have just killed me. He has gotten progressively more manic in the last year, making all our lives difficult." Wick looks down, rubbing the back of his neck with a wince.

"What happened to him? Was he… nicer before?" I hesitate to ask, not really wanting to know. I will dislike the male no matter what.

Zenik sighs, staring down at his hands. "He used to be the best Chief and father. He was kind and did everything he could to better our village and improve our lives. He had high hopes for me to find an Omega to mate before I took over but he was not pressing the issue, until about a year ago… I don't know exactly what happened but he had gone out on a hunt with a small group of his closest friends and warriors. They were only supposed to be gone for three days but a week passed before they returned without any kills." The Elf fidgets with his pockets, refusing to make eye contact. He exhales heavily, exhaustion and despair evident in his posture.

"There was... a darkness about them. Not just my father. They became cruel, tormenting the villagers who went to them for aid and... I've seen them force some of the women to do things that will haunt me." He shivers, his cheeks hollowing as he sucks in a breath. I can see the horrors pass through his eyes before he shakes his head.

"I don't know what to do, or how to fix this. I don't want to have to kill my father, but I will if I cannot figure out how to get him back... When you spoke about the evil things you'd seen. The Necromancer and the black magic User, I started to wonder if that's what happened to them." He gives me a look, eyebrows raised, as he smooths his shirt. It's hopefulness, he thinks we can help him somehow.

Shaking my head, I swallow hard. "I don't know anything about magic, all I know are the things I've experienced and what I saw as we escaped the mountains. Honestly, Brenth would be the best to ask because both him and his brother have been trained by Users in the capital. I've seen them perform incredible things with magic." Humming, I stare blankly out one of the small windows as I think. "I wonder if the black magic User cast a spell on them? Or maybe left a cursed object for them to find?"

Wick sucks in a breath, eyes wide. "You may be onto something, child. I noticed a strange necklace that Zarren has been wearing. I haven't checked the tainted warriors, but... that could be what's corrupting them."

"I know the one you speak of. I have seen the tainted ones wearing other types of jewellery with an odd stone in them... It always felt off to me, like the air around them was being pulled into the stone. It feels dark and foreboding," Zenik adds.

We're silent for a moment as we consider all the information.

"I'm sorry about your father... but do you have a plan to get me my Orcs? They aren't going to be executed are they? We need to get them. Preferably now, please," I plead, concern for my males filling me. I do not want to lose them.

Wick pats my knee in sympathy. "We will get your Orcs and get you out of here, do not worry."

"But we should help you free your father! Surely, it would be easier if you had extra help to break the curse?" I think I would feel bad if we just ran and left them to deal with their mad Chief and his tainted warriors.

Zenik shakes his head, "No, I would not forgive myself if you were injured any more because of my fathers madness. We don't even know if that is the true cause of his issues. It could be, we rip off the necklaces and bracelets and they are still filled with darkness, giving them the opportunity to attack us."

Wick nods along with him. His eyes unfocused. "This is true. But, if your Orcs truly are Users they may be able to help me sense and rip out the root of the darkness." He turns to me. "But, they did not sense it embedded in your wounds... This is all conjecture anyways, we should speak with them. If they can help... maybe we will accept aid."

Zenik pales at the thought of me staying, being in danger. Maybe he's afraid my mates will arrive before we've fixed things? But he's not denying the need for assistance either.

"Look, I want to help if we can... If Brenth thinks there's something they can do to help. I know I'm not much help in a fight. I cannot always shift my hands and I've had no training. But I wouldn't feel right just leaving you to deal with this on your own, not when this darkness keeps popping up in my life. It's like it's hunting me..." I trail off, horror dawning on me at the realization.

It *is* hunting me. Shit. What I really want to know is why. Why am I being hunted? Is it because I'm an Omega? Or is it because of the 'marker' in my blood that I overheard the dark voice muttering about?

I'm not sure I really want the answers. All I truly desire is to reunite with my mates. And get my Orcs back. They belong to me, with me.

We will help these poor foolish Elves and then we will leave, hopefully never stepping foot in this village ever again.

CH.45

I wish my mates were here. I need their comfort and safety to wrap around myself. Even sitting here, with Zenik and Wick, I feel alone. I miss my Orcs, too.

I don't even realize I'm crying until Wick hands me a piece of cloth and motions at my cheeks. I flush, annoyed with myself. Before becoming an Omega I never cried, unless I stubbed my toe really badly. Now, I'm just a mess of hormones over the stupidest things. I hate crying.

Sniffling, I manage to get a hold of myself. "Sorry. Sorry, I'm still getting used to the 'heightened emotions' of being an Omega." I finger quote the stupid words that are now haunting me. "Regardless, we're going to help. I will speak to my Orcs, I'm sure if I ask, they will gladly aid your village."

At least my little outburst has broken

the tense atmosphere. Wick smiles fondly at me, like a grandfather would a sweet child. Zenik holds back laughter, his face finally returning to its normal color. I am feeling decidedly less antagonistic towards them now.

Zenik sighs before nodding at me. "Fine, Omega. We will free your Orcs and see if they will be able to aid us in clearing the minds of our tainted brethren, and my father."

They tell me my Orcs are being held in spelled cells near the Chief's home to await their sentencing.

Before the taint, most petty crimes are a slap on the wrist. Helping in the community, building homes, working in the gardens and fishing. Other more serious crimes are usually death. Their community has been relatively peaceful until the hunt that brought black magic here.

Warriors will be guarding the prisoners, but Zenik will distract them. Wick will take me to the cells and disable the spells containing my Orcs. We'll have to be as silent as possible, which Brenth will help with once freed.

The original plan, to sneak directly out of the village and avoid capture, will not work if we plan to free the Chief from darkness. We will need somewhere to hide while we plan. Zenik suggested his home but both Wick and I agreed that would be too dangerous. His father spends too much time sticking his nose in Zenik's business. I can only hope Zarren will put off 'visiting' his Omega in the cell beneath his home.

Wick divulges there are hidden tunnels running under the exterior fence around the village. Quite a few disgruntled families have access to them and would be willing to hide us or aid in an emergency escape. Wick is also certain they can assist with removing the cursed objects from the Chief, if that's truly where the issue lies.

Zenik left hours ago to distract the guards. We wait until full dark before putting our rough plan into action.

Wick helps me into a dark colored cloak, pulling the hood up over my head, and leads me to the door. He pops his head out to scan the area before ushering me out the door and around back to the overgrown path that runs near his home.

As we circle around behind Zeniks home, we stay low behind the bushes and try to keep our steps quiet. We watch carefully, for anyone who might be searching for us. It's been hours since I escaped the windowless room and the Chief has to know I'm gone by now. But it is silent. Eerily so.

Wick moves slowly, keeping his attention on where we're going, relying on me to keep my ears and eyes open for roaming warriors. The Chief has taken extra precautions by increasing patrols around his home. He's probably worried the villagers will retaliate against the new, violent, governing procedures.

I bump into Wick's back as he stops suddenly. Grabbing on to his cloak to stop myself from falling, I peer around him and catch sight of Zarren and another warrior standing in front of a block of four cells about a yard away from the back of his home.

Wick drags me over to a thick tree, wide enough to hide both of us as he observes them. I crouch a little so I can see and catch some of the conversation.

"First light, I want this business over with. The Elves are getting restless, chafing at the restrictions I've placed on them. I really thought they'd see my way of things by now. I thought I'd made these changes slowly enough that they would barely notice. Bah, they're all self-centered cowards, they can't see the vision I have for us." Zarren rants to his warrior, who nods along with him like a good little sheep.

"I know, Chief Zarren, they'll come

around. Especially after the feast." The warrior smirks with a dark look on his face.

When I glance over at Wick, he's pale and shaking, muttering something under his breath. I tap on his arm and he just shakes his head.

They talk for a little while longer about other plans, none which sound good for the Elves who live here.

Zarren mentions that they aren't going to bother hanging them, he wants their heads on the fence posts near the gate to ward off invaders... What invaders? Brenth mentioned travellers rarely come here because they're so unfriendly. Zarren's insanity is very apparent the longer I listen.

Once they head back towards the house, we wait in the shadows of the tree until they've gone inside. Letting out a harsh exhale, I'm relieved they're gone and we're getting my Orcs out now.

There are no other guards around, Zenik seems to have them fairly occupied. Suspicion swamps me, how has Zarren not noticed the lack of guards? Is he so arrogant that he assumes no one will interfere? What if Zarren finally checks on 'his' Omega? How long will the guards stay away? Fuck. We need to move quickly.

We creep along the empty cells, not knowing which one my Orcs are in. A rustling noise ahead has us freezing mid step. I clutch at Wicks' cloak, holding my breath. Neither of us see anything in the darkness, but I hear the rustling again. It's coming from the next cell. Hopefully it's the brothers.

Moving slowly, I peer in through the bars. A lone dark shape on the ground draws my attention as they roll onto their back. It's very hard to tell who it is, but the shape seems big enough to be an Orc. I whisper *'PSST'* to get their attention.

The shape jackknifes to a sitting position and turns towards me. I still can't make out any features but forge ahead anyways, there can't be many others in here.

"Brenth? Brynd? We're here to get you out. I can't see you, come closer?"

Brenth's voice trails over to me, but not from inside this cell. "Wee One? What'r ya dooin here? Och! Get out of this mad place!" His accent thickens and makes his words hard to understand. I get the gist of it though, he wants me to leave him here.

Well, no thank you, that is not happening.

I turn back to the dark shape in the cell, which must be Brynd since he hasn't spoken.

But I'm shocked nearly onto my ass when a feminine voice replies,

"Are you here to get me out of this dreadful place too?" Her voice is seductive and smooth like warm honey, I feel light and dreamy. Wick pinches my arm, snapping me out of whatever that was.

"What the fuck was that? What did you do?" My words rush out, heart racing and palms sweating. I wave off my questions before she has a chance to answer, "If you have no plans to hurt me or mine then I see no reason we should leave you here to their madness," I'm not sure how much more stress I can handle.

She chuckles quietly. "Sorry, Doll. I forgot I wasn't trying to lure one of the warriors to free me. I have done nothing except be who I am. I wasn't even supposed to be here, but those fuck-sticks captured me and I've been caged here for the last four months." None of this has the same allure as her previous sentence. It's like she sucked up all the seduction she'd been pouring out.

There's a moment where jealousy clouds my judgement and I want to refuse her freedom. What if she tries to steal my Orcs? What if they *like* her better than me? These thoughts circle in my mind, but I could never be so horrible to someone to leave them here to die. A few deep breaths and I shake off the resentment, I will deal with everything as it comes.

My resolve firms and I glance at Wick for his input. He presses his lips tight, before nodding. "We'll get you out, Succubus. But, please, no tricks? I'm trying to prevent injuries and death."

She finally gets up and steps close to the bars, into the moonlight. My jaw drops in awe. She's the most beautiful creature I've ever seen in my life. I've never even heard of a Succubus.

"All I want is to leave this place. I have family that I'm sure is wondering why I've been missing for months. They would never find me here. We all know to avoid the Elves." She grimaces at Wick in apology.

He waves her off and steps to the lock, touching it gently before muttering something incomprehensible. The exposed area makes a few moments feel like forever as Wick works on the lock. When the lock clicks free he drops it quickly and opens the cell.

The Succubus steps out and my mouth pops open. My goodness, she's as tall as the Orcs. Her skin is a dusky pink that compliments her short purple hair. It's puffed up around her head, like a halo and I have the insane urge to pet it. I want to know if it's as bouncy as it looks. This female is stacked with muscles, definitely on par with some of my mates. It's too dark for me to make out her eyes but I bet they're as stunning as the rest of her. A long tail flicks back and forth like a cat when she turns, it has a little spade or arrowhead topping at the tip.

I think this is my first girl crush. I want to be her when I grow up, or maybe just cuddle her. She steps close to me and her scent almost knocks me off my feet. It's similar to a dark brewed morning drink that many beings use for an energy boost, called Dowen. The drink has a rich, strong, bitter smell. I don't like to drink it myself but I've always enjoyed the aroma. It brings to mind a warm home with the hustle and bustle of a busy family, like my days spent in Dani's house. The scent is happiness, to me.

She steadies me with a hand on my shoulder before leaning in, sniffing the top of my head and releasing a little purr.

"Omega. Unclaimed, Omega. What are you doing alone, Doll?"

Before the Succubus has a chance to take that any farther I interrupt her. "Nope. I have mates, too many mates actually. But I haven't got all their bites yet so my scent hasn't changed. They're on their way here actually...

You know what? It's a long story and I really want my Orcs back, soooo...." I trail off, hoping everyone will get the hint and go unlock the other cells since it looks like she was alone in this one.

Wick's already moved on, muttering over the lock on the next cell. I scurry over, excitement brimming as Brenth smiles at me from inside his cell. The moment the lock drops, he's out and has me up in his arms, squeezing me tightly, muttering something about foolish Omegas.

"Brenth, I need to breathe!" I tap on his arm, getting him to relax his grip a little.

"Right. Brynd!" We join Wick just as he unlocks the last cell, releasing my silent Orc.

I'm so happy they're free. I throw myself at Brynd, squeezing him as hard as I can while I whisper,

"Goddess, I'm so happy you're both okay. They didn't hurt you, did they?" I shuffle back far enough so I can see him sign.

"Safe, Love. No hurts. Happy you're here." My ability to understand sign has grown but Brynd keeps it simple for me, especially because we're in a bit of a rush.

We need to get to the tunnels below our helpful friends' home so I give him another tight embrace before I wave him on to follow Wick.

Wick huffs, sweat dotting his brow. "We need to move. None of you are quiet. Follow me, stay low and silent."

Brenth whispers a spell combined with a movement I recognize. Then he informs Wick our steps are now silent.

As we follow Wick away from the Chiefs home, I look back making sure our tag-along is still with us. She's there, studying me curiously with a secret smile playing on her lips.

Our exit is much faster than getting here, now that we can move without worrying about being heard.

Soon we find ourselves under one of the homes, the packed earth around us muffling all sound. I thought I might feel suffocated after my stint in the mountain caves and the Chief's prison, but this feels... less stifling. It's probably the lack of oppressive black magic in the air.

Brenth refuses to put me down and sits with me on his lap. Brynd stays close with a hand on my leg. It's as if the brothers need to be touching me, to reassure themselves that I'm here and okay.

The Succubus paces around casually, looking at the supplies that are stored down here. One wall has wooden shelving containing jars of preserved food, lanterns and a few rusty knives. Another wall has large barrels filled with water, and the other has cots.

Wick has told us we can use anything we need, but to stay here until he comes back with Zenik.

Heaving a deep sigh, I'm glad that the stress of this night is over, for now. I nuzzle into Brenth's chest and mumble out *'I need sleep'* before passing out faster than ever before. Feeling safer now that my Orcs are here.

CH.46

The Succubus is still pacing when I wake up, flinging questions at Brenth.

"So, she's your Omega? Why is her scent not altered yet from being claimed? Is she still building her pack? It is not yet complete if her scent is still so potent. Maybe she would enjoy some female company after being surrounded by so many idiotic males." She laughs, the sound throaty and enticing, sending a shiver through my body.

Trembling slightly in Brynd's arms I blink blearily, I've been shuffled around while I was sleeping.

Brenth snorts out a harsh laugh. "I do not think her other mates would enjoy having a Succubi in their pack. We have not yet claimed her, but we will. We wanted to wait until she's been reunited with her pack and introduce ourselves, hoping they will accept us. Or hoping they will accept her decision, it is the Omega's choice. But, as you know, some Alpha's can get a little... Possessive."

She laughs again, her face glowing and her eyes a dazzling glittery pink. "Yes. I do not think I belong with her anyways. While she is an alluring little thing, I do not feel that draw. The one that tells you bluntly 'this is *your* Omega'. You know?" She looks over at him and then me, "Ahhh, did you sleep well?"

Yawning, I stretch before slumping back into Brynd, snuggling into his warmth. "Surprisingly, yes. I think I was exhausted after fighting through that memory spell... and from getting out of that prison," Shuddering, I peer up at Brynd,

"I missed you both. Please do not leave me again. I am not made for this kind of stress, I miss my kitchen," I state with a heavy sigh. I'm proud of myself for fighting and for figuring out how to save myself, but I think I'd rather go back to a quieter life.

He squeezes me tightly, as if to say *'I have no plans of ever letting you go'*. In response, I pepper kisses on the closest parts of him within reach. My lips stretch into a warm grin as a flush of yellow grows over his cheeks and the tips of his ears. Brynd is very adorable for such a large, scary male.

The Succubus interrupts our sweet moment. "Thank you for the rescue, Doll. My name is Lianis, but most just call me Lia. If you haven't already been told I am a Succubus, a type of demon that lives off sex and sexual pleasure, or really, the emotions released during sex. I haven't been able to pinpoint what you are. You smell like a human Omega, but there's something else there too..." Lia scrutinizes me, eyes squinting and mouth twisted into a frown as she tries to look past my eyes, into my soul. After a moment she waves away the thought and continues, "You are a special little thing, aren't you? How many mates do you have?"

Returning her intense perusal, I try to study her objectively. But, while I find a female Alpha fascinating, my thoughts can't help drifting to *my* Alpha's. I yield to the urge and check my bonds. They no longer feel like they are covered by a veil and each of them clamours for my attention. I sense worry and a little panic, but there's also relief that the bonds are open. I direct soothing emotions at each of them. My attempts to calm their anger and concern are feeble, though. My mates are rushing to get to me, full of anger and concern.

Lia clears her throat, drawing my attention away from my bonds. I blink owlishly at her as I try to remember what she asked. *Ah, right, mates.*

"Well... If I include these two, which I do," - I give them both a sweet smile - "Then I have seven mates... no sorry, eight. I always forget about Alec since I haven't met him yet, he stayed back to run their Keep. We were on our way there when I was kidnapped. I was lucky that I caught their attention," I motion at the brothers,

"They placed a tracking charm on me and followed me to the cave system to rescue me. I've been trying to get back to my mates since, but we seem to attract the wrong attention... Well... I think I should say, *I attract* the wrong attention. Being an Omega is pretty stupid most of the time." My eyes drift as I pick at my dress.

When I peek over at Lia, she's stopped pacing and she gawps at me.

Oops, did I break her?

Snapping out of it, she shakes her head, waving an arm through the air. "Wait, wait, wait. You have how many mates? Sheesh your poor pussy! You must be exhausted *all* the time, and this coming from someone who has to fuck to live!" Laughing heartily, her face brightens, she looks a thousand times more attractive. It must be a Succubus thing.

It's my turn to gawk at her. I check both

brothers to see if they're as affected as me, but they have no reaction.

"Never mind that, what I meant to say was, what kind of trouble is following you? I know Omegas are highly desired and I have heard rumors of Omegas going missing in the last few months. But with that many mates I'm impressed that someone was able to take you. They must not be very strong males..." I think she tries to mutter that last bit to herself but it's loud enough for all of us to hear.

Gasping, I jump off Brynd's lap and stomp over to Lia. No one talks about my mates like that! "How dare you! My mates are very strong, but we'd been attacked by a massive throng of beasts and I was snagged out of a tree by a rotting griffon." My arms flail wildly as I rant at her, "My mates had been holding off the beasts but the creatures had targeted my Dragon and Gargoyle, taking them to the ground so they couldn't follow me. The only reason I know they live is because of the bond, thank the Goddess!" I'm fuming, my cheeks burn as I prop my hands on my hips with a frown. She doesn't know what I've been through, how dare she judge us.

Strong arms snatch me off my feet and cuddle me back into a warm chest. Brynd's scent soothes me, softening my anger as I nuzzle into him. Returning to his seat, he clutches me tightly, as if he thinks I might try to fight Lia.

I might, if she doesn't stop talking about my mates like that!

Meanwhile, Brenth is laughing his face off being absolutely no help at all. My glare burns a hole into the side of his head but he just starts chuckling all over again when our eyes meet. A disgruntled breath escapes me as I try not to let his laughter infect me. It's difficult and a smile wavers, growing bigger as Lia's eyes grow wide and her breath stutters.

"A Dragon! Fuck. There must have been a swarm to hold him down. Dragons are fearsome and bigger than anything I've ever seen before." She pales, freezing in place as a slight tremble works through her. "Wait. Did you say a rotting griffon? What the fuck? What kind of trouble follows you?" She blinks rapidly and swipes a hand over her hair, tugging on it a little.

I've made her panic a little and I feel kind of bad about that. Inhaling deeply, I spit out the whole story at once. "So... My mates are all apparently some elite group that works for the King..." keeping my explanation concise, I try to touch all the highlights before getting to our present.

"Anyways, then we ended up here

trapped by the madman we think has been tainted by black magic, and Brenth are you able to help Healer Wick remove the dark magic?" Sucking in air I heave a little after that spiel. I've gotten better about not just rambling random facts.

A raucous laugh escapes me at the look on everyone's faces. Surprise, shock and awe. Even my Orcs are staring at me open mouthed. When I feel Brynd shaking, I know he's laughing with me at the other two.

A yelp escapes me when a voice by the stairs speaks up.

"Quite an interesting tale. I think you are more important than anyone has realized yet," Wick states.

"Wick! What the... Why are you lurking in the dark? And don't scare me like that!" I yell at him.

He laughs lightly. "Sorry, Young One. I did not intend to scare you, but your story is fascinating. I suspected things were off after what happened with the Chief, but discovering a necromancer is involved is very concerning. And a black magic User as an accomplice? This is much worse than I thought." With furrowed brows, he purses his lips and swipes a hand through his hair, looking troubled.

Lia's expression is a mask of fear as she

states, "You are definitely important, Doll. To have the Elites as your mates? I am terrified for this village. If they get here before we figure out how to get out, your mates are going to burn this place to the ground to find you."

I guess my mates are kind of famous? Huh, who knew?

I take in Wick's grimace and ask, "Where's Zenik? Isn't he supposed to be with you?"

"Hmm... Yes, about that. His father took him to 'discuss' matters with him. I worry that we have been found out, especially if your escape has been discovered... We will continue without him." He doesn't look too concerned, so I try not to worry either. Zenik has proven to be a friend and I do not wish him harm.

Brenth speaks up, "Wick? My wee beauty here mentioned you may need my help? I was trained in mostly offensive and defensive magic. But my brother was trained in some healing, tracking, counter spells, and potions." He waves a hand over at Brynd. "Luella mentioned ya think the Chief has been tainted or cursed?"

"It was about a year ago that the Chief and a few of his closest warriors went on a hunt and returned much later acting strangely. Luella surmised cursed jewellery could be infecting their minds. I think if we remove those cursed objects and destroy them we may be able to heal their minds. I can handle the healing part, although help will be appreciated, but it's the removal that will prove difficult. I am no warrior, I will not be much help if they get violent. Which they will," he explains somberly.

Brynd gently sets me down between him and Brenth on the cot. He taps on Brenth to get his attention before signing something. His hands are moving too quickly for me to be able to understand, but I catch a word here and there. *'Want, help, hard, protect'*. I decide to wait for Brenth to translate for Wick and Lia. He nods a few times before signing something back, giving his brother a hearty slap on the back and smiles at the rest of the room.

"He wants to help. Especially if it will protect our Wee Lass, but it will be difficult because we will need to get very close to the Chief or any of the affected warriors." Pausing deep in thought, he taps a finger against his chin. "We should target the warriors first, remove the curse and heal their minds. We could use their help if we want to fix everyone before Luella's mates arrive. I do not see them waiting outside the gate." Brenth smirks at the thought of all the destruction they will bring.

Wick nods, staring at the ladder to the

hidden doorway. "Hmm, yes. That is a good plan." He addresses Lia. "Would you be willing to aid us? We could use your particular skills to lure the warriors to a secluded spot."

She smiles with delight. "Of course! It will be nice to get a little retaliation, even though I cannot kill them."

"You do know anything they did to you was likely under duress of the curse? They probably didn't mean to..." I mention hesitantly, because it's likely she has not been treated very well.

She waves a hand, her chin tipped up with an imperious look on her face. "Yes, yes I know. Although, Elves are not very kind to other beings anyways, so I will not feel bad about this."

I nod, pretending to understand. I have been very sheltered in my life, up to now.

The room is quiet as we all consider the dangers. The weight of the dirt above and around us muffles any sounds. My eyes stare blankly at the wall as I think about saving these Elves. I can't just leave them to their fate. It's not who I am.

The skittering of rats in the walls breaks the silence. When I look up, everyone's eyes are on me.

"What? Is there something on my face?" I bring my hands up to pat around searching for anything stuck to me. Brenth, Lia and Wick all chuckle lightly.

"Goddess, y'er adorable." Brenth pats my leg as Brynd rests his chin on my head.

"I know you will refuse, but it would put all of us at ease if you agreed to stay down here while we went out to do this." Wick braves.

Sighing, I drop my hands to my lap and pick at my nails. "I truly do not want to go with you to do something potentially dangerous. But, I also do not want to stay here alone... Plus, I really don't want to be split up from my Orcs. I fear they will not come back to me if I cannot see them." I know I sound silly, but my fears are true. I have gained many new fears throughout this adventure. I will have nightmares for the rest of my life, and this is not over yet, either."

They all nod or mutter an agreement before Brenth stands. "All right. No time to lose. Let's get this over with so we can get out of this Goddess forsaken place... no offence, Wick, but the welcome has been very lacking."

Wick actually snorts a laugh before choking it back. He mutters his understanding as he climbs the ladder.

Pushing the doorway open slowly, he peeks through the crack and listens for anything out of place before shoving it the rest of the way.

We all pile out of the hideaway and into the living space of Wick's friend's home. The new Elf stands a few inches above Wick. His grey eyes are distinctive against his rusty brown skin and hair. He's deep in conversation with Wick as Lia closes the hatch behind her.

"All right, Shoha says the Chief's warriors are on rotation around him. We should be able to find a few at the barracks and in the communal kitchens. If we can lure one out, there's a good spot we can bring them to in order to work our magic. Shoha wants to help too. He is friendly with many of the warriors who disagree with how the Chief has been running things. He will come with me so I can ask one of the warriors to follow me out, under the guise of needing to check him over for injuries after hauling the Orcs to the cells." He glances at Lia. "Your job will be to hide outside the doorway and mesmerize him with your allure, keeping him under while Brynd and I pull the darkness out of him."

"Wee Lass, you will stay beside me at all times. We will hide, out of view, while they bring him to us. Our job is to stay out of the way unless they need some muscle. You will stay out of reach of them, aye?" Brenth eyes me, waiting for my assent.

Nodding solemnly, I have zero desire to get in the middle of something dangerous if I can avoid it. But staying here, or in the hideaway alone, feels like a bad idea. Something in my gut is telling me not to be left behind. And if I've learned one thing since this whole mess started, it's that I need to trust my instincts, because they haven't proven me wrong yet.

CH.47

Brenth, Brynd, and I peer around a large tree trunk in a small clearing surrounded by massive trees and thick bushes.

Concern, wrinkles my brow, I fear that Lia will be seen, she is very different from the Elves and her pink skin is extremely noticeable. No one else is worried though, so I try not to let it bother me much.

Startling when I hear footsteps, I twitch, but Brenth gives an almost inaudible sigh of relief. As Lia comes into view, my body relaxes. There's a large Elven warrior following her with a dazed look, gazing at her like she's the only thing he can see. Wick and Shoha, trail them.

Once they're all concealed in our small clearing, Brynd and Wick start moving their hands and muttering something under their breath while walking around the Elf. Using magic is much stranger than I thought, all the hand waving and muttering in different languages feels foreign.

Brynd's eyes snap open and he points out a strange purple-black stone in an earring. Shoha puts on some gloves, wary of touching it. He carefully pulls the hook out of the male's ear and places it on a rock near the far edge of the clearing.

Wick continues to mutter and weave his hands around the dazed warrior, who hasn't even twitched once while we move around him.

Watching Brynd, I worry about him touching the tainted object. But he pulls out an axe, silently mutters over the dull end before he smashes it into the stone. A flash of black and purple light blinds me and a tremendous shock-wave reverberates from the stone, knocking me back into Brenth. If he hadn't been there I would have been forced right through the thick bushes.

When I can see again I fear that the shock-wave will have been felt and we will be discovered.

"Brenth, isn't that going to draw attention?" Chewing my lip, I look around furtively, trying to see out of the clearing.

"Shh... Wee One, all will be well. It likely dissipated shortly after hitting us. The evil was not pleased to be thwarted. But, I will keep my ears open for footsteps," he reassures me, patting my shoulder.

Wick slumps back after finishing whatever he did and nods at Lia to release him. Brenth brandishes his axe, pointing it at the warrior.

"What? Where am I? Who...? Wick? Shoha? What the *vell* is going on? Who are these outsiders?" The warrior holds his head as if it aches and looks around at all of us.

Wick sighs with relief before nodding at Shoha. "Tenil, thank the Goddess. What do you remember?"

"I... I was on a hunt with the Chief..." He slowly recounts before paling so much I fear he will faint. "Oh, Goddess! The things I've done. How can you even look at me? I am not fit to serve this village." Sinking to his knees, he hangs his head in despair as he remembers, as tears waver in his eyes.

Wick has recovered enough to move in and comfort the warrior. "It was not you. You'd been cursed by something. It happened while you were hunting. All of you have been cursed. You may redeem yourself by helping us free the others." This is said with kindness, but there is a thread of steel underlining the words.

"Yes! Of course! I must make this right." He looks at Lia, then the Orcs and grimaces. "I am sorry for the part I played in your captivity."

Lia waves him off haughtily. "Forget it. All is well. Let's get this over with. I need to get back to my family, I've been gone for so long they likely think I am dead."

And so it goes. We spend the whole day luring tainted warriors to our secluded spot and releasing them from the prison of their minds. It gets easier the more we free, although Wick and Brynd are looking winded and tired. We only have the Chief left and his right hand man.

At the back of my mind concern hovers, reminding me that no one has seen Zenik since yesterday. I hope he is alright.

With only two left and a group of warriors looking for redemption surrounding us, we feel secure enough to finish our task in the open.

It is an unspoken agreement amongst all of them to keep me in the centre with Brenth as we make our way to the Chiefs home.

We weren't expecting him to be waiting out front, his right hand man holding a knife to the throat of an unconscious Zenik.

"I was expecting you earlier. I do not like to be kept waiting," Zarren growls at us. Glaring harshly at Wick. "How dare you go against your Chief! You will be banished for this. Or shall I have you executed for colluding with outsiders? Just like my worthless son." He spits on the ground at Wick's feet before locking eyes with me. "And you! How the vell did a weak, pitiful Omega get out of my prison? My son refused to tell me anything, but I can only assume he was the one to free you."

Curling my lip in disgust, I refuse to answer this monster. I don't hide behind Brenth, I stand tall and snarl at him. We will see who is weak and pitiful when this is over. Familiar tingles spread through my hands and I smirk as I unsheath my claws. I doubt I will get close enough to need them but it is reassuring just the same.

Four of the freed warriors fan out around the Chief, the others brandishing their weapons, keeping me and Wick protected.

"You do not want to kill your son, Zarren. This is not you!" Wick shouts at him drawing his attention away from Lia, who is circling around and slowly moving closer to both of them.

Wick raises his voice even more as Lia releases her allure, directing it towards the

Chief and his man. It still leaks out over to the rest of us but we fight it, some of the warriors leaning closer to her but not lowering their weapons.

When it reaches the man holding the knife to Zenik, he tenses and slices into his throat a little. I suck in a breath at the blood that drips down his neck. The male fights Lia's seduction but he's slowly losing, his eyes glazing and hands going slack. He drops the knife, and Zenik crumples to the ground, still unconscious. I twitch with the need to go make sure he's okay, but Brenth drops a heavy hand on my shoulder.

The male haltingly steps towards Lia, still trying to fight the pull. Zarren is proving stronger than expected as he glares at Wick, Lia, and the rest of us.

"You think you can stop me? This is pathetic. I will call down death and you will all bow to me!" Zarren screams with bloodshot eyes, veins popping on his forehead. He weaves his hands and I watch as smoky darkness grows in between his palms, sweat dripping down his face as he fights Lia and attempts to call black magic.

Brynd is chanting over the man fighting Lia's allure. When I see him rip a ring off the man's finger and quickly smash it with his axe.

It releases a flash and shock-wave, the relief of being almost finished has my shoulders dropping.

I'm the only one who has trouble holding my ground when the shock-wave rolls over me, luckily Brenth is already holding on to me.

The male blinks out of the haze as the warriors tug him away from Lia. He starts sobbing and holding his head, screaming about voices as he's dragged away. They end up knocking him out because he needs his mind healed before he can function again. I wonder why he seems so much worse than the other Elves we freed?

Black smoke continues to grow, slowly forming into a doorway, or a portal of sorts, I don't start to panic until a malformed hoof steps out.

"Oh! Fuck! Brenth! It's one of the beasts!" Shouting, I tug on his arm and point uselessly.

Every warrior steps forward, ready to fight, watching cautiously as the beast slowly moves through the portal.

A grotesque mix of a horse's legs leads up to the body of a grey leathery skinned animal. A reptilian head appears next, the mouth lined with sharp jagged teeth designed to strip skin off bone easily.

The abomination roars a ground shaking noise as it steps through completely. More than one being here is shocked into immobility.

Just as another mutated beast begins stepping through, I catch movement behind the Chief. Shoha silently creeps up behind him. The portal snaps shut in a flash, cutting off the leg and shoulder of the second beast as Shoha smashes a rock down on the back of the Chiefs head, knocking him out cold.

No one moves except the abomination. It charges towards me and Brenth.

What is it with these fucking things and coming straight for me?

A high pitched yelp escapes me. Terror consumes my body and I freeze. The fear that this thing is going to eat me is all that my mind can focus on. But, Brenth has his axe out and ready to attack. Three of the Elven warriors join him in front of me, creating a wall of flesh.

Someone looses a few arrows that thunk wetly into the neck and side of the beast. It screeches in pain, slowing its charge which gives Brenth an opening to swing at it. He manages to slash a stripe across its chest as it dances back out of the way, moving faster than expected.

Black ichor leaks from the wounds as it

rushes towards us again. The Elven warriors step in to swipe at it as well. Each slash opens more and more wounds, slowing the beast. This one seems smarter than some of the others though, it is evading many of the oncoming strikes.

With the beast distracted, Wick quickly moves forward, meeting Brynd at the unconscious Chief. Brynd almost immediately rips off a necklace containing that same dark stone and smashes it. The power this unleashes is much stronger than the others, knocking all the Elves back, and staggering the abomination. The only ones able to withstand the sudden burst of energy are the Orcs and Lia.

Brenth takes the opportunity to bring his axe down towards the beast's head, unfortunately the beast recovers faster than expected. It manages to evade the strike and dig its vicious teeth into his leg. Even though he must be in a great deal of pain, Brenth takes the opening and slams his weapon down on its neck, lopping the head off smoothly. As it falls the teeth rip out a chunk of flesh. The sound of Brenth's grunt of pain has me moving fast in his direction. My body moves and dodges with barely a thought as hands try to stop me.

When I reach Brenth, I rip strips off my dress so I can tend to his wound. I struggle with the cloth, frustrated that my claws have receded as my emotions shifted from anger to concern. Glancing over quickly to see how the others are doing, a frown creases my face. I'm not sure I want the Chief to be alive. He's caused so much trouble. Immediately, sadness envelopes me for that thought. That's not me. I'm not so cruel. The Chief may be okay after he's cleansed.

Wick sweat profusely, looking extremely pale as he finishes working on the chief. Brynd quickly catches Wick as he loses consciousness, gently laying him on the ground beside Zenik. The rest of us stare at the severed pieces and the form of the other beast in horror and revulsion.

With a collective sigh of relief, they all lower their weapons.

After making sure Brenth is going to be okay, I go check on Zenik. The cut is fairly shallow, so I know he'll be alright. Ripping another strip off the bottom of my dress, I bandage the wound on his neck.

Brynd joins me on the ground next to Zenik. My Orc is slightly out of breath from all the effort used to break the black magic, but he looks far better off than Wick. Is it because Brynd is stronger magically? Or maybe Wick did more work... Whatever it is, I'm glad everyone is mostly alright. A few bumps and bruises are okay.

The Elves seem a little lost and somber, silence blanketing the crowd. A few faces peer out of doorways, checking to see if the danger has passed.

"What now? Is this over? Can I leave yet?" Lia breaks the tense atmosphere.

I snort while Tenil, the first warrior we freed replies, "I would be very appreciative if you would stay until they all wake. Just in case we need your skills again." His tone is even and respectful. I guess having her help save them really changes a being's mind, either that or the influence of the curse caused them to treat her so badly.

She looks at the unconscious Chief thoughtfully and nods. "Alright. In that case, I'm starving. Can we get some food over here?"

My stomach growls loudly in agreement and the solemn warriors chuckle. A blush reddens my cheeks but I'm glad I could help lighten the mood. Tenil and Shoha send a few of the warriors off to the kitchens to bring us back a feast.

Before they get too far from us though, a shadow covers us in darkness for a brief moment. A roar and a blaze of blue-black flames light up the sky as a black scaly tail passes over us.

The relieved atmosphere is silent once again as the Elves try to understand what's happening. A deafening *BOOM* shakes the world around us, anyone who was standing has been knocked to the ground, even Lia and the Orcs. My fear is reflected back at me as my eyes meet Brynd's.

This is when the screaming starts.

CH.48

Echoing screams of horror draw our attention towards the gate.
'What now?'

My body is completely still as I try to figure out what's going on. There's a tug in my chest and I look inwards. My bonds light up and laughter bursts out of me, before I start crying. My emotions are wild as the realization hits me.

"They're here!" My shout rushes out, before I jump to my feet. Nimbly dodging Brynd and Brenth's hands as I sprint for the gate.

Voices behind me yell to 'stop', 'be careful', and 'what the fuck are you doing?' but I ignore them all as I weave around flaming chunks of rubble.

Elves scream in terror as they flee the

damaged area that used to be the gate and nearby buildings. I must look like a lunatic because I can't stop laughing as I race towards the angry males at the entrance. Heavy footfalls thump behind me, catching up, but I am small and agile compared to their bulky seven foot height.

My steps slow as the destruction comes into view. A furious and beautiful Tawson strides through the gaping hole. I tug on the bond as I scream his name. As soon as I see him, I throw myself at Tawson knowing he will catch me.

The moment he sees me, his face breaks into the biggest smile I think he's ever worn. His normally stoic demeanor is thrown to the wayside when faced with his missing mate.

Tawson swings me around keeping momentum before pulling me into his chest and placing gentle kisses on my forehead, nose, cheeks, and mouth. Slick leaks from my core as I scent him for the first time in what feels like months. Before I know it, I'm crying. I'm a mess of emotions, lusty, sad, and joyful, all at once. I missed him and his seriousness, his caring and safety.

"Shh, Love. We're here. We won't ever let you go again. That was the worst thing I've ever experienced, and I live with Rafe." Nuzzling me, he takes in lungfuls of my scent.

A voice shouts with indignation, "HEY! I'm not that bad! You're just sour over that one prank where I stuck your hand..." The rest is muffled behind someone's hand.

Sniffling, I kiss Tawson everywhere I can reach. "I was so scared. I didn't know if I'd ever see you again. I wasn't sure I'd get out of that cave, but I was really lucky that the Orc brothers came to rescue me. Umm, they're mine by the way?" Phrasing it as if it's a question, I lean back to look him in the eye. "I mean, they didn't claim me yet or anything, but they do want to be a part of our pack and they're actually really great. They can Use magic and do pretty amazing things..." It's my turn to be muffled, by his lips kissing me silly.

Tawson is still smiling, laughing at my nervous rambling. "That's fine, Sweetheart. It truly is the Omegas choice, although I wouldn't mind being consulted beforehand. In this case, I am grateful they were there for you when I couldn't be." He looks over my shoulder as a shadow passes over us. "Ahh, yes. You will be needed to calm your Dragon before he burns this whole village to the ground. He's been exceptionally difficult since you were taken."

The ground shakes as the Dragon lands, and excitement has goosebumps trickling over my arms. Wiggling to get down, I'm tugged from Tawson's arms abruptly and smothered into a very hot, very naked chest. I don't even need to inhale to know it's Gin. I start crying again as I touch him everywhere, leaving kisses in my wake. I struggle to get closer to his face but he holds me so tightly as if afraid to lose me again. ,

"Gin. My grump? I'm so happy to see you're alright. I was so scared. As I was being taken away, I saw those beasts overtake you and force you to the ground. I thought you were dead for so long, before I remembered I could check on you through the bond. I missed you so much, please let me see your face," Begging and pleading, I drop kisses in between words on his chest, inhaling his scent like a drug.

Finally he lets me out of his tight grasp, eyes glistening with tears that refuse to fall. I plant kisses all over his face, crying enough for both of us.

When I finally calm down, he seems more stable but hasn't yet said a word. I look over at Tawson for answers.

He grimaces. "So, before you, Gin didn't talk much. He's never been one for words, he relies on actions and watches behaviors to judge someone. When he met you, that's the most anyone has ever heard him speak, and after you were taken... He hasn't said a word to any of us. He's been staying in his Dragon form for the most part. We were all pretty shaken from that attack," finishing softly, he gently strokes a hand over my hair.

I lift Gin's chin, forcing his eyes to mine, "Honey? Grumpy? My large, scary-sexy male? Sweetie-pie? Scrumptious? I can continue to get more ridiculous if you don't say anything." A smile ruins my attempted seriousness.

When his lips twitch, triumph flows through me and I pump my fist in the air. It's at that motion that he finally laughs. It's deep and rumbly, like a rockslide vibrating through my body. It goes straight to my core and I have to squeeze my thighs together to stem the flow of slick.

Purring when he scents my arousal, he growls, "Never. Again. Little One. You belong to me. You belong with me, and I am never letting you go again."

Sighing with relief that he's truly okay, I pat his arm. "I want to go hug Fen, Rafe and Blue. They need to touch me too, to be sure I'm real," I tell him gently.

Refusing to put me down, he makes his way over to Fen, since he's the closest. Although Rafe is right beside him. Fen must have been the one to silence whatever ridiculous thing was about to come out of his mouth.

Since Gin refuses to relinquish his hold, they take turns hugging me against him.

What I would give to be the meat in this sandwich. My cheeks burn as my thoughts turn salacious. I will never get enough of these males.

Fen steps back and runs his eyes and hands all over me, checking for injuries.

"I'm alright, Fenny. My Orcs did a very good job taking care of me, and then the healer here helped with the rest. I promise, I'm good as new!" I explain brightly, trying to put off the more serious conversation that needs to happen.

Rafe turns me towards him, a grave expression settled on his face. "Please, my Heart, I cannot take losing you. I know we haven't known each other all that long but, I love you."

A single tear of happiness escapes as I throw myself at him, plastering his face in kisses and murmuring 'I love you's' in between, making him laugh. I'm surprised Gin let me go to him.

"Oh thank the Goddess, I was worried

you weren't there yet! Whew. Okay is there a bed around here we need to reacquaint ourselves with your luscious body." He starts looking around as if a bed will magically appear, making me laugh again.

Tapping his arm, he refocuses on me. "I still haven't seen my Blue! I have to tell him how much I missed him too."

Rafe whines about putting me down, but drops me in front of Blue. Gin follows closely, rumbling a low growl the entire time I'm not in his arms.

Blue looks at me shyly, almost hesitant, as if he's afraid. I refuse to let that stand so I smother his face in kisses too. "My Blue. I missed you so much. I'm so glad you're okay, I was so worried that the black magic would be able to take you back when you shifted and ran into the fray."

"No. Claiming me completely severed the connection. But... Lu... you should hate me. I left you and you were taken. It's my fault. I just wanted to help, but I lost you and it was the worst feeling I've ever had." Letting his tears flow, unafraid of showing his emotions, he's so dejected. His head hangs, brows pinch and eyes redden from crying.

"No." Tangling my hands in his hair, I jerk his head up. "That was *not* your fault, you hear me? You did the right thing going to help them, there were too many and I can't lose any of you, okay? Plus, I was already high in the tree, the griffon would have snagged me whether you were there or not. It all happened as it was supposed to. My Orcs helped me escape and brought me to a healer. They took care of me until our pack could be reunited." Relaxing my grip, I kiss him softly, trying to impart my love for him through my lips.

His body slumps as he lets out a heavy breath, murmuring agreements into my lips.

A short yelp slips from my lips as large hands steal me from Blue's lap mid kiss. Gin quickly has me cradled in his arms again, clearly feeling needy. I indicate to Gin that he should take me to Tawson and my Orcs.

Brenth leans heavily on Brynd. Lia and the Elven warriors lingering in the background. Wick, Zenik, Zarren and a few other warriors head our way. Zarren looks a lot less murdery and more aghast at the destruction of his village.

When Gin spots the Orc brothers he lets out a deep furious growl. "The fuck are they doing here?"

I smile up at his grumpy face. "They saved me from the Necromancer and black magic User. Please be nice because they belong with us."

When he looks like he's going to disagree I cross my arms and jut my chin out, ready to argue with him. Tawson stops the argument before it even starts and introduces himself.

"Glad to meet you. I hear you will be joining us? Are you sure this madness is what you want?" He asks with a quiet laugh, throwing a thumb over his shoulder in our direction.

Brenth snorts. "Aye. Tis exactly what we need. I am Brenth and this is my brother Brynd. He is mute, but can hear ya."

Brynd waves with a shy smile and signs, "*Happy family.*"

He is the most adorable Orc I've ever seen. How can someone who's seven feet tall be adorable? Biting my lip, I fight the urge to squeal at his cuteness. I've never seen him so shy before.

Fen perks up and signs back something along the lines of, "*Welcome! Friends, new family.*" And a few other words I don't know yet. Fen's excitement over signing is infectious and the appreciation in Brynd's eyes warms my heart. The ability to communicate so clearly with someone other than his brother must be exhilarating.

"What the *Vell* is going on?" Chief Zarren shouts angrily, "Why have you destroyed my gate and attacked my village?" The Chief is furious but still weak from the healing. There's a vein in his forehead that's pulsing with his ire. But he's pretty stupid if he thinks yelling at my males will help in any way.

Before any of us have a chance to answer him Zenik steps in. "Father. You need to step back. You are still recovering from the curse and haven't quite remembered everything you've done yet. But, this damage is your fault. Please let me handle this?" He's angry with his father, yet still gentle, as if he has hope that the male he used to be is still in there, somewhere.

When he turns towards me, cradled in Gin's arm, surrounded by my mates his anger softens to guilt. As his shoulders slump, he runs a hand down his tired face.

"I am truly sorry, Luella. I am sorry you got dragged into my problems." Shifting, he addresses Tawson, who stands with his arms crossed and his face back to that default serious blankness. "You must be her head Alpha. It is wonderful to meet you, even under these unfortunate circumstances. I promise you she was, mostly, safe while in my care. You have found yourself a truly amazing mate... Would you all enjoy a chance to rest? I can have food and alekis, Elven wine, brought for you? Please follow me."

He turns to lead us away from the destruction of the gate, but pauses and summons one of the warriors. "Extra guards on the gate. You three grab others and start the clean up. You will have food and alekis brought to the guest house. And you, check if there are any wounded, Wick are you alright to heal or has the curse exhausted you?" He starts firing off orders, pointing and making demands. His Elves quickly obey.

"If there are any serious, life threatening injuries I will do what I can, but I am fairly tapped out. I'm sorry, my Chief." Wicks drooping shoulders and dark bags beneath his eyes give him a worn-out exhausted appearance. The poor Elf has been working tirelessly to hold this place together.

Brynd steps forward and signs something, but I can't see it because Gin pushes my face into his neck at the same time. Brenth translates for him, "My brother says he can help where he is able, he still has some power left. But if the injuries are small I would say to clean and wrap them until tomorrow when Wick and my brother are recovered."

The Elves disperse and Zenik leads my pack towards the home we had occupied when we first arrived.

Finally, Gin lets me up for air as we trail behind our pack and my attention is drawn to my Orcs. They're heading towards Wick and that is unacceptable. They should be with us! With me.

"Where do you think you're going?" My voice is stern as I shout in Gin's ear. The only reason I know I've surprised him is because his arms tighten around me. I bite my lip to hide a smirk before I continue, "Brenth, Brynd! You're a part of this pack. Which means you go where we go."

The grin that takes over Brenth's face is worth the grumpy scowl Gin shoots them. I need to sit down and have a talk with him. Tawson told me Omega's choose and since this is what I want Gin is going to have to get on board.

Wick waves them off with a tired smile, "Oh, go on. I'm just going to check a few things and take a nap. You can help me with some healing later."

Brenth, with some help from his brother, hustles as fast as he can limp over to us. This is the family I've chosen. It's the beginning of something wonderful and I will make sure my Orcs know they belong with us.

CH.49

After a filling meal and the divine Elven wine, I finally have the chance to tell my mates what happened after we were separated.

Our bond simmers with rage, all of my mates wear similar expressions of anger, guilt and concern. Tension leaks into the air as each pack member processes my journey. Of all my males I worried about Gin the most. He's been overprotective and very concerned with my well being right from the beginning and I was anxious about how well he would take news of my injuries.

Gin's reaction is about what I expected. He refuses to put me down, feeding me and holding me close as I recount my story. His extreme worry and guilt filter through the bond and the tremor in his hands is telling.

Arching to sit taller, I lean in and

whisper in Gin's ear, "My grumpy male. I do not want you to drown in this guilt. It was *not* your fault. There was nothing you could do. I think it's the Goddess's will, everything happens for a reason. Maybe it was so I could discover a Necromancer is aligned with the black magic User. My Orcs saved me, and that wouldn't have been possible if I hadn't been captured. Perhaps I was supposed to aid the Elven village with the dark curse. We will never really know," I pause and place a hand on his cheek making him look me in the eyes, "the most important part is that I am alive and well. You have all made it back to me. We will be okay."

I relax as the tension drains from Gin's body. These words are mainly for him, but I'm glad the rest of the room heard me too. It's important they understand how I feel and that they are not to blame. A near silent growl grumbles from his chest but he drops gentle kisses on my forehead, nose, and mouth before his dark blue eyes, lined with the yellow glow of his Dragon, meet mine.

"I will try to leave the guilt behind, but you are the most important thing to me. I will burn the world to keep you," Gin's low rumbling purr has my stomach dipping with anticipation. Everything he didn't say shines fiercely in his eyes. He will let his Dragon free to wreak havoc and destruction if I am lost to him. I don't know how he restrained his savagely protective Dragon before meeting me, but I know now that he has me, the beast will break free if anything like this happens again.

"Are you sure about the Orcs?" He adds quietly as he clutches me possessively, "I don't like them." Glowering in their directions, a trail of smoke escapes through his nose.

All eyes are on me as I emerge from my huddle with Gin. My mates gaze at me with lust burning in their eyes. While my pack looks tired and dirty from the road the tension that had lined their shoulders has eased and the desire to reconnect with me is clear.

Tawson turns to Zenik. "Thank you for making sure she was not injured while here. I am sorry your father had been cursed, but you are lucky we did not get here while he was threatening her. Had we come earlier, the Chief would be a smear on the grass... it is still a possibility," he states with zero remorse. A muscle in Tawson's jaw twitches, mouth pressed tightly together as his knuckles turn white. His fists are clenched so tightly I worry he's going to injure himself. "It is late and we have a burning need to make sure she is uninjured, please leave now. We will speak with you more in the morning."

Tawson has always been the lead, our

head Alpha, the one to take control, but watching him dismiss the Elves so easily has heat rushing through me.

Zenik does not argue, he takes the dismissal easily and waves a quick goodbye. I'm finally alone with my five mates and two Orcs. The room grows warm, or it could just be me. I have a great need to be sandwiched between my mates.

Someone better touch me soon or I'm going to have to take matters into my own hands.

Brenth cuts through the sudden lust filled tension. "We have not had a chance to properly introduce ourselves. I am Brenth and this is my brother Brynd. We want to be a part of your pack, what say you?" He is so blunt and forward. I cover my mouth to smother a snort of laughter.

They both stand rigid, Brenth still having to lean on his brother for support. Blood leaks through the fabric I'd tied around his leg. He really should get some healing, I don't like the look of it. But their eyes are focused on Tawson as they wait for his response. This is more important to them, than getting his leg fixed up. I have to refrain from rolling my eyes at the male stupidity.

Tawson rises and contemplates the brothers' proposal while pacing. Stopping in front of them both, he glances at the rest of his pack. "How do you all feel about this?"

Fen is the first to answer, "They rescued and protected our Omega, putting their lives on the line. They will make strong pack-mates and protectors for our Centre."

"Yep, what he said! Plus they are Users, that will be extremely helpful during any future attacks, even help protect the Keep once we are safely ensconced there." Rafe hops up and slaps Brynd on the back, smiling widely.

Gin just grunts, tucking his face further into my hair. "Fine. But, I don't like it." I really hope he will come to accept them. I chew my lip with apprehension.

Tawson glances at Blue with an eyebrow raised.

"Oh! Me? You, uh, you want to know what I think? Wow... Okay. Um, yes. They are noble in their actions and I can see how much they care for Lu." Blue blushes with nervousness while rushing through his words. His excitement at being included is so sweet, I will have to make sure Blue knows he is part of the pack and is an equal among my mates. I need him just as much as I need the others.

Tawson nods sharply and faces the brothers. "It seems the whole pack is, mostly, in agreement. Brenth, Brynd, you are now Pack

Foreastra. I will bring you into our pack bond in the morning. For now, we have an Omega to reconnect with and you need that leg looked at. Come."

We follow Tawson up the stairs, but before they're out of sight, I peek at my new pack mates. The shock, awe, and happiness at being accepted so easily beams from both Orcs. I think they were expecting to be rejected, considering their past. I am pleased my mates so readily acknowledged the brothers are mine. They follow behind us, dazed and content.

Gin and Rafe enjoy the Elven plumbing while bathing me. Rafe gushes about how amazing this system is and I zone out listening to the familiar cadence of their voices. It feels like I can finally relax after being on edge for so long.

The entire bath is foreplay, they do not touch me intimately, but it leaves me squirming with desire. Although, I melt when Rafe washes my hair. Tingles buzz through me as he runs his fingers through the strands. Massaging my scalp as he soaps the tresses, I moan at the sensation. He douses my growing lust with a cup full of water over my head, I think my moans get to him.

Good.

Gin hauls me out of the tub and wraps a cloth around me to soak up the water. Once I'm situated in his arms, he carries me into the bedroom near the sunken bed. It looked massive when it was just me and my Orcs, but now with the whole pack crowding in, it feels small. I hope they have a bigger bed at the Keep, the thought of any of my mates not being near me has me feeling a little unhinged.

A squeak escapes me as I'm dropped unceremoniously into the middle of the bedding, my mates disrobing around me. My instincts scream for me to take their clothing and build a nest that smells like all of us.

I need to be surrounded by them.

Deciding not to fight it, I rush Gin. My body slams into his chest knocking him onto his back as I claw at his shirt. He is not moving fast enough and I need his damn clothes! Once I've managed to yank his shirt off him I start pushing and shoving Gin out of the bed. My movements are manic and frenzied as I snarl at my males,

"Take off your pants!" Instinct has taken over. Our separation has been long and I desperately need a nest and their knots.

My Orcs are slightly off to the side and I frown, pinching my lips together.

Unacceptable. I'll be fixing that. Brynd tends to Brenth's leg wound while studying me with the same intensity as my other mates. They're all waiting for permission to enter the nest.

But first, I need more of their scents. "Brenth, Brynd, Give me your pants. Now."

No one argues with me as I make my way around the room. I gather clothing, tugging at the fabric if the males don't move fast enough. Eventually, my arms end up heavy with a pile of their scents and I can return my focus to perfecting the nest.

A low chuckle echoes around the room and Rafe steps forward, as if he thinks he can get into the bed, but I release a high pitched snarl at him until he steps back. He never loses his smile though.

"Sorry, Little Kitten. I will wait until you say so," Rafe murmurs, hands raised as he laughs in delight.

I don't pay attention to the rest of what he says. He's leaning in to talk to Fen anyways. I go back to shaping my nest, placing clothing here and there until it's just right. Kneeling in the center, I sigh with happiness at the scents and feeling of safety having all of my mates around gives me.

Glancing around, seeing them all relaxed and smiling gives me warm, happy feelings.

I beckon Gin first, knowing instinctively that he needs me the most right now. Plus, once he is settled he may be less hesitant about my Orcs. He stomps into the bed with a loud growl. The sound sends a thrill of excitement down my spine and I have to clench my thighs together at the immediate gush of liquid.

Pushing me onto my back, he encircles me with his big, hard body. Gin's encompassing scent has me relaxing completely, I can finally breathe again now that the pack is reunited. My hands roam over his hot skin, feeling him everywhere. I even sneak one down to grope his butt, enjoying the way his snarls encourage me. When I attempt to grab his throbbing cock he pins my arms to the bed beside my head.

I love when he gets a little rough with me, it makes me very hot. I can feel my cunt growing wetter and wetter, readying for his large, ribbed member.

Ducking his head down to kiss me senseless, Gin's forked tongue licks into my mouth, tasting me. Goosebumps shiver over my arms as I remember the pleasure that appendage can provide. When he trails kisses down my neck, over my collar bones to my breasts I gasp for air, or composure, I'm not sure which.

Gin nibbles his way to my nipple, sucking and biting on the tip until it is hard and red from his attention. Each bite feels as though it is connected by a cord to my clit, making it pulse in time with his bites. I'm a whimpering mess, pleading for more. My arms pull against his hold, I need to touch him, but I also enjoy being at his mercy.

My mind grows hazy as desire takes over. Flushed and panting, I arch my back encouraging him to continue. Gin's grip on me is possessive and intense. I can't help writhing with need. I want more, I want his cock. I need him inside me.

Gin moves on to lave attention on my other breast, biting and sucking, tweaking and squeezing until it matches the other. He doesn't move on until I'm squirming, searching for relief against my clit. Evading my efforts to rub up against his cock, he drives me insane.

Vaguely, I register groans from outside my Gin cocoon but pay them no mind, I am much more focused on getting that velvety hard cock inside my greedy pussy.

Before Gin moves further down my body he stops, taking in my glassy, heavy lidded eyes and smirks before calling someone over to hold my hands down.

A set of light green hands replace Gin's,

tugging my arms above my head. I look up into Tawson's upside-down face and moan. I truly love the feeling of being held down for my mates. He leans in to drop a licking kiss on my lips, muffling my whines for more.

I'm distracted from Tawson as Gin kisses down my stomach, dipping his forked tongue into my belly button. I smother a squeak, resisting the need to laugh at the ticklish sensation. Gin moves on to the crease between hip and core, lapping closer and closer to where I need him. Finally, I allow moans to slip from my lips as he licks over the space and moves towards my clit.

I almost sigh in relief but he skips over that pulsing nub of flesh. Releasing groans and growls at him, I'm cut off as Tawson's mouth presses against mine. When he runs his tongue over my bottom lip I lick out meeting him, moaning at his fresh taste and reveling in his touch.

Tawson draws back the moment Gin pulls my lower lips open and licks straight into me, allowing my moans to reverberate throughout the room. His long tongue delves deep inside me, twisting and twirling, gathering all my slick wetness. He groans deeply at my flavor, the vibration adding a delectable sensation.

"Oh, Little One, I have missed this taste. I want to keep you strapped to my face so I can snack on you all day." I clench down as soon as he shoves his tongue back inside me, the words have me thrashing, wild for him.

"Please, more. I need your cock! Gin, please!" Whining, I beg him for more. It's as if the lack of touch built up over the weeks we've been separated. Now that I feel safe, all my lust has been unleashed and I've become a begging, writhing mess.

Gin purrs and pulls back, licking all the slick off his face. He's silent as he aligns with my body, notching his cock at my opening, waiting until I'm looking him in the eye before thrusting hard, fitting himself deeply inside me.

The sudden stretch has me screaming. There's an abrupt jolt of pleasure from his violent entry. He pauses with his knot resting just outside, giving me a moment to reacquaint myself with his size. When I whimper for more he moves, pulling out slowly, before shoving back in. He rocks with an uneven rhythm, keeping me on edge, refusing to let me cum. Gin works until I'm a mess of tears and whines before he finds a steady pace, releasing little grunts of effort each time he slaps into me.

The melodic rhythm of Gin's snarls join

my mewls to create a passionate symphony of pleasure. The sounds of our bodies meeting in bliss. All of it combines to become my favorite song. Us.

So close to cumming, I beg and cry for more. Pausing with just the tip resting inside, he asks, "Do you want me to knot you, Little One? Do you need me to breed you, fill you to bursting with my hot seed?"

His words force me to grip him hard in response, trying to pull his cock deeper inside. There's a moment of apprehension as I feel his knot toy at my entrance. It's been so long, can I even handle a knot anymore? My head rolls to the side and I meet Brenth's eyes. The fire of need burning in his dark gaze sends a lick of hedonistic pleasure through me. I roll my head to the other side and Rafe's brilliant orange eyes meet mine.

"You can take it, Kitten. Let my brother in. Let Gin try to breed you," Rafe's voice is low and rumbly, a purr lacing the words, "We all know *I* will be the one to fuck a pup into you first." His smug grin is the last thing I see before I let my lids fall closed. The fact that every one of my mates are sitting around us, watching Gin fuck me roughly has my muscles tightening over the hard rod inside me.

Gin closes his eyes and grunts out,

"Vixen," before he thrusts hard and pushes fully into me. The feel of that thick bulge being forced into my already overfilled cunt compels a scream out of me. My orgasm is explosive. It hits me so hard I swear my soul leaves my body, it lingers delectably as contractions pulsate around him.

My keening moans drown out all other sounds as his cock jumps and spews seed deep inside me. His knot expands and plugs me tight, not letting any escape. My orgasm has me blind to anything else happening in the room, it goes on and on. I cling to him, my hands are now free, as I feel him continuously pump more cum into me.

The euphoria fades and I find myself on top of Gin, knot still pulsing within. My belly bulges with the amount stuffed inside me. Shifting so I can look up at him, I find his eyes already on me. He's more relaxed now, I smile and drop kisses all over his chest. He sits up so he can kiss me deeply, every movement makes his knot press on that special place inside me, forcing out another orgasm. I moan into his mouth, feeling his lips tip up in smug pride.

Laying back down, he draws me with him. My muscles are limp and sated as I melt into him.

"Shhh, I need to rest before tackling the

next cock, cocks?" I mumble into Gin's chest as I drift off, hearing a chorus of laughter from my mates. A smile graces my lips as I sleep.

CH.50

Sleep doesn't keep me under for long. I'm roused from my nap when Gin's knot releases and the deluge of cum and slick leak out of me. I lay limply on Gin's chest, my breasts crushed between us. My thighs make a weak attempt to stop the flow but someone is holding me open. Tilting my head back, twisting slightly, I find Rafe gazing intently at my cunt.

"What'r you doin?" I mumble sleepily, my words almost indecipherable. My eyes are a little bleary, but I blink away the haze.

Smirking up at me with mischief in his eyes, Rafe moves his hands down to hold open my lower lips.

"I love seeing our seed leaking out of your well used pussy." His eyes flare with lust and dazzling hellfire. The way the flames dance in his gaze, his sharper than normal canines and the intensity of his scent combined sends my mind straight to the gutter. I want him.

It's lucky that I am an Omega. I do not know if my core could take all this sex without being incredibly sore afterwards.

A breathy moan escapes when Rafe shoves two fingers inside me. Cum spills from my entrance as he forces me to leak more slick. Rafe trails his fingers through the mess and paints it over my skin.

"I want you covered with all of us by the end of the night." Rafe leans in close, his breath comes out in warm puffs against my skin as he murmurs dirty things to me, "There won't be one inch of you that doesn't have our scent marking you. *You're mine!*"

Goddess, why is that so hot? Rafe's possessive words and the smears of seed over my body tease me with the prospect of more. How can I want another knot again so badly? I'm not even in heat and I crave each and every one of these males desperately.

My body jostles from Gin's rumbly chuckle. He helps me up to my knees and pushes me back into Rafe, who gladly wraps his arms around me and falls back into the bedding. I'm happy that Gin feels more settled now.

Releasing an 'Oof' as we land, I laugh at

our silliness.

I have missed this so much, missed them so much.

Rafe crosses my arms over my chest and holds me securely. "Tawson, feel like doing the honors of prepping her delectable ass for me?" he queries cheerfully, at his words my back arches in anticipation. The thought of a cock in my ass and cunt simultaneously has my mouth watering with depraved desire.

The sounds that escape me have a few of them groaning. My eyes meet Brynd's and I almost choke on my next groan as I watch him stroke his massive cock. Movement beside him draws my attention to Brenth as he leers lasciviously at my cum smeared form. I would very much like to taste those thick green members but a rustling sound to my left brings my focus back to Rafe and Tawson.

"Pass the oil," my sexy Fae murmurs before he cups my ass.

Tawson lifts my lower half and begins licking up the mess of seed and slick smeared on my thighs. My teal haired mate consumes me, easing the stress I felt from our separation. The overwhelming need to reconnect with all my mates spurs my desire further. The feel of their hands alone soothes the jagged edges left inside me from the distance between us.

I buck against Tawson's face in surprise when his tongue licks over my clit. I'm still sensitive from Gin's knot and my legs shake as the pleasure builds.

Groans slip out as I twitch, my hands want to reach out and grab Tawson's delicately pointed ears to direct him, but Rafe's restraining hold leaves me writhing. He whispers dirty words along my neck, pausing to lick and nibble.

"Have you let either of those Orcs touch you while we were apart? No? Hmm, interesting. I am impressed with their willpower. I would not have been as respectful. But, I am a lecherous rake." Holding my arms with one hand, he lets the other roam and pluck at my nipples, enjoying my squeals.

"Look down. See how hard Tawson works that little clitty. But, he's not going to let you cum yet. We will leave you in a frenzy before filling your tight cunt and ass with our cocks. You're going to squeeze me so hard, it's been too long since someone touched you there, hmm?" He nuzzles my hair, while spouting filth and I can't get enough of it.

I'm so close to cresting over the edge when Tawson slows his ministrations. Rafe's non-stop, sexy whispers clued him into the game we're playing.

Make the Omega crazy.

Tawson gently pinches my clit between his teeth as he smears the oil over my skin, moving down to rub a slippery finger over my back hole. Even though I know what to expect, I still cry out and shift my hips up into his mouth, only encouraging him more.

Rafe distracts me with his electric touch, pleasure surges with each kiss on my neck. His skillful hands work my breasts, keeping me suspended on the edge. Tawson's tongue circles my clit and he easily slips a finger into my tight back hole. While it still feels strange, I don't mind it so much. Will I ever get used to these dark naughty thoughts? It feels so taboo, but the wickedness draws me in like a moth to flames.

Pushing a second finger in, he stretches me. I keen at the feeling, his tongue in my pussy combined with this depraved pleasure will make me detonate soon. But, he stops moving a second before I'm about to cum. I snarl at the both of them, my claws unsheathing as I thrash trying to grab at them. The surprised 'O' that Rafe makes as I almost slip free has my lips twitching into a smirk. They don't know how much stronger I have grown. Pride urges me to fight them harder, to test them. A little voice in my head says

'*Test them. Make your Alpha's prove themselves. Our mates must be strong.*'

"*Omega,*" Tawson barks, putting his potent dominance into the word, "*settle.*"

The power in his dominance sends shivers through me as my eyes roll back. Goddess, that's arousing. My head Alpha is so strong and I can tell he's still holding back.

Rafe bites down on my neck and, combined with Tawson's bark, I go limp with a faint whine. Having my males force my submission is so hot. The thought of continuing to fight crosses my mind briefly but, I want them inside me too bad to push my luck.

Tawson returns to stretching me. When he lifts his head, his mouth and chin glisten with slick. The sight has my insides clenching down on nothing. I need him to fix this empty feeling.

The fingers disappear only to be replaced by a cock. Tawson doesn't push into me yet and I whine, my mind fuzzy from the withheld orgasms.

Tawson directs Rafe's thickness and helps push my hips down so the head pops in past my tight rim. It feels too big, too much, and I tense, making it worse and better. Moaning at the thought of Tawson's hand on

Rafe's cock, I'm a little envious that I can't see it and I make sure to let them know.

"I wanna see!" The words come out on a whimpered sigh, "I wanna see you touch his cock!" A rumble seems to echo around the room, coming from every direction.

"Look here, Wee Beauty," Brenth coaxes, his voice syrupy and thick with lust as he purrs.

Rafe nudges my head in that direction and when I blink to clear the haze, my eyes first trail over Brenth's fist working his length. Rafe groans as my muscles tighten over him, the sight erotic and mouthwatering. Brenth snorts and covers himself so I will look at where he's pointing.

The sight that greets me is more than welcome. A mirror reflects the intensely arousing picture the three of us make. Rafe underneath me, mouthing along my neck, playing with my breasts while Tawson sits between our legs. His light green hand wrapped around Rafe's darkened ochre cock, feeding it into my body. My eyes squeeze shut as I moan out,

"Oh, Goddess! I need you both to fuck me. Right now!" I can't handle how good we look together. How titillating it is to see my males handling each other.

Rafe snarls in my ear, "You will take

what we give you."

Tawson must have oiled Rafe's length while I was distracted because it's slippery and slides into me far too easily. Rafe grasps my hips tightly and releases a shaky groan as his knot rubs against the tight hole.

The heat of his length inside me grows warmer, along with his fingers pressing into my hips. It doesn't burn me, he can't hurt me with his flames because I am his mate.

"You feel so good, Rafe." I moan at the new sensation, revelling in my ability to threaten my mate's restraint, "More! Please, move!"

"Fuck!" Rafe leans back to snarl, "Tawson, hurry up!" before he continues spouting his filth, "Oh, Kitten. You drive me crazy. You're so tight and hot and I want to shove my knot into your ass while he knots your cunt. You will be absolutely filthy by the time we're finished." Rafe's words are low and dark. My muscles tighten around him at the delicious threat.

"Oh Goddess! Rafe! You can't knot me there! That's-That's not allowed... is it?" I'm whining and wriggling on him, feeling him shift inside me. I try to deny how much I enjoy it, but I don't think anyone believes me.

I haven't really had the chance to adjust

to Rafe's large member in my ass when Tawson lines himself up. Rafe holds me still with teeth and hands while Tawson starts to push slowly into me.

"Fuck, Omega." Tawson grits out, "you look beautiful taking our cocks. So slippery and tight. You're radiant like this."

Between the two of them, their hardness pinning me in place while they both spout such dirty, depraved things, I think I'm going to lose my mind. I missed the way my mates ruin me. Their hands stroking the flames of my desire. I will never get enough of them.

Adding the pressure from a second cock feels like too much, and yet my body stretches easily to accommodate both of them. I close my eyes and relish the immense fullness. I can't decide if it's too much, or if I want them to move and absolutely wreck me.

There is no choice and that makes me cream even more. Submitting to the loving care of my mates is everything. I love feeling helpless as they do whatever they want to my body.

Tawson pulls his hips back quickly, immediately throwing me into a wild orgasm. Light flashes behind my eyes, blinding me to everything as I thrash and writhe. Being sandwiched between two of my males after so long is exactly what I needed. They hold me tightly between them while Tawson fucks me through it, rocking me on Rafe, prolonging the sensations.

My breath heaves when I finally come down only to be pushed up the hill again when Rafe's hard, hot length slides in opposition to Tawson's. My eyes roll back and my moans are wild and loud. I don't even care if the entire village can hear me, the world should know how good my Alpha's make me feel.

"You're so tight with a large cock in both your holes. Do you feel how we move together? We will give you so much pleasure you can't function. You're getting both knots. Gonna plug you and pump you full of our cum. Our scent will be embedded in you so deeply you'll never get it out. If it fades, we'll do it again, maybe fill your pretty mouth too." Rafe promises in a raspy tone. He releases a choppy breath while fighting his pleasure, ensuring I'm completely insensible before he cums.

Tawson speeds his thrusts and I scream my pleasure to the room. All I can do is hold on as he fucks me harder. Vaguely, I can hear the sounds of my other males touching themselves somewhere in the room and it makes me grip harder over the cocks currently destroying me.

Rafe's hold on my upper body tightens,

"Now!"

They both push, Rafe's knot pops in past my rim first. I shriek at the stretch, there is pain but mostly it makes the pleasure sharper, darker.

Tawson's knot slips into my cunt moments later and the stretch, the fullness, is overwhelming. I cum, blacking out from an overload of pleasure. There's a brief thought that this might kill me, but it's fleeting.

When I come to, they are carefully maneuvering us until we're laying on our sides. I'm securely tucked between them. Rafe lightly kisses me, his dirty mouth returns to sweet nothings, while Tawson soothes me with soft touches.

"Th…" I attempt to thank them, but my lips refuse to work. I blink sleepily at Tawson, pleased at his fond smile.

"Sleep now, Sweetheart. We've got you."

Waking in different arms is something I'm still getting used to with these males. I don't open my eyes, instead I nuzzle against the scent of peaches and cream. Brynd is so warm and makes me feel so safe. I'm excessively pleased that my mates have allowed the Orcs cuddle time. I can't wait until I have their claims on my skin as well. My thoughts drift to the brief glimpse I caught of their green cocks and my pussy clenches. The soreness reminds me that I'm not quite ready for their unique lengths. They may be a little too big for me… but if I can take Gin's fancy member then theirs should be no problem.

When I wiggle closer to him, his chest shakes and I know he's huffing out a silent chuckle. He probably remembers how I would do this every time I fell asleep between them on our journey here.

Someone coughs, clearing their throat before speaking, "Precious, you need to eat and drink something before you get some more exercise." There's laughter in his voice and a hint at what he's going to do to me when he has the chance.

Blinking into the brightness of the room, I groan as I roll over. Why is there so much light?

"Wha-? Water? Please?" My words are sluggish as I try to wake up. My dry throat doesn't help the sleepy words come any easier.

Making grabby hands at him I hope he'll hand me a waterskin. Instead, two strong hands grasp mine and yank me to my feet. I yell out my surprise at moving so quickly, and away from the warmth of Brynd and the nest.

"Noooo! Why? It was so warm and comfy. My body is so sore, Fen," Wailing out my complaints, I pout at Fen.

"You are the most precious thing I've ever seen." He just smiles, trying to hold back his laughter at my objections, "even acting like a brat, you're adorable. Come, let me take care of you. I promise to make it worth your while."

"Ugh! Fine, but you're carrying me. I don't think my legs work anymore." I grumble as Fen lifts me straight into his arms, without protest. He carries me to the bathing room and plops me on the privy. I shoo him out so I can use it in peace, we may all be very close but I refuse to have them watch me do that. When I'm done, I clean my teeth before hollering that I'm finished.

Running the bath, Fen dumps in a few different bottles of liquid that smells delicate and pleasant, making bubbles form on the surface. I squeal my delight and immediately scoop out a handful, playing with it.

Jumping when he taps me with a waterskin, I grab it greedily and immediately chug it down. I didn't notice how thirsty I've grown. Being double knotted takes a lot of work!

When I'm done Fen strips and joins me in the tub, tugging my back tight to his chest.

The hard bar of his cock rests in between my ass cheeks and I squirm as desire blooms once again. Just the thought of one of my males causes lust to warm my body. But, he ignores my wiggling and soaps up a rag.

Taking his time gently cleaning every inch of my body, he pays extra attention to my breasts and cunt. Fen may be the most quiet of my males, but he'll never pass up a chance to play with my body.

By the time I'm cleaned from head to toe, I'm warm from more than the hot water. My body noticeably leaks slick and I wonder if there will ever be a day I won't make a mess of myself.

"I will always want to make a mess of you," Fen nuzzles his face into my wet hair.

"Did I say that out loud?" A snort escapes me as my face grows warm.

"Never change, Precious. I love you just the way you are." Fen's arms pull me into his warm embrace, allowing me to hide my pleased grin in his chest.

Happiness blooms throughout my body. I know my mates love me, I can feel it in the bond, but hearing it is extra sweet.

CH.51

Fen carries me out of the bathing room and down the stairs wrapped only in a drying cloth. Frowning, I go to ask him why he walked right past the nest when my stomach growls loudly. Oops, I guess I'm hungry. I can't survive off orgasms and cock alone, although I'm pretty sure I tried when I was in heat. Laughing to myself, I should not allow my cunt to run things, I'll never get anything done.

The whole pack, plus Zenik, Wick and Lia crowd in the living space. It wasn't all that big before, but with all these large beings in here the space looks absolutely tiny.

I blush bright red when Lia and Zenik look over my bedraggled state, wearing only a drying cloth with my wet hair clinging to my shoulders.

Fen ignores them and settles himself

between Gin and Tawson, keeping me on his lap. He tips a waterskin to my lips before feeding me from the many dishes set out. With my hands trapped in the tightly wound cloth, I'm happy to let him feed me. I've gotten pretty used to all of them taking over that duty, even though I find it humorous. I mean, my hands work perfectly fine but this is one battle I do not want to fight. I'd rather save my energy for more useful purposes.

Wick speaks up first, "It's good to see you looking well, young Omega. Being reunited with your pack has truly brought some life to your skin. You really come alive in their presence. There's a vibrant glow about you that'd been missing."

"Getting dicked down by multiple Alpha's will do that to you," Lia's bold voice interjects. Her smile lively and amused.

Hiding my embarrassed laughter in the cloth, my face burns at the compliment and at Lia's blunt observation.

"Lia!" I scold, my voice muffled in the sheet, "You can't just say something like that!"

"Looks like I just did." The Succubus sports a wide grin, enjoying my flustered state.

Burrowing deeper into Fen, I'm choosing to ignore Lia for now and address the polite healer,

"Thank you, Wick. It was truly like I was missing a part of myself. I could survive but it wouldn't be living without them." Thankfully someone else takes control of the conversation before Lia has a chance to embarrass me even more.

"Wick and Zenik were just introducing Lianis to us." Tawson comments evenly, grabbing some flatbread and adding some meat and cheese to it, "this place has truly been a mystery to the rest of our Kingdom. Hiding behind enchantments and walls, no one has seen the inside of this village in more than a century,"

The tips of Zenik's ears turn a dark red as he flushes at the dig, "Yes, well, we have not had a fortunate history with the other races in this Kingdom." Clearing his throat, he pauses a moment to collect himself,

"things will be changing here. After everything with my father and this black magic, I have... encouraged him to step aside. I will be taking over as Chief of this village and I have plans to make it a more welcoming place. We will also have more stringent rules around hunts and checking for any curses or dark magic." He seems like a different person after pulling himself together, more dynamic and compelling. It's a little disconcerting, how quickly his demeanour changed since I arrived.

The room is quiet, save the sounds of our meal. Tawson considers Zenik with a shrewd look. "I think this village is fortunate to have you. You protected our mate when many others would have stolen her, and you accepted help when you needed it. This shows good character, the Elite would like to give you our backing. If you have need, we will aid you."

Zenik's eyes widen with surprise as he jerks back in his seat, a piece of fruit tumbling from his open mouth. I don't bother hiding my giggle at his reaction. Wick and Lia both gasp. I guess having the 'Elites' behind you is a good thing? I mean I've heard them call my pack the Elites, but I don't know what that really means. I get the feeling that my mates are kind of a big deal. I shrug to myself, it doesn't matter to me, as long as they are good males who treat me well, I will be happy.

Zenik stutters out a reply, "Oh...Oh! T-That's..." He releases a deep exhale. "Thank you. That means more than you know, considering our history. I will make sure the Elves are worthy of this gift. Thank you."

Wick sidles over to me, standing behind Fen. "You are a truly remarkable, little Omega." Huffing out a laugh, he smiles widely, doing a good job ignoring Gin's rumbling growl at his nearness to me. "I'm pleased to be your friend. Zenik has left supplies for all of you, I hear your journey will be long. I will see you once more before you leave, but I need to monitor the wounded." He nods to my mates before patting Zenik on the shoulder.

Pausing at Brenth, he raises an eyebrow. "How is your leg healing? I see you're able to put weight on it and move normally. So I'm guessing the healing was able to regenerate the muscle and skin that was lost?"

"Aye. It is still regenerating. That cream you gave me is doing wonders. It works slowly, but it's better than losing functionality." Brenth slaps him on the back smiling, almost knocking the slighter male over in his exuberance. "Thank you. You have shown Brynd and myself much about healing. It won't be forgotten."

Wick's cheeks redden and he mumbles out, "Anytime," before departing with one last wave at the rest of us.

Zenik spends a few more minutes thanking my mates and raining praise on the 'Elites', I'm really going to have to remember to ask them about that.

When he leaves, Lia follows and pauses at the door before, tossing me a sultry smile and wink, "Not that I doubt we would be explosive together, but I do not think we're meant to be, Doll. It has been illuminating meeting your mates, though. I did not picture your sweet little self surrounded and doted on by these hulking brutes." She throws her head back and releases a hearty cackle at the echoing growls throughout the room. Lia waves away their ire,

"Oh, don't be so fussy. You all know I'm not interested. You do have working sniffers don't you?" She cocks a hip, raising one eyebrow.

My mouth clicks shut when I realize I'm gaping at her brazenness. She's taller than a lot of them but I don't think she's as strong. I seriously love her sass, she reminds me so much of Dani. A bold, outspoken demeanor, with a beautiful soul. The comparison saddens me, I still have no idea where Dani is, or if she's even okay but I'm going to hold out hope that we'll be reunited one day.

Lia exudes allure on top of her brazenness and I'm a little in awe of her. I wish I could pull that off, but I think I would end up spanked and ruined very quickly...

Hmm... Now that's an idea.

I miss part of Tawsons response to her but catch the end of it, "-compensation. Your aid with keeping our mate safe is worth more than I can say." He's still wearing his serious face, but I catch the hint of a smile.

Lia just waves him off as she heads for the door. "Nope. Don't need it, although I may drop your name here and there just for fun. Honestly, that sweet little thing is priceless and I am pleased to call myself her friend." She stares at me fondly all bundled up on Fen's lap with both him and Gin feeding me, and smiles the first genuine smile I think I've seen on her since we met. "You find me if you ever need some girl time. You're dealing with a whoooole lot of dick and that can get tiring after a while." She blows me a kiss and sashay's out.

I can't help but laugh. She is so much more fun than I expected, although it's hard to be cheerful when fighting for our lives. I am glad to have her as a friend, especially because so many seemed leery of her and her power.

Tawson lets out a loud guffaw, startling everyone. He catches our wide-eyed stare and laughs harder. Seeing Mr. Serious let loose like this has me smiling and sniggering along with him. After a few minutes of wondering what the hell is happening, the others join in.

The moment is a pleasant release of tension due to the weeks we've been apart. Eventually, I can breathe again and sigh with happiness.

I am home. I know we still have a long journey to make it to our Keep, but as long as I am with them I know things will be okay.

The addition of two new pack members definitely surprised them, but they were fully supportive of the situation and respected my choice. Although, Gin still seems leery of the Orcs. It could be that he's just overly possessive of my time though. Dragon's aren't known for sharing. Oh well. Gin will just have to get used to the brother's being here.

When Tawson found out they were trained Users, and could find me anywhere, he was practically giddy with relief. I think being kidnapped will haunt him, all of them, for a while and knowing there's always a way to find me brings him a measure of solace.

I am done with my morning meal, and I am done with serious conversations. My eyes land on Blue, who has been quietly observing everything. The sight of my shy Beta's lips closing around a piece of fruit, the way he sucks the juices of his fingers has my core tightening. I have more males I need to reconnect with. Wiggling until I can free a hand, I point at Blue.

"Beasty! I need you." I shift in Tawson's direction, "we have some time before we have to leave right? All of you are going to fuck me until I don't know my own name anymore."

The moment my desire fills the air and hits them, everyone moves.

I'm upstairs in a flash and tossed into the nest, the cloth unravelling around me. I'm a little out of breath as I watch my males quickly strip. The vision before me must have been sent from the Goddess because there is no way this much hard, muscled flesh is real. Each of my mates are molded specifically for me. Before I'd met them, I hadn't realized that this is exactly what I craved. It's all I could ask for and more.

My hazy, lust filled eyes find Blue's, inviting him to join me. He'a a little unsure, but his hard dripping cock seems very interested. He's nervous, biting his lip, as he kneels beside me. Quietly, I ask him,

"Are you okay? Do you still question my desire for you? You silly male..." He cuts me off with a biting kiss. There's so many things I appreciate about Blue. His sweet and caring disposition, his perceptiveness, and the fact that he isn't always so gentle in the nest. Goddess, I love my Beta so much. Our pack wouldn't be the same without him.

"Blue lie down beside her, you're going to fuck her ass while I knot her sweet pussy," Fen utters softly, taking control.

When Fen gets bossy like this it does something to me, desire and arousal radiates from me. My quiet moan has a dark smirk crossing his lips. Fen sucks hard on my clit throwing me roughly into a screaming orgasm. Licking me through it, he prolongs the sensation, until I'm twitching and trying to get away.

When he sits back slightly, he thrusts three fingers into my leaking opening and narrows in on that spot inside that turns me into a mess. Fen thrusts into me until I'm whimpering and begging for more. Pulling his fingers out, he moves down to my back hole. I clench for a moment before forcing myself to relax as he fits two fingers easily inside. The pinch and burn makes me whine even as I revel in it.

Soothing kisses on my breasts distract me from what Fen is doing. Blue's lips glide lightly over my hard nipples. Shivering, I beg for him to use more pressure. I enjoy when they're rough, the barely there pressure is such a tease.

He doesn't listen, continuing to gently tickle and tempt my chest. Grabbing him, I use his hair to try and press him harder into me, but Fen shackles my hands in one of his large ones. Smirking. he continues playing with my ass.

Fen pulls his fingers out and bids Blue

to lay back. Picking me up, he puts my back to Blues chest, lining up his cock with my ass as he sinks me down onto him. The music of mine and Blues groans fill the nest. I twist towards the mirror so I can see Fen's hand on Blue's hard length. I don't know why it's so arousing, but it is. Their casual groping adds an extra layer of heat to our intimacies.

When I'm settled on him with his cock pressed as deep as he can go, Fen pulls me upright. I settle on top of Blue, facing his feet and watch, wide eyed as Fen ducks down between our legs. He swipes his tongue through my slick, barely touching my clit before he moves lower. Fen cups Blue's dark sac and rolls it in his hand before mouthing over the skin. His tongue catches the extra slick I produce at the debauched vision.

Holy fuck. This is the hottest thing I've ever experienced.

Fen alternates, tonguing my dripping slit and fondling Blue. My poor Beta sounds as though he's being tortured in all the best ways.

"F-fuck, Fen! Oh, Goddess, please! I-I can't take much more of this. I'm going to go off like a teenager seeing tits for the first time!" Blue wheezes out, his grasp on my hips tighten to the point of pain.

"Next time you will take it longer, and

hold back until I tell you, you can cum." Fen's voice is a dark rumble. His dominance leaking out as he takes control of us.

Fen relents his erotic torture and lines his cock up. My Alpha sinks into my pussy quickly with a whispered groan as he revels in the tightness of the pressure with Blue's length filling my other passage.

"Fuck, fuck, fuck, Precious. You're so tight and perfect. You're mine. Ours," he growls out, his eyes full of wicked intentions.

When Fen rocks his hips, I mewl into his neck, my claws unsheath and trail over his skin. He rumbles with delight and pushes into me faster.

Blue shifts and drives himself into me in tandem and I can't help closing my eyes as I fall into the rhythm of the push and pull. Pleasure ripples through my body, my legs twitching as I crest through one orgasm after another.

It's overwhelmingly perfect.

Reaching a hand around Fen's neck, I dig my claws into him. The pain makes him grunt and speed up his thrusts. My dominant Alpha likes a little pain, too. I'll have to remember that.

Blue breathes heavily in my ear, releasing little grunts of effort as he slides in and out of my dark passage. He mutters curses into my ear,

"Lu, Goddess, you're squeezing my cock so hard. The feel of another length moving through you is unbelievable. Fuck. I'm going to fill you with my cum and watch it leak out of you as he knots you hard."

I did not expect that from my sweet, shy, Blue, but damn! His words send me into another orgasm, my body clenching over them both.

Fen grunts and warns Blue, "I'm going to knot this clenching pussy and force both of you to cum."

The groan Blue releases sounds pained, but I know it's because he's trying to hold off his orgasm. In the next second, Fen forces his knot in, the fullness has me screaming and closing my eyes against the all consuming pleasure. His cock kicks as he spews cum deep inside my cunt.

Blue wheezes and cums in shallow thrusts, Fen's knot making it hard for him to move. I see stars as another orgasm overtakes me, my breathing shallow as I delight in the sensations.

Fen nuzzles his forehead to mine, eyes closed, breathing me in as he fills me. "Love. You are our heart. I will never allow you to be taken from us again. I... *we...* will do everything in our power to keep you safe, I promise you."

Tension lines his face, the separation has been hard on him. I don't think he will hear me if I say it's not his fault, so I just nuzzle him back and kiss him softly, trying to put all my feelings for him into it.

Fen lifts me off Blue, giving him room to slip his softened cock out of my ass. He twitches against me, still sensitive after his orgasm, and I smile into Fen's shoulder. Smug pride emanates from me, I love that I can exhaust my males with pleasure.

When Blue is free, Fen rolls and settles me on his chest, stroking down my back cooing softly, encouraging me to nap again. I know when I wake we will be leaving and the road ahead will be long and likely dangerous. This may be my last chance to rest properly, so I will take advantage.

I really wanted both my Orcs to claim me, but I think I need to have a conversation with Gin before that will happen. They have been relegated to the sidelines and forced to watch, which I truly enjoy, but I want to feel them against me too.

Lips gently placing kisses over my face pull me from a deep sleep,

"Noooo," I groan out, "I don't wanna wake up." I complain even as I search blindly for his lips on mine. Wildflowers and a fresh breeze through crowded trees invigorates me. Tawson's scent alone is enough to sweeten my grumpy morning disposition. He smiles against my lips before pulling back.

"Would you like to wash? I think I could go for a bath as well. You wouldn't mind if I joined you?" Tawson's smooth, serious voice asks.

When I open my eyes he has a 'look' in his and I think a bath with him will have very little cleaning, and I'm okay with that.

I'm eagerly nodding before even opening my mouth. "Uh-huh, yep. That sounds perfect. Let's do that." I scramble off him, his hands finally releasing me.

As I stand and step away, he slaps my ass hard enough to leave a mark and make me jump. My hands fly to the reddened flesh as I squeak and scurry into the bathing room with a laugh. He gives me a few moments to use the privy before coming in and filling the tub.

I have never bathed this much in my life, but the set up in this village is incredible. It makes it so easy to clean regularly without having to haul pails of water in and heat it over the fire.

Sinking into the hot water, my sore muscles immediately loosen. Tawson drags me onto his lap before he lathers up a rag and cleans me gently, humming some tune under his breath. It's very relaxing and my body melts into him, I trust him to keep my head above water.

There's a lot less playing in the tub than I expected, and I'm only pouting a little. I can't believe I'm still feeling lusty. My cunt should be sore and exhausted after all the knots I've taken. It must be an Omega thing.

Tawson dries, dresses me, and carries me down the stairs. Normally I'd protest, make an attempt at being independent, but I'm feeling too relaxed to argue.

He only places me on my feet when we join the others. Everyone is busy packing clothing, checking the supplies given to us by the Elves, and whatever else needs doing before we leave. Gin snags me down to his lap and feeds me from the small spread they set out for a late breakfast. I nibble mindlessly as I think about my time here.

This darkness invading our Kingdom is worrisome. How many other towns and villages have been affected that we don't know about? Why are those beasts hunting me? Or, I should say, why is the Necromancer hunting me? What did he mean by the markers in my blood? I have too many questions and no one has any answers. I can only hope our journey from here to the Keep will be easy and free of monsters.

Sitting beside Fen in the cart as we trundle out of the ruined gate, I gaze over my shoulder at my new friends and wave goodbye. There are amused smiles all around as they wave. I keep looking until they grow small in the distance.

It was quite the adventure, and I would do it again but I would leave out all the attacks and kidnapping.

All I can do is beg the Goddess that the road ahead will be quiet, but I have this nasty feeling that something bad is coming. I'm getting very sick and tired of these 'gut feelings', my lip curls in distaste. I really hope I am wrong.

I have so many questions about myself and what darkness is growing on the horizon. I can only hope that I will find some answers and the evil will leave me be.

Closing my eyes, I pray as we slowly move farther into the desert. *Please, Goddess, don't let anything bad happen to my pack. Please help us get to the Keep safely.* The unknown ahead weighs me down with a heavy foreboding feeling.

EPILOGUE

(Deep in the Mikta Mountains)

Watching him pace back and forth across the small cavern, I do my best to keep out of his way. Nothing good happens when he's angry, and he's always angry.

Huddled in the darkened corner straining to hear what he's muttering. I catch a few words; *'Fuck'*, *'need more'*, *'had the Omega'*, *'blood'*, *'genetics'*. It doesn't fully make sense to me. But, I'm assuming he's upset about the escaped Omega, we still can't figure out how she left without a trace. She wasn't accompanied by any other scents and there weren't any footprints in the dirt either. There was no indication she had help leaving.

Her cage was empty with the exception

of smeared blood and some peculiar gouges in the stone. The strange markings do not make any sense for a human Omega. They are weak and useless.

"What the fuck are you doing just standing there?" I'm jarred from my musings when He shouts, "Why haven't you figured out a way for me to get her back? We need that Omega!"

"She has been reunited with her mates." My face remains emotionless in an attempt to hide my fear while my hands grasp each other tightly behind my back, "It will be incredibly difficult to get her away from them again, especially now that they will be on high alert. That Dragon is a problem." I'm pleased when my voice doesn't shake.

"FIGURE IT THE FUCK OUT!" He spits while screaming. For a brief moment his eyes morph from green to crimson during his emotional outburst, stray stones tremble from his rage.

"Yes, Sir." I drop my eyes, not wanting to look into his furious gaze, "I'm on it. I will go and put together a plan of attack." I've found avoiding eye contact calms him, slightly.

At his growled 'GO!' I hurry out of the room and down towards the cage. I should go look through the newest monsters that he created to see if any of them could challenge a Dragon, but the Omega's escape irks me. How did she get out? How did her injuries not keep her passed out? What is she to Him? Why is she so important? What did he mean by genetics? Is he talking about the strange markers we found in her blood?

With these questions rattling around in my head, I take another look at her cage. I examine the blood smears, tracing her movements throughout her cell. She didn't get far, it seems like she only made it to the bars.

Huffing out a frustrated breath, I rake my hands through my hair and tug on the strands. How the fuck did she get out of here? My spells should have kept her contained. Nothing should have been able to get through them.

Stepping closer, I stare at the small scratches and punctures in the bars. They look... they look like they were made by sharp claws. But, it must have been a pretty small beast because they are barely big enough to see. I'm surprised I caught them.

Bringing myself closer to one of the gouges, I spot some blood inside of it. I sniff it, getting a very slight hint of the Omega's scent. Could she be more than just human? That isn't what our informant told us... He said she was weak and easily overtaken. He claimed she would be a scared, fragile mess.

I despise humans, they're all weak and whiny. I don't know why He trusted the word of this fool. And now here we are, no closer to His goals with a lost Omega.

Although, the tests we ran indicated the markers He was seeking, so maybe I'm just trying to find a reason to kill that little snake.

Upon investigating the ground outside the cage, there aren't any clues she had help escaping. No disturbance in the dirt or stones and no footprints, so how the fuck did she get out? She should not have had the strength to climb these bars, not with the injuries she sustained.

What's even more frustrating is how she got out of the cave system. It's a maze of traps and monsters that should have scented her. She had to have had help. Someone had to have followed her here and helped her escape because she was far too injured to get out on her own. I saw the infection the griffon left and knew that would keep her weak enough for us to do what we needed.

Defeating her Dragon mate will be a difficult task, so I head to the library for more research on the matter. Dragons are notoriously challenging to injure, let alone kill.

But everything has a weakness.

Everything.

I will find it, because if I don't, I'm pretty sure He is going to use me in his next round of experiments.

My thoughts drift back to the Omega as I maneuver through the corridors. One of our scouts tracked her down in the grasslands, but, those fucking Orcs were there protecting her. Where did they even come from? That little snake didn't tell us anything about Orcs. Only about her four Alpha's, and right before they left Pekayan, the pack had somehow stolen one of His beasts. That's another frustrating puzzle. It seems mysteries abound around this little Omega. The more He learns about her, the more he wants her.

His fixation is going to get me killed.

The horrendous stench permeating from monsters in passing rooms has me covering my nose in disgust. I don't think I will ever get used to the smell of the dead rotting away as they drop pieces off their bodies. It's disgusting. I'm a black magic User, so I'm perfectly fine with the abominations, but even I draw the line at the putrid abominations. I wish He would just stick to the monsters.

When I reach the library I grab a few tomes and sit. This small room containing a few shelves of forbidden grimoires and other unsavory tomes is what passes for a library in this forsaken cave.

Flipping through the pages, I try to find more information about Dragons. I doubt I will find anything useful here. In the history of this Kingdom there isn't a record of anyone properly defeating a Dragon.

Their scales are impenetrable, they are massive enough to destroy whole villages and the different types exhale specific magics to their species. Some breathe fire, ice, water, or stone, and others breathe darkness, death, and acid. They are a fascinating species that I would enjoy studying if my life weren't on the line. If I can't find a way to at least incapacitate that Dragon, I will be the next being murdered for His experiments.

He still hasn't told me why we need Omegas. I know the others were used in His experiments. They failed, and their parts were used in the next batch of monsters. But, they still turned out weak compared to the ones made from Beta and Alpha parts.

Live Alpha's are another piece that He's trying to experiment on, but they are much harder to capture. They're strong and vicious. I hate dealing with Alpha's. I'm better with the Beta's. They are much easier to control through the threat of pain and death, so much weaker.

I spend hours leafing through pages looking for anything that might help. Desperation leads me on a wild hunt through unrelated tomes where something interesting catches my eye.

Muck-worms. These strange beasts are very stupid and spend their entire lives underground. They are massive, bigger than most Dragons. With no eyes, they get around using a fascinating form of echo location. Round layered mouths house rows of jagged sharp teeth meant for tearing and grinding stone and earth. There is nothing in here about whether they can eat through anything, but being able to rip up earth and stone so easily might at least give us a chance to slow the Dragon down so we can snatch the Omega.

A plan tales form, if we trap one of these worms, I can cast a spell to mesmerize and control it. Maybe He will aid me and with a few enhancements, the creature would stand a much better chance at killing at least one of her Alpha's.

If we send a worm plus a hoard of monsters and some of the rotting beasts, I shudder at the thought of them, we should be able to separate her from the pack. My excitement peaks and a blanket of calm settles over me. This should save my skin for another few days.

The information we obtained from the Elves before those pesky Orcs and the Omega destroyed our connection to them will be invaluable. Now that we know those Orcs are Users, I can put in place some counter spells to slow their effectiveness against our creatures.

I'm annoyed that they were able to find and destroy our curse, and that they found the black infection in the Omega. If they had only let it fester and grow, we would have been able to have that little bitch walk straight to us.

Muttering to myself as I make my way back to Him. I'm ready to tell him of my plans to retrieve His property. This pack of Elites has become such a fucking nuisance. I really hope this plan works and we can get rid of a few of them.

If we can break their spirit it will be easier to fulfill His plans... I really wish He would share the master plan with me. I can't help Him if I don't know what he wants. He wastes so much of my time with stupid fucking orders. Meeting that little snake is a complete waste of my time, especially if the information is incorrect.

He's still pacing the same room I left him in, muttering and cursing Alpha's and the King. He terrifies me even though we are partners. I'm pretty sure he sees me as his lackey, though.

Clearing my throat quietly to get His attention. His head snaps over to me, his eyes glowing an eerie green that flashes with red. My heart beats faster, sweat dots my brow and my hands start shaking. I clasp them behind my back to hide it.

"What? You'd better have something good for me. I am in no mood for useless beasts. I have half a mind to use your parts in my next experiment. Might be of better use to me…" He snaps at me. Trailing off cursing under his breath, whispering about ripping my body apart to see what parts of me might be serviceable in the next monster.

I catch a few words about killing me and raising my corpse to control my magic. Fear permeates my body and I swallow hard, resisting the urge to shudder.

"Sir… I think I've found a way to separate the Omega from the pack so we can get her back." My voice is a little shaky but I hold myself together, praying that he has not decided I'm better off dead.

Pausing his ranting and pacing, he stares at me. "Well? What is it?" His voice is cutting and harsh.

Trying to swallow past my dry throat. "Muck-worms." I cough. "We trap and control a muck-worm to accompany a hoard of monsters and we might have a chance to incapacitate the Dragon and distract the rest so we can separate her from the pack."

A menacing grin creeps over his skeletal face, hidden within a deep hood. He cackles loudly, ending in a coughing fit.

"Yes. Yes, yes, perfect! I already have an idea of how to alter the muck-worm to suit our needs."

His laughter is abrasive and I bite my cheek to contain my fear. It's almost worse than his anger. But, at least he isn't murdering me to harvest my body parts.

"Excellent work, Lash. Now go speak to the pest and then find me a big one!" He orders with glee before continuing, "Yes. This is good. Well, done. I'm pleased I don't have to kill you."

And with that lovely sentiment I hurry out of His presence, stopping by my room to grab a few things. The book on muck-worms goes into my satchel so I can research where to find one and how we might trap it.

I take one of the, non-dead, flying monsters to meet with the stupid Human. My beast waits by my side at our rendezvous point. I thoroughly enjoy the humans fear as he faces me and one of my monsters.

His annoying stomping disturbs the quiet lull within the forest. Footsteps grow louder, and when he's close enough to come into view, I can't help but curl my lip in disgust at his appearance.

"What do you have for us, Jerrik?" I snap. I do not enjoy his presence. He is foul, and this is coming from someone who spends time with the deceased.

He smirks, before paling as he catches sight of the beast.

"Uh, um. Right, uh. He told me He would give me the Omega when he was done with her. So, where is she?" He demands, with an air of entitlement. The fool.

My eye twitches in irritation at his audacity. "You will have to wait. He isn't finished yet. We need more information on her. Everything about her life and habits." I do not want to tell him we lost her. He would likely say something to piss me off and I would curse him. My master isn't done with this snake yet and would be displeased if I killed him before he is used up.

I let the human talk, Jerrik's anger increases when he isn't given what he demands, but I don't care. As long as he gives me what I want, I will continue to allow him to live. I can be gracious, sometimes.

"Hey!" Jerrik's nasally tone aggravates me as I mount my monstrous steed. Now that he's done blustering about the Omega's life I can thankfully leave.

"That's it?" He continues angrily, "When am I going to get my Omega? I want that little bitch under me. She defied me too many times. I need to punish her and teach her how she's supposed to behave."

"You will get her when He is done." I level a harsh stare, letting him see my distaste as I answer, "Do you wish me to send Him so you might make your demands in person?"

Jerrik pales and steps back quickly, shaking his head. "N-no. No, that's fine. I can wait. W-when…"

"You will wait until He is finished!" My voice booms through the trees as I cut him off, even the forest inhabitants seem to shrink away from my outburst.

He scrambles back, tripping over himself in his haste to get away. Jerrik's nod is frantic and seeing him sweat brings me great pleasure.

With one last look of loathing, I kick my beast into flight. I have a worm to trap, far better company than this little fuck.

Soon, I will have that Omega back in my cage and He will let me live another day.

THE END

For now

ACKNOWLEDGE MENTS

First of all, a HUGE thank you to **you**, the reader for giving my first ever book a chance. I have always had a vivid and wild imagination full of stories. I'm so happy to finally work up the courage to actually write some of them down. It is terrifying putting something out into the world for judgement. All those what-if's bombard you, but all you can do is try. And hope people will enjoy the stories that come to life inside your mind.

Secondly, I couldn't have done this without my editor Andra (from Sinful Aloha Editing) - one day I promise I'll figure out dialogue tags and commas! But until that day you are a Goddess sent to help make my words legible. Thank you!

I couldn't have done this without my alpha reader - Ashlynn. You are amazing at finding all the little things that I could no longer see after reading and re-reading this too many times. And at finding all the repetitive words that would have made this a challenge to read. You and Andra help push me to be a better writer.

I can't forget to include a big shout-out to my beta readers: Eliana, Nicole and Stephanie for helping make the characters individuals and sound like people you'd actually want to read about!

All of you, editors, readers, alpha's and beta's are vital to helping make a book come to life instead of just words on a page. So, THANK YOU!

ABOUT THE AUTHOR

AR Lines is a daydreamer, crocheter, nerdy gamer and avid romance reader. She has been reading the romance genre since she was a teen and has always been interested in writing. As a little girl she even wrote a terrible children's book and had it published in her elementary school library. AR Lines lives in Vancouver, Canada with her husband, enjoying the mild coastal weather, beautiful beaches and mountainous nature hikes. She also has two demons masquerading as cats that she adores even though they are evil little gremlins that destroy nice things. This is her debut novel.

Find her online for updates on what's next!

Instagram: @author_arlines

Facebook: AR Lines Readers Group